RAKEMYST

Book Two of the Lissae Series

R. Lennard

Rakemyst
First published in 2019 by R. Lennard
Copyright © Rebecca Lennard, 2019
Cover Design © Vanesa Garkova, 2019
Map Design by Ricky Gunawan, 2019

Printed and bound by Blurb, Inc, San Francisco, USA
Edited by Anna at CREATING ink.
www.CREATINGink.com
Proofread by Desanka Vukelich.
Published by Rebecca Lennard.
www.lissae.com

A catalogue record for this book is available from the National Library of Australia

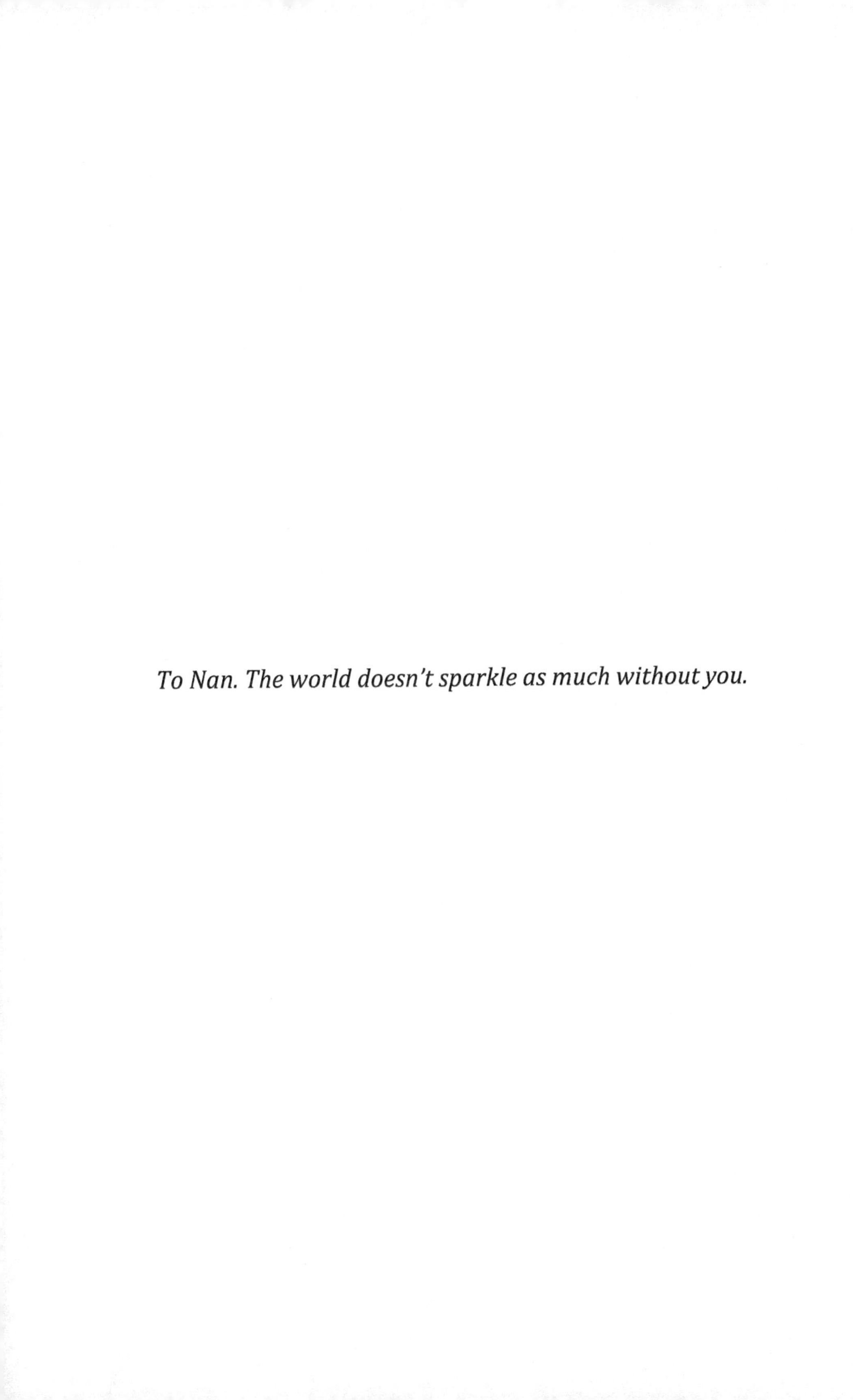

To Nan. The world doesn't sparkle as much without you.

CONTENTS

PROLOGUE

Spring 4059

Crouched behind a shrub, Fiona peered through the leaves and the shimmering of her Innarn shield. Not even a handful of strides away, a scout slunk past, his sharp eyes scouring the dense bushes before him, the *thock thock thock* of his armour belying his position.

As he passed by, Fiona could make out the individual pieces of bone that had been strung together to construct the scout's armour. Fiona fought to suppress a shudder as she wondered how many had died for his chest to be covered in an entire skeleton.

He waved an arm and continued forwards. A few minutes later, a second scout slunk along the path—this one had both legs, one arm, and half his torso covered in bone armour. He looked around as well, but missed her lurking in the bushes. He moved on, and Fiona breathed a sigh of relief. She hoped he was the last one.

Of course, the Fates weren't that kind. The ground beneath her feet shook in time with the pounding beat of an army on the march. Wave upon wave of warriors marched forwards. Fiona struggled to stay silent, her shield flickering slightly with each new line of warriors marching by the meagre protection of her shrub.

Thankfully, the army moved rapidly, their armour in different configurations, but still made of bone. Even their weapons seemed to be made of the stuff. There were swords, bows, and quivers of bone arrows gently knocking together as the soldiers moved, setting her teeth on edge.

She waited as the seemingly endless wall of warriors marched by, the noise of their armour fading into the distance, before rising on silent feet intent on following them.

As she left the shadows of the bushes, an arrow hit the ground by the side of her boot in a clear warning shot. Her eyes flicked to the treetops and fell on a lone archer, obviously charged with protecting the army's back.

"I mean you no harm," Fiona called. "Your... friends scared me. I just want to go on my way."

The next arrow landed in the dirt right next to her left foot. It took everything she had not to yelp and skitter away. She raised her hands, indicating her lack of weaponry.

There was no sound from the archer. Fiona tried to make herself look unthreatening. When the next arrow raced towards her, her only thought was that she clearly needed more practice at appearing unassuming. She arched out of the way, the arrow grazing her side.

Hissing, she retaliated, sending a jet of water towards the archer who let out a startled shriek and fell from the top of the tree. He landed on the ground with a thud. Fiona cautiously crept towards him, but before she managed to reach him, she felt the ground shake with the pounding of boots. She slipped into the bushes as three of the soldiers from the back ranks of the army appeared at their fallen comrade's side.

"Betthar!" one of them called, kneeling by the archer. "He's soaked!" he exclaimed, looking at the others, eyes wide under his skull helmet.

They glanced at each other, hands on the hilts of their weapons.

Eyes flicked around the area, scanning the cloudless sky. Sharp, panicked breaths came from one who was whipping his head back and forth, his skull helmet clattering against the oversized rib bones covering his chest.

"He's gone," the one kneeling exclaimed.

"My brother," whimpered the one with the oversized ribs.

"What do you think...?" one of the standing soldiers asked. His eyes roamed the bushes, and Fiona sunk back farther, drawing the shadows closer.

The kneeling warrior rose, his eyes narrowed. "An Innarnian killed his son," he growled. "Come. We must inform Luttrell."

The three lifted Betthar's body and trudged after the army.

With her brown cloak wrapped around her, Fiona followed a little way behind, staying close to the bushes and keeping an eye out for any other archers.

She skirted the bulk of the army, following the trio and their fallen companion with her eyes as they neared a massive Chirea, completely covered with bone. He towered over the others, and his bulk hid those behind him.

He turned to face them, and upon sighting their burden, he let loose a wail that made Fiona jump in her skin.

The whole army joined in, voices raised in unspeakable agony. Fiona clamped her hands over her ears, trying to block out the noise, tears rolling unbidden down her cheeks.

"Who did this?" the man roared. "Who killed my son?"

Uh-oh.

"An Innarnian, Luttrell. He'd been soaked straight through."

"Innarnian," Luttrell snarled. "Where would an Innarnian have come from?"

A few of the troops closest to him muttered among themselves before one was shoved forwards. "Lissae is the closest Realm, Luttrell. Maybe one came from there?" the soldier asked nervously.

Luttrell loomed over him. "Well, maybe we should pay Lissae a visit and show them that Innarnian or not, they can't get away with killing one of us... killing *my* child!" he roared.

Fiona gulped. Somehow, she didn't think that Luttrell would take kindly to the idea that she'd just been protecting herself. She needed to get back to Lissae and let Jonathan know what had happened as quickly as she could.

The counter of Books 'n' More gleamed in the late afternoon sunshine streaming in through the stained-glass windows. Dust motes danced through the air as Lissae's Altoriae leaned on the counter, her head in her hands.

Shari Dawn was using the downtime between battles to read through the list of the beings who had been Returned to them when she'd defeated Anriluka, and cross-referencing them against the adjusted map of Ronah, making sure that no one had been left out or missed.

Her Guardian, Jonathan, wasn't in the store. He was in a specially sealed room at the castle, helping the Returned residents of Ronah who had yet to move into their new houses.

The door creaked open, and a figure in a brown cloak slid inside, groaning softly, and stumbling as they passed the counter.

"Hey, are you alright?" Shari asked, as she hurried from behind the counter. She recognised the hooded figure from previous encounters.

Collapsing to the floor, the hood fell back revealing the pale face and bloodless lips of Fiona Ribeck, her hands clenched against her stomach.

In between her white-knuckled fingers, the shaft of a pale arrow was protruding.

'*Get Jonathan. The Chirea are coming,*' Fiona sent to her.

Hesitating, Shari wondered if she should send to Jon. Something about the Chirea tickled at the back of her mind though, and it wasn't good.

'*Hey Jon, what's the thing with the Chirea? Are they poisonous?*' Shari sent.

'*What? No. Why?*'

Shari started to reach out with her Innarn, ready to shift Fiona to the Healers' Centre.

"No!" Fiona gasped, eyes wide in her pale face. "The arrows are coated with something that reacts to Innarn!"

'*Can you finish up? There's a thing...*' Shari sent. She heard Jon wordlessly swearing in the back of her mind as she sent out another frantic message to Holli Doonavan, one of the head healers, before rushing to the back room in search of bandages. Arms laden with bandaging supplies, Shari skittered back towards Fiona just as Holli arrived to take over.

Muttering and grumbling, the healer laid Fiona out on the floor, cloak spread out underneath her. "You've got bandages ready? Good. Arrow out, bandage on. Ready? Now." Ruthlessly, Holli pulled the arrow from Fiona, slapping a bandage down as soon as the tip of the arrow came free. "I'll keep up the pressure; you go and get Jonathan."

Shari nodded, and shifted straight to the lower levels of Castle Bachelor. Her legs pumped as she pounded down the corridor. She skidded to a stop and banged on the door of the Barkley Room, urgency flowing through her veins.

The door swung open and Jon slipped through, closing it behind him and cutting off the view of the stunned faces peering at her as he stepped into the hall.

'*Fiona Ribeck is here. Says the Chirea are coming. She's been shot,*' Shari sent, holding out her hand. Jonathan grasped it and she shifted them back to the shop in time to see Holli and a team of healers coming through the door, Fiona on a board between them.

"She needs rest now," Holli said. "We'll keep her at the hospital until the poison is out of her system, then we'll be able to heal her properly."

"She came to talk to me," Jonathan said. At the sound of his voice, Fiona started to struggle off the board, rocking it dangerously.

"Easy!" Holli said, rushing to help the others steady it. "You can talk to her as we walk."

Jonathan gave her a grateful smile and took up position next to Fiona's head as a healer slipped smoothly out of the way. Shari took the other side and joined the healers on the trek as Fiona told them what had happened in gasping sentences. She was even paler when she was done.

Jonathan leaned over her. "Rest now. You've reported. You're safe. The healers will take care of you."

Fiona's eyes fluttered closed. Shari and Jonathan were seamlessly replaced by healers as they slipped away from her side, their eyes meeting in concern for what lay ahead.

"We'd better call Tania and..." Jonathan stopped and ran a hand over his face. "And get back to the shop."

Shari flinched, knowing that he'd been about to say *and Mitch*. Except, of course, Mitch wasn't around anymore. Jonathan's trusted apprentice rested with the Spirits of Ronah now.

Holding a hand against her twingeing chest, Shari shifted them to the front of the shop, sending Tania a message to meet them there.

'*Beat you to it!*' Tania stepped out of the back room with steaming cups of peppermint tea.

Shari took one gratefully. Taking a moment to breathe in the scented steam, she set her tea on the counter, and leaned down to clean Fiona's blood off the floor.

"Ronah filled me in," Tania said quietly as she stood with Jonathan at the end of the counter. "I'm not sure what makes the Chirea so dangerous compared to what you've already dealt with. Their armour is off-putting, but I don't see the big fuss."

"We have something the Chirea don't. The ability to tap into the Elements," Jonathan replied grimly.

"You mean Innarn?" Tania asked, wrinkling her nose in confusion.

"Yes. When someone wants something badly, there's very little they'll stop at to get it," said Jonathan, taking a sip of his drink.

"Can that happen? Can someone steal an Innarnian's powers?" Tania asked, brows drawn together in concern.

"There are old stories, but I hope that's all they are. If the Chirea got hold of a powerful Innarnian, there's no telling what they'd do," Jonathan said, his eyes tracking Shari at the other end of the bookshop.

Picking up her cup, Shari took a gulp of the scalding tea, trying to chase away the chill trickling down her spine.

CHAPTER ONE

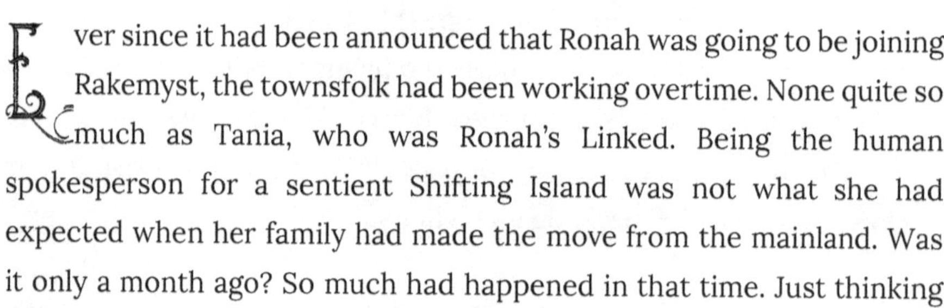

Ever since it had been announced that Ronah was going to be joining Rakemyst, the townsfolk had been working overtime. None quite so much as Tania, who was Ronah's Linked. Being the human spokesperson for a sentient Shifting Island was not what she had expected when her family had made the move from the mainland. Was it only a month ago? So much had happened in that time. Just thinking about it made Tania's head spin.

After the battle with Anriluka, Tania found Ronah's enthusiasm for joining with one of the Shifting Islands exhilarating, if not hard to block out at times. As she slipped through the door of the bookstore, thoughts of Chirea swirling through her head, Ronah sent her another image of flowers growing on the bereni trees of the Island's only school, Ridden Hall, seemingly unaware of the fate of Jonathan's scout.

'Please pick some and take them to the town square. Rakemyst is sure to appreciate them!' Ronah sent to her.

Giggling, Tania skipped her way down the street. Rakemyst was older than Ronah, and just like any other sibling, Ronah was trying to make Rakemyst proud. Tania didn't know exactly how one sentient Island made another proud, but she was sure that being Linked to Ronah meant that she was going to find out.

The preparations for joining with Rakemyst were almost done. The town square was adorned with the most beautiful, jewel-bright flowers that Tania had ever seen.

Ronah was currently growing houses as fast as she could for all the newly Returned residents, as well as preparing for the join with Rakemyst, controlling the Islands' weather, and the path they travelled around Lissae.

Tania's favourite part was watching the homes grow straight out of the ground. If she had a week or two spare, she'd watch as the houses expanded up from the earth, branches twisting into walls, stairs, and furniture, ready for a new family to move into. Tania was used to the brick-and-mortar type used on the mainland, but the most common houses on Ronah were the bereni tree, or the rezem; a type of house that looked like a big grassy hill from the outside, but was actually quite roomy and warm on the inside.

A gentle mental nudge from Ronah reminded her that they still had work to do. Tania grinned as she skipped her way to the beach end of Calloway Street. Staring at the empty residence, Tania breathed in deeply, the way that Ronah had taught her. She took a moment to stare at the scene in front of her, memorising the lines of the house, the flowers and herbs in the garden, and the curve of the land. Then she closed her eyes and breathed out. After raising her hands up to her chin, fingertips together, she slowly pushed her hands out, sensing the movements of the earth as she did so. Focusing on the way Ronah felt, the land that should be nice and smooth, and the dwelling that should now be slightly to the right of where it originally stood, she flicked a finger, and tilted her head. Opening her eyes, she nodded in satisfaction. The first part was done.

Stepping forwards onto the newly created dirt road, she repeated the action again and again, until sweat was dripping off her forehead and her arms were trembling. She sent out a message to the earth Innarn crew, who would come and pave the new road, making it accessible no matter the weather.

Growing up in a tiny village on the mainland, Innarnians had felt like mythical figures. They were people who could use Innarn and shape the Elements to their will. Far too often, Innarnians were blamed for any problem the villagers had. Moving to Ronah and living among Innarnians who were able to create things like the road she'd just made, had been a big adjustment. Ronah still had a few who were Blanks, and not all Innarnian had the same strength or the same abilities. Tania still felt a little zing of energy lighting up her nerves every time she remembered that *she* was an Innarnian. She'd heard of them, dreamed of being one, but it wasn't until her family had come to Ronah that she'd discovered she was not only able to use Innarn, but was Linked to Ronah as well.

A gentle green, healing glow surrounded her tired, trembling limbs, and she grinned, sending fond thoughts to Ronah. Spinning in a circle, arms wide, Tania laughed aloud. For a moment, she could ignore the monsters who were about to come knocking and just enjoy where she was.

Shari sped through the forest paths, pushing herself hard, trying to outrun the memories that chased her. She broke through the last of the trees and emerged into a clearing. Hands on knees, she tried to catch her breath. It took her a moment to realise that she was standing at the edge of the clearing on the highest point of Ronah.

Right at the spot where she'd first seen Mitch fall after he'd had his brain scooped out through his eye socket, was Samuel Caragnton.

The friend of her Guardian stood with his back to her, the overhead sun making his hair gleam like gold. Shari wondered how he was coping with everything that had happened since he'd arrived on Ronah. He'd hardly had the welcome wagon rolled out. She sniffed, remembering Mitch's suspicion of this man who had claimed to be Jonathan's friend.

A faint breeze whispered past Shari, carrying a noise that caused her to drop her jaw.

Sam was *humming*.

Her lip curling involuntarily, Shari frowned as she shifted away, wanting to put as much space between her and Jonathan's friend as possible. How could Sam hum when she was still grieving?

Slipping back into the room under Castle Bachelor, Jonathan apologised for his disappearing act. Concerned faces looked at him from all corners. A woman rose from her seat, facing him.

"Guardian, how can we help?" she asked, bowing her head deferentially.

Jonathan ran a tired hand over his face. After Shari had most convincingly defeated the U'tan, Anriluka had exploded, sliming the whole of Ronah with her insides. Out of the slime had risen all the meals the U'tan had eaten. There had been hordes of beings and creatures who Anriluka had digested in case of her defeat, but she had also eaten a lot of Ronah's townsfolk before she'd been banished from Lissae. Every day for the last month, he'd been to endless meetings, trying to ascertain what the Returned from Anriluka needed.

From what he understood, the Returned had lived out every day since they were first eaten in a nightmarish pocket-Realm, where they'd had to fight for their lives the whole time. If they had been killed, they were simply reborn again, often to find another horrific creature feasting on their flesh. They'd made a fortified village of sorts, but it hadn't been totally impenetrable. Anriluka had kept them like that, using any excess Innarn from them and the other creatures trapped there.

Most of the Returned wanted to resettle on Ronah. A few had asked to go to the mainland, and some wanted to leave Lissae altogether. It was a struggle for the very young, as they were now great-great-aunts and uncles, their family, friends, and playmates long dead. The older victims were swinging between wanting to take up their position as Elders and shying away from anything to do with leadership. Many of the Returned weren't able to stand bright light after living in the dimension they'd been trapped in for so long. Only a handful would talk about their time in 'captivity.'

Their long, haunted faces and empty eyes plagued Jonathan's dreams.

"I'm not sure, to be honest. Things are becoming more difficult," he admitted.

The woman raised an eyebrow. "Really?" she asked sardonically. "All of us here have sworn our oaths, Guardian. Tell us how we can help."

"I'm not sure if..."

The woman withdrew a dagger from the folds of her skirts and pressed it into the soft flesh under his jaw before walking him backwards until he hit the wall. "I'll not ask again. We have spent *lifetimes* trapped and waiting to be able to do something. You are *not* going to deny us that chance." Her voice dropped, low and menacing.

Jonathan found himself quite glad that she was on his side. Gently, he pushed her hand down. She let him, but he didn't forget the blade clenched in her fist. "We've received information that the Chirea are planning an attack on Lissae." He didn't mention how big their army was, nor the provocation for the attack. He shoved down to the deep, dark recesses of his mind how much he worried about his young charge, her shaken confidence and depression after the death of his apprentice and her friend at Anriluka's tentacles.

The woman before him nodded. "We can help with that. There are healers here who could assist yours, and fighters to join the front lines."

"Ours. We are all from Ronah, are we not?" Jonathan asked.

She dipped her head. "Shall I...?" Trailing off, she gestured to the room.

"With my thanks." He bowed his head and she strode off, no doubt ready to rally the troops.

How many of the 2198 people who had returned would fight? Ten of the largest family groups had been settled into their new houses so far, and there were a few Innarnian architects who were gathering their strength before they commenced the creation of their own houses. He was looking forward to seeing them work. Ronah hadn't had an architect since... well, not since Anriluka ate them all.

A commotion off to the side caught his attention. One of the townsfolk was shouting at a tall, thin woman. She was looking at her attacker with blank eyes, her arms wrapped protectively around her middle. Jonathan noted the glint of a blue blade resting along her ribs, hidden from her attacker, but ready to strike if he got any closer.

Squaring his shoulders, he strode over. "What's the matter, Trent?"

"This! Half of my property has been taken away because Ronah is rebuilding roads so this lot can move in and take over! How is it fair when the land that's been in my family for generations is taken from me?" Trent Shansky snarled, waving his arms, and almost knocking the woman in front of him off her feet.

Jonathan frowned. "These people are the reason you're alive. Actually, your great-great-great grandfather is over there," he said, pointing to a bearded man in a blue shirt who looked younger than Trent. "His son survived and went on to continue the family line, ensuring that you were born. Are you saying that you don't want more of your family on Ronah?"

Trent's scowl didn't change. "I have a very specific crop rotation. I make use of every part of my land. Why is Ronah taking it from me?"

"To give back to your family. If you look at the records, your land wasn't always that big," Jonathan started.

"I don't care how big or small it was in the olden days," snapped Trent. "I care about now."

Jonathan stared at him, clenching hands into fists. He worked at unlocking his jaw so he wouldn't shatter his teeth. These people had suffered so much. They'd experienced traumas so deep that he couldn't begin to comprehend, and Trent was worried about a few metres of land. "Maybe," he said, his voice deceptively calm, "Ronah can move you to a bigger block."

"I don't want a bigger block; I want *my* block the way it was. Things were just fine before this lot came back. Maybe they should all move to the mainland, or just go somewhere else," he muttered.

In a quiet voice, the woman standing next to them spoke up. "We never asked for this. We never wanted to be killed, never wanted to survive a half-life, and never dreamed that we would come back. I see now that it would have been better if we hadn't."

"No," Jonathan pleaded. "Not everyone feels like Trent."

"His anger burns me. Cuts me like a thousand knives. I cannot stay when there is so much anger directed at me. At us," she said.

Trent seemed to deflate. "I'm not angry at you. I just want to keep what is mine."

She tilted her head, a bird-like gesture. "Don't you think that we wanted to keep what was ours as well? Our lives? Our families? Anything else seems trivial to us now. Guardian, give *me* the parcel of land that this road goes on, and I'll give it back to Trent. I'll happily sleep out under the stars," she said quietly.

Jonathan bowed his head, moved.

"Good. It's settled then," Trent said, clapping his hands together, as if the whole conversation was dust he could brush away.

"While your offer is generous, if you remove the road, the people whose houses lie on the other side wouldn't be able to access them. I'm sorry, Trent, but the current plan has been finalised. I'm not sure why you didn't come to me beforehand. I know you were notified," Jonathan said.

"I was busy," Trent blustered. "Had to clean up after those creatures decimated my crops."

"They decimated our lives," said a new voice. It looked like Ashlen, his great-great-great-grandfather, had joined the conversation. He was joined by a tall teenager with ink on the skin of his biceps. Jonathan recognised him as Collis. He wasn't sure why he had come over, but if he could help to diffuse the situation, he was more than welcome.

"I'm sorry for that," Trent said, not sounding sorry at all. "But the consultation period to change the layout of Ronah should have lasted longer than a week!"

"You expect us to wait how long? We waited 328 years to be freed; what's another month?" Ashlen said. "What could it possibly matter to us, eh?"

Collis put a restraining hand on Ashlen's shoulder, and Jonathan was surprised to see the older Returned take a calming breath.

"Look, you can't just come back and think that everything is going to be the same!" Trent exclaimed.

"*Everything* has changed. Everyone we ever cared about is gone or has been affected by what has happened. Nothing is the same for us," Ashlen said sadly.

"So, because nothing is the same for you, it can't stay the same for me? Maybe I should join those going to the mainland! Maybe then I'll get my fair share of land!"

Jonathan could hear Collis grinding his teeth, but the boy stayed silent as Ashlen looked at his descendant. "If it makes you happy, then I wish you a pleasant journey."

"You'd like that, wouldn't you?" Trent growled, raising his fists, and leaning in close to Ashlen's face. "Want me to get out of your way so you can get your precious road?"

As Collis pulled Ashlen back, Tania popped into being between the two men, her eyes wide and her nose pressed against Trent's chest.

He cursed and stumbled back.

"Ronah says you need to calm down. The amount of land that she needs is only a strip off your block. It works out as far less than what your neighbours are losing. They're relocating, as are the people on the other side of them," Tania said. "Ronah has been leaving you messages and sending to you. As you haven't replied, we went ahead with the proposed changes. These people are *of Ronah*, same as you, and Ronah welcomes everyone and looks after everyone. Not just a favoured few," Tania said, her pleading eyes at odds with her commanding stance.

He harrumphed. "Suppose I can't argue with Ronah," he grumbled, "but I'm not happy about it at all!" He turned and left the room.

Tania and Jonathan both sighed. With Trent gone, the mood in the room relaxed significantly. Jonathan nudged Tania. "Good job," he said.

"My thanks," Ashlen murmured. Collis led him away, glancing back at Tania.

"That was intense. I'm sorry I didn't get here sooner," Tania said. "Ronah was keeping an eye out. I'll see if I can get the road moved slightly so it cuts less into his property, but there's no guarantee. Creating roads is hard work!"

Shari moved through the crowds on the main street, aiming for her parents' tavern. Everyone was coming to check out the preparations for the joining.

At first, she was able to pass through relatively easily, but there was a tickle of an Innarn against her shields. Turning, she saw little two-year-old Eric grinning at her.

"Ree!" he said joyfully. "No piky, Ree?" he asked, grabbing her hands.

"No spiky things today, Eric," she said. It had taken her a few precious, heart-stopping seconds to figure out that Eric referred to the twin blades on her glove as 'piky.' She was glad that the little boy didn't seem to be affected by his death at Anriluka's hands, not to mention seeing the minotaur who'd almost run him through after he'd returned.

Eric's parents came up, breathless.

"He's still escaping!" Andrew exclaimed, sweeping his son into his arms. Eric squealed with joy.

Shari grinned at the couple. "It seems like he's quite happy."

"Our little escape artist has his moments," Louise replied, a shadow flicking across her eyes.

There was an awkward silence. Shari wasn't sure what to say. Did she apologise? Did she deliver some meaningless platitude that made her feel better for saying it, but lacked any depth? She might work hard to save these people, but being on the outside of everything for so long had decimated her social skills.

Andrew cleared his throat. "Are you looking forward to the joining? You'll be able to see your father's side of the family!" he said in an obvious attempt at joviality. Louise wrung her hands together.

"It will be good to finally meet them," Shari smiled. "Dad has told me so much about them."

In a rush, Louise flung her arms around Shari. "I'm sorry!" she cried. "You saved Eric! I need to hug you!"

Shari stood stock-still, her arms stiff by her sides, her eyes wide.

People didn't touch her.

There were few on Ronah who'd ever hugged her, and certainly never in the main street where others might see—aside from her parents, of course. When Ronah's townsfolk had thought that she was a Blank, they'd avoided touching her at all, almost in fear of losing their own Innarn. It didn't work like that, but people could be funny with how they viewed things.

Louise finally let her go, her face bright red. "Thank you," she whispered again as Andrew gently led her away, looking apologetic.

Standing still for a moment as the crowd moved past allowed Shari to see the welcoming nods and smiles aimed at her. She took a deep breath and wondered if she'd ever get used to the idea that the general public would be happy in her vicinity.

Someone cleared their throat at her side. Shari turned and raised an eyebrow at Anika.

"I hope you don't expect me to hug you," Anika said out of the side of her mouth.

Shari laughed. "Nah, wouldn't want to put either of us through that."

"Good." Anika sniffed and simpered away, nose in the air.

The more things change, the more others stay the same.

On an unnamed Realm, a Ducibus opened a gateway to a purple-robed being and was promptly stabbed in both hearts.

The halls of the Ducibus were empty. No one heard the keening cry as one of their own was slaughtered.

The purple-robed being stepped through the gateway and grinned.

Chapter Two

losing her eyes, Shari let her other senses take over. The sounds of fallen twigs snapping under feet, playful shrieks, and happy laughter filled Ronah's forest as people streamed through the paths to gather at Ronah's highest point. Shari stood back from the edge of the cliff, tugging on her sleeve and failing to keep her eyes away from the spot where her friend and fellow fighter Mitch had first been killed.

Another happy shriek cut through the air. Shari opened her eyes, turning in time to see Eric being swept up into the arms of an uncle. Louise hovered off to the side. The corner of her mouth quirked, and Shari nodded to herself. Even if bad things happened, life would continue uninterrupted for others.

The din around her made it a tad easier for her to remember that. Most people were happy to put their grief aside for the night and indulge in the joy others were feeling. There was an undercurrent of uncertainty in the crowd though, stemming from those who had suffered at Anriluka's hands.

Shari spotted a few new faces. The Returned had made the trip. Some trembled and grasped hands, while others held their heads high. Most wore ink on their skin, some hidden behind the older-style tunics and dresses. Shari idly wondered if inking had been more common before Anriluka had decimated Ronah's population.

A furious satisfaction filled Shari at the thought of Anriluka's defeat. She was glad that the U'tan would never be a problem again. The destruction that had followed in the wake of Anriluka's death was still being cleaned up. The residents of Ronah deserved a night of frivolity and fun to make up for all that they had been through in the three weeks since Shari had publicly declared that she was the Altoriae.

Jonathan stepped up to her right side, and Tania Bryant took her place at Shari's left. Seeing that the Altoriae's Guild was present and accounted for, Alan Pratt thumped the ceremonial staff he was holding on a flat ziom rock. The deep boom echoed in the sudden silence. A ribbon of anticipation threaded through the crowd, winding higher and higher until the call came.

"Rakemyst is nigh!"

Cheers arose from the crowd. Shari half-heartedly joined in until Tania jostled her. She looked at the younger girl, curious.

'What are they doing?' Tania sent.

'The traditional greeting ceremony for Rakemyst. It starts off with the sighting of the Island. Then when the Islands join, there is the greeting, the reply, and the crossing. It's more fun than it sounds,' Shari sent back.

Tania frowned at her. 'You don't look like you're having fun at all.'

'I don't feel like it too much, to be honest. I'm worried about my grandfather, and I can't forget that this is where...' She couldn't even finish the thought. Shortly after the scourge that Anriluka had released had been wiped out, Shari's father had received news that her grandfather was ill. SilverCloud Dawn was an important person on his home Island of Rakemyst, and instead of travelling by conventional means, the two

Islands had conspired together to meet, allowing the Dawn family to reunite.

'*I understand being worried about your grandfather. But don't forego your favourite place on Ronah because of what happened here. Don't let Anriluka have that victory over you,*' Tania sent, laying a gentle hand on her arm.

She hadn't thought of it that way before. There was no way that she wanted to give Anriluka any sort of hold over her, not when she'd taken away so much. She nodded, knowing that Tania would understand.

Looking out at the rapidly approaching land mass before them, Shari let her mind wander, spiralling up higher and higher above the clouds to get the best view of the Islands meeting. She knew that Tania and Jon would keep her safe.

Ronah was a familiar sight. The gleaming white beaches wrapped around half the Island and gave way to houses and green pastures before the stream and forest, and the joyous mass of people perched on the edge.

Turning, Shari took in Rakemyst. The Shifting Island glided through the waves with barely any wake around the base of the grey rocky cliffs.

The main island was shrouded in fog. Shari's gaze was drawn to the tiny islands floating above the main one, some so small only a person could stand on them, others large enough to hold grand houses. The biggest one held a home three stories high, with gleaming white walls, and a tiered garden thriving with plants and birdlife.

The fog seemed to pull at her again, and Shari felt a chill go through her soul. Were the Ilutri standing in the white shroud, or were there monsters lurking in the mist?

The gap between the Islands was closing, and Shari had just enough time to get back in her body and brace herself as Rakemyst and Ronah finally touched.

A thunderous clap sounded as the base of the Islands came together. People rocked on their feet and grasped each other, laughing, or looking on in awe. Rakemyst sent the tingling noise of silvery bells at them and Ronah replied with the sizzle of lightning. The sounds echoed around the cheering crowd.

Shari expected to be excited. Those around her certainly were. Tania had tears welling in her eyes, and Jonathan had straightened his spine. She could feel his eagerness singing through their connection. The cheering crowd seemed to fade into the back of her mind as Shari stared into Rakemyst's clearing.

It was still shrouded in a thick fog.

She could just make out dark shapes moving, causing the happy anticipation to wind higher in the crowd on Ronah's side as they waited for their counterparts to respond.

As one, Ronah and her residents sent out the welcome with joyous hearts. 'Well *met!*'

There was no response.

They sent again, 'Well *met!*'

Silence.

Another frisson of unease skated down her spine. She reached out to Rakemyst but couldn't get a read on the older Island.

Elder Silverstone took a step forwards before she called out. Jonathan threw up a shield, preventing anyone from crossing to the other Shifting Island.

"Really now, Guardian," the Elder called out, frowning. He was hushed quickly by the other Elders. From the uneasy looks they shared, they knew something was wrong as well. It had been decades since the two Shifting Islands had met up, but this time there was a difference in the air that had more than a few people looking at each other uneasily.

Shari and Jonathan glanced at each other.

"Tania," Jon said in a low voice, "can Ronah hear Rakemyst?"

Glad that they had someone who was able to tap into Ronah, Shari waited as the younger girl's eyes slid closed.

"There's... static. But it feels like..." Her eyes flew open. "Like Rakemyst is in pain!"

Nodding to each other, Shari and Jon shifted across the shield, landing silently on Rakemyst. Inside the fog, the sound from the crowd behind them disappeared. Shari raised an eyebrow at Jon, who shook his head. It wasn't him creating the silence. Even knowing that Jon was only an arm's-length away, Shari struggled to make out more than just his outline. Rakemyst was renowned for fog, but she'd never heard of it being this thick before.

Together, she and Jon tried to push the concealing mist back, but it barely rippled. Dark shapes loomed across from them—trees, maybe? She couldn't tell.

'Well met, Altoriae, Guardian.' The voice in her head was old and reedy, reminding her of a water bird's call. 'It seems I require aid.'

'Well met, Rakemyst. What sort of aid do you require?'

Shari stepped closer to one of the shapes and stopped as a section of fog lifted. Jon nudged her with his mind, and she saw the spirit—a kneeling Ilutri in gleaming silver armour with his head bowed, wings folded and drooping behind him.

Shari's eyes widened. There was no record of Ronah being met by a spirit before. As she stepped forwards, her foot scuffed on the ground. The spirit looked up and spotted her. Ethereal tears made tracks down his cheeks. He lowered his head again, and for the first time, Shari saw the tip of a golden arrow protruding from his stomach.

He'd been shot. But why was he here, now?

The unknown Ilutri looked shocked for a moment before he left the ground. He hovered above their heads, before floating backwards, away from Shari and Jon.

'Defend me,' the reedy voice whispered in her mind.

Shari barely hesitated. She flicked her wrist, her glove appearing on her hand, blades out. Jon didn't question her; he merely summoned his crossbow, bolt loaded and ready to fire.

In the fog that surrounded them, the trees swayed, despite the distinct lack of breeze. She narrowed her eyes, scanning the branches, before she caught sight of two glowing spots. Squinting, she tried to see better.

An arrow streaked past her, bouncing off Jonathan's shield, landing only a handful of steps behind them.

Shouts rose from Ronah as Chirean warriors stepped forwards out of the fog, bows drawn and ready to fire. Their skeletal armour clicked with each step. Shari met the glowing eyes of the warrior closest to her and snarled.

The only thing she was going to lose today was her temper. How did the Chirea get onto Lissae?

Then there was no more time to question.

'To arms! Rakemyst has been attacked!' Jon's send rattled in her skull as he dissolved the shield, allowing Ronah's residents to shift over and join them in battle.

The Chirea let out an eerie cry and shot their arrows into the stampeding rush.

Tsunamis of earth rose to crash down on Chirean troops even as a more familiar call came from the tiny islands floating in the air above. Craning her neck, Shari recognised the Ilutri archers before the first bolts rained down. Most bounced off the bone armour, but Shari had never been so glad to see an army in her life.

The Chirea army marched relentlessly forwards, bows twanging and blades hacking the people in their way.

Shari sent a quick message out, *'Those who can shift, start moving them off Lissae. Don't let any past our ranks!'* She received a rush of affirmative answers.

From the cliffs, a phalanx of Ilutri archers rose and streaked across the sky. Arrows streamed through open air, hitting some of the Ilutri, and Shari realised that the one with the greying wings was her grandfather.

He went down in a tangle with two others but seemed as comfortable with the blade as he was the bow. SilverCloud and the other fallen were fighting back. The Chirea started disappearing, one at a time.

Shari sent out her Innarn to brush against Jonathan's, and they sent off two score. A darkly familiar presence moved behind her, Sam adding his Innarn to hers. Grabbing it, she was able to shift half the army away.

Eyes wide, gasping for breath at the rush of power that had flowed through her, she shook her hands out, her fingers still tingling.

"Shall we get the last of them?" Sam asked.

A cry from the side distracted her. A group of Chirea forcing SilverCloud and a younger Ilutri towards the forest.

Shari nodded, not trusting her voice. As she gathered Sam and Jonathan's Innarn to hers, Sam started humming, low enough to just be on the edge of her hearing. A mournful sound, echoing slightly in the decimated clearing as the last group of Chirea landed several Realms away.

Checking the battlefield was clear, she rounded on Sam, who was still humming. She shot him a filthy look before shifting away to track her parents down.

Shari arrived just in time to see a squad of Ilutri archers descending to surround her parents. Her father's feathers were barely ruffled, although he was sporting a nasty cut on a forearm. He slid a blade back into the sheath, arguing heatedly with one of the archers. Her mother's dress was ripped at the shoulder seam, and she had a sizable graze on one leg. She held a sword that her father must have conjured for her.

Arilla yelped and dropped the sword as one of the Ilutri slipped his arms around her waist and started to lift off, despite Arilla shouting and pounding on the arms that entrapped her.

"No!" Shari snarled, and thrust her hand out, twisting her wrist to make a vine spring from the earth and snake around the archer's ankle as he rose higher. He jerked, but tightened his grip on Arilla, making sure she couldn't escape his grasp. He scowled down at Shari, and another of the archers shot through the vine, allowing him to rise until they were high enough that falling would be fatal. Shari growled in aggravation, took three quick steps forwards, and jumped, creating a twister of air that pushed her as high as the Ilutri kidnapping her mother.

"Let her go!" Shari snarled.

"I'm on orders to take the Blank..." the archer replied, then yelped. Arilla had twisted and bitten him on the bicep. His grasp slipped and Arilla wriggled enough so that she started to fall.

Shari guided her twister of air, swooping in and grasping her mum's hand. Arilla held on tight, fear evident in her wide eyes, legs dangling far above the ground below. Controlling the twister to lower her back down, Shari sent a quick message to Jonathan, asking for help.

Jonathan shifted in as Shari and her mother landed, sandwiching Arilla between their backs. She shifted her father in too, so they surrounded Arilla amid the Ilutri archers. Shari flicked her wrist, her black glove reappearing, the short sword from Yessna held loosely in her other hand. Even as a shield flickered to life around them, she wondered why the Ilutri archers were trying to take her mother away.

One of the archers separated from the others. He was the one who'd carried her mother into the sky. In appearance, he was a slightly stretched version of her father. Same dark eyes, same black hair— although his was longer. His yellow armour was a lighter shade than that of the others in the group, and he carried himself with an air of superiority.

Calem looked at the Ilutri approaching and bowed his head. "Prince LoneWolf," he murmured.

Shari raised an eyebrow, but not her weapons. She didn't look away as LoneWolf turned to glare at their group, catching her eye and lifting a brow of his own when she failed to bow her head.

"Is the use of outdated nicknames any way to greet your brother?" LoneWolf looked at Calem after a long pause.

Huh. The Ilutri before her was her uncle. Well, this was some introduction.

"Was there a reason you were absconding with your sister-in-law, LoneWolf?" Jonathan asked, with only a slight prompting from Shari. Behind her back Arilla was poking her, grumbling at being shut out from what was happening.

"My brother's wife is in danger from the Chirea. We must ensure her safety for when they return. Surely you see the need to keep our people safe, Guardian?" LoneWolf asked.

"We are more than capable of keeping her safe," Shari growled.

"Ah, she speaks. No doubt you are, but our archers are the finest..." He broke off at Shari's disgusted look. "You disagree?"

"Archery is not the only way to keep someone safe. The Chireans have no Innarn. We have more defensible spots on Ronah than you have on Rakemyst," Shari argued.

"Ah, but they will not stop the Chirea. We have places in the clouds that no Blank would be able to get to," LoneWolf argued.

"Ones that I would be a veritable prisoner in," Arilla spoke up for the first time. "Been there, done that. Not interested in a repeat."

The flippant words seemed to rile LoneWolf whose dark eyes flashed.

Calem stepped forwards slightly, although not enough to leave Arilla at risk of being snatched again. "You won't be a prisoner if I'm there with you," he said, his words meant for his wife, but his eyes on his brother.

Arilla let out a shaky breath. "If you will be there... alright. I'll go."

LoneWolf seemed to run through some mental gymnastics before giving a short, sharp nod. "Follow me then, brother. If your wings still work," he said, his own wings spreading out. He leaped into the air, and with powerful downward strokes, rose higher into the sky where he hovered, waiting for Arilla and Calem to join him.

Calem turned and looked at Shari. "Stay safe and stay in contact with me, alright?"

"Will do, Dad. Send if you need a hand," Shari said. "I need to help with the tidy-up down here, but I'll join you when I can."

Arilla reached out and gripped Shari's hand hard for a moment. "I'll send a message if I need a quick escape," she winked.

Shari laughed weakly, her hand rising to the pendant that she still wore. She knew that it would glow if her mother needed her. Arilla had a matching one that she kept in a pouch on her belt.

Calem smiled grimly and wrapped his arms around Arilla. Shari and Jonathan stepped back and he took off, rising into the air to wing their way to some secret fortress above the clouds. The other Ilutri archers joined them, leaving those on land to stare up at the clearing sky.

"Well," Jonathan said after a pause. "What do you think of your uncle?"

"I think he's about as uptight as you could get without adding a stick up his—"

"Altoriae!" Elder Thorne called out. Shari looked over to see him striding towards them. "Have you heard?"

Shari tilted her head to the side, nerves jumping with anticipation. Edward Thorne only ever called her by her title when things were serious. What had happened to warrant it this time?

"It's your grandfather, SilverCloud. He's missing," Edward said.

Gasping, she took a moment to breathe. Her grandfather was the oldest of Rakemyst's Elders, and the people here looked to him for guidance. He was their leader and their conscience. The Ilutri on Rakemyst would be unsettled and restless without him. "Where was he last seen?" Shari asked.

Edward sent her the coordinates, and she nodded her thanks. 'Do you mind getting this cleaned up?' she sent to Jonathan.

'Go,' he sent back. 'I've got this. Make sure to stay objective. Your emotions will cloud your vision otherwise.'

'Emotions aren't bad, Jonathan,' Shari sent back, shooting him a look, and shifted away, blocking his response.

She needed to find SilverCloud, and not just because he was her grandfather.

CHAPTER THREE

Samuel slipped away from the crowd. Residents of both Islands were milling around, cleaning up after the preparations for the two Islands joining had been destroyed in the brief skirmish. He hummed as he wandered idly along a wide path that led him deeper into Rakemyst, wondering what secrets this isle had to offer.

Rakemyst, Samuel decided, was nothing like Ronah. If the two places were any more different, they'd belong on Realms at the opposite ends of the plain. Ronah was a confusing conglomeration of all Elements, whereas Rakemyst was a place where air Innarn was valued above all else.

There were dozens of landmasses floating in the air above them. He didn't know why they just didn't float away from the main island. Great curving walls of carved white marble topped with blue tiles made it look like the tiny islands dotting the sky were carrying clouds.

Ilutri were moving between the dwellings, some in death-defying jumps with wings pulled tight to their backs. Their backless tunics and baggy pants were cinched tight around their ankles and waists, all in shades of white, yellow, or blue, with the occasional dusky orange or night-dark blue flashing through the sky. Others wore glinting armour and carried bows, drifting between dwellings in lazy spirals, ready to shoot anything remotely bone-covered.

There was a heaviness to the air here, and he wondered if it was just him, or the aftermath of the battle. He'd have to wait and see. He'd come across a lot of beings in his long years that thought the element of air was the one to be least admired. They forgot that, just like all the other elements, air could be giving, kind, and wonderful–the waft of a tantalising scent or the much-needed breath after vigorous exercise; but it could be cruel and cutting as well–the grit and sand flung against your eyes as you struggled to see where your opponent stood or the rattling gasp as a last breath was released.

The winged beings around him moved with purpose. Every one of them seemed to know what job they needed to do. It was different for those without wings, who seemed to flutter like flags in the breeze, not making much of a headway in anything they set out to do. He would have thought, given the elements that most connected with, The Ilurti would have the air in their heads, and those from Ronah would be the ones getting things done.

Feathers of all different shades fairly littered the ground here. The winged picked them up reverently, while the wingless smoothed over the ground and regrew the plants, making sure to leave the paths wide enough for three Ilutri to fly side by side.

If he were to change form, it would be slightly less cramped here, but his wings would still tangle and tear in the branches. Samuel had thought that he would be more at home on Rakemyst, surrounded by fliers, but they were sunlight and air compared to his night and plasma.

'Well met, Traveller Samuel.' The voice was old and reedy. *'I am Rakemyst. I understand that you have an agreement with my little sister.'*

Samuel blinked. *'I do.'*

'*She is kinder than I. Do not test me, traveller.*'

There was an uncomfortable rumbling, and his breath caught, trapped in his throat for a moment too long. '*I will not. I am here to help.*'

'*Words are easy.*' Rakemyst left his mind with a huff.

Blocking the thought that he was older than the hunk of dirt, he moved off the path. There was only one low-level Innarnian who seemed interested in him—a thin youth who he'd seen with one of the Ilutri Elders before. His blue feathers were quite striking, but not nearly as much as Samuel's own wings. Doubtful that one little Innarnian could cause him problems, Sam changed into his seabird form, rising high into the sky to see if he was able to establish where the Chirea had entered, and how a Blank race had managed to come onto a Realm with as much Innarn as Lissae.

Without the fog, Rakemyst was a sight to behold. The main island was bracketed by dense forests, with a stream on one side. Farmland took up a good two thirds of the cleared space, the rest making way for what looked like a town centre. The buildings were made from the same white marble-like substance, although the rooves were green and flat. As he floated on the breeze, an Ilutri landed on a roof and jumped down to ground level. It was a rather practical design, apart from the great towering monstrosity reaching for the sky in the middle of the island.

Flying closer, he noted that the outside walls were dotted with semi-circular landing balconies. He wondered why a race so saturated with Innarn bothered with such a Blank way of building. Ilutri fluttered around the tower, making it too busy to get any closer unnoticed.

Spiralling upwards and away, Samuel noted a rather small, flat-topped floating island connected to the main one via what looked like a temporary bridge. Lazily, he drifted towards it, until he alighted on the tiny island to look closer at the bridge.

If he knew the Chirea, and he did, the bridge was made of bones—some so fresh, the meat was barely scraped off. Clearly, they'd entered from this island, but how had they arrived?

There was a retching sound from the other side of the bridge. Sam looked across and saw Jonathan rubbing Tania's back as she held her stomach, doubled over, a hand shielding her mouth in an attempt to delay the inevitable.

The girl was so dangerously naïve. It made him long to train her and introduce her to the Realms as he had been, if only to strip away the idea that everyone was out to be her friend—or worse, to be *nice* to her.

There were few other beings able to stand up to the demanding and demeaning introduction which his kin preferred, but he had an inkling she would be one of them.

His first time away from his home Realm, he'd almost starved. When his kin had found him, he'd had his maw buried in the still-cooling body of a Wastigg: a beast with a body and head like a bull, and a scorpion's tail and claws. They stood ten feet high at the withers. His bird beak had been open in a sigh. It had been his first meal in three weeks. The smell of roasting Wastigg flesh still made him drool.

He shook his head. Getting nostalgic was not going to help him figure out how the Chirea had gotten onto this tiny island in the first place. Hopping around, his claws scratched the earth, sharp eyes spying something that shouldn't have been there. Moving closer, his claw came down on a glowing purple line drawn on the ground, and he pulled back abruptly, claw curled up as it burned, the flesh bubbling.

'*Jonathan,*' he sent. '*You might want to look at this.*'

'*Where are you?*' the Guardian—his friend who wasn't a friend—sent back.

'*I'm the bird on the island across from you,*' Sam sent, millennia of practice keeping the pain out of his voice. '*There's some extremely Light plasma Innarn over here.*'

There was a vague comment of *'bird brain'* before Jonathan appeared by his side. He knelt and under the guise of checking the ground, sent a little jolt of healing Sam's way. *'Will that be enough until you change back?'* he asked.

If he had teeth, he'd be gritting them. *'It should be. I don't suppose I can slip away to somewhere Darker for a bit?'* he replied. If he could get to a Dark Realm, he'd be able to heal a lot easier than he would here.

Jonathan shook his head. *'The exits will be watched, and so will I. We'll have to wait, or you can ask Shari.'*

Sam snorted, then blinked. He didn't know birds were able to make that sound.

He couldn't risk asking Shari and her finding out. He'd just have to wait and deal with it himself. There were a few rituals to attempt, assuming he could get somewhere quiet. *'Somehow, I don't think that's a good idea.'*

"Jonathan?" called Tania. "Did you find something?"

Rising, Jonathan nodded. *'You might want to head back,'* he sent to Sam even as he called out to Tania, "Yes. We need to find Shari."

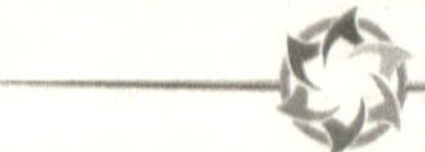

Shari stepped forwards, looking around the clearing she'd shifted into. There were signs of a struggle. Large patches of flattened grass coated with a sticky liquid gleamed in the low light of the moon. Snapped twigs were adorned with grey feathers, a single iridescent blue feather standing out in their midst. A sapling was on an unnatural lean, its green wood splintered near the top of the trunk. For a moment, all sound faded away, and Shari became hyper-focused on the blood dripping down the broken sapling before her.

A strangely familiar power skittered across her shoulders and down her spine as she stepped closer to the tree line, making the fine hairs on her arms stand up. She paused, tilting her head, her shield shimmering around her, almost invisible under the dappled shadows.

Pushing her Innarn out to scan the area for any sign of a threat, Shari snapped her hand down, her bladed glove offering a comforting weight, before making her way into the thick foliage. There were little trickles of Innarn twisting on a gentle breeze. She carefully followed the trail of Innarn to the stream that bisected Rakemyst. On the far bank was her grandfather, limping and struggling up the slippery slope.

Tilting her head, Shari took a step closer to the stream, trying to figure out how badly her grandfather was hurt when a rustling sounded to her left. Glove first, she stepped towards the noise, ready to fight. She paused at the faintest of breezes on her bare neck. The figure on the other side of the bank blinked out.

A large shape sprung at her from the bushes with a garbled yell. Shari raised her sword to parry the expected blow, only to twist away at the last second. She knew those eyes, wild as they were now. The Innarn surrounding this man, with leaves poking out of the tangles in his salted black hair, was so familiar. He failed to compensate for her side-step and stumbled forwards.

"Grandfather," she breathed. Blinking her burning eyes, she turned to him, ready to help him up, but he was already on his feet and ready to face her.

"If you want a fight, I'll fight you," SilverCloud growled at her.

Shari tilted her head and dismissed her weapons, raising her empty hands.

He paused and looked at her, sharp grey eyes evaluating her in the space of a heartbeat. His brows drew together. "Shari?" he asked, holding out his hand.

It was her first proper view of her grandfather: a scruffy unkempt mountain man. Nodding in wonder, she took his offered hand.

Only for him to flip her over his shoulder spine first into a tree trunk, driving the breath from her body.

He cackled madly and ran for the stream. "You can't fool me! She's safe on Ronah, you lying fizzpot!"

Upside down, her weight resting on her hands, Shari watched his retreat as she refilled her lungs. Snapping to her feet, she gave chase. Using her water Innarn, Shari called to the stream and bade it to carry her to the other side. With her feet only slightly wet, she landed at the tree line and followed SilverCloud's mad dash into the forest.

Twice, Shari came close to seeing her grandfather again. Once, she reached out to vainly grasp his trailing feathers, and once he shot an arrow at her from midway up a tree.

This wasn't quite how she'd imagined the first time she'd meet the most revered Elder of Rakemyst. She definitely didn't think he'd *shoot* at her.

Breathing hard, Shari stopped, allowing the thick foliage to hide her for a moment as her grandfather, on hands and knees in the clearing before her, struggled to regain his breath. He coughed a few times, spitting out blood and phlegm before slumping down onto his back, grey wings spread out beneath him.

Creeping out of the bushes, she slowly approached him, mentally preparing a shield to surround him with if he tried to take off again. When she appeared at his side, he waved a tired hand weakly.

"Vebnah's breath, you're a persistent illusion," he growled at her between pants. After leaning to the side, he spat, and the bloody saliva made Shari frown.

Crouching down beside him, she smiled. "Apparently, it's genetic." Running her eyes over his figure, she quickly catalogued his injuries.

Broken flight feathers, dislocated shoulder, and a gash on his right thigh and one on his left arm, which was turning an interesting shade of sickly green. He'd been hit by an arrow that had gone straight through the spot just under his collarbone, which was steadily leaking blood and Innarn. His limbs were covered in scrapes and cuts from the chase that he'd led her on, and internal bleeding was the likely cause of the blood he was spitting up.

"Well, get it over with then," he snarled. "This old man has no more fight left in him."

Shari frowned. He still thought that she was going to kill him. Sitting back on her heels, she sighed and held her arms out above his body, palms down. Concentrating on his wounds, she poured her Innarn into healing him. The beautiful green glow surrounded him, beating in time with his heart as he hovered just off the ground.

Gasping–likely the first proper breath he'd been able to take in a while–he opened his eyes and truly looked at her.

He reached out and trailed his fingertips down her cheek, grinning. "Shari," he said. He pushed to his feet, and she skittered backwards, giving him room to rise.

Towering above her for a moment, he gave a sudden jump and whooped in excitement as he zoomed upwards in a tight spiral. Laughing, she rose to her feet as he landed.

"I haven't felt this good since Vebnah was a babe!" he exclaimed.

Shari laughed. "So, Grandfather, shall we go back to the others?"

He shot her a heavy look. "You're really Shari?"

"Do you have any other grandchildren who can heal like that?" There was modesty, and then there was honest acknowledgement. Shari always found the latter far preferable.

"Your uncle is called *LoneWolf*. I don't have any other grandchildren." He scowled at her. She ducked her head but failed to hide her smile.

"Why would you think I was someone else?"

SilverCloud's eyes glazed for a moment. "There was another with me, and the things I saw..." He trailed off.

With a shift of her weight, Shari purposefully snapped the twig under her feet.

"Right. Come on then. Let's see what mischief has been achieved in our absence," he jokingly complained and rose into the air again.

"Do you want me to get us there faster?"

"You really are cheeky, aren't you?" he grumbled. "Just you wait! I'll beat you there, fledgling!"

Shooting him a wave, Shari called up, "See you soon!"

She shifted away from the clearing, SilverCloud's curses hanging in her ears as her laughter bubbled to the surface again.

LoneWolf rose higher in the sky, determined not to be slowed by his brother who was burdened by his human wife. He flew hard and fast towards his father's home, his phalanx keeping pace effortlessly. Looking around, he saw that his brother was keeping up too. Scowling, he huffed out a breath but was able to paste a neutral expression on as they came in for landing.

Calem, who he'd grown up knowing as SunStriker, landed gently, his wife easily finding her feet as she smiled at him.

Curling his lip, LoneWolf turned and strode towards the entrance, not bothering to see if the others were following. He signalled to the guards on the door that they were not to let anyone out once they'd entered. Walking through the wide corridors, he led the way to where his father most often dwelled.

He half expected SilverCloud to be there, the sun streaming down on him as mischief glistened in his eyes, but of course, the room was empty. His brother's wife's softly indrawn breath brought him back to the reason he was here.

He tried to see his father's room through her eyes. Bright patterns on white walls, a set of stools in the middle of the room, and a desk on the far side with an open book resting on top. Clouds drifted past, dragging his gaze to the opaque ceiling. He had grown up here, had run through the halls and played hide and seek with SunStr ... Calem.

Scowling, he turned to face his brother. "Your wife will remain inside to ensure her safety. A few of my phalanx will stay with her. If she needs any help, she can ask Belfar to send to me," he said, his eyes trained somewhere beyond his brother's left shoulder. Belfar, his lieutenant, stepped forwards and bowed his head.

"Since when do you need guards, Wolf?" Calem asked.

LoneWolf's eyes cut to his and darted away again. His spine straightened even more as his scowl deepened. "They do not guard me; they follow my leadership. As a team, it is our duty to ensure that Rakemyst's Elders are protected. Now if you'll excuse me, I have an Elder to track." He moved to sweep out of the room when a female warrior dressed in black shifted into his path. His blade was at her throat before he'd even realised that he'd moved.

"State your business," he growled at her.

'Wolf, that's...' He heard Calem moving behind him, softly groaning.

'An intruder. So soon after our father was attacked.' LoneWolf's send burned at the edges.

Calem's chuckle didn't distract him as the warrior lifted her head, her green eyes flashing dangerously at him. The handle of the blade grew hotter and hotter. She raised her eyebrows as his glove began to smoulder and he refused to draw the tip of the blade away from her neck.

Uneven boots thudded into the room. When he sensed his father's presence, LoneWolf glared harder at the little warrior before him. Belfar moved, ensuring that his father would be covered if the warrior managed to slip past.

"Is that any way to greet your niece, Wolf?" his father asked.

The warrior rolled her eyes as the handle cooled back to a normal temperature. He refrained from shaking out the pain in his hand, but did sheathe his blade, much to his father's amusement. A gentle green glow lit his injured hand. Astonished, he looked at the warrior who he now knew to be his brother's daughter. She shrugged a shoulder.

"Perhaps we should start over? I am Shari Dawn, daughter of Calem and Arilla Dawn and the Altoriae of Lissae." She gave a shallow bow and swept her arm out mockingly.

LoneWolf looked at her, taking in his diminutive niece as she straightened. He tilted his head, assessing her for an uncomfortably long period of time to see what she would do. She kept her eyes on him. After a full thirty seconds of silence, she winked. He blinked, shocked into saying, "Well met, Altoriae. I am LoneWolf, son of SilverCloud and RainbowMist Dawn. My apologies for the aborted celebrations and the not-so-friendly greeting," LoneWolf said.

"Apology accepted," she replied, giving him a winning grin.

"Now we are all acquainted, shall we find something to eat?" SilverCloud said with a smile.

Turning, LoneWolf took in his father's ripped and blood-splattered clothing, ruffled wing feathers, and unusually mussed up hair. SilverCloud met his eyes. '*I am fine. Shari healed me,*' SilverCloud sent.

Narrowing his eyes, LoneWolf looked his father over from tip to toe again. Belfar laid a hand on his arm, and LoneWolf nodded to his father and led the way to the kitchen.

Shari took a moment after they'd sat to admire the spread. Platters overflowing with osin berries, yuham cheese, crispy bread, and juicy slices of roasted vallan sat on the table next to frosty jugs of quass juice. After pouring a glass, she took a sip of the bubbly orange drink and sighed as the sweet taste rolled over her tongue. Her mother loaded up two plates, slipping one to Shari and poking her thigh to get her to eat.

The doors opened and a guard peered in, looking at LoneWolf.

SilverCloud tipped his head to the side. "You'd deny the Guardian entrance?" he said softly.

LoneWolf released a long-suffering sigh, and the guard disappeared again.

Jonathan and Tania stepped into the room as Shari took her first bite.

"Forgive our intrusion," Jonathan said, "but we have some information about the attack."

Shari looked at her Guardian, curious. Why would he mention that in front of everyone else?

'Your grandfather is the Head of the Elders on Rakemyst. Seeing the attack originated here, we need to share whatever knowledge we have with them,' Jonathan sent her.

"Come, join us and tell us what you've discovered," SilverCloud said. A lazy gesture of his hand, and two new chairs, literally made out of air, appeared.

Slipping into the seat across from her, Jonathan looked weary. Shari took a bite of vallan and fixed her gaze on him. When he made no move to fix a plate of his own, Shari shifted some morsels onto the dish before him. He dipped his head in thanks and met her gaze directly for the first time since entering the room.

She blinked.

She hadn't seen him so troubled since they'd discovered that Anriluka was part of her test to prove that she was the Altoriae.

Watching as he took a bite out of a berry and mechanically began to chew, she nodded in satisfaction. He may not be enjoying the spread before him, but at least he was eating.

"We've discovered the point of the Chirea's arrival," Jonathan said. "There is a small, flat-topped island on the west side. They've built a bridge of bones and connected it to the main island. The more concerning thing is the Light portal on the small island."

SilverCloud frowned. "Light portal?"

"Yes," Jonathan said. "There is a runic portal that is almost painfully filled with Light Innarn."

Shari raised an eyebrow. Jonathan was on the lighter side of most Grey Innarnians. If it was painful for him, then the being that opened it must have been incredibly Light.

"Do you think that the one who opened the portal is still here?" LoneWolf asked, half out of his chair. SilverCloud stared at his youngest son, and LoneWolf glared back. Shari could feel the Innarn her grandfather was extending to keep her uncle in his seat.

Jonathan closed his eyes to concentrate. Shari sensed him sending his Innarn out, searching for a Light intruder in their Realm. Last time they had done this, they'd been looking for one of their own. Shari slammed the door on those thoughts and gently pushed her Innarn into his, melding the two together. Raising their heads, their eyes locking, Shari shook her head slightly. There wasn't any sign of a Light being that wasn't meant to be here.

"No. I'm not sure that they were ever on Lissae in the first place. I believe that Lissae would have had something to say about that," Jonathan said, forcing a chuckle.

"Maybe we should ask her," Shari suggested, taking another bite.

"Lissae hasn't spoken directly to anyone in decades," LoneWolf scoffed.

"That's not true," Shari said. She opened her mouth to mention Lissae asking her to be the Altoriae, and that the Realm was the one who guided her through her early training, but paused at the mental prodding Jonathan gave her.

LoneWolf and the others waited for her to say something else.

"Ronah's very helpful though. I bet if we asked Ronah and Rakemyst, they would help out!" Tania piped up. Shari gave her a grateful look.

"Rakemyst does not interfere with the problems of his residents," Belfar said.

"But…" Tania started.

"I'm sure that Rakemyst does his bit in helping out his residents," Jon said smoothly. "It's always good to see how others do things."

'*Especially if it means avoiding their mistakes,*' Shari sent to Jon.

The Guardian tried to glare at her, but Shari resolutely ignored him and concentrated on the food in front of her, instead of on the death-grip Jon had on his fork.

SilverCloud raised an eyebrow. "Eat, Guardian. I think you will need your wits about you in the coming days."

CHAPTER FOUR

After the meal, Shari looked over at her parents. They sat with their heads bent towards each other, quietly talking. From the hard line of her mother's jaw and the soft pleading in her father's eyes, Shari knew what they were talking about.

"Time for me to patrol, I think." Scooting her chair back from the table, Shari stood. Tania hastily got to her feet, standing awkwardly next to the Altoriae. Jon patted his mouth with a napkin and gracefully rose.

"Thank you for your hospitality, Elder Dawn." Dipping his head, Jonathan pushed his chair in and reached for Shari and Tania.

"Wait!" Arilla cried. Shari looked at her mum, startled. "You don't have to go just yet. We'll come with you."

Shari smiled, tears lodging in her throat. Sometimes she hated being right. "I think you're needed here. Dad can send to me, and you can leave me messages on the screen."

Arilla grasped Shari's hand and gave it a squeeze. "This is the first time that I haven't slept under the same roof as you since you were born. You'll have to allow me a bit of leeway," she said tearfully.

Words caught behind her teeth. Shari wanted to say that she didn't spend much time sleeping at their house—most of her sleep was caught in the safety of her sanctuary. But she understood the spirit of what her mother was saying. "Only if you give me some too." Shari grinned. She kissed Arilla's cheek and hugged Calem.

"Only a send away," Calem murmured in her ear.

After nodding, Shari shifted Jonathan and Tania back with her, arriving on the clifftop where the festival of joining was meant to begin. Neither mentioned the sheen of tears she was sporting.

Jonathan was immediately hailed by the Elders and he left to inform them that the festival would go ahead the next night. Tania moved among the rest of Ronah's residents and Shari checked on the Ilutri who were milling around, looking dazed.

Summoning the feast from where it lay in stasis at the castle, Shari laid out tables full of food. The tantalising scent seemed to ease the crowd slightly, and people began to eat and talk, stiff postures slowly relaxing.

Tania sank to the ground at the edge of the cliff, letting her legs dangle off the side. Leaning back, she looked up at the stars dotting the sky and smiled sadly. Today had not gone at all the way Ronah had wanted, and she'd spent a lot of time sending to the Island, trying to get her to calm down. Ronah had been ready to jump in the fight, ready to protect her older brother, Rakemyst.

She hadn't heard anything from the other Shifting Island, and Tania wondered if it was because he found her lacking in some way. Deciding to throw caution to the wind, Tania took a deep breath and sent, *'Well met, Rakemyst.'*

A deep silence settled over her mind, and Tania huffed softly.

'*Well met, Ronah's Linked. My little sister tells me good things about you.*'

When Ronah had first sent to Tania, she'd sounded young and full of life. Rakemyst sounded a lot like her birth father's ancient grandfather. He'd been a wizened old man, bundled up in a blanket, perching on his rocking chair with a gummy grin.

'*Not quite the image I had in mind.*' Rakemyst did not seem to share Ronah's sense of humour.

'*You should be flattered. He was very dear to me. He was the one adult, apart from my mother, who made life bearable before we moved away from my father.*'

'*Well then, I thank you for the comparison.*'

Tania grinned into the night. '*I noticed you've been talking to Ronah?*'

'*She's impudent. Fighting for her residents. We're here to guide and keep the peace, not lower ourselves to hostilities.*' Rakemyst sniffed.

Struggling to maintain her composure, Tania grimaced. '*Ronah keeps the peace by making sure intruders can't hurt us.*'

'*By using you to do her fighting for her. I'm not sure I approve.*'

'*How do you keep the peace?*'

'*By negotiation.*' Rakemyst sounded haughty. Tania fought against knocking the Island off his metaphorical perch.

'*What happens when negotiation fails, and fights like the one today break out?*'

'*That is why the Ilutri train. My residents are quite skilled in combat.*'

Tania's teeth clicked together, hard, as she stopped herself from sending something which could be misconstrued. '*What about those who fell in battle?*'

The Island warbled, long and mournful. Tania patted the ground next to her in a vain attempt to soothe the grieving landmass.

'*I mourn their passing too.*'

Moving among the people, Shari healed the lightly wounded and made sure those who looked to be in shock had someone who was watching over them.

One woman, standing by herself and wringing her hands, caught Shari's attention. The Ilutri's wings were drooping dejectedly behind her, the hem of her dress ripped and muddy.

"How can I help you?" Shari asked gently.

The woman turned tear-filled eyes in Shari's direction. "You can't," she gasped. "He's gone."

Shari followed the woman's gaze to the spirit of the Ilutri archer who had warned them of the attack, an arrow still protruding from his stomach.

"He came and got me. Wanted to show me something. But his body is gone." Tears streamed down her face, matching the tracks on the archer's cheeks.

Shari's eyes flicked around. She was silent for a moment, standing awkwardly beside the grieving Ilutri. "Do you know what he was trying to show you?" She settled on asking.

The woman shook her head, but the spirit beckoned. Shari took a hesitant step forwards, and then another as the spirit started flying backwards. Breaking into a sprint to keep up, Shari found herself leaping over streams and fallen trees. After clambering up a mound of dirt, she drew to a stop, looking where the archer was pointing. A few feet away, there was a bone-covered hand sticking out of the ground.

Frowning intently at the mound, Shari tried to figure out the best way to decipher what the spirit wanted. When someone crossed over into the spirit Realm, sometimes certain functions, like speech, were lost—even if it was only a temporary thing. The spirit of the archer was going to have to mime what he wanted her to find.

He stretched out his wings and pulled at a feather. Shari tilted her head. Was he after a feather?

There was a rush of air, before the grieving Ilutri woman was beside her again. The archer pulled at a feather again, looking at the woman.

"Oh!" the woman gasped. "Meyron's golden feather!"

With her eyebrows climbing, Shari said, "Golden feather?"

Nodding, the woman said, "Yes. When he was out patrolling, he came across a pack of sinfrons. They burned his wings, and he lost a flight feather. LoneWolf had a replacement made of gold for him. When the feather grew back, Meyron kept the gold one as a reminder."

"Alright. Let's find a feather," Shari announced cheerfully, thinking about needles and haystacks. She climbed down the mound, her feet sliding on the smooth sides. It was at least as high as her house and covered the same area as the oval at Ridden Hall. She sent Jon a quick message, letting him know where she was and what she was doing, then she got to work.

Using her Innarn, she lifted some of the fallen branches, weaving them together to create a massive sieve. Making it hover in mid-air to one side, Shari used a massive blast of wind to shoot the mound up into the sky and separate it into dust. She floated it over the sieve and let it fall gently to the ground. Once the dirt had settled, she lifted the sieve and searched through it. Branches, bones, and a few bodies later, she finally found the feather. She shifted the bodies to a safe spot, and turned back to the woman, holding the feather out.

The woman stared at Shari in shock, her shaking hands reaching forwards to grasp the feather. Pausing just before she touched it, her fingers curled in, as if she was afraid it wasn't real. They stood there for a moment until a bird in a nearby tree burst into song, and she reverently slipped the feather from Shari's fingers.

Shari nodded and took a few steps back before shifting away, the woman's *thank you* echoing in her mind.

Forbidden from patrolling, Shari spent the night tossing and turning restlessly before slipping into an uneasy sleep. She woke the next morning at the insistent beeping of her alarm clock and groaned.

Staggering, she went about her morning ritual. Washing, grabbing the first clean clothing that came to hand, and stuffing food into her mouth before settling down on the balcony outside her room to call on the spirits who would come to her aid if she needed their help. With a last look in the mirror, she shrugged and used her Innarn to plait her hair as she jogged to the hospital.

After slipping inside the doors, Shari moved down the hall to where she sensed Jonathan and Fiona were. As she raised her hand to knock, the door swung open.

Motioning her into the room, Jonathan's eyes flickered to Fiona's still form. The wooden bed she was in was covered in bright, colourful quilts that had healing spells stitched directly into them. Her skin was still pallid, her eyes sunken and shadowed.

'*She is getting better,*' Jonathan sent to her. '*The healers think that the last of the poison should be flushed out of her system tonight, and then they can heal her properly.*'

Sighing, Shari eased herself into a cushy visitor's chair. '*Can I do anything?*' Her fingers itched to do something–anything to take Fiona's pain away.

Jonathan shook his head. '*The poison will react badly to any Innarn. The healers are surprised that she even managed to make it back to Ronah. Just going through the gateways should have killed her.*'

'*She's tough,*' Shari sent. '*How long has she been scouting for?*'

'*Eight years. She's the best scout I have. This is the first time she's been caught. It will shatter her confidence, you know,*' Jonathan sent.

Wondering if they were still talking about Fiona, Shari scowled his way. He raised a calm eyebrow in return. Wrinkling her nose, she rose. *'Got to get back. Next class is starting soon.'*

Jonathan nodded, and his eyes had returned to the bed before she'd left the room.

As Shari slipped out of the hospital, she came across Sam, who was humming again. She scowled at him, but he either didn't see or took no notice. Before she did something she'd regret, she shifted away, but not before seeing the brief flicker of disappointment on Sam's face.

Shaking off her foul mood, Shari made her way through Ridden Hall, heading for the classroom she'd been assigned. Soon she found herself standing before a group of kids only a few years younger than she was. It was one of the most intimidating things that Shari had ever attempted, and she had done some pretty daunting stuff.

"So, um, hi," she said, tucking a strand of hair that had escaped her plait out of the way. "I'll be your teacher today, but before I can do that, I need to know what you can do, so quick pop quiz." As the groans rose, she chanted in her head, *stick to the lesson plan, stick to the lesson plan.*

A hand hesitantly rose from someone at the back of the room.

"Yes?" she asked.

"Can we ask you questions instead?"

It was Alistair Hollingsworth. Shari kicked the guilt she felt at the way his Innarn had been awakened down low and thought, *lesson plan next time.* "You can ask, but that doesn't mean I will answer," she said, leaning back against the desk before crossing her arms over her chest and putting all her weight on one leg. She would still be able to react to a threat quicker than anyone else in the room could move, but at least she looked relaxed.

A hand shot up in the front row. Shari raised an eyebrow and nodded.

"Have you ever killed someone?"

She blinked. Dipping into the thoughts swirling around the room was almost too easy. Only three of the kids before her knew how to shield. Many of them wanted to know if she'd killed, how she'd done so, and the number of lives she'd taken. Stifling the shudder that crept under her skin and raised the fine hairs on the back of her neck, she straightened her spine, and glared at Desrick Silverstone, who'd asked the question.

"In defence of Lissae, in fighting for my life and for yours, yes, I've killed. In more ways than I want to think of, and more beings and creatures than I care to say," she said, quite proud that her voice didn't tremble and betray the faces she saw in her nightmares—the souls of those she'd killed and those she hadn't been able to save.

The nervous energy in the room dissipated, dampened by her serious tone, leaving an awkward silence.

Alistair raised his hand. "What... ahhh... what is the difference between a being and a creature?"

"A being is an entity with a higher thought process, capable of decision-making and rationalisation, such as Humans, Ilutri, Wisara, and even U'tan." A shudder went through the class, but Shari continued, "A creature is an entity that acts more on instinct than anything else—some we consider pets, some food, and some we stay well away from because we're *their* food."

The class exchanged nervous giggles and glances.

"So, being is a way to encompass all of the races that have higher thought processes without having to list them all?" Rory Ribeck clarified.

"Yes, pretty much."

"How many different races of beings are there in the Realms?" Gideon Ribeck asked.

"On Lissae alone, there are eleven races of beings. We're discovering new races all the time, so it's hard to say," Shari hedged, "In the last year, Jon... ah, the Guardian and I have identified three new races on the Realms."

Excited murmurs arose as the kids chatted about what races they wanted to meet and which ones had the best powers.

Raising his hand again, Alistair called out, "How do beings travel from one Realm to another without creatures being able to do it as well?"

Shari grinned. "The Ducibus guard the gateways between the Realms. Most beings, and all bar a few creatures, use the gateways to get from one Realm to another. Only super-strong Innarnians, or ones that have been granted special permission, can shift straight between the Realms."

Alistair narrowed his eyes at her, and even from across the room, she could see the questions swirling behind them. "What are the Ducibus?" he asked.

"No one really knows what they look like, as they all wear dark cloaks. There is a theory that they come from different Realms and are made up of all sorts of races. They ensure safe travel between Realms and that those who aren't meant to get through, don't."

"How does that explain the things from the festival then?" Alistair asked.

"Beings, Alistair," she chided gently. "The Chirea were working with a strong Innarnian who didn't need to use the gateways."

"And Anriluka?" he asked, causing several of his classmates to flinch.

Gritting her teeth for a moment, Shari took a breath and said, "Anriluka was a strong Innarnian." Not to mention that without the thirteenth Altoriae prophesy, she wouldn't have been able to break through Lissae's shields, no matter how strong she'd been. The Chirea seemed to have found a loophole with the Light Innarn they were working with, but there was no way that she was going to say anything about that to the kids. It'd scare half of them to... well. She just wasn't going to say anything.

As Alistair opened his mouth to ask another question, the bell rang. Shari didn't think she'd ever been so grateful to hear that sound. She nodded to the students as they filed past, making mental notes to check up on Tila Flint and Owen Thorne who'd appeared especially concerned about their final topic.

Once the last kid was out the door, she slumped. Rubbing a tired hand over her eyes, she pushed off the desk and slipped out. She was hoping to check on Fiona before the next class.

Someone fell in stride with her. Flicking her eyes, she snorted when she saw it was Anika. Wearing flat shoes for a change, Anika was keeping up with her while hugging a large stack of books to her chest. Shari let the silence grow. She may have saved the girl, but there was no one on Ronah who would say that the two were friends by any stretch.

"So..." Anika said, clearly uncomfortable.

"Buttons," Shari responded without thinking.

Anika stopped in her tracks. "What?"

"Sew buttons. It's something my mum says," Shari said, turning to face the girl. Despite Anika's horrific treatment at the tentacles of Anriluka, she had suffered no scarring to mark her perfect features. The sound of flesh striking flesh reverberated near them. Anika flinched and turned with wide fearful eyes to see two boys doing some sort of weird slapping game. Shari took it in, but still said nothing.

Her heart ached at the thought that Anika had suffered because she'd not been quick enough, strong enough, smart enough, to stop the torture she'd gone through.

"I wanted to say sorry," Anika mumbled.

Frowning, Shari shook her head. "Sorry for what?"

"Anriluka was my fault." It was a whisper that Shari plucked from the air.

"How do you figure that?" Shari asked.

"I... I... It doesn't matter," Anika said. "I just need you to know I'm sorry."

Shari might not understand as much as Anika did about fashion and boys and all the usual teenage girl things, but she did know about guilt. "Apology accepted."

Tossing her head, her hair falling perfectly around her face, Anika said, "Good. Now we've gotten that out of the way, let's go." She strode purposefully off, heading for the gate.

Tilting her head at the other girl, Shari said, "Where are we going?"

"To give you a makeover, of course. Saving the Realm might be hard work, but that doesn't mean you can't look good while you're doing it." The epic eye-roll from Anika was practically audible from where Shari was standing, a good five paces behind.

How on Lissae was she going to get out of this one? "Not that I don't appreciate the offer, but I have to go check on a few things before the next class."

"Oh. Well. I suppose you are pretty busy," Anika mused, taking Shari's rejection better than Shari had expected. "Next time you're free, let me know. We can't have you looking like some sort of gutter rat– you're the first Lissaen lots of beings see, you know!" Anika said. She gestured to Shari's cut-offs and T-shirt and sniffed before turning again and striding out the gate.

Dumbfounded, Shari took a moment to process what had just happened. Anika, it seemed, was being nice. Looking at the sky, Shari wondered if the Realm was ending. When the fluffy white clouds did nothing but drift past at a leisurely pace, Shari shrugged. She'd mull over Anika's behavioural shift later. Right now, she had a scout to check on.

Jonathan rubbed his eyes and stared at the Crystal Video Screen that displayed a readout of Fiona's vitals. They were steady, even if her pain was higher than it should have been. He flicked his fingers and a hardback journal appeared in his hand. Running his fingers over the embossed cover, he searched for the hidden lock and pressed it. The book sprang open even as his eyes flicked up to check on the still form laid out on the bed.

He turned the pages carefully until he came to the section he wanted. He stared at a particularly uninteresting spot on the floor for a long time, trying to get his thoughts in order before he finally glanced down at the page entitled 'Searching for the Guardian's apprentice.'

He ran a finger down the page, locating the particulars he needed to know about choosing a new apprentice before his shoulders slumped. Last time he had looked at this page, he'd been filled with excitement and hope. He needed someone willing to share the burden of protecting the Realm. It had taken eight months of searching before he'd named Mitchel as his apprentice. Shari had wanted no part of the process. There had been a whole seven candidates from outside of Ronah. Not many wanted to commit to training under such a young Guardian.

Mitchel had been consistent in the testing, putting up with the stubbornness of Mallory Harn, one of the older candidates, with good humour. He'd known Mitchel would become his apprentice when he'd seen the boy shield Mallory against attack, even when she'd been flinging hooked barbs at him from inside the shield.

Look where it had gotten him.

Jonathan ran a hand down his face and sighed. He still hoped that Mitchel would come bursting in the door, bemoaning his father's cooking, or groaning at having to do another lesson. He had always been diligent and resourceful, and Jonathan wished he'd told Mitchel as much when he'd been alive.

Having to search for another apprentice so soon was heartbreaking. There was none of the excitement this time. To add to the stress, he hadn't had to worry about another's point of view during the last search. And now, with Shari. Sighing, he ran his finger underneath the lines as he read:

Note:

The role of the Guardian's apprentice is sacred. To find a candidate with the right mix of carefulness and opportunism, stubbornness and loyalty, and respect and inquisitiveness is difficult at best. To add to this, Guardian, your Altoriae gets the final say. Far too often, I have seen my second fall in battle without an appropriate candidate to take their place. The one waiting in the wings was suitable for my Guardian, but not for me.

Remember, Altoriae, that a good fighter is not the only acceptable choice. The apprentice must complement you in all the ways that the Guardian does. You will find your fit, Altoriae, and know it to be true. Listen to your heart and spirit.

As always, may the Deities guide and guard you and yours,

– Kay'imi

This could be a problem.

CHAPTER FIVE

Tania sat in the middle of the cave, fidgeting with the hem of her shirt. Shari, a look of wonder on her face, was wandering around the perimeter, her hand petting the wall.

Turning to Tania, she asked, "Do you feel this all the time?"

"Feel what?" Tania replied, eyebrows raised.

"The souls of those who have bonded with Ronah. They are so..." Shari paused, searching for the right words. "Peaceful. Steady. Calm," she finally said, wistfully.

"Sometimes. They're like a presence in the back of my head for the most part. There, but unobtrusive, if you know what I mean," Tania replied.

"I do." Shari collapsed to the ground in a graceless heap. Tania stifled a grin, wondering how someone who moved so effortlessly in a fight could also flop around like a fish out of water. Shari shot her a look that said she'd sensed the thread of Tania's thoughts, if not the words.

"How do you cope with all the extra voices in your head?" Tania asked, hoping to distract Shari before the Altoriae dreamed up an even worse training exercise than the one she already had in mind.

Shari blinked. "Ever since I can remember, I've been hearing others in my head. At first, it was just Lissae, then it was Ronah, and then the residents of Ronah. From what I understand, one of the previous Altoriaes made sure that I was shielded until I could block everyone out myself. That way, I wasn't found out too quickly."

"And being found out quickly is bad?" Tania raised her eyebrows as she mulled over what Shari said.

Shadows passed behind Shari's eyes, and Tania shivered as the temperature dropped a couple of degrees. "Jali Thorne, the tenth Altoriae, watched her whole family, bar her sister, be decimated on the evening when they announced who she was. Her sister, Abby, was six at the time of the attack, and went on to become the next Altoriae after seeing Jali trampled by a herd of ullfin."

Tania didn't know what to say. How did you reply to that? Sorry sounded a bit trite and empty, and she couldn't think of another word.

Shari smiled at her gently.

"Do you ever worry that you can't handle all of this?" Tania blurted, blood rushing to her cheeks.

"Not really. When you've been doing this for as long as I have, you learn how to handle yourself and what your limits are. This is just a part of my life," Shari said.

"What if it's the last part?" Tania asked, wringing her hands together. Everything they were meant to be able to get through was overwhelming.

Shari looked at her. "Who knows? It may be. But somehow, I doubt it. Besides," she said, getting to her feet, "the more you train, the better you'll be able to deal. Now, up!" Grabbing Tania's hand, she hauled the smaller girl to her feet effortlessly. "Time to begin," she said, with a shark-like smile. "Today we work on your water control. Ronah is surrounded by water. She makes it rain for us and purifies our drinking water by removing the salt. You're going to start a bit easier though." Shari placed a clay pot in Tania's hands. Tania had a moment to wonder where it had come from, before Shari said, "Fill the pot with water."

Tania looked at her, then all around the cave. There wasn't water anywhere close. How could she fill it?

Shari looked at her patiently, giving her time to see if she was able to figure the puzzle out. Tania plopped to the ground, thinking over what Shari had said.

"How does Ronah make it rain?" Tania asked suddenly.

Grinning, Shari said, "There are tiny water molecules in the air all the time. Ronah forces them together into one area and when the time is right, she makes it rain."

"That's how she cleared away the goo after..." Tania paused, not able to go on. After Anriluka exploded and Ronah got slimed, she'd wanted to say. *After Mitch was killed, reformed, and killed again,* would be what Shari heard if she'd said anything.

Shari's grin became fixed, but she nodded.

"So, if I force the water molecules in the air together above the pot, it'll rain right into it and fill it up?" Her voice rose on the end, making it a question.

"Yes," Shari said. "It sounds easy, but the hard bit comes when you are trying to get the right amount. You want to be able to fill the pot, not have a few drops in the bottom, and not have it so full that it'll spill or overflow."

Nodding, Tania concentrated on the sensation of the water in the air around her. Stretching her senses, she gathered the tiny spheres together and was promptly saturated.

Not bothering to disguise her smile, Shari said, "Good try. Don't drop your focus until the pot is full though. When you're done, you need to disperse the extra molecules back into the air."

"Okay," Tania said, blowing a breath out of her puffed up cheeks. The moisture rolled around in her mouth and she wondered if she should pull the water from her own body instead of the air.

Shari frowned at her. "I know what you're thinking. Don't do it."

Tania frowned right back. "Why not? Wouldn't it be easier to control?"

"Sometimes there are reasons to use the Elements that can be found within our own bodies, but we only have a limited amount of internal resources. That's why it's important to use the Elements around us," Shari said. "With the amount that it would take to fill up this pot, you'd be left very dehydrated, your skin would start to go flaky and pull tight, and you'd likely spend the next few days guzzling water to stop a crushing headache."

Scowling, Tania nodded. "Fine," she muttered. Concentrating, she managed to fill the pot halfway before her focus broke and her arms became wet as well. She grumbled to herself, irritated that she'd lost her attention. Trying again, she drew the moisture off her arms, and made it roll in beads into the pot. It filled, right to the lip. She held it up to Shari, who beamed at her.

"Good job," Shari said. With a wave of her hand, the pot was empty once more. "Now, try again."

Tania grumbled good-naturedly but continued to practise.

She had just filled the pot for the tenth time when Shari said, "Time to stop. The festival will be starting in a moment."

Looking around with wide eyes, Tania said, "But we haven't been here that long."

"You've been at this for hours." Shari grinned at her. "It would have been time for a break anyway. I've got to go get ready. I'll see you in a bit?"

"Sure," Tania nodded. "Think I need to go dry out a bit," she said wryly.

"Good idea." Shari laughed and shifted out.

Tania looked around the cave, gave a little wave to the faces on the wall, and shifted to her room. Shari was a tough nut to crack, and Tania was determined to keep her promise to Mitch. Glad that she'd learned a bit more about the elusive Altoriae, she skipped downstairs to drink anything that wasn't water.

After getting ready, Tania shifted to the clifftops, arriving on Shari's left, while Jonathan stood on her right. All three of them were on guard. Tania knew the crowd around them were keeping an eye out as well.

Visible in the air above Rakemyst was a swarm of Ilutri flying in spectacular formations. Tania marvelled at the aerial acrobatics. Flashes of jewel-bright colours dazzled her and the rest of the crowd as Ilutri in skin-tight tops and loose pants dipped, wove, and spun in the air. Smiling so hard her cheeks ached, Tania caught a glimpse out of the corner of her eye of something and spotted an archer perched in a tree. His wings were spread wide to keep his balance as he fired an arrow into the swooping mass above him.

Taking a step forwards, she opened her mouth to call out a warning, but found herself mesmerised as the arrow passed right by the aerial dancers and exploded into bright fiery bursts. Another arrow shot through the crowded sky and burst into a different pattern, standing out lustrously against the darkening sky. Again and again the colours burst, much to the delight of the throng on the ground. Finally, with one last spectacular splash of yellow, the Ilutri all touched down and as one, swept their arms towards the crowd on Ronah's side.

Tania thought she knew what came next. She'd been watching the Silverstones, and anyone else they were able to rope in, practise as Ronah had swept through the seas. She knew the moves, had seen them rehearse in the town square yesterday, but it was only as the last hints of colour faded from the sky that their performance really took on an otherworldly perception for her.

The group stood there, hidden by coloured mist which sprung up suddenly. A deep *thump* sounded when they took a step forwards as one, the sound reverberating through the air and making her heart thud against her ribcage. Another step and another, to a beat they pounded out with their feet. The coloured fog moved with them, then spilled over the cliff as they reached the edge, revealing the performers.

A line of twenty people dressed all in yellow danced forwards, raised their hands, and blew, each sending a seed on the breeze of their breath to land on Rakemyst's side. They threw their arms up and somersaulted backwards into the air, above the heads of the other performers. The next line of people, dressed in green, stepped forwards, one hand lowered to drop their own seed as the other stretched out, reaching towards the seeds on Rakemyst's side. As tiny sprouts began to burst through the ground, the two lines of performers directly behind the front line were raised up on platforms of plasma. The second line, dressed in blue, shot water effortlessly from their fingertips to gently rain down on the sprouts. The third line, all in red, sent off sparks that heated the rapidly growing seedlings and lit the sky in beautiful bursts of flame.

With a final wave of their arms, all of the twenty earth Innarnians in the front line had their vines connected, creating a bridge. The front three lines were lifted by the air Innarnians and brought to the back, leaving the silver and purple-clad lines to step forwards together.

Twining their arms, the purple-clad people rose high above the others and as their partners in silver lifted them up, they began to chant.

The fine hair on the back of Tania's neck rose as the spirit Innarnians finished their chant and streams of silver shot out from their hands, joined by streamers from the other Elementals, which spiralled around each other to form a barrier for the sides of the bridge.

As she watched, absently rubbing away the goosebumps on her arms, Ilutri Innarnians joined in, coating the bridge in dirt that their water Innarnians turned to clay and their fire Innarnians baked.

Their plasma Elementals did something to the bottom of the bridge, and when she craned her neck, she was just able to see the supporting struts they'd added.

Each Ilutri removed a single feather, and cupped it in their hands before throwing the feathers into the sky. Spirit and air Innarnians worked together, weaving the feathers to create a covering over the top of the bridge. As the Innarn faded, the feathers glowed all on their own, lighting up the bridge in a way that she'd never expected.

Tania marvelled at the display and stood there gawking long after most of Ronah's residents had crossed the bridge to the feast that was set out on Rakemyst's side. Shari squeezed her arm and she nodded, distracted, unable to take her eyes off the bridge. She found that she was getting feedback from Ronah, who hadn't seen a display like this through the eyes of another for longer than Tania could comprehend.

She startled when the air next to her was displaced as one of the Ilutri landed.

"It is rather spectacular, isn't it?" asked the Ilutri.

Tania tore her eyes from the bridge to look at the newcomer. An elderly Ilutri lady was regally regarding the bridge. Her silvery hair was plaited in a complicated-looking bun, her yellow eyes lined with laughter wrinkles, but holding a touch of sadness. Her voice was deep and kind, and at once, even though they'd never met, Tania knew who she was.

"You're Linked with Rakemyst," she breathed.

Smiling, the lady nodded. "I am Zana Delayer, and yes, I am Linked with Rakemyst, just as you, my dear, are Linked with Ronah."

Tania nodded, mute. Did she shake hands? Did she bow—no, curtsey? She had no idea.

Zana's eyes twinkled. "You *are* a delight. Are you coming to join the festivities?"

Nodding again, Tania let Zana gently loop their arms together and they walked across the bridge made by Innarn.

Gently, Zana filled her mind with pictures of life on Rakemyst. Waking to birdsong, collecting the fruit from the highest branches of the forest trees, digging through leaf fall to find the perfect mushrooms, and flying through the sky at dusk in looping, whirling patterns.

Smiling, Tania asked, "Do you have a special spot where you talk to Rakemyst?"

Eyes twinkling, Zana showed her an image of a tiny island, just big enough to sit cross-legged. It was high in the sky, away from all the others, but directly over the heart of Rakemyst. Then it changed. Zana was standing up, tipping over the side of the island, free falling until her wings caught her, and she was streaking directly for gleaming blue tiles on the top of a spiralling tower. Landing on a balcony jutting out from the side of the tower, she strode through the white halls, heading for its centre.

The images stopped, and Tania gasped. She'd perceived everything just as Zana had. Every beat of her wings, the brush of the wind, and the *love* pouring from Rakemyst into Zana's soul. For an Island that she'd thought of as cold and slightly hostile, it was clearly not the way that Zana felt about her home at all.

Shari found herself surrounded only minutes after stepping foot on Rakemyst again. Ilutri were coming up, offering her food and drinks, occasionally from their own plates. There were gentle touches, always proceeded by a soft warning and followed by an excited hum as they wandered away to gossip and giggle with their friends.

She looked at Jonathan, who hadn't left her side, and sent to him, '*Do I have something in my hair?*'

He flicked his eyes across her and shook his head. '*Why?*'

'*People keep... touching me. I don't understand it,*' she sent back.

'*Really?*' he sent, raising an eyebrow. '*See if you can figure it out.*'

She narrowed her eyes at him but turned to greet another excited Ilutri offering her a bite to eat, which she politely declined. As they made their way through the crowd, she received offer after offer, all of which she refused. Casting her mind back, she thought of all the times when there had been a celebration on Ronah, and she'd seen Jonathan struggling to make his way through the crowds as he was stopped by person after person wanting to talk, wish him well, and offer him bites of food. This was what it was like for him. Just a few weeks ago, she'd been lamenting the lack of positive reception to the announcement that she was the Altoriae. It was a good reminder to be careful what you wished for.

Off to the side, there was a soft, quickly stifled sob. Shari stopped in her tracks, turning towards the sound. She felt Jonathan send her a query, checking if she was okay. Absently nodding, she walked across the crowd, throwing up a shield as people stepped in closer to her. Arriving at the tables loaded with food, she caught another quiet sob. Leaning down, she flipped up the tablecloth to reveal a cherubic toddler sucking on her thumb.

"What's wrong, little one?" Shari asked.

The toddler looked up, her yellow eyes glistening with unshed tears, her thumb firmly in her mouth.

"Will you come out here with me?" Shari asked, trying again.

"It's no good," said a voice from the other side of the table. To Shari's surprise, the tablecloth on the other side was lifted. Samuel Caragnton was lying on his side, leaning on his elbow, peering up at her. "I've tried bribing, threatening, and even telling her that her parents will let me eat her if she doesn't get out. She still won't move."

"Let you eat her? I think that counts as a threat," Shari said, frowning. She held out an arm and the little girl scrambled towards her, apparently eager to get away from the odd man.

"Well, I'm hungry," he grumbled, scowling at Shari.

She snorted and rose to her feet, the toddler secure on her hip, just in time to hear him start humming again. "Let's see if we can find your family, little one," Shari said, a touch too loudly as she walked away, trying to cover the sound of his inane song.

Even with a toddler on her hip, the gentle touches and awed glances didn't stop. If anything, they grew worse. One guy, a few years older than her with iridescent blue feathers lining his wings, winked at her and mouthed something. She let her eyes slide past him, hoping that he'd get the idea.

As Shari wandered through the crowd, she caught sight of the woman she'd helped find the golden feather for. Her eyes were scanning the crowd too, clearly searching for something or someone. When her eyes locked onto Shari and the toddler, she almost melted with relief.

Knowing instantly that she'd found the little one's mum, Shari headed straight for her.

"I believe that you may be looking for someone?" she said as she handed the girl over.

"That's twice in as many days," the woman said softly. "How can I thank you?"

"Just stay as safe as you can," Shari said, shaking her head. "And keep this little one safe too."

The woman nodded as the crowds closed in.

"Although if you want to cause a distraction so I can slip away, I wouldn't be opposed to it," Shari muttered.

A small grin, and a moment later, fireworks exploded overhead. As necks craned backwards, Shari tossed a wave to the woman and shifted to the edge of the gathering, grateful for the breather. After years of laughing at Jonathan for his reaction when people swarmed to him, she finally understood his dislike of large groups.

Grumbling to himself, Samuel rose to his feet. The Altoriae had taken away his reason to hide. Everywhere he looked, the winged were sizing him up. He wished he could just eat them and be done with it.

"Is it true? Can you change into a bird?" It was another one, with iridescent yellow feathers lining his wings, his eyes glazed over like the others.

"Can you?" Samuel snapped and grabbed a plate, intent on filling it with meat from the table as he had a feeling Shari would be annoyed if he decided Ilutri flesh was on the menu instead.

"I saw you change, but I don't know how you did it?" another asked. She was a tiny slip of a thing, barely old enough for the plunging top she was wearing.

He wanted to snarl at her, but the thought of further censure from Jonathan stopped him. Reaching past the girl, he tore a chunk off the roast vallan and bit into it viciously.

"You can fly in bird form. I wonder if you can fly like this?" This one was a hulking brute whose wings were dusky orange. His glazed eyes didn't change as Samuel leaned in close.

"You'll find I can do more than you think. Why don't you let these nice people enjoy their evening and stop playing puppet master?" he snarled.

The brute looked down at Samuel, his eyes still glazed. "I'm watching you." The hulking Ilutri shook his head, the glazed look disappearing as he blinked in apparent surprise to see Samuel glaring up at him. The Ilutri bravely grinned down at him. "This is a fine gathering! What do you think of our lovely isle?"

Samuel bit back another snarl and strode off. Residents from both isles skittered out of his way. The flurry of sending about him was like barbs on newly grown skin.

It would be so much easier if he could just eat them all.

CHAPTER SIX

Sitting in the comfortable chairs in Jonathan's lounge room, Samuel gratefully took the drink his host and so-called friend handed him. Glad to be off his feet and away from the endlessly questioning crowd, he took a sip of the hot drink and blinked at the surprisingly pleasant burn at the back of his throat.

"What is this?" he asked.

"Azehal. A type of spiced hot chocolate that the Ilutri make. It's one of my favourites," Jonathan said as he settled into the seat behind his desk, a cup cradled in his hands. He stared down at the crystal slabs scattered across the wooden surface and sighed. Samuel eyed them curiously. He knew they were reports from the Elders of Lissae, but the look on the Guardian's face made him wonder what they contained. Turning back to his guest, Jonathan added, "I thought you'd appreciate it after all the humming you've been doing."

"You've noticed?" Samuel asked. Jonathan nodded, but didn't say anything. Samuel squashed down the pain at his indifference before Jonathan raised his eyes from the drink.

"So, what did you think of Rakemyst?"

Sam looked away. If his 'friend' couldn't be bothered to join in the song, maybe he should re-evaluate their friendship. Again. "Airy. Their defences are weak. They expect to have the upper hand and don't know when that doesn't happen."

Jonathan dipped his head in acknowledgement. "True. The same could be said for many races."

"Sometimes, a race is just superior," Sam said, scowling.

"And sometimes they're bested by a mere human," Jonathan said, grinning at him.

Glaring at his host, Sam tried hard not to snarl, but by Jonathan's amused expression, he didn't think he'd succeeded. He'd never really had a friendship before, and if this was how friends treated each other, he didn't think he wanted to keep this one either. Rising, he felt a stab of satisfaction to see Jonathan's face falling before he stalked out of the room.

"Did you know," Jonathan said, "that friends tease each other? If the teasing is about a subject too raw, it's good to say something about it."

Stopping in the doorway, Sam said, "In the space of a few minutes, you have managed to dismiss something dear to me and insult not only me, but my entire race. This is something friends do?"

"No, Sam, that's not what I meant..."

The Guardian's words were delivered too late. Sam stalked towards the front door, threw out the remainder of his drink into the garden just outside, and shifted as soon as he'd crossed the threshold. His cup clattered to the ground.

Alistair Hollingsworth stood at the foot of the bridge that crossed between Ronah and Rakemyst and raised his hand tentatively, his fingers stretching out to touch the structure thrumming with Innarn. He stopped before he made contact, the fine hairs on his arms rising as the power that had been poured into the making of the bridge drifted over his skin. If he closed his eyes, he could feel it pulsing like a heartbeat. Was the bridge sentient like Ronah? He didn't know how to ask without sounding stupid. Maybe he'd quiz Shari after the next class.

He heard someone shifting their weight behind him and dropped his arm to his side.

"Sorry," he muttered, and stepped away so they could cross.

"I thought you'd actually managed to touch it this time," Shari said with a low laugh.

The Altoriae! Alistair turned to face her, cheeks flushing with mortification at being caught. "Shari!"

"Hi, Alistair," she said, grinning at him. "Have you been over to Rakemyst yet?"

"No," he said sullenly. "I haven't been able to."

Shari tilted her head and eyed him shrewdly. It was rather like his soul was being exposed. She held out her hand, palm up. He looked at it, then at her eyes, and back again. She raised an eyebrow and he tentatively reached out, preparing himself for the shock he felt whenever he accidentally encountered any other Innarnian.

He placed his hand in hers. There was only smooth, warm skin. His gaze flicked up to her face, astonished.

Rolling her eyes, she grumbled, "Clearly I need to go over shielding basics." As she muttered under her breath, throwing out snide little comments that had him laughing, he didn't realise that they'd stepped onto the bridge and were already a fair way across until she gently disentangled her hand from his.

Gasping, he went to grasp the rail but pulled back when it sent a shock through his hand. He flailed around, the edges of his vision going fuzzy as he panted for breath before Shari grasped his shoulders and forced him to meet her gaze.

"You are safe," she said. "Breathe. In and out; in and out. Good. Centre yourself. This bridge was made with goodwill and peace in mind. There is nothing here to hurt you."

"Not all of it," he said.

She tilted her head. He wondered if she realised that she was doing it. "What do you mean?"

"Feel it," he said. "Right there. Someone is mad, sad, and angry."

Placing her hand where he was pointing, she frowned in concentration before nodding slowly. "I can feel it." She looked off into the distance, but Alistair knew that she wasn't seeing anything before her. "I think maybe we'll try and cross the bridge tomorrow, yeah? I need to get this fixed."

Alistair hummed in agreement. She walked with him back to Ronah, and as he stepped foot on solid ground, the tension he hadn't been aware of seeped out of his shoulders.

"Why do you have to fix it?" he blurted once he was safely back on the Island.

Shari sighed. "This bridge is not only physical, but symbolic. Tomorrow, the Ilutri will use it to cross over to Ronah. There is no doubt that someone will pick up on the negative feelings here and wonder if that is what we think of them. One of the Innarnian who worked on the bridge must have been upset about the battle we faced when the two Islands first joined. Unfortunately, they weren't able to keep that out of their Innarn, but once that seed of doubt has been planted, it could grow and damage our relationship with the Ilutri."

"What's so important about the Ilutri's opinion of us?"

"We're not like the mainlanders. We do things differently— everything from the way we treat people, to the way we trade, to the way we grow crops. Those who live on the other Shifting Islands welcome us warmly, where the mainlanders scorn and dismiss us, treating us with suspicion if we dare to walk on their lands," Shari said.

Thinking back to when he lived on the mainland, he could vaguely recall a group of people coming into town to trade. They'd fascinated him as they had worn colourful, loose-fitting clothing and had danced and laughed seemingly without a care. They'd disappeared, and he wondered if the quiet, staid people he'd grown up with had run them off.

"Are you right to get home from here?" Shari asked him, jolting him from his memories.

He almost said something smart, but managed to refrain. "I'll be okay. You go do your thing and fix it."

Smiling at him gratefully, Shari nodded. He paused once or twice to look back, but she was so focused on the bridge, he doubted she even noticed.

Standing at the edge of the bridge, Shari wondered why she hadn't noticed the discord before.

'Jonathan, we have a problem. One of the Innarnians must have been in a bit of a mood when they created the bridge, and the negativity has seeped into some of the plasma. I need to remove the infected strands and replace them,' Shari sent.

'Hold on. I'll come and give you a hand,' Jonathan sent back.

'I've got this,' she sent back, impatient to start. In her mind's eye, she imagined him shrugging into a coat with his hand already on the door.

'And how was patrolling tonight?' he sent as he appeared by her side.

Sighing, she sent, *'I haven't been yet.'* Knowing what he was going to say, she grumbled, "Fine, you can help."

Laying a hand on the bridge, Jonathan concentrated. "It's spreading. We're going to need more than the two of us."

"I can handle it, Jon." She fought to keep her temper, knowing the bridge was affecting her already. He raised an eyebrow. Her gaze fell on the toes of his scuffed boots. "Or maybe I can't," she said.

"Can you identify the infected plasma?" he asked.

Nodding, she set to work on isolating the thread of dissention as Jonathan sent off a series of rapid-fire sends. Just as Tania arrived at her side, she managed to separate out the bad plasma.

"I called in some reinforcements," Tania said cheerfully, waving at a trio on the other side of the bridge. Shari spotted her grandfather, her uncle, and a willowy woman who Tania identified as Zana. Sending the Innarn equivalent of a hello their way, Shari pointed out the problem and the six of them got to work pulling out the bad thoughts and replacing them with peaceful ones.

Finally, hours later and covered with a fine sheet of sweat, they finished. The plasma had started to corrupt the vines, so half of the railing had needed to be replaced as well. The others were running on empty, but Shari had taken in some of the negativity, rather than just venting it into the atmosphere.

Shari gave a curt nod and shifted off Ronah to do her patrol, hoping that her relatives would forgive her rudeness this time around.

As exhausted as she was, she half hoped that something would run into her just so she could work her frustration out in a productive way. Stomping through the lush forest of the Light Realm, Shari was being anything but quiet; however, she failed to cross the path of anyone nefarious.

She took to her bed in the early hours of the morning, still dissatisfied.

"Good morning!" Tania was leaning against the crystal pillar outside Shari's house as the Altoriae stumbled through the door with one of her mother's fruit rolls in hand.

Nodding, Shari took a bite and fell into step with the younger girl.

"Not a morning person, huh?" Tania asked.

Chewing before she replied, Shari said, "What gave it away?"

Tania snorted. "Not sure. Could have been the bags under your eyes, or the frowny face you're rocking."

Shari raised an eyebrow but took another bite of her roll instead of the bait Tania was dangling.

"I've got to stop in at the bookstore before school. Is that where you're going too?" Tania asked as they rounded the corner.

Nodding, Shari kept chewing. She was feeling better than she was last night, but in her early morning stupor, she didn't trust her mouth not to run away and say something she'd regret.

They walked past Sam, who was humming as he swept the path outside Jonathan's store. Shari wanted to beat him over the head with what was left of her roll, but managed to refrain by stuffing a final, too-large bite into her mouth.

Tania looked like she was going to stop and say something to Sam, but Shari pulled her into the shop, not sure that she could stand his humming much longer without resorting to violence.

The bell rang out as they slipped through the door. Jonathan looked up from the front desk and smiled. "Ah! I was hoping that I'd see you both this morning. Tania, do you mind watching the shop while I talk to Shari for a moment?"

"Sure!" Tania said brightly. "I think she needs something to help wake her up before she's capable of speech though," she teased.

Shari grumbled at her wordlessly, and let Jonathan lead her to the back room.

He gestured to a seat and pushed a cup into her hands. "Drink up while I get Tania sorted."

Shari nodded, held the cup under her nose, and breathed in the steam as Jonathan slipped out the front. Idly, she stretched her senses and found herself listening to her Guardian asking Tania to start looking for the *Hekkor Mafae*–a very old, Dark book that Jonathan had been quite apprehensive about having on Ronah.

"What's the deal with the book?" Shari asked as he came back through the door.

"I swear that I'm not going to share the rest of my azehal with anyone else. None of you lot appreciate a good drink when you have it!" he griped as he took a seat opposite her.

Taking a sip, Shari hummed in appreciation. "It's delicious, Jon. Thank you." She grinned at him.

Rolling his eyes, he said, "I've been talking to the Returned, and they've been making some noise about a Dark Council that meets infrequently but is incredibly powerful. I want to know more about it, and I think that the *Hekkor Mafae* can point me in the right direction."

"Of all the Dark books, I'm sure it would be in that one. Just the name seems to sap the light from the room," Shari said, glancing around at the encroaching shadows.

Waving a negligent hand, the lights flickered brightly at Jonathan's unspoken command. "We have something serious to talk about as well."

Shaking her head, Shari said, "No."

"I can't ignore it any longer."

"I don't want to talk about it," Shari snapped.

"Life is full of things that we don't want to do," Jonathan said. "Ignoring this won't make it disappear."

"We've talked about it before. I'm not ready," Shari practically growled at him. She knew it was not Jonathan's fault, but she hated the sensation of, once again, being backed into a corner by rules that were older than the combined memory of the Shifting Islands.

"Shari," Jonathan said, letting frustration and sadness leak into his voice.

She looked at him, thinned her lips, and nodded.

"This person isn't a replacement for Mitchel. They are stepping into a role he has left empty, that's all," he said. She turned her head away and sipped from her cup. "Is there anyone you want to put forward?"

"I don't know yet," she hedged.

"We need to nominate by the end of the day," Jonathan said.

"Why can't we just say Tania and be done with it?" Shari asked.

Pinching the bridge of his nose, Jonathan said, "Because she's Linked with Ronah, Tania cannot be a candidate."

"Do we even have to have candidates? Can't we just pick someone and call it a job well done?"

"Who do you have in mind?" Jonathan asked.

"I don't know. Alistair Hollingsworth is pretty amazing. He noticed the negativity at the bridge without any training–I can't imagine what he'd be capable of when he's been trained," Shari said.

"True. But with more and more attempts on Ronah, do we have the time to train someone from the ground up?" Jonathan asked, thinking out loud.

Frowning, Shari contemplated the dark liquid, swirling it around in her cup. "Someone older then, more experienced..."

"Fiona is used to travelling the Realms, and she already has permission from the Ducibus to travel alone," he suggested.

"But after what happened with the Chirea, she might not want to join up with what are essentially the front-line troops," Shari countered.

"True," Jonathan said. "There are many viable candidates among the Ilutri archers, or General Morrow's troops."

"There are, but I don't know them," Shari said. "If I'm going to suggest a being for this test, I want it to be someone who I at least can put a name to." She fidgeted in the chair, the agitation that she hadn't managed to disperse last night visible in the slight movements.

"Well, apart from a name, what are you looking for in the candidate you put forward?" he asked.

"I don't know. What should I be looking for?" she asked.

"Someone who is a strong Innarnian, who is able to drop everything and travel, who can take directions during training, but who can also think on their feet when needed. I'd prefer a candidate who leans towards Light or Dark to complement you, but that's really neither here nor there."

"How many candidates are we meant to sift through?"

"Each Shifting Island can send one. There are six from the mainland, one from each continent, twelve from the fixed Islands, one from the Wisara, and one from the Da'mar, as well as the two we put forward," Jonathan said, hanging onto his patience.

"Thirty-five?" Shari yelped.

"At the most. Not everyone will send one."

Grumbling into her cup, she muttered, "Why do we have to announce it today?"

"Because they'll be arriving for the test next week," Jonathan said.

Curling her lip in annoyance at the whole process, she took another sip of azehal and hummed. Her eyes lit up, and she stood. "I know who I want my candidate to be."

Jonathan's head jerked back, and he frowned at her, giving her a worried look over the top of his glasses. "Who?"

"Sam." Her annoyance with the test, and the need for a new apprentice had merged with her annoyance at the man who just wouldn't stop humming. This way, maybe he'd at least give her some peace from his infernal noise.

"Shari, you can't just..." Jonathan started.

She locked her gaze on him. "Is there anything wrong with that?"

Opening his mouth and raising a finger, Jonathan stopped before he uttered a noise. Slumping in his chair, he tried again. "Picking someone out of anger or spite is not a good thing."

Tilting her head to the side, she asked, "I thought he was your friend?"

"He's more of an acquaintance really," he admitted.

"The thing that bothers me the most is that I know absolutely nothing about his past," Shari said, looking expectantly at Jon, who continued to remain stubbornly silent. She sensed nothing at all from Jon's mind, which was usually wide open to her. "Jon, can't you even tell me what he did before he came to Ronah?" She caught a flash of something like bitter irony crossing Jon's mind.

"The less you know about Sam, the better."

Shari glared at him, furious. "So you're saying that you're letting an *acquaintance* stay at your house, that your *acquaintance* helped us, and your *acquaintance* is the one who has been driving me insane because he hasn't stopped humming since Mitch died? That acquaintance?" She stormed towards the door and shoved it open. "Samuel Caragnton is my choice for candidate." She threw over her shoulder, "Acquaintance or not."

From the other side of the door, Shari heard Jonathan mutter, "Well, that could have gone better."

Chapter Seven

Sam was just about to put the broom away when Shari swept past him. She drew to a stop and rounded on him, fire flashing in her eyes. Tania, unabashed, watched them from the front desk.

"Do you know what the Guardian's apprentice must do?" she blurted.

Frowning, Sam nodded. When it became clear that she needed an answer, he said, "Learn from the Guardian."

"Learn what?" Shari bit out.

"How to protect the Altoriae," he said, puzzled.

"Do you want to do that?"

Now he was well and truly lost. "Do what?"

"Learn how to protect the... to protect me?" The feisty little human before him stepped forwards, backing him into a bookcase. He felt properly vulnerable for the first time since he'd arrived on this too-bright Realm.

He shrugged. "I think I'd already know how," he said, trying to be charming, but falling short if her glare was anything to go by.

"You are my choice for candidate," she told him.

"Okay?" He had no idea what she meant.

Rolling her eyes, she said, "That means that you have a chance to become the Guardian's apprentice and a chance to fight alongside me on the Realms. A chance to protect Lissae."

His eyes lit up, and he smirked at her. "Okay."

Shari's hard glare didn't falter. She looked him over once, bit out, "Good," then turned so fast her plaited ponytail whacked his chest.

As she walked away, he started humming again. Her steps faltered and her hands balled into fists as she stormed out of the shop, leaving Sam to wonder just what he'd agreed to.

He looked over at Tania, who shrugged. The back room was surprisingly quiet for the conflict he felt pouring out of Jonathan's mind, so he decided to pay Lizbeth a visit. Tossing a wave over his shoulder, he set out, still humming.

As he walked through the streets, he noted that people were subdued after Anriluka's attack and the subsequent fallout. All of which could have been avoided if Shari had killed the U'tan in an enclosed space, like he'd advised. If he was the apprentice, would Shari actually listen to his advice, or would she continue to ignore him?

She wasn't the only one. There were plenty of people who wouldn't meet his gaze. Some even went out of their way to avoid him. He hadn't realised how quickly he'd adapted to the friendly openness of Ronah's residents until they'd begun to treat him as an outcast. He ducked his head and shoved his hands into his pockets, humming softly as he made his way up Lizbeth's street.

Walking along her path, he was startled out of his thoughts when the door swung open.

"Hello, Samuel. I've been hoping that I'd see you today," Lizbeth said, leaning on a cane.

"What happened?" he demanded, grabbing her forearms as she listed to the side.

"Oh, I tripped over something at the festival last night and twisted my ankle. Nothing too serious. I was hoping that you'd give me a hand in the garden?" she asked.

"Garden? I don't know…"

"Oh, hush. I can show you what you need," she said. "And you can tell me what has you so troubled."

"What makes you think I'm troubled?" he countered.

Lizbeth laughed. "Because you're here, Samuel."

He couldn't really argue with that and followed the sightless woman as she led him around the side of the house to where her garden patch was.

"Find a patch where the weeds shouldn't be, and work out some of your stress on them."

Samuel looked unimpressed at the greenery. "How am I meant to do that? They're leaves," he said flatly.

"No, some of them are weeds. Weeds, you can rip and tear and shred to your heart's content." She settled into a chair.

He stared at the garden for a moment longer, poking at the soil with a finger. There were currents of Innarn under the surface of the soil. Following them, he realised that they were channels for water. Plants needed water, so the ones that shouldn't have any must be the unwanted weeds. Grasping a spiny leaf, he tugged, and it ripped off the bendy trunk. Savagely, he pulled the plant from the ground and flung it to the side.

"Shari asked me to be her candidate for the Guardian's apprentice," he growled.

Sucking in a breath, Lizbeth was silent for a long moment. "Does she know who you truly are?"

"No, I don't believe so." Unease skated down his spine. He tore another weed out.

"You know that you should tell her," Lizbeth said. "It won't end well if you don't."

"I doubt it will end well if I do." Sam laughed bitterly, tossing another weed onto the growing pile.

"That is always a possibility."

Sam snorted. It was more than a possibility. It was something that would probably end his very long life.

"Did you accept?" she pressed.

"I did, but I can always tell her I changed my mind, right?" Sam asked.

"To do so would be a grave insult," she cautioned. "Of course, it would depend on her reasons for choosing you as to how insulted she would be."

"I don't even know why she would pick me," he grumbled.

"You're clearly quite powerful. From what you've said before, you've inspired her to keep going and given her warning of a path she should avoid," she mused.

"For all the good that did," he growled, viciously pulling out a particularly stubborn weed.

"Perhaps she can see the good in you," Lizbeth suggested kindly.

Sitting back on his haunches, he turned to look at her, one eyebrow raised incredulously. "You seriously believe that?"

"Yes, Samuel Caragnton. I'm not the only one," Lizbeth said gently.

Grunting, Sam turned back to the weeds and started humming again.

"I can walk myself, thank you." Arilla smiled to hide her aggravation as an over-eager Ilutri guard took her arm to guide her down the staircase.

The hand withdrew and she flicked the hem of her too-long dress out of the way as she navigated the perilous stairs. She and Calem had been granted leave to pick up a few things from the house, and she wanted to make sure that Shari was alright. Going back to Ronah for the day, even with an armed escort, had nothing to do with wanting the comforts of home at all. Nope, not a thing.

Another Ilutri was waiting with an offered hand at the bottom of the stairs, and she smiled around gritted teeth, shaking her head as she passed by. Going from Ronah, where people generally didn't touch others aside from family and close friends, to the Ilutri, who were very hands-on, had been a bit of a shock. She didn't remember this amount of touching last time she had been on Rakemyst.

"Alright?" Calem asked her.

She glanced at him out of the corner of her eye. "Are we waiting for anyone else?" she asked instead of answering. There were far too many ears hanging off her every word.

"Just my brother," he said, then raised his chin as LoneWolf and Belfar made their way across the courtyard to them. "All set?"

"I don't feel that this is a necessary excursion," LoneWolf growled. Arilla wondered if he knew another way to talk. His voice had always sounded like he gargled with rocks every morning.

"When you have children, perhaps you will understand," Arilla glared at him. No one was standing between her and her daughter today.

Belfar made a noise suspiciously like a chuckle but turned it into a cough partway through. LoneWolf glared at them and took wing, leading them down to the bridge between the islands.

The journey seemed to take all day, but it only took an hour or so. Once they'd arrived, Arilla happily escaped to change into something more practical, leaving Calem, LoneWolf, and Belfar standing awkwardly in the lounge room.

"So, this is comfy," Belfar said as Arilla came down the stairs, eyeing the room as if he were searching out potential threats. Come to think of it, he probably was.

"It suits our needs," Arilla said easily. Their home seemed rather cramped after the breezy expanse of rooms SilverCloud had them staying in. "I just need to make sure Shari has enough to eat, then we can go. Calem, would you mind?"

He grinned at her and leaped upwards, spiralling tightly into the open space between levels. LoneWolf ground his teeth together, but Belfar had no trouble letting his jaw hang open as Calem tucked and turned just at the right point for the tip of his wing to brush against the ceiling before he spiralled down, grabbing the bags Arilla had set on the railing.

"Show off," she murmured fondly as she slipped into the kitchen.

The smell of bad cooking wafted on the breeze as Shari stormed out of the store. There was a sudden ache high in her chest, just below her throat. Laughing eyes and a kind smile flashed into her thoughts. Her gut churned and the sting of the building tears started. She managed to hold them in check by clenching her teeth and fisting her hands so hard there were bloody crescents left in her palms. She turned her face away and marched resolutely onwards. She would have time to mourn Mitch after. If there ever was an after. There seemed to be an endless list of things that she needed to do. She needed to check on Fiona, make a lesson plan, do her homework, and patrol.

Her half-made plans ground to a halt as a shape detached from the shadows and fell into step with her. *Sam.* She sensed his presence. She had another flash of Mitch asking if they could trust him.

Shari ached to round on Sam and start firing off shot after shot of the red-hot Innarn she sensed crawling beneath her skin, but Sam was humming.

Humming.

Her heart was aching so much she thought it might burst, and this bastard was *humming?*

As if able to sense her thoughts, he stopped. He froze on the path actually, although it took her a couple of paces before she realised. *Sloppy,* she thought as she turned back towards him, eyebrow raised, waiting for an explanation.

There was an awkward silence for a drawn-out moment before Sam sighed and said, "Where I come from, when someone dies, we sing a song to guide their soul to the proper burial place."

Shari tilted her head. She'd never heard of a custom like that for the dead.

"The song depends on how they die. Your friend died in battle, trying to protect everyone else on this hunk of rock. The song he gets is the one that carries the most difficult melody. I can't do it justice, so I've been going around humming it where I can, trying to get others to join in," Sam carried on, scrubbing a weary hand over his face. "Of course, no one else knows the tune, so they never join in, but I'll keep going till the song is finished."

The catch in her throat was back again. "You've been honouring Mitch?"

Sam nodded.

"Here, music is seen as a joyous thing. Something you do when you're happy. No one has been particularly happy lately, which is why no one has joined you," Shari said gently.

Sam's face, usually so inscrutable, fell. Just as quickly, his mask was back in place and he shot her a half grin. "Guess I'll keep on humming then."

"Sing me the song," Shari said.

It was his turn to tilt his head. "There are no words. I suppose it's not a song the way you would usually think of it. It's more music you make with your vocal chords."

Shari tapped her foot, waiting.

Sam sighed, and opened his mouth. A beautiful, mournful melody came pouring out, causing goosebumps to rise on Shari's skin. Her eyes slid closed. Catching the melody, her voice rose to meet his.

Farther down the street, there was the creak of a door opening, and Shari sensed a head popping out to see two souls standing in the street, heads tipped back and voices rising and falling in a haunting sound. More doors opened, and more heads appeared, until Shari could feel the people of Ronah wandering into the street, staring at their Altoriae and the newest stranger in their midst.

Shari's Innarn pulsed, and the others suddenly realised what was going on. Slowly, another voice joined in, and another, and another until there was a chorus of voices rising and falling, the sound carrying across the Island and into the hearts of the residents.

The song faded, and people stood together, loosely embracing, tear tracks and reddened eyes everywhere. Hands were squeezed in comfort. Hugs were exchanged as they made their way back into their homes, until once again, Shari and Sam were the only ones standing in the street.

Sam looked as if a great weight had been lifted from his shoulders. '*Thank you,*' he sent to her, then, eyes downcast, trying unsuccessfully to hide the trail of tears on his cheeks, he shifted out.

Shari stood alone on the street again. Stuffing her hands into her pockets, she turned and continued to walk towards her house, the tears she'd managed to hold in while she was singing slipping from her eyes unbidden.

By the time she got home, she was a bit lighter. A bit less numb. She was able to smile in delight at her mother as she slipped in through the kitchen door. She stopped by the bench and eyed the muffins her mum was putting on the cooling rack.

"I wasn't expecting you here!" Shari said, crossing to give her a hug.

"Your uncle let us out for the day. I've stocked the cupboards so you'll have enough food until the next time Mister Grumpy consents to give us our freedom," Arilla griped.

Shari laughed and turned and grabbed a muffin. "Yum, thanks, Mum," she mumbled around a mouthful.

"You're welcome. But save room for your dinner, okay?"

Shari nodded, chewing contentedly and waving as she wandered up to her room. Maybe Sam's way of mourning Mitch was unusual, but she did feel happier for the first time since he had passed.

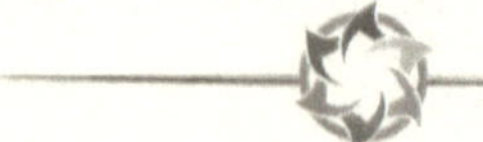

Jonathan rubbed at his tired eyes as the last orphaned child of the Returned left with tentative smiles and their adopted family. He'd had fifty-six orphans to place, and he was worn out from the emotional battering that he'd received. Oh, not all of it had been bad. Many were happy to find a family, but there were a few who hadn't yet accepted what had happened to them and were still struggling with things.

Collis Iuvo, the gangly fifteen-year-old who looked down at Jonathan from a fair height, was one of the kids who'd lost his whole immediate family. He'd elected not to move in with anyone else and wanted a little place of his own. He crossed the room to Jonathan now, squaring his shoulders as he walked.

"Hi, Collis, are you ready to get out of here?" Jonathan asked.

The kid bowed, his eyes fixed on Jonathan's chin. Jonathan saw the moment when his words made sense. "Yes. I am ready to depart, Guardian," Collis said slowly.

It was a habit that he'd noticed with many of the Returned. It was as if they were measuring their words before they spoke. He wondered if it was a generational thing. "Do you have anything here that you want to take with you?"

Silently, the boy hefted a bag that Jonathan had failed to notice over his shoulder. "Ah. Right. Let's go then." He stood and together they made their way up to the ground level of the castle and out into the air.

Despite the rooms underneath the castle being well lit, they both squinted into the sunlight until their eyes adjusted. Jonathan led the way to the rezem that had been set aside for Collis, nodding in greeting to the people they passed.

"Why do they not bow?" Collis asked suddenly.

"Bow?" Jonathan said. "I… That's not something that people do now."

"But you are the Guardian. You deserve respect," the boy said, frowning.

Jonathan took a moment to think about his answer. Clearly, this was something that bothered the taciturn boy, and he didn't deserve to be brushed off. "Respect is shown in different ways. Note how people dip their heads or smile when they pass. They move with enough room around my Innarn field and theirs, so they don't overlap. There are a few who have sent to me, asking to meet later, and if I have food for dinner tonight, or if I would like to join them for a meal. The people of Ronah may have changed in the way that they show respect, but it doesn't mean that it is no longer there," he said at last.

Collis nodded. "The people today are very different. They move like they are afraid."

"Afraid?" Jonathan said, startled.

"They are small and quiet, hunched and huddled in groups. They do not move like the people of my childhood. See? Her." He pointed at Tania, who was laughing as she chased an escaping chicken across the street. "She moves like the people I grew up with. Why does no one else?"

Jonathan shook his head. "I don't know." He didn't want to go into Tania being new to Ronah, and not having grown up with the threat of constant battles. She was not as weary of life as her peers. The thought of endless fighting would be more damaging than Collis needed at the moment.

Tania came over to them, panting, with a struggling, blue-feathered chicken tucked under her arm. "Hi, Jon," she said. Grinning brightly, she turned to Collis. "Hello, I'm Tania. I'd shake hands, but Esse would escape again."

Collis looked a bit stunned. Jonathan took pity on the boy and said, "Esse?"

"My sister says it's short for Esmeralda, but I reckon it's short for Escape Artist," she laughed.

Suddenly, Collis dropped to one knee and bowed his head. "M'lady."

"Wait. What... what just happened?" Tania said, mouth gaping.

"You speak for Ronah," Collis said. "How may I help you, m'lady?"

"Ummm..." Tania looked at Jonathan for guidance, who just shrugged. "Uh. Well, you could stand up and tell me your name?" she suggested, confusion written on her face.

Collis rose to his feet, towering over both of them. "I am Collis Iuvo, last of my clan."

"Oh. Well, pleased to meet you, Collis. Where are you heading?" She juggled Esse, who was kicking ineffectively.

"The Guardian is guiding me to my new home," he said.

"Oh, Ronah makes the best homes!" she exclaimed.

Smiling for the first time since Jonathan had met him, Collis said, "Ronah does make remarkable homes."

"Mind if I come visit you later? I have to get Esse home," she asked.

Once again, Collis seemed stumped. After a moment, he stuttered out, "I-I would be most honoured, Lady Tania."

"Great! I'll bring around some dinner as a welcome-to-the-neighbourhood thing. Mum's making vegetable stew and crispy bread tonight. See you then!" she said, and skipped away, Esse still struggling under her arm.

Jonathan gave Collis a minute to recover before leading the boy to his new home. "I'll send Tania the address, so she knows where you are."

Collis's mouth dropped open, before he nodded thoughtfully. "Of course, you are the Guardian. You are free to send to Lady Tania."

"Just Tania is fine. She doesn't stand on formalities much. Anyone can send to her; she has placed no restrictions," Jonathan said.

With wide eyes, the boy opened the door to his new house and stepped over the threshold. Jonathan grinned as Collis looked around in amazement, the bag slumping off his shoulder and hitting the floor with a muffled thud.

"This is mine?" he breathed.

"All yours, Collis. I'll let you settle in, but I'll check on you in the morning?"

Turning to him, the boy bowed. "Of course. Thank you, Guardian."

Smiling, Jonathan stepped back, and Collis reverently closed the door between them.

Walking down the path, Jonathan heard the whoop of joy Collis let out, and grinned. At least he'd made someone happy today.

The smile fell from his face. Shoving his hands in his pockets, he decided to walk back to the store, hoping that he'd be able to name his candidate by the time he got there. He'd narrowed it down to Alistair or Fiona. Perhaps he should make a quick visit to Fiona to see if she would be interested.

Mind made up, he shifted straight to the hospital. He had a potential apprentice to see.

CHAPTER EIGHT

Half an hour later, Jonathan left, dejected. Fiona had been more than shaken by her encounter, and had laughed so hard when he'd asked if she would be interested in being his candidate that Holli had kicked him out. Hopefully Alistair wouldn't laugh him all the way to the door.

Shifting, he knocked, and Tania answered, chicken absent, but a large pot in its place. "Hi, Jon. Just taking this to Collis to make sure he doesn't starve on his first night. Did you need me for something?" she asked.

"I was here to see Alistair, actually," he said.

Narrowing her eyes, Tania looked at him for a moment. "You're wasting your time, but he's in the lounge. Go on in."

Jonathan murmured his thanks as she brushed past, wondering if his idea was such a good one after all.

He found Alistair slumped in a lounge chair, slurping a drink through a straw in an obnoxious manner. Raising an eyebrow, Jonathan looked at the teen, who finally glanced over at him, and startled, sucked down the drink the wrong way before starting to choke.

Red in the face, eyes watering, Alistair managed to catch his breath. "H... Hi, Guardian," he stammered.

"Good evening, Alistair. I've come to ask you a question, if you don't mind?" Jonathan made no move to sit or enter the room any farther, although Alistair did weakly wave at the sofa.

"Of course. What is it?" The boy was so painfully eager, and so like another, Jonathan struggled to keep his mind in the present.

"Did you know that traditionally, I have an apprentice?"

"No." His head tipped to the side. With his brows drawn together, Alistair was the very study of confusion.

"I do. There's a process behind it though. The Altoriae and I choose a candidate, as do some others. I was wondering if you'd like to be my candidate?"

"What do I have to do?" he asked, wary.

"A simple test devised by myself and the Altoriae," Jonathan asked. "There is time before the test, and no pressure on you to say yes."

Taking another slurp of his drink, Alistair stared into nothingness. Jonathan knew his thoughts were whirring. He waited silently for what seemed like an age, until suddenly, Alistair announced, "I'll do it."

Blinking to try and hide his surprise, Jonathan asked, "You will?"

"I will. If it means that I have the chance to fight off the beings that are trying to destroy Lissae, then I'm all for it," he said, his jaw jutting forwards.

"I am honoured, Alistair. I shall call on you again before the test," Jonathan said, moving to take his leave.

"Wait! Do I have to do anything beforehand?"

"No. Just rest and take care of yourself. I will see you soon," Jonathan said, and slipped out the door.

Hands crammed into his pockets again, he walked down the street towards his house, deep in thought.

Sam, hidden in the shadows, slipped out behind Jonathan as he walked past. He slid from shadow to shadow, trailing him. On the rooftops, a flash and glint of wing and bow caught his attention. The edge of Samuel's blade caught the last of the evening light as the oblivious Guardian wandered towards his home.

Jonathan strode up the garden path towards the front door, intent on sitting down with a hot drink and staring into the flames of his fire when a large winged body collided with his, knocking him to the side.

"Watch out!" yelled a jittery voice belonging to the Ilutri sprawled on top of Jonathan. "I'm armed!"

"I know," said Sam, deadpan, and threw a knife, pinning his attacker's sleeve to the front door, causing him to yelp.

With all the blades that ended up being flung at his door, Jonathan found himself considering getting a metal door so that at least there would be fewer holes to repair.

"Guardian, be careful! That man is not what he seems!" the man who'd tackled him warned.

Rising, Jonathan brushed himself off. "Really, Sam? Were you not able to think of another way to get him off me?"

"Well, I could have stabbed him, but I still forget where the vital organs are for you lot. I might have hit something important," Sam said with a shrug.

"Yeah, you forget," Jonathan muttered.

"What? I'm trying to turn over a new bush."

"Leaf, Sam. Turn over a new leaf," Jonathan corrected. Together, the two turned to face the Ilutri, who'd managed to free himself from the door and was hastily trying to notch an arrow into his bow.

"Really?" Sam complained.

"Stay away, fiend! I don't know what you are, but you aren't from Lissae," the man warned, iridescent blue feathers flashing in the falling light.

Rolling his eyes, Sam said, "Have you never heard of a political refugee before?"

"Is that what you are?" Tania said from behind him, making all three men jump, and the Ilutri's notched bow let loose. The arrow flew straight towards Sam, who stepped aside instinctively, unintentionally revealing the young girl behind him.

The arrow stopped mid-air, right between Tania's startled eyes, before it clattered to the ground, the tip grazing her nose on the way down. Unbidden, Sam raised a hand to the graze, and his fingertips came away red. Tania's gaze was fixed on the drop of blood, and she missed his eyes glowing as he struggled to keep his temper.

Turning, he saw the idiot who'd shot Tania smirk. It sparked the flame burning inside him. Shadowed wings rose on his back and seemed to blot out the sky as he advanced on his soon-to-be snack.

Tania appeared before him, hands up, even as Jonathan moved so he was between Tania and the one whose feathers would become the filling for his quilt.

"Move," he growled.

"No can do. You need to stop. He didn't hurt me, not really. He was aiming at you," Tania said, trying in vain to placate him.

"All the more reason to disembowel him," he growled.

"No, it's even more reason to show that you are not a threat. Otherwise you prove him right," she said gently.

"He was following Jon, with a blade and a bow. He knocked him to the ground, and he shot you," Sam was snarling now, his eyes flashing gold as he ripped his gaze away from the idiot and settled on her face.

"I was aiming for you," the Ilutri's voice was steadier now he had two people between him and the terrifying man he'd come to warn the Guardian about.

"Hold on. What makes you think he was following me?" Jonathan asked Sam over his shoulder.

"I've been keeping an eye on you since Anriluka was defeated. It wouldn't be beyond her to have left something in hiding to attack you," Sam groused.

"What about Shari?" Jonathan asked. Sam could hear him frowning.

"Shari is more situationally aware than you give her credit for," Sam said.

Tania giggled. "Which means you tried to follow her, and she knew you were there."

"I've been shadowing this oaf for weeks and he hasn't even noticed till tonight," Sam muttered.

Jonathan looked at him out of the corner of his eye and started to say something when the garden gate squeaked closed, startling them all.

"Are you having a party without me?" Shari asked as she strode up the path. Sam was pleased to see that she made no move to conceal her shield from the newcomer. When she caught sight of the arrow they'd left on the ground, she stepped around it, pushing her shield out effortlessly to encompass Jonathan, Tania, and even him.

Perhaps the Altoriae had been serious about him being her candidate?

He didn't have any more time to think about it, as she saw Tania's face. The graze was glowing gently as Ronah healed her, but it was not soon enough to hide it from Shari. Narrowing her eyes, she took in the bow held loosely by the foolish Ilutri and before any of them were able to stop her, his back was against the door, her forearm blocking his windpipe.

"Just who do you think you are?" Shari snarled at him.

Sam shot a rather superior, satisfied look at Jonathan. The little Altoriae was doing exactly what he'd wanted to do—albeit with the tuzar's intestines still inside his quivering belly.

'I'm protecting the Guardian!' the imbecile broadcasted.

'Wrong answer. Try again.' Sam sensed that Shari was holding herself back from crushing the windpipe of the now snivelling cretin.

'I am Therdon of the Ilutri. I came to help the Guardian!'

Shari eased off. "Jon?"

"I saw him at the festival, but we did not speak," Jonathan said, shaking his head.

Pulling her arm away, she straightened, managing to loom over the shaking Ilutri despite him being a good foot taller than her. "Next time you want to help, you announce your intentions first. Now, want to tell me why you shot my friend?" she said as she casually pulled Sam's knife from the door and started twirling it between her fingers.

"I wasn't trying to," Therdon said, his voice only slightly shaking. "I was aiming for him," he added, pointing at Sam.

"So, instead of aiming for Ronah's Linked, you aimed for *my* candidate?" Shari asked, her tone conversational with a hint of violence.

Therdon gulped. He'd finally caught the hint. He pulled his tunic straight and stiffened his spine. "I was unaware that I was aiming at a fellow candidate."

Jaws dropped and eyebrows rose. Only Jonathan remained composed.

"Well, candidate Therdon, we look forward to formally meeting you before the test. If you'll excuse us, we are retiring for the evening," Jon said smoothly. He nodded to the Ilutri and slid by him to enter the house, the two girls following. Tania wore a nervous grin and Shari outright glared. Sam began to follow when the idiot spoke again.

"And where is he going?"

"I am going to sit at the Guardian's table and sleep in the bed he is providing me," Sam said, baring his teeth in a parody grin.

"Candidates can't stay with the Guardian!" Therdon protested.

"Oh, I'm not staying with him. I live with him." Sam showed more teeth before shouldering the yelping Ilutri out of the way and shutting the door in his face.

Jonathan looked at him askance, but Sam saw him stifling a grin. Beyond, he saw the girls kicking off their shoes and getting the fire started.

"So, you've been following me around?" Jon asked.

"Of course. You're my meal ticket," Sam said, trying to play down his self-appointed protection duty.

Narrowing his eyes, Jonathan looked at him for a long moment. Sam knew it would be so easy to dip into the human's thoughts and fish out what he was thinking, but he decided against it. Instead he silently endured the appraising gaze of the second-most powerful person of Lissae in silence. After a long minute, Jonathan nodded and turned, leading the way into the kitchen.

If Sam got a bigger portion that night, no one said a word about it.

After they'd all eaten, Sam and Tania retreated to the lounge room, while Shari and Jon disappeared to patrol.

Tania was unusually quiet, gazing into the flickering flames, her arms around her legs and her head resting on her knees.

Sprawled out on the couch, Sam poked at her with a foot. "Why are you troubled?"

Tania sighed, but didn't answer.

He poked her again.

She turned to look at him, and he sat up swiftly, alarmed by her leaking eyes. It took him a moment to remember that humans released emotions that way. Really, he didn't understand why bloodletting wasn't a more widely accepted emotional release. Particularly if it was someone else's blood.

"I should have died tonight," she whispered.

Samuel looked deep into the eyes of the girl before him. There was sadness in them, and a hint of fear. Fear that Tania would die a screaming, horrible death like Mitch had. "You know something?"

"What?"

"We create our own reality. You continue to think that way, and I guarantee you, that is exactly how you will die."

Tania looked shocked. "How can you say that?"

"Because it's natural to fear death. It's natural to have these thoughts after something like this happens, and because..." Sam leaned forwards and whispered into the girl's ear, "...because you might just have cause to worry."

Sam watched, satisfied his warning had been delivered, as Tania shivered as if a cold chill leaped like lightning up her spine. Rising, he gave a bow and retreated, leaving her to mull over his words.

CHAPTER NINE

"What exactly happened tonight?" Shari asked as soon as she and Jon were back from patrol. Shifting them to the back room of the book store, she threw herself into an arm chair, legs dangling over one arm.

"Therdon thought I was in danger. He pushed me out of the way as Sam came through the gate behind me. Sam was being his usual obstinate self and stirred him up. Just as Tania arrived, Therdon shot at Sam, who stepped aside. The arrow scraped Tania's nose. Sam was furious. He was going to rip Therdon apart," Jon said.

Shari scoffed. "I doubt that he would…"

"Think about it, Shari. Sam is… different from us," her Guardian said.

"Different how?" she asked. Jon ran a hand over his face, and she snorted. "Fine. Don't tell me. I suppose you can at least let me know how this test takes place, or is that something else you can't tell me?" Shari asked bitterly as she picked at a loose thread on her chair.

"It's not my place to tell you about Sam," Jon said. "His secrets are his own."

"And you hold them too," Shari pointed out.

"But talking about the test is something we need to do."

Rising, Shari wandered around Jonathan's home office. "What do I need to know?" she asked as she fiddled with a statuette of Na'reh.

"The test is quite formal. It's made up of three main parts: the opening, testing, and closing. There can be as many tests as you wish during the testing phase, but it must be decided beforehand and announced during the opening. Meeting the candidates and announcing the rules of the tests also occur at the opening. At the close, you announce the winning candidate."

"Hold up. Why do I have to announce who wins?" Shari asked, frowning.

"Ultimately, it's up to you," Jonathan said.

"Then why can't I just announce it now?"

"The reason we have tests to decide on the apprentice is so we can see the other candidates in action during the testing and decide if they are better suited to the role," he said, turning to watch her idly flicking through a book.

She made a humming noise of agreement, her gaze fixed on the book before her. Shari had barely asked Jon any questions about his life in the whole time she'd known him. She couldn't avoid the one burning the tip of her tongue now. "Did you have to go through the tests?"

Jonathan's head snapped up. "My testing wasn't as formal," he spoke carefully, "It was more about survival than rounds in arenas. Joshua was more the trial-by-fire type. And there wasn't an Altoriae to choose."

Shari's eyes went wide. "Do you regret the way you were tested?"

"Nothing about my testing was under controlled circumstances. I was literally trained and put on patrol before my tenth birthday. It is not something I feel necessary to put another being through." Jonathan's eyes fell on the crackling fire, which jumped and danced higher as he watched.

"Did Mitch go through the tests?"

"Of a sort," Jonathan said carefully. "I devised three tests of my own for the candidates to attempt. Traditionally, testing only happens when the Altoriae is around."

"I was around!" Shari protested, snapping the book closed.

"But not ready to announce yourself."

Groaning, Shari put the book back and moved away from the desk.

Jonathan watched her, trying to figure out if his amusement or frustration was greater. "Are you going to update the Handbook tonight?"

Sighing, Shari nodded. Updating the Altoriae's Handbook was one of her duties. It had been handed down right from the first Altoriae, Kay'imi, and contained a wealth of information about all sorts of things across the Realms, including the lives of the Altoriae who'd come before her.

"I'll do it after I patrol tomorrow," she said.

"I'm patrolling tomorrow," Jonathan said.

She shrugged. "I'm too restless to write now," she admitted.

"I've heard reports that the Chirea have been sighted on Gerhar," Jonathan said.

"Gerhar? But that's right near us." Shari frowned.

"I know. If you're after somewhere to burn off some energy, I think that would be the place." Jonathan nodded and rose from the chair. "I'll leave you to it then," he said, and quietly left the room.

Shari's black leathers appeared. The yellow blade Yessna, second in command of the U'sala, had given her, was safe in its scabbard by her hip, and Sam's blade from the door was in her hand. She looked out of the darkened windows to see her reflection staring back at her. She touched the mask hiding her face, debating whether she should leave it on or take it off.

For a long moment, she stood undecided, before she shook her head and shifted away, mask still in place.

Shari arrived in a wheat field on the Realm of Gerhar. Turning, she spotted a small town close by, dark grey clouds looming ominously overhead. Banishing her mask and using her Innarn, she created a cloak to cover her leathers.

"Well, at least ya aren't one of them," said a voice behind her. "Any chance you can stop the rain before it gets here? We need this crop more than ever."

Shari spotted a waving stalk of wheat among a flattened patch. Peering over the tall grass, she could just make out the brim of a hat and the flash of a blade.

"I can stop the rain," Shari promised, "if you can give me some information."

"Nuthin's ever free, is it?" muttered the woman as she rose to her feet. "What'd ya wan'ta know?"

"Have the Chirea been through here?" Shari asked.

The woman scowled at her. "A'course they've been through 'ere. Destroyed tha town and tha crops on tha other side. Half thems who survived has left, fearin' they'd be back."

"Are you afraid they'll be back?" Shari asked.

The woman scowled harder. "I've lost ever'thin' else to 'em. Don't much matter if I lose ma life as well."

Shocked, Shari found she had nothing to say. A grief that deep would not be consoled with mere words. Instead, she turned her face to the sky and, palms raised, scattered the moisture from the fat grey rainclouds.

As she let go of her control on the clouds, they began to disperse, and the sky turned blue again. The woman lifted her face in wonder, one hand raised to block out the sudden glare of the sun.

"Well, ya best come in a'fore we both get burned ou' here," the woman said, and hefting her scythe, she led Shari towards the town.

Following along, Shari took note of the town before her. The buildings had yellow clay walls and thatched rooftops, blending almost seamlessly with the environment around them. As they got closer, she could make out chunks of missing wall, and darker patches of thatch where rooves had been repaired. Curtains were pulled aside, and faces peered out at them. She pulled her cloak a bit closer but didn't dismiss her weapons.

The woman led her down a cobbled road, leaning heavily on the handle of her scythe, the blade pointed forwards. She heaved herself up the single step to a door and beckoned Shari to follow.

"What else are ya wantin' to know about 'em?" the woman asked as she hung her hat and stomped her boots on the woven grass mat.

"How long ago did they come through?" Shari trailed behind the woman, who moved farther into the house, heading for the kitchen.

"A coupla days. Jus' after they'd killed off as many of ma kin as they could, they stomped the way they came, heading back inta the forest. It was early mornin' when they left." The woman's hands paused on the glowing kettle, as she got lost for a moment, looked into the past. She shook her head as steam started whistling out of the spout. "That afternoon, jus' after we'd finished cleanin' up, there was a horrible howlin'. Made us all cry, it did."

Brows drawing together, Shari figured that that was probably when the Chirean leader had been told of his son's death. Letting her mind rise out of her body for a moment, she took a quick look at the thick blanket of trees that stretched from horizon to horizon, and failed to spot an entry point.

"Can you point me in the direction they went?" Shari asked, snapping back into her body.

The woman shook her head. "I ain't pointin' ya to ya death." She poured the tea into a mug and handed it to Shari, the steam rising in lazy spirals.

"I'm tougher than I look," she said as she took the cup with a grin.

"I know," the woman said as she poured another for herself. "But tha Chirea, they don't play fair. They'll have ya bones if ya go after them."

"You've lost so much. Surely you can understand wanting to protect what's left?" Shari asked gently.

Glancing away, the woman snorted. "Fine. I'll show ya the way, but ya come an' ask ta see me a'fore ya go back to ya Realm," the woman grumbled.

Shari nodded, and sipped her tea. It was light and minty, warming her from the inside out. She sat in silence with her host for a while before the woman rose and led her out the door.

Walking through the town, Shari saw up close the devastation that the Chirea had wrought. Crumbling walls, arrows still protruding from the rooftops, and the wary looks on the faces of those they passed. Just as Shari wondered if they'd appreciate her help, they arrived at the edge of the town.

"Ma name's Ebb. Ya remember ta ask for me," Ebb warned.

"Of course," Shari said, bowing her head.

"They wen' sou' east. When ya get closer to tha tree line, ya can see tha break tha scum carved inta them." Ebb scowled, as if it were a personal affront.

"Thank you," Shari said. "I'll come back when I'm done."

Ebb nodded, and Shari shifted away.

At the tree line, Shari saw what Ebb meant. The forest bore a scar where the Chirea had forced their way through. The trees were weeping. She wished she could help. Whispering words of comfort, she walked into the forest, keeping her steps light.

Two hours later, she came across a clearing where the grass had been flattened. The air was heavy with grief, threatening to smother her. Ignoring it, she moved through the open space, seeking to find what had happened after Fiona had left.

A twig snapped under her foot, and suddenly, she found herself lofted into the air by her ankle, her cloak wrapping around her head, cutting off her vision. Cursing, she banished the cloak in time to see a jolt of plasma headed right for her face.

Yelping, she twisted, swinging like a pendulum as jolt after jolt came her way. Using her momentum, Shari swung herself up onto the branch above her. With one arch of Sam's blade, she sliced through the rope. Grinning, she decided to ask him where he'd gotten the knife as she slipped it into a sheath. As she flicked her wrist, a glove with two long blades appeared. Dropping to the ground, she looked around for her attacker.

It really wasn't hard.

They gave away their position when another bolt of plasma came streaming towards her head. Shifting, she appeared behind the purple-robed being. The being was taller than her, and broader. She had to stretch to touch the tips of the bladed glove at the juncture between its head and shoulders.

"I suggest you stop," Shari said.

The being froze. For a short moment, they both stood frozen before the being lashed out, kicking backwards, and rolling away from her.

Dodging the kick, Shari aimed a jet of water at the plasma user, which they sidestepped then shoved their hands into the soil.

Automatically, Shari's hand rose to her ears as the trees began to scream in agony, their branches whipping through the air as they writhed in pain. Dropping her hands, Shari found herself alone in the clearing.

Shaken, she reached into the soil and drew forwards the plasma from the tree roots, flinching at the first touch. The Innarn was so Light, it almost burned her. Her leathers started to smoulder at the pure amount of power she was handling. Gritting her teeth, she pulled the

Light plasma from the roots and shot it into the sky where it cracked like lightning.

The trees wept. Shari did her best to soothe them, and then started the long trudge back to the town. After having power that Light pass through her, she didn't know if it was safe for her to shift back. Idly, she beat at her smoking jacket as she concentrated only on putting one foot in front of the other.

Halfway back, Shari received a send from one of the Ducibus. *'Well met, Altoriae. The plasma Innarnian you just encountered has left the Realm.'*

Sighing in relief, she sent her thanks back down the link. Her feet picked up the pace as the town got closer.

At the sight of the first building, she stopped and straightened herself. Her leathers had stopped smoking, and she rolled her weary shoulders back to stand straight as she made her way to Ebb's house.

Two wrong turns later, she knocked at the right door and it swung open.

"Did ya find what ya needed?" Ebb asked, before she caught sight of Shari's face. "Wha' happened to ya?" the woman demanded.

"I'm not really sure," Shari said, swaying. "Just wanted you to know I'm still alive, and I hope you don't think it rude of me, but I'm going to head home."

"Ya need to come in an' rest!" Ebb demanded.

"Thank you, really, but I've been gone too long as it is," Shari protested, even as Ebb grabbed her by the arm and led her inside, pushing her down to sit in a chair.

Moments later, she had a patterned plate with a thick slice of bread and cream shoved under her nose, and a mug thudded onto the table before her.

"Eat," Ebb demanded.

Shari gave in and ate, feeling better with each bite.

"So, wha' happened?" Ebb asked when Shari had finished the last bite.

"There was a plasma Innarnian there. They tried to kill the trees," Shari said. Ebb gasped, her hand flying to her throat. "The forest is fine. I made sure of it."

"But look at ya!" Ebb exclaimed.

Shari shook her head. She didn't really want to know what she looked like at that moment. "I'll be okay. Thank you for the food. I need to get back."

"Wha' abou' tha plasma Innarnian?" Ebb asked.

"I don't know where they went, but they aren't on Gerhar at the moment," Shari said.

Ebb nodded. "If they come back, we'll be waitin'," she said darkly.

Smiling, Shari rose. "Thank you again," she said, and slipped out the door before Ebb could say another word.

Shifting back to Ronah, Shari paused as she caught sight of her sooty reflection swaying wearily. She had said she'd update the book, but she thought of a thousand other things she wanted to do right now—and crawling into bed was at the top of the list. Even so, she flicked a finger and her leathers morphed back into her normal clothes. She crossed the room to where the Handbook was waiting for her.

Picking up the pen, she turned to a blank page and started writing.

It seems like an impossible task, saving the world every day. I am finding it entirely possible, just very, very tiring.

Shari paused, wondering what she should write next. Because of her job description, nothing she did was private. Her journal would be passed on to the next Altoriae. She knew that some of the Altoriaes before her had attempted to keep private journals, because she had read them.

The hard part of this calling—if you wish to call it that—is that it is soul-crushing, and mind-numbingly repetitive. It's always the same old story—bad guy tries to take over the Realm, I shove them back into theirs. Why don't the bad guys help save our Realm for once, instead of trying to take it over? There are worse things I could wish for, aren't there?

Hoping that Jon would be satisfied, she put the pen down, shifted straight to her room, and flopped onto her bed, asleep before her head hit the pillow.

Arilla sighed and brushed her hair out of her eyes. With the extra bodies on Ronah, the lunchtime rush at the tavern was becoming impossible.

Another customer signalled for service, and she hurried over, stepping through the narrow gaps between tables. They'd had to add more seating to meet demand, but even now, there wasn't enough. With her and Calem forced to choose between staying on Rakemyst, and enduring heavily armed guards glowering as they lined the back wall, there weren't many chances to fix the problem.

One last twist and she was at the customer's side, taking their order with a smile. It was on her way back to the kitchen that she knocked into a large clay pitcher, sending it flying.

Strong hands caught it before it landed, setting it safely on the table.

"Well met, mother of the Altoriae."

"Uh. Well met, stranger who rescues jug."

The gangly boy laughed. "I can do more than that if you need some help?" He indicated the crowd, and Arilla spotted the ink on his biceps peeking out from under the sleeves of his tunic.

Another three hands shot up, and Arilla had to stifle a groan. "Call me Arilla and get a tray. You're hired."

The boy bowed, and a serving tray floated into his hands.

"Don't touch my books. You'll mess my system up," she warned, pointing to the library area that had all but been swallowed by tables of hungry people.

He nodded.

"Oh, what's your name?"

"Collis Iuvo," the boy said as he moved to the next waiting customer.

Escaping into the heat of the kitchen, she passed an order slip to Calem. "This is getting crazy. We're four times as busy now as we were before."

Before Shari had announced she was the Altoriae. Before her test. Before the Returned. Before Ronah and Rakemyst had joined.

Brushing the hair out of her eyes, Arilla blew out a breath. "I know. I've just hired someone else to help. He's one of the Returned. Collis Iuvo."

Hugging her to his side, Calem kissed the top of her head. "If you think that he's a good fit for the tavern, then we can give it a go. You have impeccable instincts about people."

Nudging him with her hip and picking up a plate of food, she laughed. "You're just saying that because I picked you."

Chuckling, Calem swatted at her as three order slips came floating in the air, passing through the door with ease.

"May I enter?" Collis asked.

Calem raised his eyebrows at her, and she shrugged a shoulder. "You may."

Collis pushed through the swinging doors. "One of the tables is asking for cooled water. Do you have jugs that you prefer to use?"

Tilting his head, Calem stared at Collis, and the two fell silent. Arilla rolled her eyes and left the two Innarnians to communicate while she took out the orders that were ready.

Collis joined her with food for another table, effortlessly serving customers as if he'd been working at the tavern for years instead of minutes.

Grinning, Arilla took the next lot of orders, happy with their newest staff member.

The next morning when Shari's alarm clock went off, she threw it against the wall without looking. She didn't want to get up until noon. Someone tutted, and she shot upright, knife flying from her fingers before she could think.

There was wet squelch, followed by a shriek, and Shari opened her eyes to see Therdon holding his arm and looking at her with wide eyes and a quivering chin. LoneWolf burst into the room and Shari looked at them both in confusion.

Shari wanted to scream, but managed to keep her voice low and even. "What in Na'reh's name are you doing in my room?"

LoneWolf turned narrowed eyes onto Therdon, who paled even further and stared at the ground. "I wouldn't mind knowing the same thing," he growled.

"I came in to wake her. She didn't answer when I knocked," Therdon stammered.

If she had been a bit more awake, Shari probably would have thrown another knife at him. "So, you thought it was okay to enter without invitation?"

The younger Ilutri didn't answer. LoneWolf grabbed him by the scruff of the neck and pulled him out, calling over his shoulder, "Time to get up, Altoriae. Elder Dawn wants to see you."

Flicking the covers aside and swinging her legs out of bed, she stifled the groan. She was sore all over from last night. Grandfather summoning her or not, she was still going to get clean before she went anywhere.

Clean, dressed, and ready to face the day, Shari dropped over the side of the railing rather than walking down the stairs. Therdon yelped, and LoneWolf rolled his eyes.

"If your highness is ready?" LoneWolf grumbled.

"Lead the way, lowly soldier," Shari joked, her nose in the air. LoneWolf smirked at her, while Therdon looked horrified.

"Perhaps shifting would get us there quicker?" her uncle asked with a quirk of his brow.

Trying to mask how tired she was, she nodded. "As you wish," Shari murmured, and shifted them to SilverCloud's study. A gold-fletched arrow slammed into the column in front of them, inches away from SilverCloud's head. Slashing out with Yessna's sword, Shari spun, facing the retreating attacker. She flung the sword at his back.

It glanced off the bone armour, but the force knocked the intruder to the ground where he lay, gasping for breath.

CHAPTER TEN

The attacker's loud breathing echoed in the silent room. SilverCloud sat at his desk, hands clasped together as he peered at the Chirea. Only his greying skin and the faint tremor in his wings told of his shock.

SilverCloud was bracketed on one side by Arilla and Calem, and on the other by LoneWolf whose arms were loose and ready to defend if the glare he was sporting didn't kill the attacker first. Belfar, Therdon, and another Ilutri archer joined Shari, Jon, and Tania at staring down the attacker.

Even with their combined glaring, the attacker snorted and looked at the floor rather than meeting their gazes.

"Why?" Arilla said, her voice cracking like a whip through the silence.

Glaring up at her from under his matted hair, the intruder spat rather than answer her question. Shari's hackles rose, but she didn't let it show.

Therdon seemed to have no such compulsion. He strode forwards and slapped the Chirea, cutting his hand open on a tooth protruding from the skeletal jaw protecting the attacker's face.

Rolling her eyes at him, Shari wanted to ask why the Ilutri thought that this fool would be a good candidate as apprentice. Belfar looked at her as if he'd heard her thoughts and shrugged minutely. She shook her head as Therdon yelled in the Chirea's face.

"May I?" the other archer asked suddenly. She stepped forwards as Therdon stepped back.

"Well met, Chirea. I am Varlee of the Ilutri. Why did you try to kill our Elder?" she said, squatting down to stare into the attacker's eyes, her wings spread out behind her.

He snarled at her.

"You do not wish to answer?" she asked, tilting her head to the side. She reached out and, lightning quick, plucked a small bone from his chest armour. "How about now?" she asked as he gasped.

Eyes like flint, he watched as she plucked bone after piece of bone from his chest plate, leaving him sweating and shaking.

"Do you know," she said as she worked, "the Chirea gather the bones from the fallen not just as a gruesome display of their prowess, but also because they believe the bones retain the strength of their prey? Personally, I wouldn't want the bones of the fallen. The fallen are weak; they have been felled in battle. I'd go after the bones of those who were still alive."

The Chirea gave a shuddering gasp as Varlee wrenched a large rib off his chest plate and cast it carelessly aside.

"What do you think? After I remove all the bones that make up your armour, I'll start on the ones inside you, yes?"

Another rib came free.

"The only question, of course, is should I start with the little bones or the big ones? I mean, finger bones make a nice necklace and all, but spines can make a good bow."

Shari placed a hand on Tania, who was slowly turning green. Another rib joined the growing pile at Varlee's feet. If Shari bit the inside of her cheek any harder, she was going to be missing a chunk that even her Innarn couldn't heal. Shari didn't agree with the Ilutri methods—torture wasn't a good look on anyone—but so long as she was on Rakemyst, she wasn't in a position to ask them to stop.

"One of you killed Luttrell's son," the Chirea gasped out.

Varlee stopped. "And?"

"And I was ordered to kill the weakest member of your tribe!"

Sitting back on her heels, Varlee tilted her head. "You think that SilverCloud is weak?"

The Chirea didn't answer. He was covered in sweat, panting heavily. The loss of his armour affected him in a way Shari wouldn't have considered. She made a mental note of it and set part of her mind working on how to use it in battle.

Reaching out a hand, Varlee stopped when the attacker practically yelled, "He is dying. The dying are always the weakest!"

All eyes turned to SilverCloud, bar Varlee, who was regarding the attacker with interest. "Strange. I've found that the dying are usually the ones who cling to life with the most desperation."

Without another word, she left the attacker. "What would you have us do with him?" she asked SilverCloud as the Chirea frantically scrambled to gather the pile of bones before him.

"Shari, if you wouldn't mind?"

"Of course," Shari said, and shifted the Chirea away just as his fingers closed over the largest rib. She took some satisfaction that the majority of his chest plate remained on the floor.

"So, you're dying. Want to tell us about it?" Varlee said, her odd silver eyes regarding the Elder behind the desk.

"I've no bones for you to pull on, Varlee," SilverCloud said, sounding more exhausted than Shari felt. "I am dying. You've all known for quite a while."

Stepping forwards, Shari asked, "What of?"

SilverCloud smiled at her, though it didn't reach his eyes. "Something even you can't heal, Altoriae. Old age. I can feel myself slipping away day after day."

There was a sudden lump in her throat that she found it difficult to catch her breath around. Heavy silence fell in the room, the occupants lost in their own thoughts. Arilla and Calem clasped hands, staring at each other, and Shari knew they were unsure what to say. Belfar clapped LoneWolf on the back and left his hand there, lending support without hesitation.

"There are worse ways to go, you gloomy lot. Now, what should we do about this latest threat?" her grandfather said, clapping his hands together.

"Belfar and Varlee will be with you around the clock," LoneWolf said immediately.

SilverCloud scoffed, but Calem nodded. "I think it's for the best. Besides, if you want old age to be your demise, you've survived too long to scorn protection now."

Shari was impressed at how quickly the brothers managed to sidestep his objections.

"What of Arilla?" asked SilverCloud.

Her mother startled. "Arilla is right here, and I need protecting far less than you do," she said proudly.

"I will watch her," Calem and LoneWolf said at the same time.

Shari and SilverCloud rolled their eyes in tandem when the brothers scowled at each other, their momentary truce lost.

"I'm rather interested in this arrow," Jon said, trying to diffuse the tension. He and Varlee both crossed the room to look at where it stuck out of the column. When he reached to pull it free, Varlee's hand shot out and grabbed his wrist.

"Do not touch, Guardian. Can you not feel it?" she said.

He paused, and as Shari crossed the room to stand by him, he gasped. Reaching out, Shari sensed the arrow tugging at her Innarn, and she stumbled back, shields coming up in full force.

"What is that?" she breathed.

Turning to regard the Altoriae, Varlee said, "This arrow is typically called a soul seeker. The gold fletching gives it away. If this arrow had hit SilverCloud, it would have gathered his Innarn and infused it in the first Blank to touch it."

"Wait, what?" Therdon asked. "That can't be real. That's a bedtime story for children!"

"All tales have a basis of truth hidden somewhere in them. The soul-seeker arrow is real. The only question is, where did our Chirea friend get it from?"

"Shari, can you bring him back?"

Stepping away from the unnerving arrow, she reached out, trying to track down the Chirea she'd sent away to the cells at the bottom of Castle Bachelor. Frowning, she concentrated harder, seeking out his life force to get a lock on him.

There!

She pulled him back to SilverCloud's office, only for him to take one last shuddering breath around the bone protruding from his stomach.

Tania groaned and turned away. Arilla and Therdon both went an alarming shade of white, while the others in the room looked unflinchingly at the dead Chirea. Shari found it odd to think that she was among other battle-hardened warriors.

"We should not have let him out of our sight," Varlee said.

"It's a bit too late to go over our mistakes now. We must be on our guard. There may be other Chirea hiding on our Isle."

"Or on Ronah," Calem noted.

Her features hardening, Tania said, "Not if I can help it."

"Perhaps we should call Zana, and the Linked can work together to flush out any of the other Chirea?" Therdon offered.

Shari stared at him, stunned. Maybe this was why they'd named the seemingly incompetent Ilutri as their candidate. She and Jonathan shared a look and smiled grimly.

"Whatever I can do to make sure that they're stopped," Tania said, her jaw jutting out.

Hours later, Tania was seated across from Zana, exhausted. Together they'd worked at scouring their respective Islands to no avail.

Shari's mum came in and placed a platter with two bowls of kunun soup and plates of crisped bread in front of them. The thick orange soup had never smelled so good.

"Here," she said, "I thought you could use a break."

"Our thanks," Zana said, then paused, a puzzled frown on her face. "I cannot feel you."

Arilla shrugged. "I'm right here."

Zana seemed to sweep away the thought with a brush of her hand. "No. Your Innarn. I can't feel it."

"That's because I don't have any," Arilla said with a tight smile.

Getting to her feet, Zana circled Arilla like she was a specimen to be studied. "You are like a blank spot in my mind. I can see you, but not feel you." She whirled, looking at Tania, eyes alight with excitement. "We have been approaching this wrong the whole time. We are not looking for something; we are searching for its absence."

Tania looked at the older woman, running the thought through her head. She reached out to Ronah, searching for her own mother, and found her, knowing it was her because of the lack of Innarn, the blank spot in her mind.

"Of course! Thank you, Mrs Dawn!"

Together, Tania and Zana reached out. Within the hour, they'd identified more than a dozen Chirea who'd been hiding since the attack. They were all equipped with one of the golden soul-seeker arrows.

It was only when LoneWolf bowed in thanks as they handed over the map showing the locations of the hidden Chirea, and strode off, wings held up proudly behind him, that Tania felt she could breathe again.

Slipping out of Elder Dawn's house, Tania sighed. She was so glad she'd been able to help, and to stop what would have been a series of horrific attacks. As she looked up at the clear blue sky, she laughed in delight when an Ilutri flew by.

Rakemyst was a place where air Innarn was so obvious it was like—well, like air. The Ilutri seemed to use their Innarn for everything. People still walked from place to place on Ronah, whereas the Ilutri seemed happier to fly or hover.

The gardens were different too. On Ronah, they were beautiful, full of colours and scents, but Rakemyst felt like a realm apart.

As Tania walked through the garden that bordered SilverCloud's home, all sorts of small creatures buzzed, flapped, flittered, and flew around her. Walking past a bush brought a storm of butterflies fleeing from its leaves. They paused, and almost seemed to be dancing in front of her for a moment, drawing forth another joyful laugh.

It was cut off halfway through.

"Thought you would get all of us, did you, girlie?" asked a voice. Her hair was wrenched back. "Now, how abouts you come along with me? There's a good girlie."

Heart in her throat, Tania wanted to cry out but found she couldn't. Angry tears gathered, but she fought them down. No way was she going to show how scared she was.

'Ronah?' she sent.

'Tania!' Ronah picked up on her fear, and she could feel her Island reaching out for her, but on Rakemyst, she was too far away.

'Can you warn them?'

'I will, I will,' Ronah trailed off.

Tania tried not to stumble as her captor shoved her in the direction of SilverCloud's home. With a vicious grip on her hair and the edge of a blade resting painfully along her hip, she had no choice but to walk.

Shari turned as the doors were shoved open. Tania stumbled through and fell to the ground. SilverCloud rose, but before anyone moved, a gold-fletched arrow was pointed directly at Tania's heart.

"Reckon you lot can stop this one?" A voice taunted them from behind the partly open door. "I think I'm close enough to take her out before you can work any of your fancy Innarn tricks."

Frowning, Shari crept closer to the door. Before she pulled it open, there was an almighty clang. The arrow started dipping closer to Tania as her attacker slumped into view, eyes rolling back and fingers going lax around the shaft. Shari flung out a hand. A vine sprang from her fingertips, shot across the floor, and lassoed Tania's ankles, pulling her safely out of the way even as a slim hand reached around the door and grasped the arrow before it fell any farther.

The whole room drew in a breath.

Arilla poked her head around the door, metal serving tray in one hand, arrow in the other. "Like I was going to let it touch her," she scoffed.

Jaws dropped. Calem was the first to recover, crossing to his wife. He reached out to pluck the arrow from her hand, but she drew it away.

"It can't hurt me," she said, "and I won't let it hurt you." The Chirea at Arilla's feet groaned. "You can take care of this one, though."

Calem laughed, relieved. "Of course." With a display of the Innarn he so rarely used around his wife, he lifted the Chirea into the middle of the room and stripped him of his armour. Guards poured in, pointing standard arrows in the direction of the latest attacker.

Shari freed Tania from the vines. "What happened? Are you hurt?"

Eyes welling up, Tania sniffled to keep the tears at bay. "It was like he was waiting for me, outside in the gardens."

Wrapping her arms around the younger girl to offer her comfort, Shari eyed the Chirea over Tania's shoulder. Stripped of his armour, he looked rather insect-like, with a segmented torso, long thin limbs sprawled out, and a triangular head lolling to the side. His skin was a very pale green, criss-crossed with dirt and red streaks from where his armour hadn't covered his hide.

Tania sniffled again, then straightened, frowning. "I can feel him now—feel the absence. Why couldn't I before?"

Varlee swept into the room. "That's exactly what I plan on finding out."

Hours later, the Dawn family, Jonathan, Tania, Zana, and Belfar sat chatting around SilverCloud's dining table, waiting for news, and trying to pass the time.

LoneWolf was seated opposite Shari. He was the first to notice that she was struggling, her breath coming out in small panting gasps that she attempted to conceal. Innarnians who were empathic were great at sharing positive emotions and soothing negative ones, but the anxiousness spiralled in her so tightly, it probably felt as if there wasn't enough air in the whole Realm.

His chair scraped back as he stood abruptly. "Apologies," he said. Every eye was on him, bar his niece's. "I just realised that half of us here have not seen Rakemyst lit up at night. If you'll follow me?"

The others rose from the table, the Guardian placing a hand on the Altoriae's shoulder when she made no effort to move. Giving her a gentle pat, he followed the group over to the expansive windows and made the appropriate noises of awe as LoneWolf slipped back to his niece.

"Surely you have dealt with overwhelming emotions before?" LoneWolf asked as he crafted a mental shield out of air Innarn and laid it across her back like a cloak, where it was absorbed slowly. Her breathing evened out and colour came back into her cheeks.

"I have. It's just, most of the time, I can do something about them. I'm not used to relying on others to do my work," she said eventually, answering a question he'd almost forgotten he'd asked.

"Not a team player then?" he said, one corner of his mouth quirking upwards.

Shari snorted. "Hardly. I don't like putting others at risk. Jonathan makes me work with him, and because of tradition, I do."

"And not because you've become fond of him or because he's capable, confident, and good to fight alongside?" LoneWolf asked, his gaze straying to Belfar. He and his childhood friend had had many of the same issues.

"Well, there is that," Shari grumbled.

If LoneWolf was a jovial sort of Ilutri, he would have laughed. Instead, he nodded and said, "I, too, find it difficult to work with others."

"Really?" she snarked at him. "Your name didn't give that away at all."

He turned his head and was silent for a moment. "Do you know that when the Ilutri reach adulthood, there is a ceremony to mark the passing of child to adult?"

Silently, Shari nodded.

"During that ceremony, an Ilutri can choose a new name to show the world who they plan to be. Many don't change, comfortable in their own skin. Some do," he said.

The force of her gaze landed on him. Even shielded, her Innarn was a formidable thing, giving weight to her contemplation. "What was your name beforehand?"

"Your father was one who changed his name," he said, instead of answering. "He chose SunStriker. I was to be StarBorn. Two years later, he met your mother. In their commitment ceremony, a week before my coming of age, he chose the name he bears now. I only found out when he spoke the word." The loneliness and despair that he'd experienced almost twenty years ago was still bitter and real in the present moment.

"Maybe in your commitment ceremony, you can change your name to better suit who you want to become," she said gently.

He couldn't help but scoff. "Who would want to put up with me?"

"I could think of a few people." Shari smiled as Belfar crossed the room to them.

"Come, Altoriae. The view tonight is amazing!"

Belfar was right—the view of Rakemyst was indeed amazing. Lights in the trees twinkled below them, but it was the sight of the aurora above them that took her breath away. Blues, greens, purples, reds, yellows, oranges and silvers all wove like ribbons through the sky in a mesmerising display.

The anxiety in the room dropped, along with Shari's hunched shoulders, as they all stood by the window, watching the sparkling lights dancing through the night.

"It's so beautiful. How does it happen?" Tania breathed.

"Throughout the day, Ilutri are expected to use a certain amount of Innarn. Some days, they don't use all that much, so they release it into the sky to create displays of lights," SilverCloud said. "The lights weave their way over Rakemyst, and when the display is over, the Innarn settles down onto us, strengthening the shields on the Island."

"Beautiful and practical," Shari admired.

"That," SilverCloud said, "is the essence of the Ilutri."

CHAPTER ELEVEN

It wasn't until the next morning that Varlee got back to them, and she was spitting mad. The Chirea had used the blood and bone of some of the Ilutri guards who had gone searching for others of his kind.

Shari shuddered. More death, and more loss. Still, she was teaching at the school, followed with her first patrollers' training session today. She was struggling to get ready on time, her mind flicking between her uncle's revelation and the thought of how hard and fast her father must have fallen for her mother. She couldn't really wrap her mind around it and spent far too long staring off into the distance, trying to understand.

It was only when the clock chimed the hour that she realised that she was running late. Frantically, she gathered her books and shifted to the front of the school.

Juggling the books in her arms, Shari rushed through the corridors of Ridden Hall in so much of a hurry, she had the breath knocked out of her when she collided with another fast-moving body.

"You!" she exclaimed, forgetting for a moment her books and her classes. She stared at Sam as he knelt to retrieve her fallen things. "What are you doing here?"

Sam seemed amused by her reaction. She knelt beside him, gathering her things haphazardly. Her hands seemed unable to work properly. She kept fumbling and it appeared that she was dropping two books for every one she picked up.

"I teach here now," Sam said.

"You teach here? What subject?" she asked.

Flashing his teeth as he grinned, he replied, "Defensive Innarn." At her startled gasp, he rolled his eyes. "I know, I know, but Jonathan tells me that I should be a 'useful citizen' so here I am." He spread his hands out, inviting her gaze.

"No, it's not about what Jonathan said," she said, looking away, just catching the disappointed look on his face as he dropped his hands. "It's just that one of my traditional duties is to teach—and my class is defensive Innarn." Taking a deep breath, she smiled and dared to meet his eyes. "Looks like we'll be teaching the same class."

He smiled back in a lazy way that set her blood boiling. Why was it that in a fit of pique she had chosen this incredibly difficult person to be her candidate?

"Assuming that we can arrive on time," Sam said.

"Oh no!" Once more, Shari found herself rushing through the corridors, this time with a person she'd been trying to avoid at her side. She had often wished the corridors of the school didn't have an anti-Innarn charm placed on them. Otherwise she would teleport straight to class—and away from Sam for long enough to clear her head.

'*What was your plan for this lesson?*' Shari sent as they scurried towards the classroom.

'*Learning how to craft their first weapon.*'

'*Really?*'

'*You can never start too young.*' Sam grinned at her as he pushed the door of the classroom open.

'*I'm only surprised, because that's exactly what I thought this lesson should be about.*' She didn't have time to mull over the appraising look Sam sent her way as she stepped into the room, twenty pairs of eyes locking onto her immediately.

The fine hairs on the back of her neck rose at the attention. She was hard-pressed to not draw her weapons.

Sam stepped past her and clapped, the sound drawing the attention of the eight-year-olds to him.

"Well met, hatchlings. Today, we get to play with blades."

Samuel looked at Shari, a genuine smile crossing his features. Their first lesson together had gone rather well. He took that as a positive sign.

"So, where did you get the knife?" Shari asked him, jolting him from his thoughts. There was an edge to her voice that made him worry.

He blinked slowly, rather than stating his surprise as she slowly twirled the knife in her hands. He badly wanted to reach out and grab the weapon, or to warn her that a single nick would be deadly, but remembered who he was looking at.

"I made it," he said, when he found that he could talk without making a fool of himself.

"Is that why you chose crafting weapons as a lesson today?"

"Partly," he admitted, shrugging. "But mostly because there is a distinct lack of claw and fang on this Realm, and the hatchlings need to learn how to make them if they can't grow them."

Shari blinked, and he knew she was trying to parse his meaning. He realised that she had been frustrated during many points of the lesson, most notably when one of the boys had sliced off the dangling hair of a classmate. He had taken it in his stride, showing the child that the use of weapons had consequences, without shedding a drop of blood. He thought he'd done quite well.

"Can you teach me how to make one? It's exquisite," Shari said, grasping the blade and holding the handle out to him.

Carefully, he took it from her, making sure it wouldn't slice her skin. "Maybe one day," he hedged. *Maybe never*, he said in his head. A human wouldn't be able to make a knife like this. They didn't have all the right appendages to complete the delicate, three-week ritual that the blade required. Nor did they have the constitution to stand in the lava falls of Beloster as the sharp edge of the blade was forged.

She smiled at him, a little stiffly, but it was still a smile. "Well, I'm sure we'll have time," she said, and turned to start packing her things away.

She wanted to spend more time together? His grin widened. Nothing would be able to wipe it off his face. He started humming softly.

'*Shari, training starts in ten!*'

Except maybe that. Samuel heard Jon's broadcast and looked up at Shari.

"I'm not sure I want to go to this training," Shari grumbled, turning to leave the room. Pausing at the threshold, she looked back over her shoulder at Sam. "Don't forget, you have to be there too. You're my candidate; it's about time you show everyone what you can do."

He gave her a mock salute. "Of course, little Altoriae."

She raised her eyes skyward in exasperation and left the room.

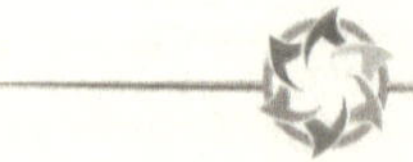

Once a month, Jonathan trained with the Innarnians on Ronah who helped him to patrol the Realms. The patrollers met every other night, but the formal training session with Jonathan was important—not just so the Guardian would be able to see their strengths and weaknesses, but so he could point out areas for them to improve, and organise the most optimal patrol groups. This was the first patrollers' training session Shari had ever been to, and she wasn't about to admit just how nervous she actually was.

She had debated the best entrance to use—should she slip in through the side door, or walk in with Jon? She'd agonised over wearing her leathers or regular clothes, and fretted about the idea of making some sort of inspirational speech like several of the previous Altoriaes. In the end, she'd decided to enter with Jon, wear regular clothes, and not make a speech. She had to remember that she knew what she was doing, and that she was good at it, because if she wasn't, there wouldn't be anyone left to teach.

She took a deep breath and stepped up next to Jon. They entered the training ground together.

Shari immediately wished she'd slipped in through the side door.

The noise stopped. Every single person turned to face them. Innarn fairly buzzed around the training ground. There were people seated in the bleachers, ready and eager to watch.

'*Is this normal?*' Shari sent to Jon. It seemed like the whole town had turned up. There were even some of the Returned, ready to join the patrols.

'*Ahhh, not quite,*' Jon hedged. From what Jon had told her about the training, usually only three quarters of the people showed up, and he'd never made any mention of watchers crowding the stands to peer at them as the patrollers went through their paces.

She had to admit, she felt more than a bit judged.

Someone in the closest group of people pushed forwards to greet her. It was Elizabeth Ribeck, from school. They had been in the same class, and more than once, Elizabeth had stood up for Shari when no one else would.

"Well met, Altoriae! We're so excited to train with you," Elizabeth said, her words filled with joy and anticipation. In a lower voice, she added, "Aram said he watched you take out two sedolics—one behind you and one in front. I can't wait to see what you'll teach us. I know you'll be great!" Elizabeth beamed at her before bouncing back to her group, ready to train before Shari could formulate a response.

'*Are you ready?*' Jon sent.

'*Let's do this,*' Shari sent back.

Jonathan stepped up onto a small platform, Shari by his side. With all eyes on them, Jonathan said, "Well met, all. Split into your patrol groups and we'll work on combining and lifting today. There have been a few instances in the reports that show we all need to work on them. The Altoriae is joining us, so try your hardest. Alright, let's get started."

They broke into groups of five. The training ground quickly filled with the sound of quiet chatter while the groups worked out the best way to approach the Guardian's task.

Shari held her position, standing next to Jon for the next few minutes and giving everyone a bit of breathing space. As the first person was lifted into the air, she stepped down from the platform and moved among the crowd, making mental notes on what to improve, or little tweaks that could be made to increase or refine the patrollers' Innarn.

As she got closer to Elizabeth's group, she saw that they were lifting Elizabeth. One of the Thorne boys, Eli, had his hands raised to control the speed of the twister of air that Elizabeth was seated on. He looked over his shoulder and spotted Shari.

He lost control, and the twister tilted wildly. Elizabeth let out an, "Eep!" but before she made another sound, Shari flicked her finger and the twister straightened itself.

"You need to concentrate, no matter what," Shari said gently.

"Sorry, Altoriae, I couldn't take my eyes off you," Eli said, leaning closer to her and ignoring the girl who was starting to spin in mid-air.

She tilted her head, running through the exchange. '*Jon, is he flirting with me?*'

'*Yes, Shari,*' Jon sent back. She heard the laughter in his mind and knew it was aimed at the hapless teen before her.

"You're here to work with your group, not to stare at me. Concentrate, or you will end up being the reason your group dies."

"Of course, Altoriae," he said, flicking his eyes downwards, then back at Elizabeth, before he once more gazed over at Shari, running his tongue across his bottom lip.

She raised her eyebrows, unimpressed. Eli quickly looked away.

Slipping into the shadows, she slid up to Niketta while Eli craned his neck, apparently searching for her, and sent, '*Play dead.*'

Niketta dropped soundlessly to the ground, her tongue lolling out of her mouth for effect.

Eli didn't even notice; he was too busy scanning the crowd for the Altoriae.

'*Play dead,*' Shari sent to Jasper Ribeck, who promptly collapsed face first to the ground. Shari whipped away before Eli turned. With two teammates down for the count, he found himself struggling to hold the twister in place and signalled to let it down.

"That's not funny, you know," he said loudly. The groups closest to him turned to see what the commotion was about. With the moving bodies, Shari scooped up two pebbles and flicked one at Elizabeth.

'*You're dead too,*' Shari sent her. Elizabeth did a credible job slumping over and listing to one side as the twister became unbalanced again.

Bernard Doonavan, the only other member of Eli's group who was left, made a big deal of looking around. "Save me, Eli!" he mock whispered, as Shari pinged him in the spine with a pebble.

'*Dead,*' she sent him.

Whipping his head around, Eli was trying frantically to see where the attacks were coming from. He wasn't watching the sky though, so Shari shifted into the airspace directly above him and dropped onto his shoulders. She twisted as they fell, so she was leaning over his face, sitting on his chest when they landed.

"Dead. Your whole team dead, because you couldn't keep focus," Shari scolded. "Aren't you glad that I'm not actually here to hurt you, but to train you to be better? Now," she said as she got to her feet, leaning heavily on Eli's solar plexus and driving the breath out of him once more, "again, everyone. Next person who gets distracted will cop more than a pebble to the spine!"

Jon looked at her from across the training ground and nodded his approval. She basked in it for a moment, before turning back to see who else she could spot slacking off.

"Jon! I think I've got a lead!" Tania said, pushing the door to the back room of Books 'n' More open. Nose buried in a book, she said excitedly, "It's taken me a while, but I think I've tracked down the location of the *Hekkor Mafae* to a Realm called Lefo." When she raised her head, Jonathan was seated across the table from her half-brother, Alistair. "Al? What are you doing here?"

"Alistair and I were going over the rules of the test," Jonathan said.

"What test?" Tania asked, frowning, the *Hekkor Mafae* flying from her mind.

"The apprentice's test," Alistair said. "I'm the Guardian's candidate."

Tania said, "Really?" drawing the word out. Jon and Alistair both shivered as the room dropped a few degrees. "Having one person in my family in constant danger isn't enough, Guardian?"

"Tania, the moment you were Linked to Ronah, the danger for your family increased. The danger for anyone living on Lissae is a constant thing as the threats against the Realm are increasing all the time. When the Guardian who trained me was an apprentice, Lissae faced a serious threat about once a season. Now it's a day every other week when it's quiet. Is it not better to have someone else in your family prepared to protect themselves than it is for them to all be targets and unable to do anything about it?" Jonathan pleaded.

She glared at him. Frost formed across Jonathan's glasses.

"I will need some time to think about this," Tania said, her words careful and slow, because she dearly wanted to say something else entirely.

Slipping back out the door, she returned to the counter. Gritting her teeth and balling her hands, she willed the tears away. She was stronger than this. The burning in the back of her throat made her want to lash out instead of cry. Hurt that Alistair didn't tell her, and upset that Jonathan hadn't heeded her warning, she slumped, her head almost touching the countertop.

The bell above the door tinkled, signalling a customer.

For a moment, Tania wanted to run. She even took a half-step away towards the back room. Gulping back her tears, she straightened her spine and turned around to see Collis regarding her curiously.

She saw the thoughts flickering behind his eyes. Slowly, he approached her. "Well met, Ronah's Linked. How can I help?" he asked.

Tania's lower lip trembled for a moment before she gained control of herself again. "There's dusting to be done, if you're keen."

"That is not what I meant." He frowned at her.

"I know," she admitted, her eyes sliding away to watch the dust motes dancing in the air.

"Come with me," he said, reaching for her.

Regarding his outstretched hand in astonishment, she reached out hesitantly and took it. '*Taking a break,*' she sent to Jonathan as Collis led her from the store.

"You are mad at the Guardian," Collis said as they walked towards the town square.

"Yes," Tania admitted.

"Why?"

"Because! Because we are children asked to fight against enemies who aren't playing by the rules, and it's not fair!" Puffing out a breath, Tania forced herself not to grind her teeth together.

Collis's slate-grey eyes regarded her.

"He's asked my brother to be his candidate!" she growled and turned away.

"This is an honour," he said, nodding to himself.

"It might be for you, but Alistair..." Tania trailed off, not sure how to express her thoughts.

"Have you asked your brother his thoughts?" Collis asked.

"No." Tania sulked. "I only just found out."

"Perhaps he thinks it's an honour as well?" he said.

Tania's shoulders dropped. "Maybe he does. I think I just need to be angry about this for a minute more."

"Be productive in your anger," he suggested.

"Be productive..." Tania muttered. They were standing in the beautiful town square, a place that still took her breath away, all bright, vibrant colours, trickling water, and laughing people. She squinted into the sunlight. "Productive... it's hard to be productive with this glare," she said, raising a hand to shield her eyes.

Collis waited patiently by her side, although she sensed that he wanted to say something.

It really was quite difficult to see around the glare of the late afternoon sun. Maybe something to block it out? She threw up her hands, envisioning the wispy curtains that covered the windows of the Ilutri homes, but making them sturdier and thicker. Vines shot from the ground as she frowned in concentration. She created a canopy over the heads of the crowd with cloths of blues, oranges, and pinks rising on the vines to reduce the glare.

Dropping her hands and panting, she said, "How did I do that?"

'*With a little help*,' Ronah sent to her, sounding more than a bit smug.

'*Thank you*,' Tania sent back.

"Better?" Collis asked.

"Better," she confirmed. Tania was surprised to note that she was ready to face Jonathan without rage cursing through her veins.

CHAPTER TWELVE

"Elder Dawn! Elder Dawn!"

The frantic cry of the messenger scattered around the antechamber's great domed ceiling before rebounding in a distorted echo.

Calem watched in silence as SilverCloud raised a single eyebrow at the messenger. The winged man was shaking beneath his robes. "Sir—they've come!"

Only Calem was close enough to hear his father's swiftly indrawn breath. "The Chirea?"

The messenger nodded, his startling blue eyes gazing firmly at the floor, allowing the greatest Elder the Ilutri race had seen in many a century time to plan in relative privacy. Calem, wise to the ways of his father, allowed himself a mental snort. 'Relative' was the right word, as there were no less than ten of his father's private guard in the room, with another twenty outside. Yet another ten guards were with Arilla, ensuring her security despite her desire for solitude.

"What would you do?" his father said into the silence.

The messenger raised his eyes for a moment despite the strict training all Ilutri received, mouth open in shock. His wide eyes darted to the side, and when he seemed to realise that the Elder meant Calem, his sigh of relief was almost audible. He, for one, clearly did not want the weight of the Island's residents resting on his shoulders.

Calem winked at the messenger, who swiftly lowered his eyes again. Languidly, he said, "Well, I'd ask where they arrived to start with."

SilverCloud sniffed and muttered, "Impudent," but Calem heard as well as felt the amusement rolling off his father in waves. Louder, he added, "They arrived on the lowest joining point to Ronah. Correct, Kesim?"

Seeming startled that the Elder knew his name, the messenger replied in the affirmative and bowed.

Calem mentally flicked through the knowledge they had gained of the Chirea. Their armour made it damn near impossible to run them through with the arrows or bladed weapons the Ilutri favoured.

The only thing able to make a dent was—surprisingly—unblessed raw steel. The type of weapon the Blank possessed in abundance and the one sort of weapon that was not only exceedingly rare on Rakemyst, but nigh on useless under normal circumstances. He knew of only two swords on the Island like that, which was hardly useful during a mass attack.

"I would ask Rakemyst to produce the weapons we need, and fast. I would send whoever we could spare to where the Chirea have landed and try to push them out with force. And if Rakemyst were agreeable, I'd get him to help in the attack... but from what I understand he is not as willing as Ronah in these matters," Calem said, breaking into SilverCloud's reflections.

"Correct. Kesim, see it is done."

The messenger startled, bowed, and left the room, wings beating hard as he lifted into the air in an obvious effort to speed his frantic rush to fulfil his Elder's demands.

For the first time in ninety years, Rakemyst's residents were able to prepare for a battle, unlike the surprise fight they'd experienced the night they'd joined up with Ronah.

SilverCloud's grey eyes met his son's darker ones. "What are you waiting for? You said, '*whoever we could spare.*'"

Sparing the time to shoot a grin at his father, Calem strode out of the antechamber, invisible wings unfurling behind him. Reaching the entrance arch, he turned and addressed his father, "I suppose you want to see how your granddaughter fights?"

Seeing the Elder's affirmative nod, Calem sped off to find his wife and daughter.

As Shari headed for Rakemyst, she saw her father winging his way towards her. Half of Ronah's residents followed behind her, ready to defend their home, their Realm.

At the edge of the clearing stood a group of soldiers, with a brightly dressed person in the middle at the front. When she recognised her mother, Shari's jaw dropped, and she instinctively shifted across the field to her. "Mum, what are you doing here?"

"This is my Realm too, Shari. I might not be able to go on patrol, and I might not be able to go off-Realm, but when the fighting happens here, you can bet that I'm going to be a part of it," Arilla said, her jaw set, sword in hand. Shari recognised it as the one that usually took pride of place over the doorway of The Quiver and Quill Tavern.

"Do you know what you're doing with that?" Shari asked, eyeing the sharp blade.

"Usually the one I train with is smaller, but that's a copy of this one. It can't be much different, right?"

Shari found that she couldn't say anything much to that. She caught her uncle's eye and nodded as her father landed and wrapped his arms around her and Arilla.

Residents of Ronah and Rakemyst alike milled around, falling into their assigned groups, visibly trying to prepare themselves for a battle that they didn't want to fight. The gentle clink of armour and rustle of feathers filled the normally tranquil glade.

Just when she noticed the abrupt silence of the insect life, the Chirea arrived.

Calem and Shari broke away from Arilla. The phalanx of guards closed around her mother and Shari saw her uncle landing by Arilla's side.

The Chirea roared, and Shari sent out orders, even as she started compressing the ground under the topsoil where the intruders stood, squeezing it down so there was just a thin layer of dirt between the Chirea's feet and a chasm. As the Ilutri started raining down arrows, she gave a final push and two thirds of the Chirea shrieked as the ground fell out from under them, the soil that Shari had pulled aside slamming back into place, compressing them like an oversized vice.

Her mum winced.

Shari concentrated instead on the Chirea who'd managed to escape her trap. The Ilutri guarding her mum sent out another volley of arrows, while Shari focused on slowing them down by making it rain heavily right over the top of them. Thick mud clung to the Chirea's legs. They roared in frustration.

Shari had time for a satisfied grin before her mother gasped and pointed. Following her line of sight, the grin fell off Shari's face. Her soil vice hadn't done much good. The arms of several Chirea could be seen as they dug themselves out.

'*Fire and plasma Innarnians, bake the ground!*' Shari sent out.

Blast after blast of plasma Innarn pelted the ground where the Chirea were buried. Massive fireballs rained down, throwing up embers as they hit the ground.

'*Water Innarnian, protect the trees!*' Jon countered.

A group of five Chirea formed a V, the largest soldier at the point charging straight at Shari. Yellow blade in her left hand, bladed glove on her right, Shari set her feet and prepared for the fight only to see her mother step up to her side. The broadsword she wielded looking ungainly and too big in her hands.

There was no more time to think. The Chirea were on them. Shari sent out a flurry of fast little plasma bolts designed to hurt and distract, aiming for anything not protected by the Chirean's armour. Her sword slashed out, cutting the ties holding an arm brace together. Shari dove in with the blades of the glove and the Chirea screamed at the same time her mother did.

Turning, Shari saw Arilla raise her sword, but her mother's opponent was clearly trained, and she saw exactly where the blade was going to land–straight through Arilla's chest.

Time slowed down. Tears blurred her vision as Shari wrenched her glove free and turned to block the blow with her sword, leaving her back exposed.

Of course, the Chirea struck, sinking the blade in the spot where her shield had been the weakest as a child, burying it to the hilt right next to her spine.

Shari took a rattling, wet breath as she sank to her knees, her mother's horrified face filling her vision.

Someone was screaming, but Shari wasn't sure who.

Her sight was tunnelling, but she still clearly saw the sword coming over her shoulder, aimed once more for Arilla.

Well, that won't do, she thought. Even as her vision narrowed to the glint of the blade passing by her, she gathered a speck of Innarn from everyone present and used it to create an air twister that pushed the Chirea back into the centre of the clearing where they'd started. As the Realm went black, she could only hope that she'd done enough to save her mother.

Calem Dawn looked down at their daughter's prone form and roared with fury. The other Ilutri nearby watched on in shock as he gathered their child in his arms. Pushing off from the ground, he rose into the air, frantically winging his way to the palace.

Arilla stared at the speck growing smaller in the sky, wishing with all her being that her husband and daughter would survive this horrible, bloody fight. With fury pulsing through her veins, she raised her sword and charged at their oncoming enemy.

The Ilutri appeared to be astonished as the featherless wife of Calem Dawn led their charge into battle. Their surprise was short-lived, however, and they were only a heartbeat behind her, half of their ranks rising into the air to attack from above.

The Chirea looked on in shock at the approaching army. They had expected their attack on the daughter to have demoralised if not completely stopped the Ilutri. As the Head Advisor of their forces gaped at the army closing in on them, a hand clapped down hard on his shoulder, spinning him around.

"What did I tell you about parents' love for their child?" Luttrell said in a snide voice.

Luttrell took great pleasure in thrusting his sword through the fool's gut before twisting it and slashing, effectively halving the meddlesome male from inside out. The commander of the Chirea was smart enough to realise that this was quite possibly the last thing he would do, so he ordered a tactical–although some might have called it frantic–retreat of his troops.

In a stunning display of purple mist, the Chirean army disappeared from Lissae and left for their own Realm, pulled away by a Light Innarnian that no one could see.

The sudden disappearance of their foes when Arilla was less than a foot away from striking the closest one made her scream in frustration. The Ilutri troops, a tad more disciplined than the High Priest's emotional wife, were no less disappointed than she was, although they were less inclined to show it. As one, the aerial warriors turned on the tip of their wings to fly back to Rakemyst and inform the Elders of their foes' retreat.

LoneWolf landed silently next to Arilla. "We should head back to my brother," he said as he looked onto the now empty battlefield.

Heart lurching in her chest, Arilla realised that her child could–at that very moment–be dying. "Is there a quick way for me to get back?"

Black eyes met her green ones, and for a single moment, Arilla read the despair that the winged man beside her hid so well from the world.

"Tradition dictates that I cannot." His silky voice, so like her husband's, slid over her, leaving in its wake crushing desolation. "Would you like me to wing ahead and return to tell you the news?"

Startled, Arilla met his eyes again, and while she couldn't define what she saw there, she knew the unexpected offer was genuine. "Yes. Please." Her voice dropped to a whisper. Immediately, LoneWolf rose into the air, his powerful wings propelling him forwards.

He paused, hovering above her for a moment before frowning and landing behind her. "Does it not hurt?"

"Does what hurt?"

A finger poked at her shoulder, and a line of fire seemed to follow it. Craning her neck as far as she could, Arilla was just able to see the line of deep red staining the back of her shirt.

"Huh."

Even though he was behind her, Arilla knew LoneWolf was rolling his eyes. Perhaps he would be able to give her a lift after all?

Bands of steel seemed to wrap around her, and Arilla tried not to squirm in LoneWolf's grasp.

Arilla reverently hoped that Lissae still had a few miracles tucked up her proverbial sleeve and that one of those miracles had Shari's name on it.

It would only be when she was hoping for the impossible that a stray arrow would hit her ride.

Clenching her teeth to stop the building scream, Arilla could do no more than watch as Belfar came to their rescue, swatting their attacker away like they were little more than a bug.

Arilla held on tight until LoneWolf set them down on a tiny floating island surrounded with high hedges.

The centre of the island held a twister of air that LoneWolf hurried her into.

Belfar landed just as Arilla stepped through the doorway and looked over her shoulder. Both Ilutri were pale. Looking around, Arilla half expected to see Shari lurking in the spartan room. When her daughter was nowhere to be found, Arilla gritted her teeth and turned back to the two Ilutri.

"Where are your healing supplies?"

Brushing past LoneWolf, Belfar headed straight for a concealed cupboard on the far wall. LoneWolf was rapidly losing colour.

"Sit," Arilla commanded. She wondered if Lissae's other miracle would be her brother-by-marriage obeying her. He staggered over to a long, low ottoman and all but collapsed.

A harried Belfar came back over, laying out bandages, herbs, and healing instruments on a nearby table.

Looking at LoneWolf's thigh, it was easy to see where the arrow had scraped it. "All this fuss. It's just a scratch," Arilla teased him. Admittedly, with the blood still oozing out, it was far more than *just a scratch.*

"Did you see the arrow?" LoneWolf ground out.

"It was white," Arilla said. The image of it spiralling past her, slick with his blood, was not something she was going to forget.

The tension in the room seemed to dissipate.

"Can I help you now?" she asked.

He nodded his consent, and Belfar stepped forwards, using a dagger to cut away LoneWolf's ruined pants.

Perching on the edge of the ottoman next to him, Arilla went to work, grinding up red moss and tura bark with the mortar and pestle. "Belfar, could you add some water?" Arilla asked, holding out the mortar.

A thin stream of water trickled from Belfar's fingertips and into the mixture until Arilla nodded. She slathered the paste onto LoneWolf's leg. He grunted, and Arilla shared a grin with Belfar.

"I'll get you a drink, shall I?" Belfar said. He slipped away as Arilla encouraged LoneWolf to lift his leg so she was able to bandage it.

"Belfar is an amazing partner," Arilla said.

"You would know all about that, wouldn't you?" LoneWolf asked.

"What do you mean?"

"You bring out the best in... Calem."

Arilla raised her eyebrows. It was the first time she'd ever heard LoneWolf call him that.

"I've watched you these past days. The way you stand for him, with him. He'd give his life for you, and I believe you'd give your life for him." LoneWolf grunted again as Arilla wound the bandage too tight. As she loosened it off, he looked outside. "All these wasted years that I should have spent being around my niece, helping to guide her, train her... spending time with my brother... with you."

"There's still time. How does that feel?" she asked.

Prodding the bandage with a fingertip, he nodded. "Where did you learn that? I've heard tales of the old ways of healing, but I have never seen it done."

Looking away, Arilla twisted to poke at the wound on her back. It wasn't deep, and there was enough moss and bark to make another poultice. She set to work as she said, "As a mother, and especially as a Blank, you have to understand your strengths and weaknesses and learn other ways of doing things in order to protect your family." She quirked a corner of her mouth up. "There's more to life than throwing your Innarn around, you know."

LoneWolf winced, and Arilla wondered if it was her words or his wounds that troubled him. After pushing himself upright, he motioned for her to turn around. Arilla slipped the shoulder of her shirt out of the way, and LoneWolf gently pressed the poultice onto her back.

The silence was stifling. "Why did you choose LoneWolf?" Arilla flinched as a fire flared to life in the hearth across the room. Clearly, she'd overstepped a boundary.

"I guess..." LoneWolf paused, as he stuck the gauze to the poultice to keep it in place. "That's what it felt like. After Calem left, he took my trust, my love, and a part of me with him. Caring for anyone but myself became a burden. I suppose I didn't want to hurt like that again." He pressed down the last of the gauze. Arilla found herself holding her breath.

"I pushed everyone who cared about me away. It was easier to become the leader, the head of the family, the lone warrior." Yawning, he summoned another pair of pants directly onto his legs. "It's easier to be LoneWolf when I'm alone."

Her heart ached. She'd never meant to cause anyone pain, least of all a member of her husband's family. After adjusting her shirt, Arilla busied herself in tidying up the healing supplies.

Belfar rounded the corner and stepped into the room, bowls of stew in hand, eyes instantly fixing on LoneWolf.

"You're more loved than you realise, Wolf," Arilla whispered, winking at him.

Gathering up the mortar and pestle, Arilla drifted over to Belfar, asking where the kitchen was. The Ilutri nodded over his shoulder and Arilla slipped from the room, leaving the two together. Poking her head back around the corner, she was just in time to see LoneWolf take the bowl of stew from Belfar, their fingers lingering as they met.

Heads bowed together, wings entangling, they spoke quietly as LoneWolf ate. Arilla grinned to herself as she slipped into the kitchen.

From across the field, Jonathan saw his Altoriae fall.

Even as he led the charge from Ronah's side, he watched Calem lift his daughter and wing her to safety. He could feel her tenacious hold on life slipping away. Much like Arilla, he wanted to scream in frustration when the Chirea disappeared. Instead, he shifted directly to Shari's side, where SilverCloud and Calem were already hovering over her.

Her breaths were coming in quick rattling gasps. Looking at how bad the wound was, he was surprised that she could breathe at all.

Lifting his hand, he poured everything he had into healing her. Long moments passed before Shari, bathed in a green light, took a deep, rattle-free breath. Jonathan bowed his head, glad the blade hadn't been coated in the same poison that stopped Innarn healing when Fiona had been attacked. He continued to knit muscle and bone back together. It was ten long minutes before he was satisfied enough with his work that he started on her skin.

"Wait," SilverCloud rasped, his voice thick with tears. "What's this?"

Shari's armour had been split by the blade and showed her scarred back.

"That is part of her story," Jonathan said, as he pushed more healing towards his charge, pulling her skin back together. Finally, he made sure that there was no infection and sat back on his heels, exhausted.

"Thank you, Jonathan," Calem said.

"You are welcome." He rose to his feet, a tad unsteady. "Now, I want to talk to those guards."

"You and me both," Calem growled.

"I will stay here and keep watch," SilverCloud said.

The two men nodded and marched out of the room.

Jonathan wandered into the halls of the Ducibus. He had healed Shari to the best of his abilities, and he was sure that Tania and Ronah had pushed an extra bit of Innarn his way. Now, he needed to find out why the Chirea seemed to have unlimited access to Ronah and Rakemyst.

A small, robed being stepped away from one of the doors and bowed at him.

Returning the bow, Jonathan sent, '*I need to speak with Pala.*'

The head beneath the hood dipped, and the Ducibus stepped back. Jonathan settled in to wait, trying to come to terms with almost losing the Altoriae. If he had been slower, or the blade had been poisoned, or if... Scenarios raced through his head, and they all had Shari's death in common.

A small hand on his shoulder jolted him out of his thoughts.

Turning, he took in the Ducibus before him. Something about the way the robe fell indicated that the being was tripodal. '*You're not Pala.*'

'*Well met, Guardian. I'm afraid that Pala is otherwise occupied at the moment. How can we help?*'

Pala had never been *otherwise occupied*. Jonathan's mind raced, and his breathing sped up. 'Is *Pala* safe?' His send was harsh and rusty around the edges, showing his concern.

The hood nodded. '*Ze is seeing to the arrangements for the passing of one of our own.*'

Bowing his head, Jonathan sighed. '*I am sorry for your loss. I grieve with you.*'

'*We thank you. But our loss is not why you came.*'

Jonathan felt sick at his own self-absorption. '*I apologise.*' He cleared his throat and ran a hand over his face, trying to settle himself. He needed to make an appointment with his Mind Healer again. '*I wanted to know if you have any information as to how the Chirea are entering Lissae?*'

His send had an instantaneous effect. All the Ducibus keened, a sound that made his joints go weak and his eyes tear up. He braced himself against the wall, and let the tears fall.

'*Do you know how we work, Guardian?*'

Scrubbing at the tears on his face, he shook his head.

'*Pala is the one who watches Lissae's gateway.*'

Jonathan waited for more information, but the ideas slowly clicked in his grief-stricken mind as the keening subsided. '*Because Pala has been otherwise occupied, there has been no one to watch Lissae's gateway.*'

The hood nodded again.

'*Why is Pala seeing to the arrangements?*'

'*He is now the senior Ducibus. He has been watching Lissae's door four thousand and fifty-nine years.*'

"Since the dawn of time," Jonathan whispered.

'*Since the dawn of your time,*' the Ducibus gently corrected.

'*And now the Chirea are through?*'

'*They have had the aid of a Light Innarnian. They have created a runic portal into Lissae that overrides the use of the gateways.*'

Jonathan sucked in a breath. He didn't know that the gateways could be overridden like that. *'How can I stop them from entering again?'*

The hallway grew colder around him.

'Kill the Light Innarnian.'

It was dusk before Shari stirred. SilverCloud's eyes flicked to her as her hand twitched on the blankets covering her.

"Get Arilla and Calem," he snapped at a guard, who winged out of the room.

Eyes fluttering open, Shari frowned. "Mum?"

"She's coming." SilverCloud held out a trembling hand and rested it lightly against Shari's cheek, his wan smile slipping from his face, a frown taking its place.

"Grandfather?" Shari asked.

"Why do you hide your true self, even now, when your people have accepted who you are?" he asked, the concern and confusion easy to read.

Shari lifted a shoulder to shrug and winced. "Habit, I suppose."

"Do you ever remove the glamour?"

"The glamour?" she asked, as he held a water bubble to her lips. She slurped.

"The one to hide your scars," he said. Her eyes sliding away from his was answer enough. "Not even when you are alone?"

"Honestly, I've been using it so long, it's like asking me if I'll shave my head," Shari said, trying to be blasé about it.

SilverCloud's eyes held a depth of sadness. "Will you remove it so I can see the scars you've gained in battle?"

"It's not pretty, Grandfather," she muttered, her eyes sliding away from his again.

He tilted his head. "Do you think your scars make you ugly? Is that why you've worn the glamour for so long?"

Her eyes welled up.

"Oh, child, scars don't make you ugly; they only show how strong you've been to survive so much," he said, stroking her cheek.

Shari turned her head away, looking at the view outside. "Let's just say I'm really strong."

"Shari." SilverCloud's voice carried that warning note that parents everywhere got when their child was about to be disobedient.

Sighing, she dropped the glamour and turned to him.

His eyes took in her face for a long moment. "Very strong indeed," he murmured.

Her glamour slid back into place as her mother entered the room. "Shari!" she gasped, falling to her knees beside Shari's bed.

"Are you okay?" Shari asked.

"I think I should be asking that," Arilla murmured. "I thought you were going to die." Her eyes welled up.

"Oh, Mum. I've had worse," Shari said, with a small smile.

"Well, I can yell at you for that later," Arilla said, leaning over the bed to carefully hug her daughter. "Right now, we can just do this."

"Where's Dad?" Shari asked.

"Here, Shari," Calem said.

Shari released the breath they hadn't been aware she was holding. "And Jon?"

"Can't get rid of me," her Guardian said, grinning over her dad's shoulder.

"What about the Chirea?" she asked, gently pushing her mother back, sitting up in the bed. She barely hid a wince as she did so, and Arilla made noises in protest.

"Gone. A Light Innarnian drew them back. I've spoken to the Ducibus about why they have unlimited access to Ronah," Jon replied. SilverCloud could sense the Guardian sending Shari the information.

"We should have done that before. Right. Let's go find the Light Innarnian," Shari said, swinging her legs off the bed. Arilla sat back on her heels, astonished. Taking a few uneasy steps, Shari found her stride and made her way to the door.

"You need to replace your armour, Shari," Jonathan called.

With a wave of a negligent hand, a new set of clean, tear-free armour appeared. She looked down, as if to inspect it, and nodded, satisfied. "Sorted. No more time to waste."

"Shari Dawn, you get your butt back into this bed, or... or..." Arilla choked on a sob.

Turning, the Altoriae walked back towards her mother, putting her hands on her shoulders. SilverCloud was a bit sad to see that they were already the same height. He'd lost so much time looking after Rakemyst, that he'd missed his granddaughter growing up.

"I have never had the luxury of taking time to heal. There have been days when I've gone to school after being slashed, stabbed, burned, torn, and mended back up. There have been nights when I haven't been able to sleep on my back, or side, or front because I'm trying not to open a wound worse than the one I got today."

"Yesterday," SilverCloud said softly. He could feel tears making tracks down his face.

"Yesterday," Shari allowed. "I heal quickly and recover fast, and I'm ready to go and defend again in next to no time at all. And I tell you what— the Chirea aren't coming anywhere near you again."

"Shari," Arilla whispered brokenly.

"This is what I do, Mum, and I'm good at it. I know you might not like it, but if it means keeping you, Dad, and everyone else on Lissae safe, then of course I'm going to do it," Shari said. She gave her mum and dad a hug and slipped from the room, Jonathan by her side.

From the shadows, Sam watched, frowning. The Guardian and the Altoriae exited the room, and strode confidently down the hallway.

He could see where her Innarn was still healing the wound.

Following them around the corner, he was surprised to see Shari slump.

"I've got this, Shari. You can rest," Jonathan said, a gentle hand on her shoulder.

"I know. But, Jon, they almost got Mum," she muttered, sounding broken.

"Oh, Shari, I know," he said, and wrapped an arm around his charge.

Still wrapped in shadows, Sam frowned harder.

SilverCloud sat in his study, alone, staring sightlessly outside as the sky became lighter as the sun rose, warming the Realm. He turned slightly.

"Just another day," he murmured. He reached out a hand, and let it fall. How often had he sat in his study, RainbowMist by his side, and uttered that line? Had her take his hand and smile as she said it back to him? She'd been gone for so long, yet he couldn't bring himself to break the habit.

Last night had shaken him. To see the Altoriae walk off a wound that would have felled even the strongest Innarnian he knew was humbling. That she was his granddaughter made his eyes mist up, and a ball lodge somewhere in the vicinity of his lower intestines. Grown she may be, and understand the importance of her role he might, seeing what she considered to be a regular day first-hand was dreadful. He had no desire to even think of what she considered a truly awful day to be like.

Sighing, he looked down at the paperwork scattered across his desk. Rubbing at the persistent ache in his chest, he coughed, and settled himself to start working out the mess before him. He picked up a quill and dipped it in the ink but stared unseeing into the distance as ink dripped down, unheeded.

He'd pushed the attack he'd suffered to one side in order to concentrate on the little slice of life he had left. The healers had confirmed his thoughts the day before Shari had completed her quest to prove she was the Altoriae. He was at the end of his lifetime, and he wouldn't see the year out. He'd be lucky to witness Rakemyst meet with Talhan, the next Shifting Island in the chain.

Therdon knocked on the door of his study. "Elder Dawn?" he said, tremor clear in his voice.

"Come in," SilverCloud said.

The Ilutri candidate made his way into the room, stuttering apologies for interrupting. SilverCloud wondered how this bumbling fledgling was the best of them. He'd let the other Elders make the decision for the candidate, and now he was wondering if he shouldn't have stepped in and had his say after all.

"How can I help you?" SilverCloud asked, steel in his voice. The Ilutri knew that his morning was sacrosanct. Long had he seen the dawn of each new day with his wife. Now, he saw the sun light up the sky alone, and he needed a few minutes more to mourn the loss of her at his side. Not for long now. They'd be reunited soon enough.

"I was wondering, Elder, if you could suggest a way that I can impress the Altoriae. I get the feeling that I haven't done very well so far and want to make up for any bad impression that I have given her," Therdon said, his chest puffing out slightly as he spoke, all pomp with no substance.

"Listen to her, and to the Guardian. Obey the rules of the apprentice test, and leave them be unless they call for you," SilverCloud said. Surely such advice should be unnecessary?

"But Elder..." protested Therdon.

Apparently not. SilverCloud fixed the boy with a glare.

He shrank in on himself. "As you will it. I don't suppose there's any chance of you putting in a good word for me?" Therdon said with a small smile.

"I would do for you as I would for any other Ilutri candidate, within the rules of the test," SilverCloud said.

"You would not use your influence on the Altoriae?" Therdon wheedled.

SilverCloud looked at the boy with ice in his gaze.

The Ilutri candidate turned into a bumbling fool once more. "Of... of course you wouldn't do that, Elder! Ha ha. Just a little joke, yes? I will, uh, return to my duties." Therdon gave a little bow and fled the room.

SilverCloud shook his head and sighed.

CHAPTER THIRTEEN

"Mum, I'm fine," Shari grumbled.

"Just a few more bites. You need to get your strength back," Arilla said, spooning another heaped serving of porridge into Shari's bowl.

Rolling her eyes, Shari took another bite.

Calem made eye contact with his daughter.

'This is the third bowl she's made me this morning,' she sent to him.

Calem chuckled. "Arilla, ease off the girl, or she'll be too full to fight!"

Apparently, this was the wrong thing to say, as his wife whipped away her bowl and placed the pot in front of Shari. "Eat!"

"Mum," Shari sighed.

Calem waggled her eyebrows at her and Shari nodded. As Arilla went to walk past him, he grabbed her around the waist and pulled her into his lap, peppering her face with kisses. He felt Shari shifting the rest of her porridge somewhere else.

Wiping her face with a napkin, she pushed her chair back and rose. "Thanks, Mum. I feel loads better. I've got to run though; I have a meeting with the Elders. Bye!" she said and shifted out before she could be reprimanded.

Arilla glared at her husband. "Did she really eat all that?"

Calem peered into the empty pot. "It's all gone."

Arilla narrowed her eyes at him. "I know when you two are up to something," she groused, turning back to the kitchen to get her own breakfast.

"I know that last night scared you," he said to her back. "Adeon knows, it scared me too."

She seemed to deflate. "Did you see her scars?" she whispered.

Calem stood and wrapped his arms around her. "I missed that bit."

"Her back is littered with them. So are her arms. Gods know where else," she said, brokenly.

"Scars tell a story of survival, of overcoming the odds in battle and living another day," Calem said.

"I know all that," Arilla said, whirling to face him, "but why does she hide them from us?"

"Probably doesn't want us to worry even more than we already do," he said.

Arilla nodded and buried her face in his shirt. Rubbing his wife's back as she released all the fear she held, he saw again in his mind's eye his daughter falling under the blade of the Chirea and shuddered. He wished, just as much as Arilla, that Shari would never have to face a situation like that again, but he knew she would. He was torn between wanting to fight at her side and a conversation that he'd had with her not long after Jonathan had let her secret slip.

Shari had begged for him not to patrol any longer. She wanted him to stay at home and protect Arilla. What kind of father had to bow down and concede to his daughter's wishes to *not* fight to protect Lissae?

He had spoken to the Guardian at length, trying to come to terms with the idea, before he had finally, begrudgingly agreed. Now, he thought he understood. Seeing both Shari and Arilla under attack and being too far away to prevent it, watching Shari fall and seeing the Chirea's last, desperate strike before they'd been blown back, had turned his insides into ice. Arilla and Shari were his world, and they had both been so close to falling. He supposed Shari felt much the same way as he did.

His arms tightened around Arilla, and he swore that he would do anything to make sure that Shari would never have to worry about Arilla being safe again; he would always be at her side to protect her.

Shari shifted to Ronah's town hall, and slipped inside, managing a small smile for the Elders gathered in the waiting room as she stood by Jonathan's side. He'd waited by the door for her. She concentrated on keeping her back straight and head up, despite being intimidated by the people around her.

Elders from all over Lissae were here, representing every race, continent, and Island, both Shifting and Fixed. Elder Silverstone was in his element, greeting everyone and making connections as easily as he breathed. She spied her grandfather among the masses and sent him a greeting, which he returned with a smile. Beside some of the Elders were their candidates. With almost seventy people in the room, Shari was uncomfortable at being hemmed in, but she breathed through it and allowed herself to relax her mental hold on her Innarn weapons. It wouldn't do to call them forwards and cause an incident the first time she met the rest of Lissae's Elders.

'What are we waiting for?' she sent to Jonathan.

'There are a few stragglers,' he sent back. *'Not all of the candidates are here today—one is coming by boat.'*

Shari raised an eyebrow but sent her acknowledgement back. So far, she'd managed to forego all but the most recent political meetings. This was the first time that the Elders from most of Lissae had met her. She saw General Morrow and dipped her head, feeling the gentle brush of his send against her mental shields. Jonathan had been quite firm that she was not to send with anyone bar himself or her candidate during the meeting. The General gave a nod and a small smile to show he understood and turned back to the Satyr who stood with him, conversing in low tones. *She must be Ginorti's candidate*, Shari thought.

'That's Elani,' Jon sent to her. 'She's quite a talented earth Innarnian.'

Speaking of candidates, Sam should be here by now. As if her thoughts had conjured him, the door opened and Sam strode in, looking like he owned the place. He glanced over the occupants of the room before strutting over and standing before Shari, giving her a short bow. She tried desperately not to show her surprise at the action, especially when all eyes were on her.

"Well met, Altoriae," he rumbled.

"Well met, candidate," she returned. The noise level of the room increased significantly, both spoken and sent. Sam smirked and moved to stand behind her, flexing his muscles and showing off. His Innarn seemed Darker than ever, and Shari pushed her second thoughts aside. It was a tad too late to change her mind now. Sam's bulk behind her set the fine hairs on the back of her neck standing to attention.

Shari passed the time by appraising the other people in the room. General Morrow stood by his candidate, a lithe Satyr with ropy muscles and clear, green eyes. She laughed at something the General said before her gaze flicked over to Shari, and she bowed her head slightly, still grinning. Shari grinned back, her eyes flicking to her grandfather and Therdon, who was nervously picking invisible bits of lint off the sleeve of his backless coat, his ruffled wings a contrast to her grandfather's smooth feathers.

Elder Thorne moved away to chat with others in the room, and Jonathan slipped into her mind to point out the others in the room.

Shari's gaze slipped to a short, round woman dressed in browns and greens who was standing by a lanky teenager with a scared face who towered over her.

'*Elder Naday and candidate Burke from Rohinda,*' Jonathan sent. '*Burke has received high test scores in sword, melee weapons, and bow. He is capable in earth, water, and spirit Innarn.*'

Burke looked at ease with his surroundings, and stoically endured the comments from the others—both spoken and sent—about his frightening countenance. He had the aura of someone confident and capable. Shari found that she was looking forward to seeing him in action.

Standing next to him was another teenager, dressed to attract attention in outlandishly loud colours that clashed with his red skin and purple eyes. He was tugging on the neck of his high-collared shirt, drifts of plasma Innarn lazily moving through his hair. Burke flinched, and moved away from the other teen without drawing attention to his actions.

'*The one Burke moved away from is candidate Mu, a Zindarian from Nindonia. Mu is here with Elder Camilla and is highly adept at plasma and fire Innarn,*' Jonathan sent.

'*He may be adept, but he lacks control,*' Shari sent back, as Mu continued to tug at his collar, his discomfort visible in every line of his body. A tall, stately woman in equally lurid colours turned to him and slapped his hand away. '*Is the Elder his mother?*' Shari sent.

Jon took a moment, clearly thinking back through the information on the candidates he'd compiled. '*His aunt.*'

Ah. That explained the woman fussing at Mu's collar, even as Shari felt her put out a dampening field to contain the plasma leaking from Mu.

Elder Camilla turned back to a group of Elders on her left and resumed chatting. Shari noted that, of the group, only Camilla had a candidate with her. '*Elder May, a Uleulan from Gondnotia; Elder Adorjan,*' *a human from Island Yaston; Elder Irepani, a Satyr from Island Hulios; and Elder Bellesi, a human from Akoren.'* Jonathan sent.

Shari blinked. She'd expected some of the mainlanders to come without candidates but hadn't expected one of the Shifting Islands not to offer a candidate. As if Elder Bellesi noticed her gaze, the Elder caught her eye and nodded. Shari nodded back, offering a small smile. The Elder's face remained impassive as the conversation flowed around the small group.

The door opened, and a woman wearing white slipped into the room, her feet barely touching the ground until she alighted next to Elder Bellesi, who raised an eyebrow in Shari's direction before greeting the newcomer.

'Candidate Caeli of Akoren. The best air Innarnian user in Lissae,' Jon offered.

Shari was suitably impressed. Just by looking at her, you had the feeling that Caeli was made of air. The lightweight fabric of her dress lent to the impression, swaying as if there were a gentle breeze in the room, the hem not even tangling on the roots growing from the limbs of the Kumaru beside her.

'Elder Willow and candidate Haran of Dento,' Jon sent.

Haran was easily the tallest being in the room, and the broadest. The Kumaru were a race that prided themselves on their connection to the earth and spirit Innarn, so much so that they were the embodiment of that duality—spirits housed in tree-like bodies. They were one of the longest-living races on Lissae, but Shari had never once seen one off-Realm before.

'Is he seriously a candidate?' Shari asked.

'Haran is known among the Kumaru as someone who introduces innovations and change. He is the oldest of the candidates at one hundred and fifty-three, and is highly proficient with weapons, and earth and spirit Innarn,' Jon sent back.

'So, he wouldn't have a problem going off-Realm? And one hundred and fifty-three—what does that equate to for a human?' Shari sent.

'I'm not sure if he would have any issues going off-Realm. I suppose we'll find out. One hundred and fifty-three years for a Kumaru is about mid-twenties for a human,' Jon sent back.

Shari saw two of the Wisaras hidden behind Haran's bulk. Elder Garayen she recognised as the one who had granted her boon after passing the Wisara's test. There was a younger Wisara with him whose features Shari couldn't make out.

'Who is the Wisara's candidate?' Shari asked.

'Dealon, Braden's daughter. She is surprisingly good with weapons, a skilled water Innarnian and she is quick; I've seen her fight.'

Shari nodded to herself. Quick was good—it was the difference between coming back after a patrol and not. A group moved in front of Haran, blocking her view of the Wisara. Focusing on them, she blinked at the hostility they were sending her way.

'Elders from the mainlands—Ben from Kenorvia, Suni from Lawrgaea, and Gwyn from Vendalbara. They aren't big fans of us,' Jon sent.

Sam was bristling behind her. Sending calming thoughts his way, she replied to Jon, 'Why are they here then?'

'To see you fail,' Sam butted in.

Turning her head to look at him out of the corner of her eye, she gave a smile that was brittle around the edges and failed to reach her eyes. 'Well, that's clearly not going to happen. Jon, can we have one of Ronah's Elders escort them away before the testing without causing an incident?'

Jon winced. 'Not really,' he sent back.

'It would be such a shame if they were called away,' Sam mused darkly.

Shari was a tad surprised to see her Guardian considering the option, but she decided to dwell on it later. She'd barely covered half the room. 'Is there anyone else who hasn't submitted a candidate?' she asked.

'*Island Jinkor didn't send an Elder or a candidate, Island Opestila's Elder Fru sent regrets at not being able to attend and informed me that the people of Opestila didn't believe they had a viable candidate,*' Jon sent. That was more than fair enough. Apart from the trio of mainland Elders, there was the expectation that those without candidates would express some sort of remorse at not having anyone suitable enough to join in the fight to protect Lissae.

'*Candidate Sulak of the Da'mar came by himself, as did candidate Talofa of the Uleulan from Island Sulanta.*'

Raising her eyebrows, she sought out the humanoid with a lizard-like, flat head that ended in a thick snout. His amber eyes caught hers from across the room and he dipped his head. Shari sent him a smile in return, unsurprised to see that he had throwing knives strapped to his thighs.

'*Sulak is skilled in melee weapons, earth and fire Innarn,*' Jon sent. '*Talofa has trained since she was three in water and spirit Innarn, and long-range weapons.*'

Seeking out the Uleulan candidate, Shari almost skipped her. She was, by far, the youngest in the room, and stood no higher than the bottom of Shari's ribs. Like most of her race, her skin was so translucent, you were able to make out the pulsing veins underneath it, even from across the room. Talofa stood alone, her four arms crossed, single eye focused on the windowsill above and behind Shari's head. There seemed to be a bubble of space around the girl that none of the others in the room dared to breech. Shari tried to ignore the tug on her heartstrings at the sight of this silent, aloof girl, but let her gaze wander away, giving the child as much privacy as she could in the crowded space.

'*Elder Cameron and candidate Josie from Nelonia are on Talofa's right. Josie is half-human, half-Ilutri, and highly skilled with earth and air Innarn, as well as a competent sword fighter, and incredibly accurate with long-range projectiles,*' Jon continued.

The Nelonian Elder was a balding, thickset man of average height who was hissing into the ear of his unfortunate candidate, who looked bored out of her mind. Josie was flicking what looked to be a metal feather through her fingers at rapid speed. Light glinted off her nose ring and the dangling silver hoops that lined her jacket.

'Elder Jillon and candidate Esme from Talhan are both half-humans as well. Esme is a highly regarded archer and has come first in all her tests for water, earth, and fire Innarn.'

The pair from Talhan were closest to the middle of the room, seemingly at ease with the large crowd and the various races in the room. Elder Jillon's white hair glinted almost as brightly as Esme's red locks did. Esme wore form-fitting blue leather, and had a quiver shrugged over her shoulder and a bag by her feet. The fletchings of the arrows glinted like a rainbow under the light. It looked like she'd infused some crystals into their feathers. Shari wondered how they would fly. Esme was gesturing with her hands, clearly sending something to Elder Jillon who was frowning at her.

Jon didn't give her time to dwell on the silent conversation between the pair. *'Next to them is Elder Doss and candidate Wesin, both half-Daens from Island Muhara. Elder Doss is talking to Elder Billi, a Daen from Cantash. Her candidate will be arriving by boat later in the week.'*

Elder Doss looked like he was more than half-Daen. Short, lithe, and animated, he was bouncing on his toes as he described something to his fellow Elder. Wesin was taking the room in, no doubt trying to size up his competition. He was wearing green sephina silk that made his blue eyes stand out in his tanned face.

'Elder Stuart from Island Tevon stands with his back to Elder Billi. With him is his candidate, Lira, who is reportedly the best of all the Tevon in weapons and Innarn,' Jon sent.

Shari tilted her head slightly as she took in Lira, who looked only a few years older than she was. Lira was formally dressed, her high collar and long robes immaculate, as was her hair and make-up. She appeared to be studying her nails, but Shari caught sight of a tiny flicker of silvery flame. Lira looked straight at Shari and winked, before closing her hand, ending her Innarnian trick.

Fighting not to grin, Shari let her gaze slip away to the people on the right of Lira. The two were clearly half-Satyrs, and the younger looked almost as nervous as Therdon, who was standing next to him.

'That's Elder Mason, half-Satyr from Island Vutana and his candidate, Reon,' Jon sent.

'Does Reon even want to be here?' Shari asked. Sam snorted, clearly still privy to their conversation.

'I can't be sure, but his test scores are high. By scores alone, he's ranked third out of all the candidates.'

One of the difficult things with sending had always been controlling how you reacted to the conversation in your head. Most people had difficulty concealing when they were sending purely because of their facial expressions.

Shari was not most people. She'd spent the majority of her life hiding her ability to send and was well versed in not showing it. Still, her jaw almost dropped open.

Luckily, Alistair had chosen that moment to open the door with a bit more force than was necessary.

"Oops," he said. "Sorry."

A stunned crowd watched as the slip of a boy nervously made his way to the Guardian.

"Hello, Jon," he said cheerfully.

Jon bowed his head. "Candidate," he intoned.

The silence was greater than when Shari had greeted Sam.

"Guardian," Alistair said, and took up his stance behind Jon, trying to mimic Sam and failing. His presence screamed of nerves, compared to Sam's menace.

Others in the room kept sneaking glances at them but remained talking among themselves. He was saved from further scrutiny when a group of four entered.

'*Who are they?*' Shari asked.

'*Elder Kestra and candidate Raven from Island Freeson. Raven is a highly adaptable air and fire Innarn, specialising in traps and tracking. Elder Zetta and candidate Ness from Island Omina. Ness is an earth and plasma Innarnian who ranks in the top ten Realm-wide for swordplay.*'

'*And the two hiding in the corner?*'

'*That is Elder Ulsi and candidate Bren, Weavers from Vannali. Bren has the second highest score all round.*'

Shari studied the Weavers, surprised that they'd come, as they were notoriously reclusive. She couldn't make out a single feature, as they were hidden behind white-hooded cloaks.

'*Who has the highest score?*' Shari turned to look at Jon, curious.

"That would be me," Sam rumbled next to her ear.

Frowning, Shari wondered why Jon would try to talk her out of Sam being her candidate if he had such a high score. Before she could ask, Jon cleared his throat, and immediately, silence fell.

"Well met, Altoriae, Elders of Lissae, and candidates. We have gathered today to discuss the test which will be undertaken for the apprentice of the Guardian. Please take a seat, and we shall begin," Jonathan said.

He summoned a seat for himself and one for Shari, who watched as others attempted to do the same. Talofa was the first to conjure her seat, a beautiful creation of coral that moulded to her form and lifted her so she was at eye level with everyone else in the room. The others weren't far behind. Shari noted that while there were a couple of Elders who expected their candidates to make seats for them, only SilverCloud had to make a seat for his candidate.

"The Altoriae and I have created a series of simple tests to discover who will become the next apprentice. Despite being straightforward on the surface, they will stretch the candidates to the limit and ensure that only the best will be chosen to fight and train alongside the Altoriae," Jon said.

Shari got the feeling that he was enjoying drawing out the announcement. Reaching out her senses, she prepared to capture the emotions of the candidates when he told them what the test was.

"Testing will be comprised of three trials. During the first trial, you will be put into simulation patrol groups where you will go up against a being and attempt to shield them for a set period."

There was a great deal of unsettled murmuring, but Jon simply waited for the noise to die down before he continued. "One candidate from each trial will be chosen to enter the second trial, where you will work with the Altoriae in a group in order to defeat some of Ronah's most experienced crack troops."

"For the final trial, the candidates will..."

'The pause for dramatic effect is a bit much,' Shari sent.

Jon chuckled in her head before continuing, "... attempt to overpower the Altoriae one-on-one."

Noise exploded through the room. Chairs were scraped back as people shot to their feet, quick to voice their protests. Through the pandemonium, Shari caught sight of SilverCloud's pale, thin-lipped face. His displeasure came across loud and clear. Beside her, almost overriding SilverCloud's fear, worry, and hurt, was a dark cloud of anxiety and panic from Sam.

'How am I meant to fight you when you were the one who chose me to be your candidate?' Sam sent to her.

'You must. Time to see if your tough-guy attitude is accurate or not,' Shari sent back.

The volume of the room was decreasing slightly. Sulak stepped up to her and bowed low. "Altoriae, I have much to offer in the way of protecting Lissae. While I am honoured to fight alongside you, I will not fight against you. I withdraw my candidacy," the Da'mar said.

"Sulak of the Da'mar, I thank you for your efforts and understand your reasoning. I release you from your candidacy," Shari said formally, loud enough for the others to hear.

'*I do hope that your people were able to return to their homes?*' she sent to him.

'*The threat passed, and we are safe again, Altoriae,*' he sent back, even as he said, "I thank you, and bid thee well, Altoriae, Guardian."

Sulak walked out of the hall, head held high, knives clanking softly as he went.

"Are there any other candidates who do not agree to the terms of the test?" Jon asked.

Esme stood up, lifting her bag as she did so. "My apologies, Altoriae. I will fight *for* you, fight *with* you, and *train* with you, but I will not fight *you*. I have pledged to do you no harm, and even the chance of being on your elite team cannot change that pledge."

"Esme from Talhan, I thank you for your efforts and understand your reasoning. I release you from your candidacy," Shari said formally, slightly disappointed that she wouldn't get the chance to go up against her.

Esme bowed, and left the room with Elder Jillon trailing behind her. As most eyes were on the pair, Shari was sure she was one of the few who witnessed the brief struggle between Reon and Elder Mason when the candidate tried to rise to his feet and the Elder forcefully pulled him down. Reon slumped in his seat, defeated.

Beside her, Sam snorted. '*You will squash him like a bug.*'

'*And how do you think you'll fare?*' Shari sent back with a grin. Thunder cracked through the clear sky outside, the sudden rush of electricity in the air causing people to cry out, and the fine hairs on Shari's arms to stand on end.

'You'd do well not to fight me, Altoriae. Perhaps, as I am your candidate, it would be better for me to fight your Guardian?' Sam sent, leaning into her personal space.

She had talked to Jonathan, and they had come to the tentative agreement that Sam should indeed try to overpower Jon, but his tone and the way he worded his 'request' made Shari snarl. 'Scared to lose?' she sent back. 'You'll be fighting me, candidate, just like everyone else.'

On her other side, Jon groaned softly.

The noise settled down, even though the air still tingled, and the ozone was on every tastebud in the room.

"Candidates, you will be given time to settle in. The Altoriae and I will post a notice with the times of your trials. Please enjoy Ronah's hospitality while you are here," Jonathan said before he rose. Shari could tell that he was as eager as she was to get the meeting over with.

Shari got to her feet smoothly and nodded at the crowd. "I thank you for your time and look forward to facing you soon. I bid thee well," she said, and shifted out when the weight of so many eyes became too much for her.

CHAPTER FOURTEEN

onathan sighed as he strode down the road towards Books 'n' More. Many of the Elders had wanted a private talk with the Altoriae, trying to put a good word in for their candidate, but when she'd shifted out, he'd had to come up with excuses while trying to keep a pleasant smile on his face. He'd hoped that once Shari's identity as Altoriae had been announced he wouldn't have to face events like that by himself. Clearly, that wasn't the case just yet.

There were so many little tasks weighing on him at that moment, that he wondered how he was going to get everything done. The relocations, the trial schedule, the book order for the store, not to mention the special-order book that Isobelle Thorne was after.

As he walked in, his eyes alighted on Tania, and he wondered if there was a chance that a tiny part of his burden would be lifted.

"Tania, can I speak to you for a moment?" Jonathan asked.

Tania placed the last book on the shelf. "Sure," she said, and followed him out the back.

"I know that you've already sworn the vows, so while the ceremony is taking place, I have a small job for you to do," he said to her, fiddling with the papers on his desk.

"Small job?" she asked, raising her eyebrows.

"I want you to retrieve the *Hekkor Mafae* for me," he said.

"That's your definition of a 'small job'?" she snorted incredulously.

"Perhaps that was a bit of an understatement," he admitted, rubbing a hand over his face.

She rolled her eyes. "Fine," she said. "I can leave now, if you like."

"Excellent. Here," he said, and handed her a pack. "Remember, don't touch the book with your bare hands. There may be some sort of trap on it. Use this instead," Jonathan said, showing her a piece of sephina silk in the pack's main compartment.

Tania looked at him dubiously but shrugged. "Okay."

"To get to Lefo, you'll have to use one of the Ducibus' doorways," Jonathan told her.

"How do I do that?" she asked.

"Come with me," he said.

Tania and Jon walked through Ronah to the museum. Along one of the hallways, a right turn at the end, then left brought them before a red door. Jon opened it and she gasped. There was a long passageway, with doors on each side. Before each door, there stood a short, cloaked being, its hood drawn low so you couldn't make out any features.

They walked down the hallway almost to the end, passing so many doors, Tania lost count. Each door was different, but they all had a small plaque in the centre and another on the wall beside it. She desperately wanted to ask what it all was, but Jonathan didn't say a word, so she let the questions burn the tip of her tongue as they continued forwards.

"Luca, here, will take you to Lefo," Jon said.

The Ducibus bowed at her, and she bowed back. She had the impression that Luca was pleased with her.

"Good luck," Jonathan said.

"Thanks," Tania replied, and gulped as Luca opened the door. "I'll be back by the time the ceremony is over!"

Jonathan shifted straight from the museum to Shari's lounge room, where she was carefully doing up the straps on her boots, her fingers slow and sure, showing her intent. Inwardly, he smiled. Clearly, she'd been practising the slow meditation that he'd been teaching her, even if she normally didn't let him see it.

"Are you ready for the Allegiance Ceremony?" he asked quietly.

Instead of answering him, Shari stood and stretched her hands to the sky, bringing them down slowly as she breathed out. The creation of the bridge between the Shifting Islands was the first part and was a more joyful expression of the Islands meeting up again.

He knew the Allegiance Ceremony was going to be the very thing she most wanted to skip out on, full of bureaucracy and politics. The Handbook had gone over them in detail, mentioning all the vows that the previous Altoriaes had received at each one over the years.

Taking another deep breath, she nodded. "I'm ready. Are we walking, or shall I shift us in?"

"I think that it would be appropriate to shift this time," he said.

"Alright, here we go then," she said.

Between one breath and the next, they were standing on the middle of the bridge between Ronah and Rakemyst. The clearings on each side were packed with people, all of whom were dressed in their finest.

Jonathan surreptitiously tugged on his ceremonial robes. Shari flicked her cloak and dropped the shield he hadn't been aware was up, revealing them to the crowded masses.

The crowds cheered as the Elders from the Islands moved to the bridge, standing to span the distance between Shari and the people they represented.

As requested, Elder Dawn from Rakemyst and Elder Thorne from Ronah were closest to Shari, with Jonathan standing in his place beside her. Elder Silverstone had put up a fuss, but when Jonathan had said that Shari was the one who'd decided the order of the Elders, he'd conceded, and had withdrawn to brood in silence.

Together, the two closest Elders raised their hands, and the crowds fell silent. Speaking in unison, the Elders said and sent into the crowd, "We have gathered today to acknowledge that the Altoriae is once again here, ready to defend Lissae. We have come together, members of two of Lissae's Sentient Islands, to pledge our allegiance to Lissae once more, and to our Altoriae for the first time. We are pleased to introduce you to Shari Sky Aonarach Mair Dawn!"

Dipping into Shari's thoughts, Jonathan was startled to realise that it was only his hand on her back that ensured that she didn't crumple under the onslaught of noise and the feeling of thousands of people sending joyous thoughts her way. He knew she'd read the accounts of the Allegiance Ceremonies of the previous Altoriaes in the Handbook and hadn't really understood how overwhelming it could be. She dealt with an onslaught of negative emotions from all sorts of reprehensible beings fighting their way towards Lissae on a regular basis and had thought herself immune to large outpourings of emotions. As she fought the tears welling in her eyes, she realised that she was wrong.

Jonathan found himself humbled.

He stood by her, ensuring that she kept her composure throughout the ceremony. Afterwards, the different clans came up to swear their special vows to the Altoriae. She accepted each one gracefully, despite the anxiety Jonathan could feel pulsing down their link.

Finally, her uncle stepped before her. The pressure on Jonathan's hand increased as she leaned back, seeking more support.

"Altoriae," LoneWolf said, bowing.

Shari dipped her head. "LoneWolf Dawn."

"I have heard many give you vows to protect the Islands, the Realm, and yourself. Many have vowed not to second-guess your orders, but to jump in with both feet before engaging a brain cell," he said. Jonathan caught the corner of Shari's mouth kicking up, but she quickly smoothed out her expression. "I have come instead to give you a different kind of vow. Altoriae, I vow to challenge you if I believe you are wrong, and I vow to protect your family when you can't be there to do so. Do you accept my vows?"

For the first time all day, Shari's chin trembled and the tears she'd been holding back escaped. "Yes," she gasped. "Yes, LoneWolf Dawn, I accept your vows and offer my own. I vow that I will listen to your challenges and I vow to give you leave to protect my family, and not fight you on it too much."

LoneWolf smiled at her and bowed again. "Be well, Altoriae," he said, and strode away.

Shari leaned back against Jonathan, seeking comfort from a totally vulnerable position, something Jonathan had never realised that she refrained from until now. Blown away, he rested his other hand on her shoulder.

Looking around, he noticed that the clearings were mostly empty, except for a seabird, watching them from a rock on Ronah's side.

The scent of stale sweat and day-old urine assaulted Tania's senses. Nose crinkling, she strode forwards, determined to reach the far side of the cavernous room. The faces carved in the brown stone flickered in the torchlight, their eyes seeming to follow her progress. A different sort of

Innarn flowed across the wall about a quarter of the way from the top. Sending out mental feelers, she found an irregularity in the stone, and she set about searching for the trigger to release the entrance to the hidden compartment.

Caught up in her search, it took her a moment to register when a hand appeared below one of the faces, followed by an arm, a foot, and a leg until a rocky golem took a step, heavy feet echoing on the floor, bringing her attention swiftly to the new being in the room.

"Oh, hello," she said, her voice only wavering slightly.

"Password," the golem stated.

"Password?" she asked. "I... uh... there's a password?"

She watched in amazement as a hand appeared out of the stonework to the golem's left, followed swiftly by another golem.

"Password," they said in unison, their voices ringing in the otherwise empty room.

"Do I get a hint?" she asked, her voice rising.

Another hand pushed against stone, another golem, standing next to the other two. "Password," they said.

Inside her mind, there was a slightly panicked voice saying, *Password? What password?*

"Uh, dark?" she guessed.

The golems paused, but when she didn't say anything else, they took another step forwards, and another one joined their ranks. "Password," they said.

"Dark, dark, dark... it's on the tip of my tongue," she grinned up at the golems, who stepped closer. Frantically, she sent to Jon, *'There's a password and these golem creatures, and I think they're going to squash me! Help!'*

'It starts with dark!' she sent to Jon. Aloud, she said, "Dark... book?"

Again, the golems paused, but they frowned and moved towards her, yet another stepping out of the stone to join them. "Password," they said.

"Dark…" she had nothing. Looking behind her, there were only five steps between her and the wall, and only three between her and the golems. Another seven guesses before they smooshed her. "Night?"

Another step, another golem, and another demand for the password she didn't know.

'I'm looking for it, Tania. I know I've seen something about it,' Jon sent to her, sounding like he was lost in the research.

She tried saying nothing, but the golems waited five minutes and took a step forwards anyway. She skittered backwards. "Okay, okay, I'm thinking here. I'm thinking that the password starts with dark and isn't book or light or…"

The golems paused, for the briefest moment.

'Jon, there's something about light in it too!' she sent.

Moving forwards and pushing her back a step, the golems seemed to be growing impatient with her. "Password!"

'Hurry, Jon!' she begged. Perhaps distracting them with inane prattle would work? "Password, I know the password. It's on the tip of my tongue. Just having trouble getting the words out, is all. The password is the easiest thing in the… Oh look, behind you!"

But behind them was another golem forming, and the line took another step forwards.

"Sorry, thought I saw a bug. I love bugs! They scurry along, so busy with their lives, totally unaware that they could be squashed at any moment." She was feeling a bit like a bug right now, if she was honest. "Oh, but we were talking about the password!"

They stepped closer.

'Please?!' Tania sent to him. "It's dark…"

'*Darkness in the light!*' Jon sent, as the golems took one last step forwards and she moved back, her back hitting the wall.

'*I hope you're right!*' she sent to him. Raising her chin, she said, "Darkness in the light."

The golem right in front of her took a final step forwards, and Tania whimpered as it raised an arm above her head, the other hand crossing its chest. Trying not to gag at the smell, she watched in surprise as its thick fingers reached in and depressed a switch in its armpit.

There was a whooshing noise behind her, and a gust of stale air. The golems stepped back slowly, one by one sinking back into the wall, their faces once more locked in stone.

Turning, Tania saw the book nestled in the alcove behind her. The scaled black leather was a spot of darkness among the pale stone. She reached out, but remembered Jon's warning just in time, and carefully pulled the cloth from her pack and wrapped the black book in it securely. It seemed to weigh more than its size indicated, and she could feel the scales on the cover pulsing underneath the cloth.

With one last look around the place, she hugged the book carefully to her chest, and left as fast as possible, the eyes of the golems tracking her progress back through the room.

After running all the way to the Ducibus who was waiting for her, she gasped out, "Back to Ronah!" and they were on their way.

"Thank you, Luca!" she said, and tore down the hallway and out of the museum. Pausing for a moment to catch her breath, she took off for the bookstore.

She raced through the store, out of breath, and skidded into the back room where she slapped the book down onto Jonathan's desk and said, "I never want to see another golem armpit again."

Jonathan looked at the book. He unwrapped the cloth reverently, his hand hovering over the cover, brow furrowed. "This isn't quite what I was after," he said slowly.

Tania deflated, sinking into the chair behind her. "What?" she said faintly.

"You've done an amazing job to get it," he said, as he stretched out one lone finger to touch the cover.

Tania found herself holding her breath, waiting for something horrible to happen, but when the cover opened and nothing bar a low mournful wail sounded, she breathed a sigh of relief.

"However, this isn't the *Hekkor Mafae*."

"But..." she spluttered.

"I thought I had sent you to the right place. It looks like it's going to be a challenge to find it—the book you brought back has a list of where the copies of the *Hekkor Mafae* are found." Jonathan flicked through the pages as Tania sat and stewed over the futility of her journey, not to mention getting all up in a golem's armpit. If the book of where to find the book that they were actually after was guarded by golems, what exactly would be guarding the book itself?

"Hmmm," Jonathan said, finger skimming across the page as he read. "Looks like we may need Luca's help again."

Tania scrubbed a hand over her face. She was grotty and tired and really wanted to collapse onto her soft, soft bed. Visions of white sheets and a rainbow quilt danced behind her eyes as she heaved herself to her feet. "Where do I need to go?" she asked.

"You don't have to go now. Why don't you rest while I figure out where the most available copy is?" Jonathan said, his eyes sliding away from hers.

"Like you don't already know," Tania scoffed. "I'll be in and out, and back before bed." Her feet ached, but she stiffened her spine and made a concentrated effort not to shift her weight to give away how sore she was. Feeling her feet tingle, she glanced down and saw Ronah's green glow gently seeping from her shoes.

Jonathan sighed and rubbed a hand across his face. Tania looked at him and frowned. She'd only known him for a short time, but it was as if he'd aged a good five years. Reaching out with her mind, she poked at Ronah, asking her Island if she could heal the Guardian.

'*I am sorry, Tania, but the Guardian will not let me heal all of his wounds. Some are in his Innarn and some just can't be healed until he is ready,*' Ronah sent to her regretfully.

'*Can you heal him slowly, the way he heals Shari?*' she sent back.

Ronah startled. '*You know about that?*'

'*If you know about it, I do,*' Tania reminded Ronah. The Island agreed. Tania found that if she squinted and tilted her head just right, she could see a faint green outline around the Guardian. She nodded in satisfaction.

"Thank you, Tania. It'll be good to get this sorted once and for all," Jonathan said.

'*Wait, what did I miss?*' Tania sent to Ronah.

'*You just agreed to go to Vastilda to retrieve the Hekkor Mafae,*' the Island sent back. Tania had the distinct impression that Ronah was laughing at her, even though there was an underlying edge of concern to her tone.

"Yes, super good. Umm, can I ask Luca to get me there?" she asked. She wanted to get the task over with, and if she never had to see or think about the blasted dark book again, it would be too soon.

"Yes, Luca would be the best bet. You know how to get there okay?" Jonathan asked, concerned.

"I'll be fine. If I'm not home for dinner, let my parents know I'll be late," Tania said, heading for the door.

"Vastilda's time runs three times slower than ours," he warned as he passed her a map.

"Oh. Don't send out a search party till breakfast then!" she said cheerfully and slipped from the back room.

The moment that she was out of the store, she got Ronah to shift her to the museum and set about tracking down the Ducibus Luca.

Sam grinned as he strutted down the streets of Ronah. He had discovered a weakness about the Altoriae he didn't think that she knew she had. *Family*. He shuddered.

Family left a bad taste in his mouth. His family was pretty much non-existent by this Realm's standards. He didn't know his parents, and his chosen mate had been labelled as an outcast as others of his race had not wanted him to breed, fearing him to be too powerful.

He had only one ally among his own race, but dared not contact him as there was no doubt that Gazn would use the information to attack. Sam didn't want that to happen, not when he was so close to having the Altoriae's ear.

There was no one to tell his good fortune to, but the strut didn't leave his stride. He'd never been one for bragging about his knowledge anyway.

CHAPTER FIFTEEN

Tania's footsteps echoed eerily as she made her way towards the darkest part of the Ducibus' lair. Turning down the last hallway, she found herself reading each plaque as she went, despite Jonathan's wish for her to hurry. She started to commit them to memory, and tried to figure out what was beyond each of the doors.

Obirium's plaque stood next to a door of deep black wood that seemed to glow. The sign for Eazithan was bronze, matching the hinges and handle on the bristlehide-covered door. Panagar's plaque was shining an orange light that made Tania think of warm fires and a cup of the azehal Jon favoured. As she got closer to the metal door, she shivered. Maybe more like a cup of poison than azehal, she amended.

Hurrying past the doorways to Hinioxar, Dakleozen, Gihalan, and Tiaclorune, the Ducibus guarding the doors didn't seem to move, and none spoke, even though she offered tentative greetings to each one. As she slowed down, the sign for Baenge caught her eye. It seemed to be made of a giant shell. Tania wondered what kind of Realm could possibly have a door like that. Her feet carried her forwards to the next door made of ice. She found that she couldn't go any farther. Reading the plaque on the side, she realised why.

"So, this is the way to Vastilda?" she said, half to herself. Out of nowhere, a hand grasped her elbow. Tania jumped a foot into the air, and collapsed, palm over her racing heart, before looking with wide eyes at the Ducibus who had to be Luca.

"By Zoemer's Rocks! Warn me next time!" she scolded.

The Ducibus stood there, seemingly impervious to her ire. Despite Luca's hood hiding the expression he was wearing, she frowned at him as she rose to her feet. "Stop laughing at me," Tania grumbled.

A sound like rocks tumbling over each other and birds twittering in a valley filled the hallway. Blinking, Tania looked around and realised that all the Ducibus were laughing at her.

"Huh," she said, stunned. Immediately, the hall fell silent again, and she found that she missed the noise. "Don't stop," she begged.

As one, the Ducibus bowed, and Luca moved to place his hand on the door. He paused for a moment, the dark opening of his hood swinging around to face her.

He stood as if frozen. Tania guessed he was asking her if she was sure that this was a place that she wanted to go.

"I have to, don't I? The Guardian's given me a job to do, and I can't let him down," she said softly.

Still, Luca didn't move.

"What should I do then? Tell him I'm too tired? Too scared? Not ready enough? Nothing about being away from Ronah makes me feel ready enough, but I'm still going to jump in and give it a go," Tania said. "I never once thought that I'd be able to do anything like this, and I find that I can't wait to see what's on the other side of each and every one of these doors. There is so much to discover, so many different ways of living and being, and so very much to learn. That's why I want to do this, that's why I'm here—because maybe if I show Jonathan that I can do this, he'll teach me more—and I want to know it all!"

Luca's hooded head nodded once. Slowly, his hand reached forwards and touched the door. Tania watched it spring open in awe. She couldn't wait to find out what was on the other side. Stepping through the doorway, a tingle overcame her body and she looked down to find herself decked out in cold-weather gear.

"Thanks, Luca!" she called back, and took her first step onto a new world, her heart light, and her head just the tiniest bit giddy.

Amara Telka leaned over the side of the boat, gripping the railing tightly in both hands and wishing her stomach would settle, wishing there was another way for her to reach Ronah, wishing that she hadn't been chosen to represent the Daens as their candidate for the Guardian's apprentice. Why she'd been picked, she wasn't sure, and at this rate, she doubted that she'd ever make landfall.

The boat rocked unpleasantly, sending up a spray of saltwater. Amara wrinkled her nose and dared to turn her back to the ocean. Lifting her face to the sun, she luxuriated in the warmth, using her Innarn to steam the water from her clothes.

A Wisara sailor passed by her and grinned. "Not enjoying the trip, are you?" he asked.

"Much prefer land," she said, fighting to keep her lunch in and get the words out.

His lotus leaf shirt glistened wetly in the sun. "I wouldn't trade the ocean for the land, and you're the other way around." He leaned on the railing beside her and took a deep breath. "This is what I love."

Turning, Amara looked back out at the endless blue choppy waves. "This?"

Laughing, he shook his head, the roots that made up his hair making a wet, slapping noise as he moved. "Lissae. We're all different, every one of us, yet we can still get along."

"Well, most of us do," Amara said, frowning.

The sailor glanced at her out of the corner of his eye. "Might want to put that out," he said softly.

"Huh?" Looking at her hand, she realised that it was smouldering slightly. "Oh, sorry," she said contritely, clenching her fingers in a tight fist, and putting out the embers that had lit on her hand.

Her uncontrollable fire was what had forced her to travel by boat. The last time she'd travelled by slipstream, the poor air Innarnian at the starting point had suffered serious burns and spent a month recovering under the gaze of watchful healers. Amara never wanted that to happen again. Her Elder refused to shift with her after she'd accidentally set her instructor's hair on fire while attempting a tandem shift for the first time, and she couldn't go by herself without seeing the place first. Flicking the last of the embers from her fingertips into the sea, Amara watched through lowered lashes as the sailor gently lifted some water from the ocean and let it slip over the scorch mark on the railing.

"The ones who work at getting along are the only beings worth worrying about," he said softly, patting her hand, and slipping away silently.

Amara stayed for a while longer, looking out at the waves and fighting nausea caused by more than the rocking boat. What were a few salty tears to the vastness of the ocean behind her?

Six hours later, Tania's fingers were frozen, her feet were wet, and her nose was tingling. Vastilda was decidedly less exciting than she'd imagined it to be, and far colder than anywhere she'd ever been. She was following the map Jonathan had given her, but four hours in, realised that she'd been looking at it upside down. As she'd turned to start trudging back, it had started snowing, severely limiting her visibility. On the horizon, she saw the shape of the hills that the Ducibus' doorway had led her through, but that seemed very far away now.

Tania sneezed and sneezed again, stopping to rub a mittened hand across her aching nose.

Later, she'd look back at that second sneeze as the thing that saved her life, because in the instant after she rubbed her nose, her eyes went wide as an axe blade hit the ground in front of her.

There was a grunt from the handle side of the axe and a gurgling noise from the other side.

"Hoping to get her pack, I was," came a deep grumble from the being holding the axe handle. Thick, pale green fingers clenched and pulled the axe from the ground.

"Missed it, you did," came the reply.

Tania shot forwards, her legs pumping hard, even as she was picked up by the hood on her jacket. Yelping, she clawed at the fabric as she was dragged backwards. The being with the axe swung it up over her shoulder and started stomping along behind her.

"Not breathing it is," axe man said.

"Need it breathing?" her captor asked.

She nodded and ended up coughing as the hood tightened more.

"Maybe," axe man said.

The hood holder dropped her, and she fell into the snow in a grateful heap, drawing in deep, gasping breaths. The two stood over her, blocking out the weak light from the sun. They were taller than she'd first thought, standing around nine feet high. Each being had a single eye centred in the middle of its head, two tiny holes to breath out of, and slit-like mouths. They had two extra arms each as well, and her captor seemed female, while she was pretty sure the one with the axe was male.

"Breathing, puny one?" her captor asked.

Tania nodded, and thought about getting to her feet, if only to get out of the snow seeping into her clothes and freezing her bones, but her limbs felt like jelly and the cold had sapped all her strength away.

As hands wrapped around her upper arms and she was hauled upright, Tania wondered how she was going to get out of this one.

"Land-ho!" came the call, and Amara almost cried in relief. Travelling by boat was not something that she ever wanted to do again.

She shook her limbs out, trying to get her head on straight. Her talk with the sailor had got her mind stuck in the past, and it wasn't safe for anyone on board if she stayed there. It was only the endless expanse of water that had kept her fire Innarn in check. Maybe Phoenix was right, and this was the best thing for her. It sure was a good way for her to learn how to keep her temper in check.

Her family were among the few Daens who had lived on the mainland. They'd been happy there for generations, before a village had sprung up about an hour's walk away when Amara had been a babe. By the time she was ten, the human village had been encroaching on their borders. On her thirteenth birthday, tempers had boiled over, and the Blank humans had stormed the Daen village in order to claim it as their own.

Thankfully, she didn't remember much of that day, apart from the roaring fire that her parents had sent streaming towards her. The fire had burned hot and fast, carrying her away from the fighting and onto the shore that was so many clicks away, she couldn't have walked back to the village she'd called home in a week.

She'd waited on the beach, alone and hungry, for two days. She'd used her Innarn to keep warm but had been wary of the water lapping at her toes, and worried about who might follow the burn trail through the forest to her.

There was a vague memory of her reaching out, trying to send to her parents and getting a scary blank blackness in place of their comforting warm thoughts. She shuddered, and turned her face to the sun again, hoping its rays would dry the tears on her face.

On the second day, she'd started broadcasting, hoping that someone, anyone, would hear her. That evening, a man had appeared on the far end of her beach. Gus had taken her in and welcomed her into his family without a second thought. He and his family lived a day's walk from the beach and used Innarn freely in a manner that Amara only just remembered from her early childhood.

Gus had been the kindest human Amara had ever met. He'd gone out of his way to contact the Daens on Cantash to let them know that she was alright, and when she'd reached her sixteenth birthday, he had tearfully sent her to train at the Daen academy, where she'd worked hard to master her fire Innarn.

Now, all her hard work had paid off, and she was in sight of Ronah, ready to show the Guardian that Amara Telka would be the best apprentice he'd ever laid eyes on.

Tania was trying hard not to stare at the backside of the being who had her slung over a shoulder again. Mind you, she was more than thankful that she was over the top set of shoulders, and sandwiched in between two sets of armpits. She'd had enough of armpits for one day.

Her captor dropped her without warning, and Tania yelped as she hit the ground hard. She staggered to stand as the clicking of heeled feet on the rough stone floor entered the room and headed straight for her.

"Well, well, well. Who do we have here?" said a high-pitched voice, face hidden in the folds of a fur-lined white cloak.

Tania tried not to giggle, she really did, but the being sounded like one of the overacted bad guys from a Silverstone Clan show. She turned her giggle into a cough, but still, the room became colder.

"Hmmm." The being came closer, and a long, thin purple finger poked her cheek. "Not enough meat on this one. Why is it here?" the cloaked figure asked her guards.

"Caught it snooping," axe man said.

"Caught it sneaking," her captor finished.

"I asked you to find me some food, not a sneak!" the being snapped.

"Sneak is good eating," axe man grumbled.

Her captor poked at her. "Not this sneak," she groused.

"I was not sneaking!" Tania said, slapping away the fingers poking her.

All three stopped and stared at her. Axe man closed his mouth with an audible snap and stepped up close to her. In the heat of the room, her eyes watered from the smell of four unwashed armpits.

"Sneak can speak," he said, eyes narrowed.

"Of course I can speak," Tania snapped back. She was tired and sore, and thoughts of diplomacy had fled her head the second they'd mentioned eating her.

"Sneak can't speak," snorted her captor. "This not sneak."

"Well," said the high-pitched one, "if it is not a sneak, what is it then?"

"I'm a traveller who got lost," Tania admitted.

The long, purple fingers grasped the edges of the hood and pushed it back, revealing a large, bald head and a face that was dominated by four black eyes, all intently focused on her. "A traveller," the being said. It sniffed the air and raised its chin. "From the Grey Realms. Kill it."

Tania had time for nothing more than an indrawn breath before her arms were grasped and she was dragged away.

CHAPTER SIXTEEN

Taking a deep breath, Amara hesitantly placed her booted foot on the white sand of Ronah's beach. She was here. Shouldering her pack, she walked up the dunes, towards the street where people were going about their daily business. Overwhelmed, she paused when she reached the cobbled stones of the street.

Sailors from the boat milled around her, pushing past with boxes and chests of goods to deliver, careful not to jostle her, letting her take in the sights. Oh, and what sights there were!

Her human family had lived in stone cottages and were brilliant earth Innarnians. Cantash, where she'd lived with the Daens, was warm and cosy, with houses made of fire and stone. When she'd first arrived, she'd seen it as a marvel of Innarnian construction, but this... If Cantash was a marvel, then Ronah was simply otherworldly. Structures made of every conceivable Innarn lined the streets. People wearing bright colours and using their Innarn freely streamed past her and gently sent thoughts of welcome her way.

Bouncing on her feet, Amara couldn't have been more delighted. She was finally here! Holding the strap of her pack securely, she headed for the town square, where she was to meet the Elders.

"Wait!" Tania screamed. Axe man stopped, but his companion kept going. There was a moment when Tania feared that they would rip out her arms, but her captor halted on the wrong side of painful.

"I can go," she babbled. "I'll leave, won't say a word about you, get out while the going's good, yeah?"

The purple one took a step forwards and sneered at her. "You are not food. You are not a sneak. You are of no use, so your bones can fuel my fire."

"What if I bring back food? I can do that. Lots of food at home," Tania said quickly. Clenching her jaw tight to stop her teeth from chattering, she'd thought when the Chirea grabbed her, it was bad. But she'd never been so terrified in her life.

"What kind of food?" the purple one asked.

"I... what do you like to eat?" Tania said. She'd promise to bring back a moon for them to gob on at this point. *'Jon!'* she whimpered.

"Pedutia," the being said.

"Pedutia. Sure. I can get that." She was nodding so hard her eyes were rattling in their sockets. She had no idea what pedutia was, but surely Jonathan would know?

"What about us?" grumbled her captor.

'Jon, please answer!' she sent.

"You'd eat dirt if you could get to it," the purple one sneered.

'Tania? What's wrong?'

"Mmm," axe man said. "Likes the worms in it."

Tania hid her thoughts on worm-filled dirt for dinner, but ultimately, so long as she wasn't on the menu, she was happy. *'In a bit of trouble. Okay, a lot of trouble.'*

"If we let you go, how do we know that you'll come back?" the purple one asked, ignoring the worm comment altogether.

"I will, I promise," Tania insisted.

'What sort of trouble?' She could almost hear Jon's frown.

"Promises are empty words," the purple one sneered.

Rapidly considering her options, Tania gasped out, "I have friends, allies. Let me send them a message and they'll bring the pedutia and you can let me go."

"Wormy dirt too," axe man insisted.

"Yes, that too," Tania said. "Please?" she begged the purple one. Her arms were still being stretched to the limit. Tears were welling in her eyes. She tensed, preparing for any decision.

The purple one grinned, showing off dull, flat teeth. "Fine. But I want enough to last the winter."

"How long does the winter go for here?"

Another grin accompanied the evil glint in its eyes. "Centuries."

Tania gulped. "Okay, I can ask for that."

"Send your message," the purple one snarled.

Shari looked at Jonathan in horror. "You did what?" she hissed.

"I asked Tania to go to Vastilda," he said, rubbing the back of his neck uncomfortably.

"You asked the person Linked with Ronah to go to a Dark, Ice Realm," Shari hid her face in her hands, not sure how to ask why he'd been so stupid. "Tell me you at least sent someone with her."

"Well..."

Shooting her Guardian a withering glance, she grabbed his arm, ready to shift them straight to Vastilda. Before she got the chance, the bell over the front door sounded. Jon gave her a helpless look. Shari tried her hardest not to snarl at him, but at the rate he left the back room, she had a feeling that she hadn't succeeded.

Pacing around the back, Shari found herself tugging at her hair, trying to understand what could have made Jonathan think it was any sort of a good idea to send an undertrained, Linked person to a Realm that was darker than anywhere she'd ever been. On Vastilda, Tania's link with Ronah would become tenuous, and without the training, she would struggle to perform even the easiest Innarn. Shari tugged her hair again, before forcing her arms down by her side. As Jonathan served his customer and closed the store, she prodded his mind and found out that Tania had been missing for over eighteen hours. That was far, far too long.

Shari ached to kick something, to dive into the Dark Realm and check to see if the girl who was fast becoming her friend was okay. Jonathan slipped through the back door, breathless.

"Shop is all closed up, so we can..." He froze, and Shari, still half-Linked with his mind, heard Tania's message.

'Jonathan, I've come across a few... friends? Let's say friends, who are a bit hungry. They're after some pedutia and some wormy dirt. Easy, right? Ha ha. Um, they need a fair bit—like, a century's worth. Can you bring some to the hills about two hours north of the door into Vastilda?'

'Are you okay?' Jonathan sent back.

Shari thought he sounded far too calm.

'Just fine. Except I don't really know what pedutia is, and the dude with the axe keeps licking his lips when he looks at me.'

'Pedutia is a plant. I know where we can get some. Enough dirt to last centuries would be too heavy to carry, but I...'

'Don't worry, I've got it,' Shari broke in.

'Hey Shari, I...'

'Who are you?' asked another voice.

'I am Lissae's Altoriae and I...' Shari never got to finish. There was the mental equivalent of static, and her horrified eyes met Jonathan's.

Just as Shari clamped a hand on Jon, ready to shift them out, Sam burst through the door and clapped Jon's shoulder. There was an aborted scream, and then Shari and Jon were alone on the icy slope of a hill in the Dark Realm where Tania was trapped.

Samuel had burst through the back door to remind Jonathan to send out a search party for his little worker. Seeing Jon seated in front of him, he reached out to clap him on the shoulder and Shari's Innarn swirled around him, trying to shift him off Lissae.

Thanks to Jonathan's binding bloody promise, he couldn't leave the Realm without direct permission from the meddlesome human, and so far, he'd been smart enough not to try.

Being caught in the shield created by the promise was like having a giant's hand scoop him up and drag him across a cheese grater. Unfortunately, said giant had left him hanging a good twenty feet up, and he crashed to the ground before his heart caught its next beat. He lay there, stunned, and struggling to breathe as his vision became fuzzy around the edges.

Just before Sam lost consciousness, he cursed the fragility of his mortal frame.

There was a sideways tug as Shari and Jon shifted to Vastilda. She pushed more of her Innarn into the shift, frantic to keep them intact and on track. As they arrived on the frozen Realm, she landed heavily, stumbling under her Guardian's weight.

Jonathan found his feet first and pulled himself up. Shari let herself droop for a moment, hands on bent knees, shoulders hunched as she drew gasping breaths in, fog unfurling from her mouth as she breathed out. She gave herself half a minute to recover, her Innarn creeping out, searching for a grounding point on a Realm with weather wildly different than she was used to.

There, over the distant horizon, was a gnarled tree with a single green leaf trembling in the freezing wind. Locking on it, she took a steadying breath in, and drew herself straight.

"What in Na'reh's name was that?" she asked Jon, bewildered.

Her Guardian ran a hand over his face. Tilting her head, she wondered for the first time if he was hiding something from her.

"Someone who didn't have authorisation to leave Lissae tried to shift out with us," he said at last.

"Without authorisation? Who..." But before Shari finished her sentence, she heard a high-pitched whining sound. Eyes snapping up, she spotted a ball and chain heading straight for the back of Jon's head. She dove towards him, tackling him around the waist. They ended up in a tangle of limbs, watching as the ball and chain smashed to the ground behind them, kicking up a shower of snow.

"We need to find Tania," Shari said, untangling herself from him and staying low, scanning the area to see where the projectile had come from.

'Tania?' Jon sent. Shari piggybacked off his send, trying to pinpoint her friend's location.

Friend. The thought distracted her for a moment. Could she call Tania a friend? The last person she'd thought of as a friend... well, Mitch's end hadn't been pretty.

Perhaps she was better keeping people at arm's-length.

'Jonathan?' Tania sent back, incredulous. 'Be careful. It's a trap!'

Shari rolled her eyes. *Of course, it was a trap.* Another ball and chain whizzed overhead, landing closer than the last. Concentrating hard, she fixed on Tania's location, grabbed Jonathan around the ankle, and shifted them there.

It was only a quirk of the way they'd initially fallen that caused Shari to grab Jon's ankle. That little quirk meant that her hand wasn't crushed under the heavy metal cage which had come crashing down on her Guardian's ribs the instant they'd landed.

Watching Jon fade from consciousness, Shari started to curse.

She was interrupted by a high-pitched voice saying, "Are you the only bipedal ones of your kind?"

Shari snarled and reached out a hand to help concentrate her Innarn as she lifted the heavy cage off Jon and sent it slamming into a wall.

"Now, now, that won't do," scolded a cold voice. Looking up, Shari saw a four-eyed purple being who had been holding Tania captive. The being glided forwards and lifted Shari's chin with a long, thin finger. "The Altoriae, I presume?"

Shari glared in response. The being seemed to take her silence as confirmation.

"There have been whispers on the Realms that the Altoriae had reappeared. War'Jan has a bounty on your head, one that will keep us in pedutia for millennia. Once we turn you in, we'll never go hungry again," the being's eyes glistened with want.

Raising an eyebrow, Shari peered at the face of her captor. She felt Jon trying to force himself back to consciousness, and fear emanating from Tania. Concentrating on her captor, she sent her Innarn spiralling out, trying to sense how many other people were with the purple being.

"Someone is sneaking," said a voice.

"Someone is snooping," said another voice.

Two lumbering beings stepped out of the shadows. They stood head and shoulders above everyone else in the room, their four arms bulging with muscles. One held an axe loosely in one hand, and the other held a spoon big enough to be considered a shovel.

"Wormy dirt here yet?" the female holding the shovel asked.

The purple being rolled all four eyes. "No, Besfu, they have failed to deliver the wormy dirt. When we hand them over to War'Jan, you'll get all the wormy dirt you could ever want."

Besfu dropped her shovel. Her tiny eyes opened wide. "War'Jan? No, no, War'Jan!"

Shari frowned. Who could make a four-armed Vastildian cyclops afraid?

Axe man stepped forwards. "War'Jan bring wormy dirt? Bah! War'Jan turn *us* into wormy dirt!"

The purple being turned to Besfu and axe man. "Enough!"

"You know, we can match whatever War'Jan has to offer," Shari said conversationally.

Narrowing her eyes, the purple one turned back to Shari. "You think you can do that? What we want is much, and you are few."

"We are few here, but many at home. We can supply all the pedutia and dirt you want," Shari affirmed. Tania nodded along frantically. Jon groaned faintly, and Shari fought to ignore him. She didn't dare try to heal him yet, as much as she was aching to. Taking their physical bodies such a long distance had put a strain on her that she hadn't expected.

The purple one glared at her. "I don't believe you. No one trades for nothing."

"The book," Tania gasped out.

Shari frowned. '*What book?*' she sent to Tania.

"You have a book. The *Hekkor Mafae*. Trade us that for the pedutia and let us go. We won't tell anyone," Tania said between shaky breaths.

There was a long moment of silence. The purple one regarded each of the Lissaens by turn, its eyes lingering the longest on Shari. Just when Shari thought she might break from the strain of the silence, the purple one said, "Fetch it, Opar."

"I is not fetching the thing, Kinsa," axe man said, shuddering. His lower arms wrapped around his torso, the upper arms passing his axe back and forth nervously.

"Do you want wormy dirt or not?" the purple one, Kinsa, growled at him.

Shuffling his axe a few more times, Opar grumbled and lumbered off. Silence descended once again, broken occasionally by Besfu licking her lips. Shari wasn't sure what the attraction of wormy dirt was, but clearly it was Besfu's favourite meal.

Opar came back into the cave on tiptoe, one of his upper arms extended right out, a black book dangling from his fingertips. He flicked it at Shari as soon as she was in range, totally bypassing Kinsa.

Shari didn't pause to consider her luck. Simultaneously, she snatched the book out of the air with her gloved hand, sent out a thread of purple Innarn and coiled it around Tania's wrist, slapped her free hand onto Jonathan's ankle, and shifted them straight to the hospital on Ronah.

Kinsa's furious shout followed them out of the Realm and was ringing in Shari's ears as she collapsed onto the hospital floor in a tangle of limbs.

Amara greeted the Elders with a smile and winced as they barely acknowledged her. The trio of Elders who'd come to meet her gave her the blank-faced stares of someone sending rapidly to others. Were they sending about her, or was this a test?

Shifting her weight from foot to foot, she wondered if it would be rude to put her pack down. She'd come with the intention to stay, even if she wasn't the successful candidate. Her whole life was in her pack. Was it just a little bit sad? Twenty-seven, and the totality of her life to date fit on her back. Her eyebrows twitched up. Others might think it sad, but she found it comfortable—it meant that she could move where she wanted to, without the hassle of having to get others to help. Mind you, she was a deft hand at shrinking things, so that was useful.

The Elders were still lost in their heads, so Amara slipped the pack from her shoulders and rested it on the ground, taking the time to look around. Ronah sure was different to Cantash, and to the mainland. That wasn't a surprise, really. She'd heard stories of Ronah for so long, and the Wisara brought pictures when they visited. It was almost as if she'd been here before.

There was a sudden buzz against her mental shields that caused her hand to reflexively tighten on her pack, a tiny flicker of flame escaping her fingertips before she regained control and called it back.

From the send-chatter buzzing around her, the Altoriae and Guardian had just arrived in the hospital, severely injured. Amara frowned, concerned for them. She itched to go and see if she could help, but the Elders had put out a request that people go about their business as usual, with promises on updates of their conditions. Nodding to herself, Amara conceded that was fair. No doubt there would be a swarm of people wanting to help and send good wishes.

That didn't stop her head snapping up to the sky as a dark shadow swooped over her, the sound of wings beating hard filling her ears. Astounded, she watched an Ilutri carrying a human in his arms, winging across the sky faster than sparks flew from a fire.

Eyebrows almost at her hairline and mouth agape, she said, "Well, that was something you don't see every day."

"Apologies, candidate. If you'll follow me, I'll see you to your quarters." Elder Billi stepped away from the other two and indicated for Amara to follow. "The Islands are in a bit of an uproar at the moment, but I'm sure it'll settle down soon."

They walked up the main street of Ronah, Amara trying not to gape as the castle came into view.

"That is where the candidates are staying. Your room is next to mine. You'll be free to mingle with the others, but be on your guard at all times."

"Have you met the Altoriae?"

"Yes. She seems... competent, if unorthodox in her methods. From what I know of you, you'll be a good fit for her." The Elder smiled to take the sting out of her words.

"I can't wait to meet her!" Amara skipped, and promptly tripped over. Springing back up again, she grinned as the Elder shook her head.

"Maybe she can teach you to not trip over air."

Amara laughed. "If you can't do that, there's no hope!"

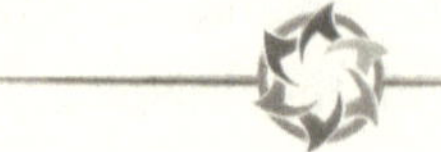

Shari's arms fell stiffly by her sides as Jonathan was carted away. She'd done her best to heal his ribs, but after shifting three people over such a massive distance, she thought that it would be better if healers took over for the delicate part of repairing the punctured lung and internal bleeding that she'd uncovered.

'Ronah, can you trace where I shifted in from, and send enough pedutia and dirt with worms to last three beings for a century or two? Or, at least organise it to happen for me?' Shari sent to the Island as she looked down at the book in her hands.

The cover of the book was black—the blackest black she'd ever seen. It seemed to draw all the shadows in the room into it. The normally cheery waiting area seemed to be dull and distant now. The old leather binding creaked as Shari turned it over in her hands to get a better look at it, the yellowing pages indicating it was ancient. The silver writing on the cover twisted as she watched, changing from a script she couldn't read to *Hekkor Mafae*. Wondering exactly how sentient this book was, Shari found herself desperate to set it down, but she dare not for fear of how it would affect anyone else.

Tania sat on the ground next to her, surrounded by Ronah's glow, steadily healing. She'd suffered a touch of frostbite and some strained muscles from Besfu and Opar using her as a tug toy. Shari grinned fondly at Ronah's Linked.

Holli Doonavan strode over to her and handed her a gently smoking cup. "Drink," the healer said sternly.

Taking the cup in one hand, Shari downed the faintly glowing blue liquid, wrinkling her nose slightly at the salty taste. "What is this?"

"The latest in healing advances from Talhan. It's infused with femto-crystals that will help to recover from any damage you've sustained. It should assist you to recuperate a bit quicker. Try and align with the Elements tonight, and you'll be back to full strength by morning."

"Thanks, Holli," Shari said, grinning.

The worried look didn't leave the healer's face. "You stretched yourself too far, Altoriae. Especially in a Dark Realm. It is imperative that you take the time to recover tonight, or else it may take you weeks, and I'm not sure that's a good idea with everything that's been happening lately."

Shari nodded solemnly. "I will rest, healer. You have my word."

Holli held her gaze a moment longer and nodded, striding off to tend to her other patients. Shari allowed herself a moment to close her eyes. She opened them when she heard the door move and blinked hard to make sure she wasn't seeing things.

Samuel had stepped out of a room and was limping towards them.

"Sam?" she asked.

He glowered at her, eyes flicking down to the book cradled in her arms, his mouth dropping and his eyebrows rising. It took him a long moment before he swallowed and all but growled at her, "Tell Jonathan I'm trying out my new house tonight," before limping through the door.

Shari blinked at his abrupt exit. She opened her mouth to call out to him but caught the hint of blood on the cuff of his sleeve and decided not to.

"It isn't finished yet," Tania said.

"Sorry? What isn't finished?" Shari asked. She guessed she was only getting half of the story.

"Sam's house. Ronah has... just finished the bed. There are walls, a roof, and a door, so it's a start. We were meant to have another few days yet, but I think that I can finish it off while he sleeps," Tania replied, getting to her feet.

"Don't strain yourself," Shari warned.

Tania tried to laugh. "I think I've done enough of that for one day," she said. "Are you going to wait here?"

Shari nodded.

"Okay. Well, I'm going home." After heading for the door, her steps dragging, she turned back and said, "Don't bug the healers too much."

"I'll try not to," Shari replied, a ghost of a smile crossing her face.

"Did you want me to talk to Sam tomorrow? He doesn't seem very happy with you at the moment."

"Yes, thanks. I'm not sure what happened," Shari said, subconsciously beating out an anxious rhythm on her thigh.

"Will do. Try and get some rest," Tania said, and slipped out the door.

Shari's smile melted away. Rest. When was the last time she'd done that?

The sound of pounding feet and the cry of, "Shari!" came from the hallway. Her mother and father burst in, only to stumble to a halt as Holli descended on them, scowling.

"We're at capacity, and I know that you'll respect the patients who are resting." The healer glared.

Giggling quietly as her father straightened up and tucked his wings away while her mother threw her windblown hair into a quick bun, Shari couldn't help but be touched by their concern.

"Sorry, Healer. We heard that Shari was here?" her father asked. Holli gestured down the hallway to where she was standing.

Giving a little wave, Shari was promptly smothered, one parent either side of her, squeezing her ribs hard enough that she couldn't help but gasp for air.

'Too tight!' she sent to her dad.

The pressure around her ribs lessened, and he sent back, 'Sorry, little one. We were so worried!'

"I'm fine," she said aloud. "Jonathan is pretty banged up though. I'm just waiting to see that he's in recovery, and I'll head home."

"We'll stay with you," her mum said.

"What about SilverCloud?" she asked.

"LoneWolf is with him tonight. He'll send me if anything happens," her dad replied.

"I have to check on Fiona as well. I want to make sure she's okay," Shari said.

Crista Edwards popped up in front of them. "Altoriae? Healer Doonavan said that you'd want an update?" he said hesitantly.

"Yes, please," Shari said.

Gently tapping at Shari's mental shields, Crista sent, 'The Guardian is now in recovery. We have immobilised him for the night while his ribs reset. He suffered two shattered ribs, three cracked ribs, a punctured lung, and internal bleeding. We have set his bones, repaired his lung, and fixed *the bleed. For anyone else, we would recommend at least three weeks of light duty, but as he is the Guardian, we're only requiring him to visit for ten minutes a day for the recovery period so we can monitor him.'*

Shari felt quite weak. The corners of her mouth turned down and she had to close her eyes to stop the rush of guilt that overcame her. Jonathan had been injured because she wasn't quick enough.

'He will heal because of you too, Altoriae,' Crista sent gently.

Shari nodded abruptly. *'Can you tell me about Fiona?'*

'She has been released but is still on the Island. Her Innarn is back up to full strength...' The healer paused, and Shari softly prodded him to finish his thought. *'The incident has shaken her. I worry for her state of mind.'*

'I'll check up on her,' Shari promised.

'Tomorrow,' Crista sent. "Tonight, you must rest," he said aloud.

"We'll make sure she does. Thank you, Healer Edwards." Her mum stepped up and wrapped an arm around her shoulders.

"Aw, Mum!" Shari moaned, even as she leaned into the hug.

"Faker," her mum said fondly. "Now, bed for you. You can come back in the morning after you rest!"

With a final round of thanks to the healer, the Dawn family went home together, Shari feeling more at peace than she had in a long time.

CHAPTER SEVENTEEN

Samuel groaned and rolled onto his belly, pulling his pillow over his head at the persistent knocking on his door. He thought strongly about dismembering the creature disturbing his rest but found that he didn't even have the energy to swing his legs off the side of the bed without his head spinning.

"G'way!" he grumbled loudly towards the direction of his door.

"Shan't!" a sing-song voice said. "I have food!"

He grumbled again, but his stomach clenched, painfully reminding him that this form needed food more often than he was used to. "Fine," he said. "Come in!"

Tania entered, carrying a large bowl that smelled like cooked vegetables.

"What is this?" he asked, his head swimming as he shakily regained his balance.

"One of Mum's concoctions. It's a vegetable stew. Meant to be good if you're not feeling great," she said, handing him the bowl and conjuring a stool to sit on.

"I'm more of a carnivore," he said, looking at her and raising an eyebrow.

She had the nerve to roll her eyes. "Just try it. It's tasty," she said, shoving a spoon into his hand.

Scooping up some of the vegetables, he eyed them warily. In all his long life, he had yet to find plant matter appetising. Still, it appeared that the little female was trying to be friendly, so he gamely put the spoon into his mouth, fully expecting not to be able to swallow.

Flavour like no other exploded over his tongue. Samuel's eyes closed involuntarily, and his bones melted. He slumped back against the wall, breathing through his mouth, trying to chase the taste. "What was that?"

Tania shrugged. "No idea, to be honest. Mum just throws things into a pot and creates the most mouth-watering things you will ever eat."

Sam would have nodded but was too busy spooning the last of the stew into his mouth.

The little female grinned, clearly pleased that he'd finished his meal. "I've got seconds, but it's best if you wait till later to eat it," she said. From her expression, it looked like she was amused with his disappointment. Leaning closer to him, she whispered, "It'll taste even better then."

He scowled at her, "Food does not taste good later."

"I was right about the stew, wasn't I? Trust me," she said blithely, and turned away to place the earthenware pot in a cupboard he'd not noticed before.

"When did that happen?" he blurted.

"Ronah hadn't quite finished your house last night, but we've been working on it while you were asleep," Tania replied.

Sam blinked, not sure what to say. Going through past conversations, he realised that some form of thanks was required. "Aren't you tired?" came out of his mouth instead. He scowled at himself but smoothed over his expression as she turned around.

"Why?" she said. Sam blinked again, not aware that the tiny female could go from open to guarded so quickly. He nodded in approval.

"Did you not have a rather eventful time on Vastilda?" he prodded.

It was the girl's turn to scowl. She turned away from him and fussed with something on the newly created bench in what was to be his kitchen. "You could say that." She turned back, her hands full of bandages. "How about I tell you while I swap your bandages over?"

Glaring, he remembered the stew, and softened his gaze. "Fine," he said shortly.

"Jon asked me to travel to Vastilda to get a book for him. I ran into some beings who weren't too happy to see me, and they ransomed me for some food. I don't think they'd eaten in a while," the girl said. She shuddered, but her hands remained steady as she wrapped the bandage around his calf. "I don't get why I understood the beings on Vastilda. It doesn't make sense," Tania groused at Sam as she moved to re-bandage the gash on his arm.

"Has no one bothered to tell you yet?" he said, glaring at her as she prodded his wound.

He could tell by the bunching of her arm muscles that she wanted to poke at him, but to his surprise, she kept her hands steady and light. "Tell me what?" she asked, trying not to speak through her teeth.

"Lissae is the Mother Realm," he said, as if that explained everything. She raised her eyebrows at him. He rolled his eyes and continued, "Any spoken language has roots from this Realm. Written ones too, but written language can change faster than the spoken word. Travelling with Shari, Jonathan, or one of the Ducibus ensures that you'll be able to understand the language on the Realm you're travelling to. Physical language, like the Veti Cant, doesn't translate and must be learned, and some regional dialects and slang can be difficult, but most things will translate."

"What happens if I just slipped through one of the doorways? Would it work then?"

Sam laughed as he shoved back from the table and staggered over to the couch. Tania smiled gently at him, and he had the impression that she was glad he was getting better.

"There is no way in the Realms that you would be able to just 'slip through' a Ducibus' doorway. Although, I'd like to see you try." He lay back, exhausted by his display of mirth, and full from his meal.

"Maybe some other time," she said. "Rest now. Someone will be by later to check on you."

"I suppose Jonathan's annoyed that I'm not under his watchful eye anymore," he drawled as his eyes slipped shut.

Whatever Tania's response was, he missed it as he fell into sleep.

When Jonathan woke up, his mind was drifting enough that the pain in his chest was a distant, niggly thing that was easy to ignore. What wasn't so easy to dismiss was the curled-up form of the Altoriae in the chair at the end of his bed.

Lifting his head, Jonathan heard a groan as his body protested. It took him a moment to realise that he was the one who had made the noise. It took him another long minute to realise that he'd woken his charge, and she was looking at him, concern and guilt swimming down the link that was feeling cloudy, no doubt due to the pain medicine that the healers would have given him.

"Well met, Altoriae," he croaked. A glass with a long stem appeared in front of him. He gratefully took a sip.

"Well met, Guardian," Shari said softly, her guilt at not acting fast enough to prevent his injury surrounding him.

"It can't have been that bad," Jonathan said.

She gave him the stare she'd used to quieten down the Dark Army on Neharn. He gulped. "Your injuries should see you staying in the hospital for the next three weeks."

Frowning, Jonathan went to raise himself to his elbows, and couldn't manage to hide the wince at the movement. Shari pushed him gently back on the bed with her Innarn, even going as far as fluffing the pillow before she set his head down. "As it is," she continued, "you are you, and the healers know that you are more stubborn about doing your duty to the Realm than even I am." She ignored his snort at this, but quirked the corners of her mouth up. "And they have said that you are to come in once a day for ten minutes until they tell you otherwise. I can break you out of here as soon as they check you over."

"Break out isn't quite the phrase I would use, Altoriae," said Healer Edwards as he slipped in the door.

"Ah, but it appeals to his sense of adventure," Shari said, her body relaxing back into her chair. She wouldn't fool the healer and she didn't fool Jonathan. Her Innarn was fairly humming, a clear warning that she was on guard.

"Be at ease, Altoriae," Crista said. "I've come to help."

"Do you blame me, Crista? The Guardian has long been a target, and I will take no risks with his safety," Shari said. The blade Yessna had given to her appeared, and she started twirling it between her fingers.

The healer heaved a sigh. "As you wish, Altoriae," he said, then turned his back and ignored her to tend to his patient. Jonathan wasn't sure if he should be amused at Crista's audacity, or worried for his safety.

Hiding his winces and grunts as the healer poked and prodded at his ribs earned him a raised eyebrow and a slight shake of Crista's head. Clearly, the medicine was affecting his reaction time.

"You must keep your ribs strapped, and as immobile as possible. No off-Realm travel unless necessary," said Crista, ignoring Shari's snort of derision in the background. "I mean it. I know life and death is your trade, and I'm more than grateful for what you both do, but if you stress your ribs unnecessarily, at best, it's a longer healing period, and I don't think I need to explain the worst case to either of you." He turned to Shari. "Altoriae, make sure he rests, please."

Shari narrowed her eyes at the healer, holding his gaze for a beat or two longer than necessary before nodding abruptly. "I will."

"Good," the healer said, all smiles. "Now, I'll leave you to get the Guardian home safely. If you can ensure his landing, you'll be free to shift out from here."

"Thank you, Healer," Shari said, before prodding Jonathan, who echoed her.

Crista slipped from the room as quietly as he'd entered.

"Ready to go home?" Shari asked. Jonathan nodded, and found himself stretched out on the couch in his lounge room.

Shari fussed over him before sitting on the low table in the middle of the room and looking at him intently. "I have a question for you."

The way that she spoke, Jonathan found that he was suddenly glad he was laid up on the couch. The last time Shari had used that tone with him, she'd soundly trounced him in training, and had managed to break his arm in three places because he hadn't been able to block in time.

"Yes?" he said warily.

She attempted to smile, but it came out as more of a grimace that made him snap his teeth together in order to stop the automatic apology from spilling from his lips. "Why did you send Tania off-Realm?"

"Because I needed the–"

"And you didn't go because...?"

"I had to deal with the–"

"That's not good enough."

"Shari," he said warningly, struggling to try and sit up. Thunder rumbled through the air as dark clouds formed inside his lounge room.

"Don't you 'Shari' me," she bit off. "You've been busy, dealing with the Returned, with the Joining Ceremony, with the attacks on Rakemyst. I get that. But nowhere in that mess of things does it give you the right to send the one Linked with Ronah off-Realm."

Jonathan blinked, and lay back again. Somehow, in among all the things he'd had to do, he'd forgotten who Tania was. She had, in his mind, become a temporary replacement for the apprentice who he'd lost. "I…" he started to say.

"No," Shari said gently. She'd read his confusion and apology through their link before he'd even been aware of it. "Let's just agree that you won't send Tania off-Realm again, okay?"

"I can do that," he said, guilt and sadness washing over him like a tsunami.

Shari put her hand on his forehead, acknowledging and drawing out the negative feelings, leaving him with an echo and a bitter reminder of how wrong he'd been that twinged every time he breathed.

"Rest," she said, putting up wards to protect him even as he slipped back into sleep.

Tania sidled out of Sam's front door and down the path.

"Well met, m'lady," Collis greeted her as she hit the main street. He was sweeping the sidewalk outside the tavern. One look at her face and he put the broom down, falling into step beside her.

Together they walked in silence, Tania letting her feet lead the way. When they reached the beach, she slipped her shoes off, and wandered down the dunes, allowing the waves to lap at her toes and her feet to sink into the sand. Collis's shoes seemed to melt away and he sighed blissfully as the water reached his ankles.

"I don't think I've ever been so scared," she whispered. Collis stood beside her, silent. "I thought I was going to die. I couldn't tap into my Innarn, but it was like all the fear had chased it away."

"'Tis not true," Collis said.

"What do you mean?" Tania asked, eyes brimming with tears she refused to allow to spill over.

"You are bound with Ronah, just like my mother. Your Innarn will be strongest when you are on the isle you are Linked to. The farther away from Ronah you are, the weaker your Innarn will be. How far away were you when you feared death?" he asked, gazing out at the ocean.

"A long way away. On a Dark Realm," she said.

Collis's eyebrows shot up, and he hissed in a breath. "You should not be leaving Lissae *at all*. What were you doing on a Dark Realm?"

"The Guardian asked me to get something..." she said weakly, turning to face Collis. She didn't know that she wasn't meant to leave the Realm.

Fury burned in his eyes, but his voice was calm. "Next time the Guardian asks you to go off-Realm, please allow me to take your place."

"Collis, you don't have to do that," she protested.

"If the Guardian won't take your role seriously, then yes, I do," he said evenly, but Tania sensed the Innarn flexing under his skin, making the air between them ripple.

"I don't understand," she said. "What is so bad about being off-Realm?"

"Ronah is bound to you. Upon your death, your soul joins with the others to help give Ronah a greater understanding of her residents and you live on, helping newcomers settle, and ensuring that Ronah can aid her residents any way they need. If you die off-Realm..." He shook his head sadly. "I saw it happen once when I was a boy. My father was the first to be Linked to Ronah. He was taken off-Realm and killed. Ronah went into mourning so deep it lasted years. Our crops failed; our seasons shifted. Life was hard. The Elders didn't know what to do as there hadn't been another time like it. The Isle only really recovered when my mother joined with her, but even then it took years for things to come back to what they were like before my father was killed."

Tania looked at her toes and processed his words. "Why didn't Ronah try to stop me then?"

'*You were gone too quickly. I did not think you would leave,*' Ronah sent. '*I sensed your fear but could do nothing.*' Ronah showed her the frustration the Island had experienced when she'd been away.

"But I've gone off-Realm before!" she protested.

"While it might have been dangerous, you might not have felt like you wouldn't make it back before," Collis countered.

"True," Tania said, her shoulders slumping. "But isn't part of being bound to Ronah defending her?"

"Never at the cost of your life," Collis said. "Your passing is meant to be peaceful, after a life well lived."

Tania wrapped her arms around herself and snorted. "I don't know if that will happen. Things seem..." she trailed off, not sure how to end the sentence.

"Scary?" a new voice chimed in. "Difficult? Dangerous?" Shari said as she joined them by the edge of the water.

"All of the above," Tania admitted with a wry twist of her mouth.

"You aren't going off-Realm again. That's not your place, and Jonathan should never have sent you," Shari said, her eyes steely as she looked out at the waves.

"But..." Tania was ready to protest.

Collis gently overrode her, and said, "Thank you, Altoriae."

Shari turned to them and held Collis's gaze. "You're offering to protect Tania, aren't you?"

The tall Innarnian dipped his head in acknowledgement.

Nodding, Shari said, "Good. If there are any issues, come to me."

"As you wish, Altoriae," Collis said.

"Don't I get a say in this?" Tania asked. She felt like a little kid with the grown-ups talking about her over the top of her head.

Shari shook her head sadly. "Not really. I wish I could say that you have the freedom to do what you want, when you want to. But this is another part and parcel of being someone important. For what it's worth, I do understand how you feel."

"There's so much more I want to see," Tania said softly. "It's like a whole new world had opened up to me, and now the door is being slammed closed in my face."

"There's more than one way to travel the Realms, you know," Shari said. "I'll teach you to Astral travel, and then you can explore as much as you want."

"Are you sure that's wise, Altoriae?" Collis asked.

"Better than her sneaking off without telling anyone," Shari retorted.

"I wouldn't do that!" Tania protested.

"Given enough motivation, anyone would," Shari said. "Na'reh knows I do it all the time."

Tania kind of liked the idea that she and Shari were looking out for each other. And she was quite happy to add Collis to their ragtag band.

CHAPTER EIGHTEEN

As Shari, Tania, and Collis walked up the main street of Ronah, there was the growing noise of a large gathering near the town hall.

"The trial times have been posted," Shari said to the others. She stood back to watch the crowd with Tania by her side, trying to keep track of the responses from the candidates.

Shari had worked on the list last night, determined to post the thing and get the test for the next apprentice out of the way. She hoped that Jonathan would be proud she wasn't shirking her duties.

Most of the visiting Elders were happy to stand back, but Elder Mason and Elder Camilla were jostling among the candidates trying in vain to see the list.

"Well met, all!" called out Mayor Pratt, moving to stand beside the list. The candidates begrudgingly let him through. Scanning the list, he sent images of it floating above the heads of the assembled crowd so they could all see:

First round:

Talofa from Sulanta

Alistair from Ronah

Raven from Freeson

Dealon of the Wisara

Burke from Rohinda

Second round:

Josie from Nelonia

Ness from Omina

Lira from Tevon

Mu from Nindonia

Wesin from Muhara

Third round:

Elani from Ginorti

Reon from Vutana

Caeli from Akoren

Therdon from Rakemyst

Fourth round:

Amara from Cantash

Bren from Vannali

Haran from Dento

Samuel from Ronah

"Please remember, everyone, the rules of engagement state that the aim is to surround the Altoriae in a shield for a minimum of one minute. This is not a fight to the death; we don't want to send anyone home in a body bag," Alan continued.

Shari buried her head in her hands and groaned.

"How are you going to fight them all?" Tania asked softly.

Shari shrugged. "Just another day."

"Are you concerned about a particular candidate?" Collis asked.

Drawing in a breath, Shari frowned. She'd found the applications for candidates that Jonathan had left in his office and looked them over as she'd been making up the list. "I suppose the fourth round will be the hardest. Bren and Sam are the top two on paper, but I haven't seen either of them fight, so it will be a challenging match."

"Have you seen *any* of them fight?" Tania asked.

"A few. I've seen your brother training with Jon," Shari admitted.

"Please..." Tania started to say, then stopped herself. She wouldn't beg on Alistair's behalf.

"I'm adapting the training ground for each round. Ronah said she will help me put it together. I can't guarantee that your brother won't come out scratched and bruised, but he'll be able to walk for sure," Shari said gently.

"Playing favourites already, Altoriae?" asked a lilting voice.

Shari looked at Caeli, who'd drifted over to them from the other candidates. "Hardly, candidate," she said, raising her chin. "I am going up against eighteen competitors of different skill sets and abilities. The test for each candidate is designed to play both to their strengths and against their weaknesses. Do you know how long ago the Guardian's candidate discovered he was an Innarnian?"

Caeli looked at her with wide eyes. Whatever response she'd been expecting from the Altoriae, this was not it.

"Not that long ago. He's been training for less than a week. If I were to submit him to the same test that I would give to an experienced Innarnian, someone like you, for example, we wouldn't be able to scrape him off the floor before the next trial began. 'Favourites' is not the word for it, candidate. Adaptability is," Shari said.

A few of the other candidates had gathered around. Some looked relieved at the idea of different trials, while others were sizing her up. She dipped her head to them and strode away from the crowd, Tania and Collis keeping pace with her.

As she left, she heard someone say, "These trials are all fun and games until she obliterates you from existence."

The crowd of candidates tittered uneasily as Shari fought to hide her smirk. She didn't want to hurt anyone, but she did need to know just how far these people were willing to go to protect their Realm, and if they thought that she would obliterate them, then they'd fight all the harder.

"I will be training Rakemyst and Ronah residents at the castle in half an hour if anyone else would like to attend," she threw back over her shoulder, sending a buzz through the candidates and Elders alike.

"Are the Returned invited to this training, Altoriae?" asked Collis.

"Of course. There may be some who do not wish to attend though," Shari said. The Returned had seen enough fighting to cover too many lifetimes.

"I will spread the word. I bid thee both well," Collis said, bowing his head and walking briskly towards the castle where the Returned still liked to gather.

"I heard something about the Altoriae living at the castle," Tania said, frowning.

Shari sighed. "It's long been a tradition that the Altoriae and her family live in the castle. It makes warding Ronah and all of the Shifting Islands easier, with it being the centre point."

"Have you ever seen the Islands come together?" Tania asked.

"No," Shari said, shaking her head. "I wish that I could see it one day. Mind you, if each time a new Island joined, we had to fight a group like the Chirea, I could do without it happening."

Tania shuddered. "Me too."

With Jonathan still on enforced bed rest, there was no one to shield Shari from the crowd that had gathered in the castle training ground. She took a deep breath and moved into the light, a little uneasy when the volume dropped so quickly at the sight of her. Usually that meant she was in for a massive fight. It was hard to resist the urge to summon her blade. Gritting her teeth, she only just managed to avoid flexing her hand in front of the crowd.

"Well met, all. Today, we're going to be practising shields," she stated. There was a murmur of disappointment from where the candidates were gathered that she managed to ignore. "It is one thing to be able to create a personal shield, but to create a shield with a team is quite another. It's something else entirely when you have to work with beings you've never met, and likely won't see again, but with training and practice, it is quite possible."

There were more than a few disbelieving looks, but she masterfully tuned them out. "Now, Blanks off the training ground. All able-bodied Innarnians are practising today. Spread out, arms at shoulder height. You should be able to touch the fingertips of those beside you."

Clearly, the training ground wasn't meant to hold this many people. The lines were so close, toes were getting stepped on.

"One moment, please," Shari said. '*Ronah, a little help?*' She felt the Island groan, and then the space between the lines increased so they were far enough apart that everyone, even the Kumaru, could swing their arms without hitting any of their neighbours. A few of the mainlanders looked astonished at the increase in space, but those from the Shifting Islands took it in stride.

"That's better. Now, show me the shield that you use for defence, please," Shari called out, projecting her voice so those in the back of the ground were able to hear her.

Shields of all types of Innarn sprang up, sizes and densities varying greatly. Shari cast a critical eye over them, seeking out weak spots and determining where they were strongest. The crowd before her was a huge mix of Innarn abilities, so an attack to incapacitate one may end up injuring others. She narrowed her eyes for a moment, deciding how to proceed.

"Right," she said, under her breath. She let her Innarn seep out in invisible streamers, settling thickly above the highest heads in the crowd before letting it drop.

Alarmed cries sounded as candidates struggled under the weight of the shield that Shari had released, some even buckling at the knees and falling to the ground. A quick glance around showed that all the candidates were still among the standing, as were the Elders and those who Jon considered to be the elite guard of Lissae—those of Ronah who most often went on patrol. There were also a lot of Ilutri left standing, her father and uncle among them, although LoneWolf was looking a little strained.

Pulling her Innarn back, she said, "How did I cause you to stumble or to fall?"

For a moment, it seemed as if no one would answer, and then Ness, the candidate from Omina, stepped forwards.

"You used your shield offensively, the way you would use it to hit someone in a swordfight," she said.

"Correct," Shari said with a nod. "Your Innarn is like any weapon. It can be used offensively or defensively, for good or for bad. The trick is to be able to look at a situation and judge how to adapt what you know to suit what you need in that moment." Gazing at the eager faces taking in her words, Shari found she needed to move.

"We have quite a mix of Innarnians here today. I want you to group together with those of your major Innarn. If you have more than one major, pick the one with the strongest shield. Air here," she said, standing at the far left of the training ground. "Earth here," she said a few metres to the right. "Fire here." A few metres more. "Plasma there, then spirit and water."

There was a general shuffling. Spirit was the smallest line, but it was also one of the hardest of the Innarn skills to master.

"Anyone else comfortable in creating a spirit shield?"

A dozen others shuffled in from other lines.

"Good. Now, I want all the first-in-lines to join into one group, then the second-in-lines, and so on until you're all grouped up. There should be six to a group." Standing at the head of each line, the candidates looked at each other, sizing up their competition-turned-teammates.

This is, Shari thought, *a lot like herding fritos.*

The candidates reluctantly formed the first three groups, while the residents of Ronah milled around, grumbling about who they were grouped with.

Shari shot a blast of plasma Innarn at the sky, lighting it up and causing an ear-shattering *crack* that got everyone's attention.

"There will be times when you are patrolling with a group of people who you don't want to be with, or who you don't like, and really? I don't care. You are all Lissaens, regardless of what differences you may have; that is the one thing you have in common. We are here to train, and I do not have time for idle gossip. Are we clear?" Shari allowed her Innarn to drift around her in lazy spirals that had some people gasping.

"Now, you have five minutes to come up with a shield that will hold against my attack. Candidates." Shari tried to stifle the quirk of her lip when they all, bar Sam, snapped to attention, their gazes fixed on her every move. His wink told her she hadn't quite succeeded in hiding her smile in time. "Your groups have three minutes. I suggest you move!"

There were no grumbles from the three candidate groups, or from the others, and Shari was thankful. She didn't quite understand why you'd come to a training session and then complain about actually having to train.

Shari kept an eye on the candidates as she moved around the training ground, noting those who were working well with others, and those who weren't. She was particularly interested in the group with Sam and Bren, the Weaver. They were joined by Ness, Burke, Lira and Raven.

Raven was saying, "I don't see why I can't do the fire shield. Clearly mine is stronger than Burke's."

"Because you are doing the air shield, and Burke is doing earth and it's Bren who's doing fire," Ness snapped at him.

Sam was pinching the bridge of his nose in a move so like Jon that Shari's mind almost wandered, but she pulled herself back. He was vibrating with suppressed emotion, yet when he spoke, his voice was steady. "Burke, earth shield. Ness, plasma. Lira, water. Bren, fire. And Raven, stop filling the air with your complaints and raise your shield instead!" Sam barked, a flash of gold slipping over his eyes.

Beneath his hood, Bren tilted his head and eyed Sam consideringly. "Where are you from, candidate Samuel?" Bren asked as his shield sparked to life.

"I came here with the Wisara," Sam replied, spirit Innarn swirling around the group.

"A non-answer," Bren said, with a nod. "And before the Wisara, where were you from?"

"I'm a traveller. My feet take me where the road goes," Sam said with a shrug, the only sign he was unhappy with the questioning was the slight tightening around his eyes.

"Are we just going to talk, or are we going to practise?" Lira asked, her water shield condensing around them.

"I don't know about you lot, but I want to show the Altoriae just how good I am," Raven said, preening.

Shari rolled her eyes and moved onto the next group of candidates, who were attempting to meld their Innarn into one shield, rather than create the multiples that the first group were doing. It was a difficult task even for those who knew each other and had trained for years.

"Again!" Wesin was shouting.

Reon flinched from the noise, while Amara, the Daen candidate who'd arrived late, shot the Wesin a glare just as hot as the fire Innarn that flared blue at her fingertips.

Reon let the spirit Innarn drift from his fingers, Talofa and Elani both bent down, Elani drawing the earth up, while Talofa drew on the droplets of water trapped in Elani's earth. Therdon swirled the air around them, actually managing to add to the shield. Amara skilfully wove her plasma in, holding the other Innarn together until Wesin slammed his fire into the Shield and the Innarn fell apart.

Burke, from the first group, moved so the embers of the dying shield wouldn't fall on him, shooting Wesin a glare as he did so.

"Again!" Wesin shouted. Shari sighed and moved along to check out the final group of candidates.

Haran was confidently instructing his group, although Josie and Caeli seemed to be brushing off his words for the most part. "Fire, plasma and earth, go!" he said, and the group disappeared behind a thick shield of lava. From inside the first shield, a second burst through, made of spirit, air, and water. They circled in opposite directions to each other. Shari raised her eyebrows, impressed. If they managed to hold it...

Of course, it didn't last. Mu's plasma started to break away from the inner shield. Haran pulled his spirit shield back just in time. The lava cracked, the pressure becoming too much, and Shari caught the eruption just as it shot an out-of-control geyser straight into the patrol groups. She let it hang for a moment before drawing the tumultuous Innarn away from those staring up in horror, many of whom hadn't raised their shields despite the danger.

Her gaze flicked to Burke who, although he was pale, was shielding not only himself, but his whole group under a thick earth shield. There were a few others who'd thought to shield those around them as well, mostly patrol veterans.

Alistair, who didn't seem to realise that Shari had taken control of the lava geyser, stretched out his hand and pulled it back, drawing the flames and the heat of the fire Innarn into him. Josie got the idea and pulled back the earth Innarn, leaving only Mu's crackling plasma behind. Shari sent it shooting up to the sky as if that was what she'd intended to do all along.

Shaking her head, she looked at the other patrol groups. Despite their initial grumbling, most of them were working well together. She paused to watch Edward show Cassie how to adjust for the speed of the spinning shield. Edward threw her a wink, and she laughed. She was glad to see him in good humour.

Tila Flint and Owen Thorne were together with a few of the older residents of Ronah. Tila was chewing on her lip as her spirit Innarn shimmered and fell before it could join the shield. Owen was too busy rubbing her back to add his own Innarn to the rest of their group.

'*Tila, what's wrong?*' Shari asked.

'*Spirit has always been my strongest Innarn, but after...*' Tears spilled over, making silent tracks down her face. '*After Anriluka, I know how some of the spirits come about, and I just can't bring myself to call on them.*'

Shari's heart ached. '*Remember that not all of the spirits have died in battle, and only those who want to help, will.*'

'I know, but...'

Sighing gently, Shari let her Innarn mix in with Tila's, and found the spirits that Tila was calling on. '*Your Great-Aunt only wants to help you succeed. Libon, a Satyr who died from old age, thinks the way you contact the spirits is peaceful, and he wants to be a part of that. Clarin was a*

Da'mar, and she thinks that your heart is the most precious thing. They all want to add to your shield.'

Despite her quivering chin, Tila met Shari's gaze. 'They do?'

Smiling gently, Shari nodded.

'*See. Shielding is good, Tila,*' Owen sent gently. '*Come on, let's show the old guards how we do it!*'

Nodding, Tila sent a stream of spirit Innarn out again. It flickered only briefly before melding seamlessly with the shield. Her team members cheered and Owen grinned as he added his fire to the rest.

Turning from the group, Shari hid her own smile. "Candidates, practice time is up. Let's see what you've got," she said. A few of the closest groups paused to watch, but as she turned to look at them, they suddenly found a reason to turn back to their training.

"Reon, Wesin, Talofa, Elani, Therdon and Amara. You're up."

The group stepped forwards, clearly nervous.

"See if you can hold me back," Shari said. "Shield up now."

Just like when they were practising, their shield fell apart as soon as Wesin tried to slam his fire on top of the rest.

"Show me where you went wrong," Shari said. As predicted, the others worked together harmoniously, but when it came time for Wesin to add the flames, she stepped in and stayed his hand.

"Slowly. You want the warmth of a fireplace and a hot drink, not the fury of a blacksmith's furnace," Shari said.

Wesin narrowed his eyes for a moment as if trying to decide if she was serious. Finally, he nodded, and eased his fire into the shield. It held, much to the delight of the others in his group.

"Good," Shari said. "Now let's see if you can withstand me." Taking a step back, Shari threw blasts of different Innarn at them, testing for weak spots. Shari saw a gap where the plasma and air had not quite merged, and she shot a jet of water through it, spraying the group. Reon reacted quickly and attempted to adapt the shield so he was covering the weak spot, but Shari drew on Talofa's water, making it bubble up inside the shield. It reached their ankles before anyone noticed that there was something wrong. The eyes of the other groups were on the candidates, but Shari didn't relent. She wanted to see what this group would do.

Talofa was trying to draw the water back to her, but it continued rising, even as she blasted against it, attempting to create a bubble inside the water to protect them from the rising tide. Elani used the earth to soak up some of the water, turning her part of the shield into mud.

Therdon started working with Talofa to create a bubble that would hold, while Reon and Amara pushed the water away using their chosen method of shielding.

It was then that Wesin struck, deciding that he could burn the water away. Forcefully, he grabbed Amara's hand. Pulling on her connection to the plasma in the shield and drawing on his own fire, he sent ball after ball of superheated fire into the water.

Shari's mouth dropped open in shock, as did a lot of others. The inside of the shield started to steam up, and frantic screams were building in the throats of the candidates. Slashing her hand in the air, she cancelled her attack and pulled the Innarn from the shield outwards.

The group collapsed in a heap, gasping for air and whimpering or outright crying as the breeze slid past reddened, parboiled skin.

"What were you thinking?" she hissed, stalking forwards, and lifting Wesin by his shirt. A few of the watchers moved to stop her but were held back.

"It's the bird's fault," Wesin sneered. "Don't blame me."

"What?" Shari said, drawing back in confusion, her hand still fisted in his shirt.

"Birdbrain should have been able to use the steam to strengthen the shield instead of letting it cook us," the half-Daen said.

"You would blame another for your mistake?" Shari said, her voice deceptively soft.

Behind Wesin, some of the residents of Ronah stepped back, gulping.

"It wasn't my mistake; it was his," Wesin insisted, blue eyes flashing. Therdon lowered his head, ready to take the blame. As much as Shari was unimpressed by the Ilutri's candidate, she couldn't let that stand.

Shari let go of his shirt and turned away from the thoughtless boy. She took a deep breath. Clearly the half-Daen didn't want to learn from his mistakes, nor could he even see that he'd made one, despite the others from his group spluttering on the ground around him.

Turning to face him again, she bowed and said, "I thank you for your time, candidate. I release you from your candidacy."

"What? Wait! No!"

Shari shifted him out before he made another sound. She looked at the remnants of Wesin's group. Amara was moving among them, taking the fire out of their skin, and sending gentle waves of healing their way as she touched them. She looked up at the Altoriae, her face fierce.

"It was not Therdon's fault, Altoriae," Amara said.

Tilting her head, Shari regarded the Daen before her. Even as she spoke, Amara was still healing the others, despite her own blistered, red skin.

"I know it wasn't. Wesin of Muhara is no longer a candidate," Shari said, sending a wave of healing over the rest of the group, Amara included. The girl closed her eyes and sighed with relief.

Shari nodded, satisfied, then turned to the next group.

"Samuel, Ness, Lira, Raven, Burke and Bren. Let's see how you lot fare against me," she said with a grin.

Sam seemed ready with a brazen comeback, but she shot him a warning look. He winked instead and turned to give a terse nod to his group, who raised their shields as one.

Impressed, Shari let herself admire the six shields for a moment before she went to work taking them apart.

Raven's air shield was the outermost one and was helping to keep Bren's fire shield sparking nicely. Shari slammed into both with another powerful jet of water. It took a few seconds, but the air shield faltered, and the fire was put out barely a breath later. Lira was able to take a few drops of the jet and add them to her water shield, but Shari pulled the rest back and attacked with a rapidly fired flurry of pebbles that sent so many ripples through the shield there wasn't enough water holding it together and it streamed away.

The plasma shield held together by Ness was strong, but no match for the streams of spirit that Shari sent shooting her way, swirling around the shield, and carrying the streaks of plasma high into the sky. That left just Burke's earth shield and Sam's spirit one.

Shari took a step to the side and thrust her arms out, the heels of her hands together, fire blasting from her palms. Burke paled, but the earth shield he'd created stayed strong. Sam placed his hand on Burke's shoulder, which made the Rohindian falter, and his shield crumbled to dust. Sam frowned, but stood tall, surrounded by the rest of his group as Shari battered his shield.

Throwing a flurry of different Innarn bolts at Sam's shield, Shari had to admit that she'd never come across a shield so powerful before. Eyes narrowing, she reached out to detect the edges of the shield even as she was pummelling at it with boulders that were doing little more than breaking into shards.

There was the weakness. From deep down inside herself, Shari pulled on the Light Innarn. She thought of the lightest Realms she'd visited, of the wonderful, generous Light Innarnian who had shown her their tricks and how she had made them her own. She sent a sliver of Light Innarn that pierced Sam's shield like a balloon.

There was silence for a moment as the rest of his group slumped in defeat. Sam remained standing tall, staring at her before he gave her a mocking bow.

Shari regarded him for a long moment and had the horrible feeling that he'd let her win. "Well done, candidates. You held up admirably."

The group looked at each other, relieved, as Shari moved on to the last lot of candidates.

"Haran, Caeli, Mu, Alistair, Dealon and Josie. Can you do better than the others?"

"Of course we can, Altoriae," Caeli said, her hair flicking out behind her, the hem of her dress snapping at her feet.

"The first group lasted for thirty-eight seconds. The second for two minutes thirty. You'll have to last longer than that. Ready?" Shari said, and attacked at once, firing a jet of water at the group.

The outer shield sprung up fast, Haran's spirit shield surrounding them all, with Caeli's air and Dealon's water rushing to join in. Shari's jet of water ended up absorbed into the shield, strengthening it.

Three heartbeats later, Alistair's fire, Mu's plasma and Josie's earth had joined together again. The shields spun slowly, making it hard to find and fix on a weak spot. Shari wondered who had decided to do that.

To keep their Innarn joined and spinning like that took a lot of effort. If they were out on the battlefield, Shari would have let them wear themselves out trying to maintain the shield, but as it was, she had to see if she was able to take it down quicker than the others.

The biggest problem was the inner shield was solid, giving her no clear sight on those inside it. She didn't want a repeat of their practice, nor one of Wesin's group. But her biggest problem was also theirs, as they didn't know what she was firing at them until it hit.

Dealon had been able to absorb her jet of water, but could Caeli handle extra air blown her way? Shari raised her arm and twirled it like she was going to throw a rope, and instead a twister of air fled her fingers and rushed to batter against the outer shield. Caeli was struggling to absorb it all and the exact moment that the Akoren candidate crumpled to the ground as she failed, the outer shield slipped apart like leaves falling from the winter-cold branches of a tree.

Instead of leaving Mu, Alistair, and Josie to bear the brunt of her next attack, Haran and Dealon pulled back their Innarn and pushed it towards the inner shield, surprising Shari. It was a good tactic, and both candidates rose several places in her esteem by their actions.

Still, it was closing in on the two-minute mark, and she needed to get their shield down. The easy way would be to push as much fire as possible at Alistair, but that would be no way of testing the other candidates, so she started sending bolt after bolt of plasma at them.

Mu managed to catch the first three bolts but faltered on the fourth and broke on the fifth. He sank down on one knee, but heaved himself up, face flushed and panting, pushing his plasma back into the shield. But he was weaker now, and easy to distract.

Shari sent another jet of water straight at Dealon, then a sneaky little side bolt of plasma that caught Mu unaware. Unable to counter in time, it struck the shield with a tremendous *crack* that echoed through the training ground.

Right on the two-minute-thirty mark, the shield crumbled, revealing Shari's grinning face.

"Well done, candidates. You succeeded in matching the time of the previous group," she said.

Haran and the others were silent for a moment, before Alistair let out a cheer. The others laughed in surprise and joined in cheering with him.

Shari raised her eyes to the rest of the training ground to see who she could test next.

The patrol groups seemed bolstered by the candidates' successes, and as Shari worked her way around all the other groups, she made sure to add in appropriate words of support and the occasional cautioning phrase. She was most impressed with Edward's group, who succeeded in beating the candidates' time by a second, and she'd battered their shield with all she had.

Hands on hips as she caught her breath, she grinned at Edward, Cassie, Trent, Aram, and Uista. Dripping with sweat, they grinned back.

"I think that will do for today. You've all done exceptionally well," Shari said. "Please make sure to keep practising. The Guardian will be contacting you about the patrol schedules. I bid thee well."

"I bid thee well," echoed from around the training ground, and Shari slipped away before anyone was able to corner her.

CHAPTER NINETEEN

"I enjoyed training yesterday," Sam said as he joined Shari on the walk to the classroom.

"Huh? Oh, thanks," Shari said distractedly. The training had been a good exercise to get rid of the excess Innarn she had floating around. She was tense and tired of trying to solve all the riddles that were thrown her way.

"Did you not enjoy it?" Sam asked.

"Oh, no, I did. It was a useful exercise. I'm just distracted," she said as she slipped into the classroom, relieved to find it empty for the moment.

"Distracted by what?" Sam asked. He was doing well to only show a hint of annoyance in his voice.

"I still can't figure out who War'Jan is," Shari burst out.

Sam's head snapped up. "War'Jan?"

For a moment, Shari swore that the fear she'd seen on Besfu's face was mirrored on Sam's. But she blinked, and it was gone. "The beings who captured Tania were saying that War'Jan has a bounty on my head. I'm trying to figure out who would do that?"

"Put a bounty on your head? Can you think of no one?" Sam asked, lips twisting into a sardonic smile.

Shari shrugged a shoulder and put her books on the desk. "Well, when you put it that way."

There was no more time to talk as students started filing in. Shari looked at the tiny first-year students and wondered if she'd ever been that small.

"Today, we are going to work on shielding," Shari said as the students milled around, gazing at her in awe. "Find a spot to get comfortable, and we'll see how well you can shield."

"Like at the training?" a voice piped up. Lucian Ribeck had shot up since the last time she'd seen him. He grinned at her, teeth white against his ebony skin.

She couldn't help but smile. "Not quite like that yet. When you've practised more, you'll be able to shield like that, but for now, we're practising on creating a personal shield."

There was more than one disappointed groan.

She knew her smile was brittle around the edges. Surely even kids this tiny realised that they couldn't just jump into doing something as advanced as shielding with others when they didn't even have the knowledge to shield themselves properly.

Sam broke the silence before she had a chance to. "Everyone, up! In lines according to the Innarn shield you'll be working on today," he said. The kids scrambled to do as he'd said, tiny chests puffing out with pride when he commended them for their quick actions. Sam looked to Shari, waiting for her to tell the kids what to do next.

"Okay. The best way to shield is to think of the things that make you feel the safest. Feel them right in the centre of your chest, at the deepest point of where you hold your breath. Hold that feeling tight, then push it out through your skin with your Innarn," Shari said.

The kids blinked up at her like they didn't understand what she was talking about.

"Um, isn't there a move that we should do?" one of the braver kids asked.

Shari and Sam shared a confused look. "A move?" Sam asked.

"Yeah, 'cause when Da shields at home, he does this." Lucian jammed his arms straight down by his sides before raising them skywards in a circling motion, palms up right before he abruptly clapped his hands together, a few droplets landing on his upturned face.

A few of the other kids gasped and applauded, and Shari found herself impressed. "Does he do that every time?"

Lucian nodded. Most of the other kids frantically bobbed their heads with him.

"Does this move have a name?" Shari asked, suspecting she was doing something wrong.

More nodding. "Da calls it his 'personal shield move'," Lucian said.

Shari fought to keep her expression neutral. "Did you want to see my personal shield move?"

The kids gazed at her, eyes wide, mouths agape, nodding frantically. Shari blinked and her shield bubbled to the surface, shimmering in the air before drifting away like smoke on the breeze.

There was a moment of silence before Quintin blurted out, "But you didn't do anything!"

"Didn't I?" Shari asked, eyebrow raised.

"You blinked," came the quiet voice of Laura Winter from the back of the room.

"Yes," Shari said with a smile, "I blinked. Your parents may be trying to show you the way they learned to shield, but I'll be showing you the way that works for me. If you'd prefer to do one or the other, it doesn't bother me, so long as you end up able to shield."

A few of the kids looked like they didn't know what to do with that news, but others were rapidly blinking, trying to mimic her technique. A few tried to copy Lucian, all with varying rates of success. Shari moved among the kids, encouraging them, and gently correcting them on their technique, while Sam took the other side of the room.

Sam frowned and crouched down by a child who was huddled against the wall, looking crossly out at her classmates. Honestly, humanoid children were more dramatic than even their adult counterparts. The youngling's scowl was fierce enough that he found himself impressed.

"Do you have a good reason for not trying?" he asked.

"No," the child replied, scowl turned on him. This was the one who'd seen Shari's move. Clearly the child was bright.

He scowled back. "That is not an acceptable answer. Get to your feet and try."

"Why bother?" she sneered.

Sam scowled even harder, leaned closer, and let a hint of menace into his voice. "Because if you don't, I might just decide that you are snack-sized."

She blinked at him, clearly curious, but decidedly unafraid. "I've tried. I've tried so hard I thought my skin was going to rip right off. I don't want to feel like that again," she said, eyes sliding away from his as she admitted what she thought was a flaw.

Sam let a thread of his Innarn out to brush against hers, trying to guess the best way to help her. To his surprise, she was Darker than any other being he'd met on Lissae.

"You, little one, are not like the others. You're trying to flex muscles you don't have. You need to try a different way. Let me see." He wove his

Innarn around hers, seeking her strength and using his own to ignore her weaknesses. "Ah, there it is," he murmured.

"Where?" the child said, glancing at the skin of her hand like it held the answers.

"You will be a strong spirit Innarnian one day, if you train hard and stay focused on your studies. To succeed, you need to use spirit Innarn the way that the rest use the air to breathe. There are many spirits both here on Ronah and in the Realms. If you ask, they will Shield you. Always ask, however, because if you order them, they could just as easily destroy you," he warned softly.

He wasn't quite sure that a human child's eyes were meant to get that big.

"I... I can do that," she said softly. She stood up, back straight, and closed her eyes, whispering under her breath.

Suddenly, delighted, she let out a cry.

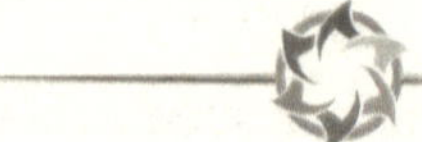

From the other side of the room, Shari looked over to see Sam standing proudly next to Laura, who had a shimmering silvery shield surrounding her, about a finger space from her skin. Her eyes were lit up with its glow.

Shari beamed at her. "And that is how you do it!"

Laura looked at Sam and smiled, gap-toothed and blindingly bright as the shield gently twisted around her.

Samuel packed up slowly after the kids left the class, finding that he had more trouble concentrating than he'd expected. Shari's voice saying War'Jan's name was burned into his memory. He had assumed he would be able to escape the old ghosts which had insisted on haunting him through the Realms for a while. Apparently, he was wrong.

He picked up his belongings and turned to leave, only to stop at the sight of one of the kids loitering in the doorway. Briefly, annoyance flared bright in his mind, but he reminded himself that he was meant to be trying to show how well he could fit in.

"Did you forget something?" he asked, keeping the irritation out of his voice.

The child flushed and ducked her head. Maybe he wasn't as adept at modulating his voice as he thought he was.

"No, but I wanted to say thank you," she said. Sam narrowed his eyes before he placed her as the only student who had successfully shielded.

"What for? Your success was your own," he said, gathering up his books, ready to leave the room.

"I'm the odd one out, just like you," Laura said.

Samuel froze. "What do you mean?"

"Everyone else on Ronah is a Grey or Light Innarn. Us, we're Dark Innarn. What you said made so much more sense than anything anyone else has. I hope you teach all my Innarn classes!" Suddenly, she darted forwards and hugged him around the middle, before rushing out of the room.

Samuel found himself stunned, returning the blade that had appeared in his hand at the child's unexpected move to the lining of his sleeve almost absently. He tried to think back to what he'd said to her and failed. Bemused, he stood by the desk for a moment longer before shaking himself and moving on to his next job for the day.

Trying to figure out how to keep War'Jan off his tail and away from the Altoriae.

Jonathan stood carefully by the side of the bed, weak limbs trembling. He steadied himself with a deep breath, but his ribs burned with a fiery pain that made him gasp aloud.

As if the noise had summoned her, Shari shifted into his lounge room, frowning at him. "What are you doing out of bed?"

Gritting his teeth, Jonathan shuffled forwards, leaving the room. "Attending to nature's call," he muttered back at her. When he was lying down, he would grumble about the many days of bedrest weakening his muscles, but as it was, it took all his energy to just move.

When he finally shuffled back into the room, eyes on the couch and spine straight only because hunching his shoulders made his ribs scream, he sensed Shari watching him. Mercifully, she waited until he was horizontal before she said anything.

"The shield training went well," she said lightly.

Jonathan slowly let out the breath he hadn't been aware he was holding in.

"Although we're down a candidate," she added, almost as an afterthought.

"Who?" Jonathan asked, shifting in the bed to try and relieve the pressure on his ribs. He gave it up as a bad joke and pushed himself upright using his Innarn.

"Wesin of Muhara," Shari said, sending flashes of Wesin's behaviour during training. "I'll not work with someone who doesn't think of others."

Struggling to keep the words trapped behind his teeth, he wondered what she'd think of working with someone whose first thought was of the nutritional value of others. She frowned at him like she'd seen a glimpse of his thoughts and he buried them, as he so frequently seemed to be doing these days.

"How did class go?" Jonathan asked.

Shari frowned and rubbed her hand across her face. Jonathan quirked the corner of his mouth, seeing her use one of his own tells. He wondered if it was intentional.

"I didn't know people did big, elaborate movements when creating shields, and the kids called me out on it. I feel a bit like a fool, I suppose."

It was Jonathan's turn to frown at her. "You aren't a fool. Some parents make elaborate movements to demonstrate to their kids what may be required when calling on a particular type of Innarn. As the child learns control, the movements become smaller and more subtle. There are very few who learn the way you did."

"Then how am I meant to teach?" she said, exasperated.

"When it came up in class today, what did you say?"

"I told them I don't care how they do it, so long as they end up with a shield," Shari said, worried now she looked back that she'd said something wrong.

"That is the perfect answer," Jonathan said, smiling at her. "Perhaps it needs a little rewording, because you do care, and saying you don't could be misconstrued."

Shari rolled her eyes. "Yeah, I guess so." Her eyes flicked to the timepiece on the wall. "I'd better get going. You need to rest up. Crista said you could start exercising tomorrow if you rest today."

Jonathan bowed his head, groaning. What he wouldn't do to be able to move freely again! But at the same time, he knew he would be in for a Realm of hurt during training with Shari tomorrow.

"Alright, I'll rest," Jonathan said, lying back as Shari gave him one last smile and slipped out the door.

Not a moment later, someone else slipped into the room, sliding along the shadows.

"Well met, Fiona," Jonathan said, his eyes still closed.

"Guardian," the scout replied, seeming unsurprised that she'd been recognised. She took up sentry position in the far corner of the room, back to the wall, but eyes able to scan the room from door to windows and back again easily.

"Aren't you meant to be resting as well?" Jonathan asked.

Fiona snorted. "Yeah, 'cause that's going to happen."

Jonathan chuckled, then hissed in pain.

"You're getting weak, letting a few busted ribs hold you down," she said. Jonathan didn't have to open his eyes to know she was looking down her nose at him.

For a long moment, he wondered if he should reply. "The next few days should be a bit quieter," he said softly. "I'll be more help if I can heal during the lull, rather than struggling to keep up now and breaking apart when the storm catches us."

"Any idea when that storm is going to hit?"

"I managed to recover the book that should tell us when, but haven't dared to look at it yet," he admitted.

"Is that the thing that feels like the deepest Dark, shrouded in shadows?" Fiona shivered, rubbing her arms.

"That'd be the one. I think I'm going to need all my strength just to be able to open it," he admitted. Neither of them mentioned the tremor in his voice.

There was an uneasy silence for a long moment that was broken by Fiona abruptly saying, "Give it to me."

"What?" Jonathan opened his eyes at last to see Fiona standing in the corner, surrounded by shadows, only her arm in the light. Her hand was outstretched as if he would place the book in it that very moment. "No, Fiona. That book is a weapon that must be handled with the utmost care."

"And you think I can't do that?" she asked, snorting in derision. "Remember who trained me? I can handle anything you send my way."

"Just because you can doesn't mean you should have to," Jonathan argued.

Fiona clenched her jaw, teeth grinding. "How important is this book?"

"It holds the key to the next attack on Lissae," Jonathan admitted.

"Lissae is always under attack," Fiona protested. "You don't need a book to know when the beings from other Realms will decide our grass is greener."

Jonathan sighed. "The next co-ordinated attack from the Dark beings."

Fiona's hand dropped limply to her side.

"The *Hekkor Mafae* contains all the information about the Dark races, including their council. It tells us when it happens, where it happens, who'll be there and what they're voting on," Jonathan rubbed a tired hand over his face.

"But... an attack like that can't possibly happen," Fiona protested.

"You were there for the aftermath of Raval," Jonathan said, "You know it can happen."

"Raval? That was only..." She broke off, and Jonathan knew that she was revisiting the site in her mind. Two years after she'd become Jonathan's scout, they'd received word of the attack. She'd visited Raval under his orders. The utter chaos and devastation that she'd seen on the once popular and thriving Realm, reducing it to cinders that still burned today, all at the hands of the largest Dark Army they'd ever encountered, still haunted her dreams.

"Raval was a practice run. And a message. The Leader of the Realm had 'insulted' War'Jan by failing to pay the required tithe to the Q'Aralide. War'Jan formally requested the Dark Council that the Realm be made to pay. The Q'Aralide are nothing if not thorough," Jonathan said.

"And terrifying, and deadly," Fiona muttered.

"War'Jan's request was granted, and an army comprised of beings from all over the Dark Realms descended on Raval and made an example of the Realm. There are very few now, who won't honour deals made with the Dark Realms," Jonathan finished.

"You think this army is heading here?" she asked.

"No, but the way our luck is going at the moment, I would prefer to make sure," he said.

"I can find someone to translate if you like?" she said.

"I've got that covered, thanks, Fiona. You need to finish healing just as much as I do," Jonathan replied.

"I am fine," she protested, "Totally healed."

"The mind needs healing just as much as the body does, Fi," he said gently.

She scowled at him. "My mind is as sharp and steady as ever," she said. Neither of them mentioned her hand trembling on the hilt of her dagger.

"There are dark days coming, Fi. I want... I *need* us both to get through them," he said softly.

"I'll get through them just fine, even if I have to drag you kicking and screaming out the other side," she snarled and slipped out the window, done with the conversation.

Jonathan found he didn't have to stretch his Innarn too far to sense the sadness and terror leaking from Fiona's eyes as she lay huddled under his windowsill.

CHAPTER TWENTY

hari caught Fiona slumped under the window, counting the blades of grass near her feet.

As she settled down beside her, Fiona flinched.

"Easy, it's just me," Shari said.

Fiona snorted. "Says one of the most dangerous beings on the Realms."

"I'm no danger to you," Shari protested.

"And I thank Lissae for that every day," Fiona said back, discreetly wiping at the dried tear tracks on her cheeks.

The corner of the Altoriae's mouth twitched, but she didn't say a word, just sat and stared off into the distance.

"Shouldn't you be at school?" Fiona asked.

"Probably," Shari said. "I think that saving the Realm is a bit of a higher priority than either teaching or my grades at the moment. I haven't been a student in class since the Islands joined."

Fiona nodded, conceding the point.

"How are you holding up?" Shari asked.

The scout glanced at Shari out of the corner of her eye. "Do you know the reason Jonathan originally asked me to be a scout?" she asked.

"Your ability to answer a question with another unrelated question?" Shari guessed with a sigh.

Fiona held out her hand and watched the shadows from the leaves above dance over her pale skin. "I can call to the shadows to cloak me. Apparently, it's rare. Some air Innarnians can do it—it's highly complicated and beings under twenty shouldn't be able to use it at all. Not for me. I was some sort of prodigy—although at the time, I only wanted to use it to win hide and seek," Fiona said with a bitter laugh. "The shadows mean that I can hide wherever the light doesn't fall. Look around, Altoriae. There are plenty of places that the light isn't falling, even now, in the middle of the day."

Shari took in the tree-covered hill around them. Shadows dappled the ground, and there were still spots of darkness under seats and near buildings. There were plenty of places for someone to get lost in, if they could use the shadows to hide.

"Now?" Fiona said, eyes still fixed on her hand as she twisted it to watch the play of shadows. For a moment, her hand flickered, as if it wasn't there, and then it was back again. Shari's eyes flew to the scout's face. Fiona was pale and panting, sweat beading on her forehead as if the effort had exhausted her.

"What happened?" Shari asked.

"When the Chirea shot me, it was like the ability to use the shadows was left in the dust where my blood soaked the ground. I don't know if I'll ever be able to use them the same way again," Fiona admitted. With a bitter, barking laugh, she added, "Some scout I'll be."

As focused on Fiona as she was, Shari still heard the tell-tale whistle of air. She shoved the scout to the side, the force of her movement dropping her to the ground as well. There was a dull *thunk* above her head and she looked up to see an arrow made of bone protruding from the wall, right where Fiona's heart would have been.

Bits and pieces clicked together in Shari's mind. The "old stories" that Jonathan had mentioned. The Chirea scout no one had been able to see. Fiona's missing abilities. Looked like they weren't just stories.

"If I needed to, how would I flush you out?" Shari hissed in Fiona's ear.

"Make the shadows disappear," Fiona hissed back. "Most beings try to use fire, but that throws up a different sort of shadow. Makes it easier to run and hide again."

Shari's eyes narrowed. She grabbed Fiona by the belts criss-crossing the front of her shirt and heaved with her air Innarn, pushing them both out of the way of the next arrow in the nick of time.

"Hide," Shari commanded, "Keep Jon safe."

Using her air Innarn she floated to her feet, her eyes fixed on the shadowy hilltop before her. Dramatically, she threw both of her arms upwards, fingers curled, palms to the sky. Lightning crackled from her fingertips, arcing from one hand to the other as she took a step forward. She straightened her fingers, and sheets of plasma danced among the treetops.

Keeping her left hand raised, Shari looked around, searching for the Chirea she knew was hiding. Calling to her short blade, Shari drew it as she stalked forwards. If the Chirea were coming to finish Fiona off to get the rest of her powers, they'd have to go through her first.

An arrow came at her, aiming for her exposed left side. Shari swivelled and knocked the arrow aside with a swipe of her sword. The Chirea drew the next arrow, seemingly unaware that the never-ending sheet lightning had exposed their position. Shari glared at the bone-clad archer before flipping her sword so she held the tip of the blade in her hand. The sheet lightning flashed as she lined up her shot. The archer met her eyes and she let the blade go. The Chirea fumbled with the arrow and tripped, trying to get out of the way. The blade landed and Shari flinched from the sight for a moment. Instead of going through a hole in the abdominal armour as she'd intended, the trip meant that the Chirea now had a gruesome pointy hat.

Shari forced herself to move forwards, cancelling the lightning with a flick of her fingers. She reached the lifeless Chirea's side and crouched down. It was almost anticlimactic, until she noticed a shadowy form rising from the Chirea's blood. Shari squinted as it rose higher. Almost at eye level, the shape started swirling around, acting as if it were confused, or looking for someone.

Tilting her head, Shari reached for Fiona instinctively, shifting her into the clearing.

"Wha..." the scout started to say. The shadowy shape zoomed towards her, and into her mouth. Fiona coughed and gagged before slumping to the floor next to the Chirea who'd attempted to take her life.

For a moment, Shari wondered if she'd done the right thing. Maybe the Chirea could use spirit Innarn differently and it was the dead archer who'd just taken over Fiona? Maybe they released a toxic gas on death, ready to hunt down the last person they'd been assigned to kill? Maybe...

Before her mind conjured even more unlikely scenarios, Fiona sat bolt upright with a gasp. "What in Vebnah's name was that?"

"I... I'm not sure," Shari admitted.

Fiona looked at the downed archer by Shari's feet and drew in a breath before disappearing.

There was silence for a second as Shari reached out with her Innarn, sensing the scout. "Fiona?" It hadn't felt like she'd shifted out.

"I'm right here... ha!" Fiona said, reappearing. She was staring at her hand. The shadows gathered over her palm again, and she vanished. "Will you look at that," said a disembodied voice.

"Would if I could," Shari quipped.

Firm arms wrapped around her middle, and Shari startled, tripping backwards. Fiona, still cloaked in shadows, kept them balanced.

"I don't know how you did it, but thank Vebnah, 'cause I'm back!" Fiona breathed. "I'm going to find where the rest of these Innarn stealers are hiding, and they'd better hope that they're far away from Lissae, Altoriae, or I'm going to make them wish they were."

Shari was released, and she heard the crunching of Fiona's steps on the fallen leaves until the only sound at the top of the hill was her ragged breathing.

Fiona slipped along the Ducibus' hallway, suppressing a relieved laugh at being able to slide through the shadows with ease again.

She made it to the doorway, nodding to the Ducibus who stood beside it. "I need to go back," she said to the silent guard.

The Ducibus she'd called Glen in her head looked at her, the features under his hood not giving away a single thought, but neither did it make a move towards the door.

Fiona sighed and rolled her head to the side. Glen blinked once, slowly enough that she could have counted the sparse lashes on each eyelid. She grinned fiercely, knowing that it meant that Glen would let her through. She may still be feeling a bit ragged around the edges, but if she was able to retrieve what she needed from her base, then she would be much better equipped to find the Chirea.

Glen looked at the door, and it swung open.

"Thank you. I'll bring you back some of those flowers you like," Fiona promised as she slipped through the doorway, breathing out frost as the door soundlessly closed behind her.

The glare of the icy terrain made her shield her eyes. Squinting, she saw the roof of her cabin in the distance. The cold didn't have a chance to seep through her Innarn-protected layers, but it did bite at her face and make the exposed skin of her hands tingle as she rubbed them together briskly. Setting off, she waded through the snow, delighting in the way it flew into pieces in the air due to her kicking boots, before settling back down to blanket the landscape again.

Reaching the door of her cabin, she let fire stream from her palms, melting the snow to get the door open. Slipping inside, she kicked the white powder from her boots and went searching for the device she was after.

A few years ago, on a scouting mission from Jonathan, she'd stumbled across an old Innarnian on a deeper Grey Realm who was sure that someone was out to get his treasures. She'd helped him create a series of diversions that he hadn't been able to manage with just one person, and in return, he'd gifted her a slate-grey slab of Crystal. It had similar properties to those that were used on Lissae, but he'd done some tinkering that meant it showed those who she was trying to track down. She was hoping that it would help the Altoriae find the Chirea without them getting wind of it first.

There it was, behind a multicoloured throw rug that she'd got from a thankful young man from Luerix who'd woven it himself.

Snatching the slab up, she raced back to the door, only to stop short at the site of Glen filling her doorway.

"What...?" she started to say, but watched, speechless, as the tip of something sharp appeared through the chest of Glen's robes. A horrid gurgling sounded, and that was all Fiona needed to move. She leaped over the couch that dominated the room and slapped a hand down hard on the low table in front of it, activating the defences that drove spikes straight out of her doorways and windows. She had three seconds to get up the stairs before she'd be cut off.

Fiona was glad that she wasn't breathing hard when she reached the top of the stairs and grabbed one of the decorative vases that lined the banister. Long ago, she'd filled them with various brews that weren't too friendly to flesh or bone, and now she was thankful for her foresight as she threw the first one behind at the Chirea who was chasing her up the stairs. It grunted at the impact. Fiona grabbed another one in each hand, shoving one beneath her cloak and sprinting towards the far end of the hallway. She had to slam through the only remaining window that had yet to have the bars come down, blocking anyone from getting in or out.

She had less than ten seconds. Directly below the bars she spotted the bone-white skull helmet of the second Chirea as it climbed the side of her wall. Fiona lobbed the vase that held the bone-dissolving brew directly at the being's back. It landed with a satisfying thud right before she hit the snowdrift.

Scurrying to regain her feet, she bolted to the doorway back to Ronah. After years of working with the Ducibus, she knew that once a Ducibus was killed, she only had three minutes to get back through the doorway before it closed off. Eventually, she'd be able to return here, but it would take a lot of convincing for the Ducibus to want to step foot where one of their own had fallen. The only consolation she would be able to offer was that she'd managed to take out two of the scum-suckers who had murdered Glen.

Her side was aching, and breathing was becoming harder as her body was no longer used to such prolonged exertion. Clearly, she needed to train more if she got out of shape this quickly.

Fiona made it to the doorway and slid through into the corridor back at the museum, hitting the wall on the other side with a hard thud. She stood on shaking legs and turned back to see the Chirea she must have hit with the bone-dissolving brew stalking towards her, its white hide gleaming in the weak sunlight. It reached a hand out just as the doorway started to flicker, indicating that the Ducibus' Innarn which held it open was failing.

The Chirea came closer still, and Fiona stepped forwards, facing her fears with narrowed eyes. "I hope you freeze," she snarled, as the scene before her faded, leaving her facing a blank wall.

By Na'reh's ghosts, she'd really liked Glen. He may not have been the most expressive or verbal of the guides, but he'd been the one assigned to the doorway of her own private pocket Realm for as long as she'd had it.

At least she'd managed to trap two of the Chirea in their own version of hell. She couldn't imagine that bone armour was very warm. By now her cabin would be all locked up, and they wouldn't have any way of getting into it. She'd only wished that the bone-dissolving brew had damaged its hide as well, but her concoctions didn't work that way. They were made to target specific things. She should have lobbed the others at the scum-suckers as well.

Pulling the slab from beneath her cloak, she grumbled at being chased away from the closest thing she'd had to a home since she started scouting for Jonathan.

The Crystal slab shimmered for a moment before showing the Chirea at the doorway, clutching its arm, which now ended in a stump. The snow by its bone-covered feet was stained dark with blood and it was swaying on the spot. When the doorway closed, it must have been trying to reach through it. Clearly the Chirea hadn't had a clue.

The other one, who'd been inside her cabin, was now lying unmoving in the snowbank outside it, two more of its comrades crouched beside the still body, heads raised, and helmets removed, showing hide even paler than the bone that covered it.

It was hard to feel sympathetic for the beings who'd just killed one of her friends. Jaw clenched, she slid the slab back into her cloak and started the long walk past all of Glen's companions, murmuring words of his bravery to them as she passed by. She wanted to stay and help the Ducibus to grieve, but knew she wouldn't be welcome. When she reached the end of the corridor, all that was left of her tears were tracks down her flushed face. Sniffing inelegantly, she strode towards the centre of town, intent on reaching the Guardian before she did anything else.

Jonathan was sitting down to eat a bowl of broth and a hunk of fresh bread beside it. Just as he lifted the first spoonful to his mouth, he heard his front door open and close. Flicking his Innarn through the house, he sensed Fiona's Innarn signature by the front door.

"Come into the kitchen," he called out, and mentally pulled another bowl from the cupboard and filled it with the broth that Arilla Dawn had prepared for him. Collis had delivered it directly to his door.

Fiona slipped into the room, her feet soundless. Sighing blissfully, she settled into the chair opposite him, and took up her spoon. She ate quickly, as though she was worried someone was going to snatch the bowl from her hands.

It reminded him of the first time he'd seen her, not long after she'd chosen to leave her parents' house. She'd discovered that living away from her family was more difficult than she'd anticipated, even on an Island as wonderful as Ronah. The challenge was more than someone of ten years had been expecting. Jonathan had offered to feed her, and she'd eaten with a speed that had rendered him so stunned, she'd slipped his own bowl out of his senseless fingers and finished his portion too before he'd had the chance to blink.

"Bad day?" he said gently.

"They killed Gl... the Ducibus who guarded my door," she said, her voice cracking.

Jonathan's shoulders fell. "Zoemer's Rocks. How did they..."

"Followed me. Must have forced him through the doorway. Killed him at the entrance to the cabin," Fiona said, bitterness evident in her voice before she cleared her throat and added, "We need to guard the Ducibus. If the Chirea go after them..."

Jonathan sent Shari a quick update. He sensed her sending a request out to the Ribeck Clan even as she scolded him for not resting. *'I'll rest if you do next time you're injured,'* he retorted.

'I'm always injured. Make that severely injured, and we've got a deal,' Shari sent back.

'Done,' he replied, then brought his focus back to Fiona, who was on her second bowl of broth, his bread mysteriously absent. He grinned at her fondly.

She raised her eyebrows at him. "Don't you want to know why I went to the cabin?"

"I figured that you'd tell me anyway," Jonathan said easily, levitating more bread out of his pantry and onto his plate.

"This," Fiona said, draining the bowl in one last gulp, and pulling a slab of grey Crystal from her cloak.

"What is that?" he asked, frowning so hard, his eyes ached.

"It lets you see anyone you concentrate on. You just touch it with bare skin. Like this," she said, laying a hand along the edge and drawing forth the image of three Chirea, one lying prone in the snow with a comrade on each side, all three seemingly frozen solid. The only indication that it wasn't a picture was the snow falling, slowly burying the trio.

Jonathan's eyebrows rose and he reached out and stroked a finger along the side of the slab. The image shifted to show Shari in a heated discussion with Gideon Ribeck, who was nodding and looking at the Altoriae as if she was the best thing in the world.

Fiona made a rude noise. Jon grinned at her. He knew that she contributed as much to Shari's success in foiling most of the attacks on Lissae as he did. As a scout, she was relegated to the background, preferring the shadows to the spotlight. He knew that Fiona was aware, through her years of observation, that the Altoriae wasn't a fan of the spotlight either. She also knew that wouldn't stop half the population of Lissae fawning over the girl. Fiona's hand flittered up to the clasp that held her cloak together. It was a silvery leather badge shaped to look like a fawn. It was her only piece of adornment, and the final gift that her mother had given her.

"Do you remember the Chirea leader?" Jonathan asked.

Making another rude noise, Fiona laid her hand on the side of the slab again.

There was a swirl of yellow before his face came into focus. He was scowling at something. His mouth appeared to be moving, but Fiona found that she couldn't read his lips due to the skull he was using as a helmet. Frustrated, she backed away from him, hoping to glean any information about where he was.

The image refocused, and in the background, there was an instantly recognisable mountain range.

Jonathan hissed in a breath. "Is that the Niverwell Ranges?"

Fiona hummed in agreement.

"But that means that the Chirea may be working with the Harvvens," Jonathan said, aghast.

"Not just that," Fiona said, arching a brow.

Jonathan blinked a few times, putting his slow realisation down to the fact that he was still healing. "We know where they are."

His scout grinned at him.

'*Shari!*' Jonathan sent out, '*We've found the Chirea!*'

Gideon Ribeck was looking at her like she'd created the sun and moons. He'd sought her out under the pretence that he required pointers on his earth shield, but had done little more than make eyes at her since she'd started talking.

'*Shari!*' Jonathan sent out. '*I've found the Chirea!*'

"Excuse me." Shari turned away from Gideon. '*Where?*' she sent back to Jonathan.

'*On Iabovar, about sixteen clicks from Niverwell Ranges,*' Jonathan sent back.

'*Gotcha,*' Shari said with a fierce grin. She was familiar with Iabovar, and confident that she knew the rough area where the Chirea were camped, after seeing the image in Jonathan's head.

'*Shar...*' Jonathan sent as she shifted away. '*Ri, don't go in without—Oh, for Adeon's sake! Get back here!*' Jonathan sent. His fury burned at her senses through their mental link.

'*Just having a quick look. Now hush,*' Shari sent back.

There was a brief grumbling in the back of her mind before she slipped through the trees to try and get a closer glimpse of the place where the Chirea had holed up.

As always, the silhouette of the Niverwell Ranges was breathtaking. The whistling that was caused by air rushing through tiny holes in the mountains was muted at a distance, but still made tears well in Shari's eyes. Local legends said the whistling was due to the souls of the departed trying to contact their living relatives. The romantic side of Shari thought that was beautiful, but the practical side knew the static build-up of two Elements crashing together was actually the cause of the hair raising on the back of her neck.

"Boo," said a deep voice from behind her.

Or it could be because someone was trying to sneak up on her.

She let out a noise of distress but refused to jump. A heavy hand came down on her shoulder, causing her knees to buckle under the weight.

"I think you should come with me," the voice said. The hand increased pressure on her shoulder, forcing her to turn and march farther into the trees, away from the Chirea camp.

As she was forced along, Shari sent out her Innarn in a vain attempt to get a sense of her captor. Due to all the Innarn in the air, it was difficult for her to achieve a lock on him.

He led her deeper into the trees, until eventually she spotted a vibrant green flickering through the red leaves. They got closer to the flickering, and just as Shari had decided to take herself out of her captor's care, beings of all races started dropping down from the surrounding trees. She was given a huge push and thrust into the clearing where the green flickering was strongest.

"Well, I'm glad that I spread word as to what you looked like," said a familiar voice. "Or we'd be enjoying some roast Lissaen right about now."

Shari grinned. "You could try," she said.

Yessna purred, "It would be a good fight. I wondered how long it would be before you arrived."

"Had a bit going on. Sorry I'm late," Shari said flippantly.

The second in charge of the U'sala looked at her with wide eyes. "You do not seem very sorry yet."

"Ignore her. She's had her whiskers in a twist for a week now," grumbled Jeran. The tripodal Wikkur stomped out of a tent, a long-range projectile weapon strapped to one side of his belt. "We did expect you here a wee bit sooner though, lass."

"I really did get held up," Shari protested. She wasn't about to tell the leader of the U'sala all the issues that had occurred since the last time they'd met.

"Humph. Never mind. You're here now, so we can attack," he said decisively.

"I'm sorry, what?"

"Those Chirea scum are working their way across the Realms. Last month, something changed an' they made a beeline right to your doorstep. This is their base camp. Took three years and scores of my best to track the ruddy thing down. But with you here, we finally have the chance to attack and do some damage," Jeran said.

Shari blinked, and opened her mouth, but closed it again, lost for words.

"I think the healer needs sustenance first, Jeran," Yessna interrupted smoothly. "And perhaps a debrief?"

"Fine, fine. Not that there's much taste in the sustenance around here. Bloody tree-sucking, leaf-biting..." his grumbles followed him into the tent, cutting off as the flap fell closed.

Yessna beckoned her forward towards the green fire in the middle of the rather impressive camp. It was ringed by a group of tents as red and mottled as the leaves around them. Beings of all races were ducking in and out of the tents, casually carting all manner of weapons around. They passed a couple of groups who were fighting in soundproof bubbles, which Shari studied with unabashed curiosity, trying to pick the fighting styles and abilities that came from so many different Realms. She lost count.

"Is this all of the U'sala?" she asked Yessna as the Ferah led her closer to the fire.

"Hardly," Yessna snorted. "This is about a quarter of our forces. Some are on clean-up detail in other Realms that the Chirea have hit. These are mostly our crack troops. We have been slowly preparing for battle against the Chirea but wanted your input once we had confirmation that they had infiltrated Lissae."

"Why me? How did you know?" Shari asked, just as her gaze fell on an odd-looking skull. It took her a moment to realise that the reason it looked so odd was that there was another skull within it. The top one had been offset in such a way that if you were to take a quick glance, you might mistake the whole setup as a creature that had teeth around a full half of its face.

"Ah. I, uh, think you need to work on your decorating a little bit." Shari would never understand the desire to view the deceased within the walls of your own dwelling.

Yessna snorted. "You have fought these beings more than once. We have lost many to them, and none have been able to return with their mind still enough their own to tell us of the Chirea's weaknesses or strategies."

Shari took a seat on a log and sighed. Resting her elbows on her knees, she gratefully took a cup from Yessna. Sniffing the drink within, Shari sighed again. Spice, honey, and some sort of citrus tang. With the sizzle of flaming fat falling from the haunch on the spit above the fire punctuating her words, Shari took a sip of her drink before she began to tell the second in command of the U'sala what she knew.

"You mean the Chirea have soul-stealer arrows? How? They're a Q'Aralide creation!"

"I don't know. It's more than a bit concerning though." A plate of fire-roasted root vegetables was handed to her, and Shari took it gratefully. "We know the removal of even a single bone from their armour causes intense damage to them. It isn't helpful unless we can figure out how to utilise it on a large scale during battle."

Taking out a knife, Yessna cut off a hunk of the meat from the spit. Remembering the Chirean skull, Shari shook her head swiftly, and the Ferah laughed at her. "What would you do if you did not have to fight the bone warriors?"

Refraining from a biting comment, Shari said, "We're in the middle of testing for the Guardian's new apprentice."

Another of the U'sala sat heavily on the log next to Yessna, the green fire making the blue skin of his bare chest look sickly, despite the muscles on his muscles. The opened purple robe seemed to catch the light of the fire as he carved a chunk of meat off and bit into it.

The second in command rolled her eyes. "Altoriae, meet Kodan of the U'sala. Kodan, mind your manners, you tuzar's arse."

"You're one to talk. She doesn't even have any meat!" Kodan leaned forwards, long silver hair swinging dangerously close to the flames. "Altoriae, would you care for some roasted ruzayra?"

"No, thank you, Kodan."

The silver-haired U'sala flashed her a smile and sat back on his log, flicking his mane behind his pointed ears.

"What's this about an apprentice?"

"The Guardian of Lissae is testing for an apprentice at the moment." Shari popped the last of the roasted vegetables in her mouth and sighed in contentment.

"And does the apprentice get to work with you?" Kodan lowered his voice and leaned forwards, the muscles of his arms flexing under the sleeveless robe.

Jeran stomped up behind her, preventing her from having to answer. "What are we waiting for? If we burn away the sinew holding their armour together, we should be able to drop platoons at a time. We're ready whenever you lot have finished stuffing your faces."

Blinking, Shari hardly believed her luck. *Being asked to fight alongside the U'sala? How could she say no to that?*

'No. *Just like that,*' Jonathan sent her. She choked on air and started coughing violently, hardly the image of a seasoned warrior. Jeran was looking at her, concerned, while she had a sneaking suspicion that Yessna knew what was going on, judging by her smirk.

'*Did you forget that you had a link open?*' Jonathan asked, mild amusement evident in his tone.

'No,' Shari sent back. "Went down the wrong way, sorry," she gasped aloud, gratefully accepting a cup from Kodan, who gave her a devastatingly charming smile.

"Humans," said Jeran, "Full of design flaws, you lot are. What were the Weavers thinking of, putting breathing and eating pipes so close together?"

Shari took a sip to ease her stinging throat.

'*Come back, Shari,*' Jonathan sent. '*Fiona has been searching around for more Chirea, and I think we've found an issue.*'

'*How urgent is this issue?*' she asked.

'*Middling,*' he replied.

'*Then I can lend a hand here until it becomes urgent, yes?*'

His mental sigh reverberated around her skull, but he sent a begrudging agreement to her plan. '*Keep the link open,*' he reminded her.

'*Of course,*' she sent back with a roll of her eyes.

"So, how do you need my help?" Shari asked, finishing her drink, and putting the cup down.

Jeran grinned, and Kodan rubbed his hands together in glee.

Less than ten minutes later, the whole camp was packed up, and the U'sala were edging through the trees, feet silent on the forest floor, bodies cloaked in shields Shari had specially conjured for them.

They arrived at the edge of the forest, Shari counting her breaths as the rest of the U'sala moved into place. Smoke from the camp tickled her nose as she watched the beings who'd tried to kill her grandfather. The Chirea camp was full to bursting, with lots of chattering reaching her ears and warriors bustling between structures, but she couldn't shake the sensation that something was off about the whole setup.

Frowning at the camp for a long minute, she turned to Yessna and asked, "Where are the guards?" She used the Veti Cant to sign. It was something that all the U'sala were familiar with.

Out of the corner of her eye, she saw the issue.

The camp was empty.

Shari straightened her spine in realisation. Whoever had done the illusion was amazingly talented. She faced the camp again, but now she knew the truth, she saw the slight blur around the edges of the Chirea as they moved around, and tasted the slight tang that came with Innarn-created scents.

Swiftly, she signed to Yessna, who signed to Kodan, who signed to the next U'sala and the next, until the whole U'sala crack force who'd surrounded the camp knew what was going on.

"That is why there are no guards," Yessna said bitterly.

Shari scowled at the camp, strangely disappointed that she wouldn't be able to introduce some of the Chirea to the afterlife. Standing up, she strode forwards, not worrying about stealth any longer. She paused for a moment to detect the Innarn that had created such an elaborate illusion. She pushed with her own Innarn, and it shattered just as Yessna called out a warning.

Too late.

As the illusion shattered, so did the bars that made up the cage that held some of the Realms' most dangerous creatures. A herd of fulni.

"Not again," Shari muttered, drawing the blade that Yessna had gifted her. The Ferah grinned at the Altoriae carrying her blade, fangs flashing and eyes sparkling in delight.

"Let's make sure these feseor stay extinct!" Kodan said, wading into the fray.

CHAPTER TWENTY-ONE

What had Jonathan expected the Altoriae to do? Wait?

Fiona gave the Guardian an incredulous look as he grumbled to himself after Shari shifted out. Surely as Guardian, he knew the girl better than that. She did, and she'd only heard anecdotal stories and met her a handful of times.

Finally, he started to tidy up the kitchen while Fiona set to work seeing if she could find if there were any other Chirea on Lissae.

She caught sight of two, both of whom were in relatively easy-to-contain spaces on Rakemyst. Frowning, she wondered where the other Chirea were. Surely, they wouldn't leave behind just two scouts? Well, six, if you counted the frozen ones stuck in her pocket Realm. Six was not a lot to leave behind. Pushing harder, the scene on the slab changed, and she caught her breath.

"Jonathan," she whimpered.

His head snapped up and he hurried towards her, breath escaping him in a rush when he saw what was on the slab.

The Chirea were marching through the Ducibus' hall.

Jonathan frantically started shifting people out of the Chirea's way and into Castle Bachelor until they were able to come up with a better plan. Fiona kept an eye on the Chirea's forces, beads of sweat dotting her brow as she watched more and more of the bone warriors marching through the wide-open doorway. She hoped that the Ducibus were somewhere safe, because she couldn't see them in the hall at all.

What if they... what if the Chirea... Panic clawed at her throat, and her vision started to go black around the edges. She grabbed her wrist with her free hand, trying to focus on her pulse, but it was thready, and it seemed like there was a thick blanket between her fingers and her skin. Her breath caught in her throat, and her limbs just seemed to go weak, like her bones had been dissolved.

Gasping for air, she was sure there wasn't enough in the room. She stood, trying to reach the back door. There'd be air outside, right? But her legs failed to hold her up, and she collapsed beside the bench, elbows clattering against it so hard, she'd have bruises later.

Her vision narrowed even farther, spots now dancing in the blackness, and her mind shut down totally when large hands wrapped around her biceps and pulled her upright.

Breath coming in heaving gasps, Fiona slowly regained her sense of self and found that she was bundled in a thick, warm blanket, lying on Jonathan's lounge, not quite sure how she'd gotten there. She was safe. Closing her eyes, she fought to find her centre.

When she felt ready, Fiona's gaze landed on Jonathan's white face. Figuring there would be little chance to rest with the Chirea around, she rose shakily to her feet.

Jonathan made a noise of protest, and holding a hand up, she gritted her teeth and said, "The best way to stop the gozochas in my head is to face them."

The Guardian paused, and she knew that he desperately wanted to say something, but thankfully, he refrained.

As she drew in a shaky breath, Fiona's skin felt too old for her bones. She kept her eyes on the flickering flames in the fireplace across from her, but out of the corner of her eye, she saw Jonathan's head snap up.

"They've reached the bridge," he said.

Eyes widening, chin quivering slightly, Fiona steeled her nerves. "Go. I'll be along soon."

Looking as if he wanted to reassure her, he hesitated, before nodding and shifting out.

On Rakemyst's side of the bridge, there was a veritable army ready to face the Chirea who stood on Ronah.

As Jonathan looked at the horde before him, their bone armour clicking as they moved, Samuel came to stand by his side.

"There is something not right about this," Samuel said in his ear. "The Chirea would not attack in this fashion."

"They're noted for their full-frontal attacks. So what exactly do you mean?" Jonathan said, his crossbow at the ready.

"This unnecessarily puts the lives of many at risk. The Chirea prefer a guaranteed outcome, and this battle is not guaranteed. There are too many variables, and they're in a weak position, flanked on both sides. I don't like this," Samuel muttered.

"If it gives us the advantage, I like it just fine," Jonathan said, raising his crossbow as the first of the Chirea started to cross the bridge.

Others around them raised their weapons and readied their Innarn, but before anyone got off a shot, Samuel shouted out, "Wait!"

Ears ringing, Jonathan considered jabbing his elbow into his visitor's gut, but refrained.

"Why?" he growled.

"Look at their outline," Samuel insisted.

Jonathan grumbled, but did as he was told. Squinting and pushing his glasses up his nose, he finally understood what Sam had seen. The slight blur around the Chirea, the clicking armour sounding muffled, and finally, the majority of Ronah's residents on the far side of the Chirea, taking aim at them.

Hastily, he threw up a shield right in the middle of the bridge. Innarn blasts hit it from both sides, and the Chirea army disappeared as if they'd never been there.

Beings on both sides stood around, shocked, trying to come to grips with the disappearing army.

Jonathan looked at Samuel. "This is an awfully big drawcard, isn't it?"

"Got everyone down here and away from the towns," Samuel said with a nod.

"Leaving our most vulnerable citizens ripe for the taking," Jonathan said bitterly. He broadcasted an order to immediately shift back to the towns and ensure that everyone was safe.

Of course, that meant he sent to Shari as well, without really meaning to.

She appeared by his side. "What'd I miss?" she asked, puffing out a breath to get the hair off her face. Sweaty and smudged with dirt, it looked like she'd found her own set of troubles.

"Chirea staged a big illusion to get everyone here. We're thinking that they may be attacking the towns," Samuel said.

"Or my grandfather's place," Shari said, twisting her mouth. She grabbed fistfuls of their shirts, and shifted them directly into SilverCloud's office, only to slump between them, her eyes locked onto her grandfather.

Samuel looked down and almost dropped Shari completely. The golden tip of the soul-stealer arrow was sticking out of her chest. He looked at Jonathan, horror clear on his face.

Shari gasped, a wet, sickly noise, eyes wide.

Jonathan snapped his head to the other side of the room in time to see a Chirea start sprinting towards them. Without thinking, he shifted Shari to another room, and summoning all his concentration, he used his Innarn to pull a steel blade from the floor of SilverCloud's office, swinging it and delivering a stunning blow to the charging Chirea.

The bone warrior landed, limbs akimbo on the floor, a massive gash in its abdominal armour. Jonathan smiled viciously and took up a protective stance in front of a stunned SilverCloud.

Arilla looked up, stunned as Shari and Ronah's newcomer, Samuel, landed in the room next to her. Shari made a horrid noise and Arilla dropped the glass she was holding, hurrying over to her daughter.

"What...?" she started to ask.

"Touch... touch the arrow," Samuel told her, his voice thick.

Looking down, she spotted the gold arrow sticking out of her daughter's chest. "Shari!"

"Do it!" Samuel said, his voice hoarse. "If you don't, I will. Please." He dragged his gaze away from the glinting tip and locked them onto Arilla. "Hurry," he begged, eyes golden in the dimming light.

Tentatively, Arilla reached out and touched the arrow, surprised that it wasn't covered in blood. As soon as her skin encountered it, a burning sensation ran up her arm and through her body, the pain causing her to cry out, head tipped back, and eyes screwed shut from the onslaught of feedback her nerves were sending her.

"Got it," Samuel said, although he sounded a long, long way away.

Shari gasped wetly, and Arilla forced her eyes open. Her baby was hurt again. She never wanted to see her little girl like this, blood and some colourless fluid rushing out of her in a seemingly never-ending stream. Some instinct made her raise her hands, green light pouring out of them and surrounding Shari.

As the glow from around her daughter disappeared, Samuel held out his hand to her. Not really understanding why, Arilla grasped him tightly. He eased Shari down to the floor and held onto her hand as well. He started chanting in a language that Arilla didn't recognise as she sank to her knees beside them, eyes on her daughter's ashen form. Outside in the hall, the fighting started to sound more muted the longer that Samuel chanted.

An age or a minute later—it felt like both—Samuel gasped out one last, guttural word.

Arilla screamed.

Shari's eyes snapped open, her free hand coming up to grab another of those horrid golden arrows barely a breath away from Samuel's chest.

The trio turned to look at the Chirea in the doorway, bow notched and ready to take another shot. Its eyes went wide underneath the skull helmet and it backed out of the room, clearly not ready to take them on.

Rising shakily to their feet, Arilla found that she almost missed the fire that had been coursing through her veins before.

"What happened?" Shari asked, sounding as if she hadn't had a drink for weeks.

Arilla could sense the quick back and forth between the two, but she couldn't keep her eyes off her daughter.

Shari was rather animated as she sent to Samuel, her face going pale, her eyebrows raising, her mouth open in disbelief before she closed her eyes and the shutter came down.

"Keep my mother safe," she said aloud as she dropped Samuel's hand and started towards the entrance of the room.

"Shari..." Samuel said.

"I mean it, Sam. If even a hair is so much as out of place, you're out of the running as apprentice. Keep her safe," she said, and darting back, she delivered a quick kiss onto Arilla's cheek before turning and jogging out of the room.

Samuel groaned and slapped a hand over his face. Arilla grinned and walked away, but forgot that he still had hold of her hand.

"Oh no. You aren't going anywhere," he growled at her.

Smirking at him, she raised her hand and scuffed it through her hair, tangling it. Narrowing his eyes, he growled at her, before he pulled her roughly into his arms.

Arilla started to squirm out of his grasp, but it suddenly felt like she was spread thin. She was everywhere at the same time, her molecules fragmented all over Lissae. Trying to latch onto something familiar to stop the weird feeling, she ran her eyes over the room.

She was somewhere she'd never been before.

"Did you just shift with me?" Arilla gasped, pushing away from Samuel.

He grunted in the affirmative.

"Huh." She'd always wondered what shifting was like, and now she'd done it, she wasn't too keen on a repeat. Hastily, she patted herself down to make sure that she was still in one piece.

"Stay here," he growled at her, and moved away from the furniture, ready to shift out of the room.

"But my hair's mussed up," she said, grinning at him.

Groaning, he slapped something onto the wooden table and shifted away.

Arilla bounced lightly on her toes. She fairly buzzed with energy. Running around the whole Realm wouldn't tire her out! Looking around the room, it seemed quite bland and boring. There were no windows, and no door. It was lit by harsh, artificial lights that reminded her a bit of her childhood before they'd had crystal lights installed.

The walls and ceiling were compacted dirt, but the room was quite sizable. The furniture was all rough-hewn wood, and it looked as if someone who wasn't quite skilled had put it together. There was a pallet bed, a dresser, and a table. Sitting innocuously on the table was a brush.

Grinning, Arilla picked it up and brushed her hair, moving to sit on the surprisingly comfortable bed. Her arms became tired and her eyelids drooped before she was even half done, and she tipped over and fell asleep as her head hit the pillow.

Tania skittered to a stop in an archway of Zana's garden and gaped. Rakemyst's Linked was floating above the ground, wings gently fluttering in the twister of air that surrounded her, leaves and flowers twining around her, her hair wisps in the breeze.

Closing her jaw with a snap, Tania said, "Uh, Zana, I wondered if I could get your help?"

Zana lazily opened her eyes, staring at Tania from below her half-lids. "I am helping," Zana said, her voice a melody that spoke of ages.

"Rakemyst needs defending," Tania said, frowning.

"I am lending strength, little one," Zana said, and her eyes slid closed.

For a moment, Tania stood in the archway, surprise and frustration playing across her features. Hands still clenched into fists, she sighed and asked Ronah to shift her away. If Zana wouldn't help, she would have to work twice as hard.

Arriving at Ronah's side of the bridge, Tania took her position, and was surprised to find Alistair stepping up next to her.

"What are you doing?" she snapped.

Alistair didn't flinch from her harsh tone. "I'm protecting Ronah and my family. Just like you."

Taking in his serious expression, Tania wondered what the Realm was coming to when a boy was more likely to step up than Rakemyst's own Linked.

Snorting, she focused on the other side of the bridge and readied herself for the battle to come.

Sam shifted back to Jonathan's side in time to deflect a blow aimed at the Guardian's back. They worked together to drive the Chirea from the room. Sam found that his arms were straining and limbs trembling after using such a massive amount of effort in order to transfer Shari's stolen Innarn from her mother back to her.

"What are you doing here?" Jonathan asked, panting.

"Saving your thick skull, as always," Sam snarked back.

"Where's Shari?" Jonathan asked, readying his sword as another Chirea came in the door, yelling.

"She's around here somewhere," he replied, flicking a knife into the miniscule gap between two ribs that were wrapped around the second Chirea's chest.

"Somewhere?" Jonathan snarled, pulling his blade out of a Chirea's stomach, and slicing down into her unprotected thigh.

"Well, she left the room after I—Stay still, Chirean. I'm trying to hit you!—After I healed her. Gotcha!" Sam crowed as the third Chirea went down.

"You healed her? But it was a soul stealer!" Jonathan said, ducking as his eighth opponent took a wild swing and ended up run through from groin to neck by the Guardian's sword.

"Who do you think made them?" Samuel growled.

"Well, I'd sure like to know, so I can kick their arse. That hurt," Shari said as she skittered into the room.

Sam's lips clamped shut. No way was he owning up to making the thrice-damned thing now. A few millennia ago, he'd made the soul-stealer arrows on War'Jan's orders. Of course, to cover his own hide, he'd made a ritual to counteract the effect of the arrow and because of that, his mate had become an outcast, banished from the clan. Gritting his teeth, he let loose a veritable storm of throwing knives at the next wave of intruders.

"What I'd like to know," Shari said, only his keen ears picking up the hint of a gasp, "is why you are here and not with my mother?"

"I put her somewhere safe. No one knows where she is but me, and I'm the only one who can get her back," he said, using the blockage of bodies at the door to take a breath.

Amara skittered into the hallway outside the room, her eyes going wide as she spotted them inside. "Altoriae, the biggest Chirea I've ever seen is heading right for your grandfather!"

Shari's eyes were large in her still pale face. Even as she reached out with her Innarn, she gathered Jon, Sam, and Amara and shifted them to her grandfather's side, just in time for a lumbering brute, covered head to toe in bone, to come into view. From the image Fiona had shown her, this had to be Luttrell, leader of the Chirea.

The most massive Chirea Amara had ever seen sized them up from across the clearing. More and more Chirea strode out of the forest and stood beside him. Amara edged to the side, not wanting to burn anyone in her group. Other candidates arrived to surround SilverCloud. The fear emanating off the Elder and the Guardian left a nasty taste at the back of her mouth. The thought of this being a test was squashed before it could fully form. She doubted that they'd bring in beings as dangerous as the Chirea for a mere trial.

The big Chirea took a step forwards, and Amara pulled a dagger out of the sheath strapped to her thigh. For every step the Chirea made, Amara moved closer to the edge of the group, hoping that she'd be able to round on him and take him out from behind.

"You killed my son," the big Chirea growled. "Washed him out of the trees and thought no more about it."

"And in return, you've killed my people," SilverCloud said. "I never saw your son, in the trees or on the ground."

"Liar!" he roared, stepping closer still. Amara found herself hemmed in, the other candidates unintentionally blocking her way to the fringes of the group. She couldn't get them to move without making a scene, so she started moving back to where she'd been before.

"My son died," the Chirea said, his voice breaking. "He was beloved by his people. By *me*."

"How many sons have you killed to avenge him? How many daughters? Husbands? Wives? Brothers? Sisters? All of whom were beloved by their people. And yet, still you aren't satisfied," SilverCloud countered.

"Fancy words, birdman," he snarled, and drew a massive bone sword from the sheath at his waist. "I won't be satisfied until every last stinking Innarnian is lying dead at my feet," he growled, and started running forwards.

Amara gasped, and struggled to get closer to Elder Dawn. To do what, she wasn't quite sure, but she didn't want to see him die. Others were readying their Innarn and trying to call their weapons forward when the leader of the Chirea was only a few steps away.

Amateurs, she thought, and then, to her mortification, she tripped over Therdon's outstretched foot and stumbled forwards, thrusting her arm into the air so she wouldn't stab someone.

The blade pierced into something, and she grabbed hold of it with her other hand. The smooth, worn bone under her fingers made her eyes go wide.

Black blood was pouring down her arm and dripping off her elbow onto the ground below. Horrified, she gazed into the surprised face of the big Chirea. Her dagger, buried to the hilt high in his thigh, was pushing apart two bones of his armour. The blade barely fit in the gap. Pulling it out with a gasp, Amara scurried away from him.

The Chirea ineffectively slapped a bone-covered hand over the wound. He staggered forwards, swinging wildly with his sword before he slumped to his knees in a growing pool of blood.

"Luttrell!" A Chirea from the other side of the clearing screamed. Their forces swarmed closer, tripping each other up in the attempt to get to their leader.

The big guy staggered to his feet, disorientation clear on his face, and turned to face his comrades. He took two giant, staggering steps, before he collapsed face down and didn't move again.

Shari rushed forwards, hands glowing green, seemingly intent on trying to heal the Chirean leader.

"Luttrell!" came the mournful cry from the army across the clearing.

The Altoriae fell to her knees when the Chirea let loose the most soul-breaking sound Amara had ever heard.

Clamping her hands over her ears did little to deafen the noise. It did, however, give her a headache when she clocked herself with the hilt of her own dagger.

Without warning, the sound cut off. Amara opened her eyes, unaware she'd closed them. The Chirea on the other side of the clearing were gone.

The candidates and the Ilutri stood around for a moment, shocked. The silent clearing erupted into cheers and she was hoisted into the arms of her fellow candidates and held above their heads as they celebrated her accidental victory.

Blood coating her arm, her dagger pointed to the sky so she didn't stab at any of the hands that were bouncing her around, Amara found that she didn't know if she should laugh or cry.

The residents of Rakemyst and Ronah cheered their victory, despite the current of unease that was running through the crowd. It had been so easy for the Chirea to almost get them to fire on each other. Only the quick thinking of the Guardian had stopped them. In spite of their victory, the mood on both sides of the bridge was despondent, and people were refusing to look at each other.

Collis Iuvo strode forwards, long strides eating up the ground until he stood in the middle of the bridge, where he sank down and folded his legs. Closing his eyes, he started projecting thoughts of happy times he'd shared with others until his memories burst from him in silver wisps, dancing and laughing.

Residents of Ronah and Rakemyst slowly looked up at the noise, some frowning at the daring of the young Returned until others dropped to the ground, their own joyful memories joining the ones Collis displayed.

A wispy girl with a flaring skirt danced in circles next to a boy drawing an arrow. An old lady was whittling next to a man bent low, his fingers digging into the soil. A palon raced along the ground, snapping playfully at the heels of a tall girl who stretched up to greet the sun.

Slowly, the mood of the crowd changed, and as the happy memories were shared, the guilt and frustration that the battle had caused began to bleed into the mix, until apologies and forgiveness were offered and received. Happy, silly memories took over again, and the residents of the two Shifting Islands took the afternoon to enjoy the peace while they could.

CHAPTER TWENTY-TWO

"So," Shari said to Sam as she watched the others celebrating, "when are you going to bring my mother back?"

"I'll get her now and meet you in SilverCloud's office?" Sam said, swaying slightly on his feet.

Shari nodded and shifted Jonathan and her grandfather back to his office, anxiously waiting for her mother to arrive. She sent her father an update, and sensed him getting closer.

Sam arrived at the same time Calem did, with Arilla cradled carefully in his arms. He passed her to Calem and stumbled over to sink down into a chair.

"Want to explain?" Shari said, nudging his foot with her own.

Running a trembling hand over his face, he nodded. "The soul-stealer arrow has a counter curse, if you will. Many years ago, I happened on the counter, and knew that if a Blank like Arilla would touch the arrow and then willingly give up the Innarn back to Shari, I would be able to enact it. Under ideal circumstances, it takes a lot out of the caster, and with the battle going on, it wasn't quite as ideal as I'd have liked."

"I don't understand," Arilla said weakly.

Sam sighed. "For a moment, you held Shari's Innarn. You even used it when you healed her. But I took it out of you and put it back in Shari."

Shari blinked at him. She'd never heard of any being having the powers to do something like that. It almost seemed unnatural, but the lack of Innarn was just like when she'd been on Xaviour with Yessna. The rush of it coming back was just like coming home.

"After you gave it back to Shari, it was like I was a kid coming down from a sugar high," Arilla admitted, snuggling deeper into Calem's arms.

"Your body isn't used to Innarn. Essentially, I suppose you were," Jon theorised.

"How could you shift with her?" Calem asked.

"There's a... residue, for lack of a better word, that means for the next few days, an Innarnian will be able to shift with Arilla," he said, and added in a grumble that Shari was able to pick up only because she was standing right next to him, "as well as do all the other tricks that you lot like so much."

"I have to say, shifting is not all it's cracked up to be," Arilla grumbled. "It feels like I'm being spread like fine jam over all of Lissae."

"Yeah, it kind of does sometimes," Shari said. "I suppose it depends on who you're shifting with."

"Well, I've got two legs, and I'm quite happy to use them to get to where I need to go," Arilla said with a grin.

"Do you think that we've succeeded in stopping the Chirea from coming back?" Calem asked, bringing the mood of the room down.

"No, I don't think so. If their revenge for the leader's son was wiping us all out, I think their revenge for their leader is going to be much worse," Jon said.

"Well, as horrible as that is, we can still take a breather while they regroup," Arilla reminded them.

"True," Shari said, her gaze on her grandfather, who'd been surprisingly quiet the whole time. SilverCloud grinned at her, but it didn't reach his eyes. Shari couldn't help but worry about him as he tipped his cup at her and took a sip.

Later that night, Shari walked into Ronah's town square and saw the candidates were all there, surrounded by the Ilutri and townsfolk from Ronah alike.

Amara, the Daen who'd saved the day, was half hidden in the shadows cast by the new shade coverings Tania had created.

"Not big on parties?" Shari asked, sliding in next to her.

"Me? Not really," Amara said, sipping from the drink she held loosely in her hand.

"How are you after today?"

Shrugging one shoulder, Amara took a bigger gulp of her drink. "Every time I close my eyes, I see his blood dripping down my arm. If I look into the mirror, I see it splattered on my face. How am I? Glad to be here, certainly, but a mess at the moment. A proper mess."

"That's how I feel most days, to be honest," Shari admitted. "It helps, you know, to talk to someone about it. It doesn't do any good to keep feelings like that bottled up inside."

Amara took another drink. "I'll... I'll think about it. It feels... raw. Like the painful edge of a wound."

"Trust me, I know," Shari murmured.

Tania slipped in on Amara's other side. "There are way too many people here," the younger girl said, her eyes wide.

Shari and Amara both laughed, a slightly bitter tinge to the sound.

"They're celebrating the win, not knowing that the battle is far from over yet," Shari said.

"You think they'll be back?" Amara asked.

"Revenge is something the Chirea live for. They practically breathe it," Shari said, taking the drink that Tania offered her. "They'll be back."

Groaning, Amara tipped her head to look up at the shade coverings. "I know that being the apprentice to the Guardian is a difficult, dangerous job, but I think I'm only now beginning to appreciate exactly how much danger I'll be in if I'm chosen."

"I wish you'd tell my brother that. He thinks it's a duty, or that it'll all be fun and games and accolades when he saves the day," Tania grumbled.

"Your brother is a candidate?" Amara asked.

"Alistair is the Guardian's candidate," Shari said, ignoring the face that Tania pulled.

"I didn't see him in the clearing with the other candidates," Amara said, frowning as she struggled to recall the mousy boy being there.

"He wasn't; he was guarding Ronah's side of the bridge with me," Tania said.

"Were any of the other candidates there?" Shari asked.

"Talofa, Raven, and Ness were," Tania replied. "Although Raven doesn't seem to be much of a team player."

Shari nodded, absentmindedly fiddling with her cup. "Are all of the candidates here tonight?"

"Hold on," Tania said. She blinked slowly a few times. "Yes, although Sam is hiding in the shadows on the other side of the square."

'Jon, all the candidates are in the square.' Shari sent, gritting her teeth.

'Excellent. Time to announce the trial then,' he sent back.

Doing her best not to groan, Shari sent back an affirmative, and readied herself for Jonathan's entrance.

A few minutes later, the bustling crowd seemed to move as one to the far side of the square. Shari watched, a small smirk on her lips, as the candidates descended on the Guardian. Suddenly, she gave a yelp and disappeared from her comfortable hiding spot, arriving at Jonathan's side.

'Not *nice*,' she grumbled at him.

Biting back a smile, Jonathan called out, "Well met, candidates!"

"Well met!" they all but screamed back, high on victory and survival.

"I have come to announce that the official testing for my apprentice will begin in two days' time," he said, his voice modified so that it filled every corner of the square. "Remember, the last candidate standing in each round will be one of the finalists up for consideration as my apprentice," he added. *'I feel like one of the Silverstone Clan,'* he sent to Shari, his thoughts giddy.

She giggled quietly as the candidates were chattering and sending loudly among themselves for a moment but quietened down when they realised that Jon had more to say.

"In the first trial, the candidates will face off with one of the most difficult to defeat beings on all the Realms." He let the silence hang for a moment. *'It is kind of fun,'* he admitted to her.

Shari could pick the name of random beings the crowd were sending to each other. One stood out, and she snorted at the idea. *As if they'd bring in a Q'Aralide for them to fight!*

"You know this being; you've seen her in action. The one you'll have to defeat is the Altoriae!"

The candidates went wild, some jumping up and down, clearly hopped up on more than just the victory from earlier in the day. Others were looking at each other, the shade covers adding interesting pastel colouring over their paling features.

"So, candidates, get your rest and be ready to fight, because you need to be at your best to even come close to defeating her!"

"Guardian!" came a cry from behind Shari.

She turned, and her face lit up in a delighted grin. "Yessna!" she said.

The Ferah was walking towards them, a hooded figure at her side.

"Guardian," Yessna said, bowing slightly at the waist as she drew to a stop. "Healer," she smirked at Shari.

Shari rolled her eyes, and grinned.

"Yessna of the U'sala," Jon said, turning to face her. "It is a pleasure to see you again."

"Well met. Are you announcing the trial for your apprentice?" Yessna said. "Must candidates only be from Lissae?"

Jon drew his head back. "I suppose so. There's never been a candidate from another Realm," he mused aloud.

"We are allies, are we not?" Yessna asked.

"We are," Jon replied, masterfully ignoring the gasps from the crowd.

"Then will you accept the one the U'sala put forward as a candidate?" she asked.

'Shari? Did you know anything about this?' Jon sent her.

Busy trying to peer under the hood of the purple robe, Shari took a moment to respond. 'Not a clue,' she admitted.

'Are you for or against an off-Realm candidate?'

'For. The U'sala would not try to hurt us.'

"Yes, we will accept a candidate put forward by the U'sala," Jon said.

"Very well," Yessna said. "Meet Kodan, the candidate for the U'sala."

The being at her side drew back his hood, the blue skin of his bare chest glinting in the light. He bowed, silver hair flashing. When Kodan straightened up, he winked at Shari, who rolled her eyes again. *Honestly, one battle together, and he thought they were friends? He'd have to try harder than that.*

He grinned wider at her disinterest, or perhaps it was at the clamouring from the other candidates behind them. "Well met, Guardian, Altoriae, fellow candidates. I look forward to joining you in battle," he rumbled, drowning out the upset voices of the others.

Shari watched in amusement as he made his way towards the other candidates. He seemed eager to get to know his opponents, although Shari studied how he covered it with charm and flashes of his broadsword that were meant to distract.

Jonathan looked back at Yessna. "Will you be staying to watch the trials?"

The Ferah snorted. "Kodan can handle himself. He may return to the U'sala if he is not successful, or he may stay here and help to defend Lissae if you find him acceptable."

"Is this his choice?" Shari asked.

"Indeed, healer. Not everyone is as satisfied with the roving lifestyle of the U'sala as I am. Kodan asked to be named as candidate and will happily stay here if allowed," Yessna said. "His absence is a great loss to the U'sala, but Kodan's wishes are far more important than any desire to tether him."

"I understand," Jonathan said.

'I hope you remember that next time you try to tether me to a training schedule,' Shari sent to him, only half teasing. He shot her a disgruntled look out of the corner of his eye.

"Fight well, live free," Yessna said, then shifted away.

Shari turned to see Kodan looking right at her. He smirked and returned to chatting with the circle of candidates who'd surrounded him.

Jonathan cleared his throat. "Kodan will be taking Wesin's place in the first trial. I suggest you get a few good nights' rest, so everyone is healed and ready to go. We shall see you in the training ground."

Shari shifted them to Jon's lounge room before the candidates were able to mob them for more information, stumbling slightly on a cushion that was on the floor instead of on the couch.

Catching her by her shoulders, Jon steadied her on her feet. "Are you okay?"

"I'm tired," she said, "but I'm okay." She caught his look and rolled her eyes. "Really. When Mum healed me... I've never felt so good. It's like she put all her love into that healing. And look," Shari said, shoving her sleeve up, and baring her forearm in his direction. He peered over it, trying to see what she did. There were a few scars, but otherwise, her skin was unmarked.

"What am I looking at?" he asked, shaking his head.

"I don't have my glamour on," she said.

Frowning, Jonathan looked at her face. The claw marks from the iomnuroz were gone, and although the slash mark she'd retained from the battle on Crihimos was still there, it was lighter. There were a few other scars that she'd gained from over the years, but it did seem that there were significantly less than the last time Jon had seen her without her glamour. "A mother's love," he murmured, and she grinned at him.

"Talking about healing, how is Fiona going?"

"She's... recovering. She's been through a lot recently."

"I know the feeling," Shari mumbled. "Well, we should get some rest. It will be good for all of us." There was a snort from the other side of the wall, and Shari knew Fiona had received her message to rest. "Go, sleep. I will see you in the morning. We need to set up the training ground for the trial," Shari said, heading towards the door.

"Good night, Shari," he said.

"Night, Jon," she replied, and slipped away.

Shari pottered around for a while, eating one of the savoury scones that her mum had left behind and tidying up the house a bit. She was tired, but still too wired to sleep. Just as she was deciding to turn in, there was a knock at her door.

Stretching out her Innarn, Shari rolled her eyes when she realised who it was. "Kodan, what are you doing here?" she asked as she opened the door.

"Hoping you have a spare bed?" he asked, grinning unashamedly at her. The hood of his robe was pushed back, and his hair gleamed under the glow of the crystal light.

Shari sighed and rolled her eyes again. "One good deed deserves another, I suppose. Come on in," she said, holding the door open wider.

He squeezed past her and into the house.

Therdon cursed as the door closed and he couldn't hear what the Altoriae was saying to the new candidate. He'd decided to keep an eye on the big blue Sebbolen the instant the Guardian had accepted him, but Therdon had never dreamed that the Altoriae would welcome the Sebbolen into her house when she'd made such a fuss of *him* just being in her room.

Well, if the Altoriae was so determined to let her guard down and allow the new candidate into her home and her life, Therdon was just the one to take him out of both.

Chapter Twenty-Three

When Shari stepped outside in the morning, the last person she expected to see was Anika. Nodding to the other girl, she set out for the training ground.

Anika fell into step with her. "So, like, I know you've been busy, but we still need to do that makeover," Anika said.

It took a few steps for Shari to gather her thoughts, and not drop her jaw. "Maybe after the new apprentice is announced?" Shari tried to be diplomatic. The second-last thing she wanted to do right now was organise a makeover—the last thing would be *having* the makeover.

"After would be too late! There'll be all sorts of dignitaries there, especially now there's an off-Realm candidate. Oh, I saw him last night; he's got muscles *everywhere!* You're so lucky to work with him!" Anika gushed.

Shari frowned. Yes, she was lucky to work with Kodan, because he had years of experience with the U'sala. It didn't have anything to do with his fitness level.

"Anyway," Anika said, flapping her hand as if to wave away the stray thought, "I was thinking, I know that you like your hair up, and I can work with that. Would you consider wearing a dress? Or a skirt? No. No, okay, that makes it a bit harder, but still something I can deal with. How much time do you usually spend on make-up?"

"I hate to break it to you, Anika, but I don't use make-up," Shari said, trying not to grit her teeth.

"But your skin always looks so flawless! I mean, the bags under your eyes need work some days, but most of the time, ugh. I'm so jealous of you! But hey, you know, I've found this awesome concealer that covers scars..."

Shari rounded on her, consciously unclenching her fists. "Anika, I don't want to cover my scars anymore."

"Oh. Really? I hate my scars," Anika said so softly that Shari barely heard it. "Every time I look in the mirror, I see *her* again."

"Yeah, and you know what? You're still here, and she's not. Your scars say that you survived. That you are strong. And that is nothing to be ashamed of or cover up."

"How can you say that? I've never seen yours," Anika said, her nose in the air.

"'Cause I just figured it out myself," Shari admitted. They walked along in silence for a moment.

"Still, I think we should..." Anika started again.

Shari didn't quite stifle her groan this time, and Anika spun to face her. "Look, Miss High and Mighty," she snapped. "I can't fight, I can't defend. I can't even lift a lipstick tube anymore! There is literally nothing that I can do to protect Ronah or Lissae. Looking good doesn't take Innarn, and it's something that I excel at. People take you seriously when you look good. They want to spend more time with you, and they think your ideas are worth something. Or at least something more than someone who is rocking the gutter rat look the way you usually do! I want... no, I need to do something to help!" Anika's eyes were blazing.

Blinking, Shari took a step back. "You're good at more than just make-up, Anika..."

"And what if I don't want to do anything else? What if that's what I want to do?" Anika said hotly, as if she expected Shari to argue.

"Then do it," Shari shrugged a shoulder. "I'm not going to stop you."

Narrowing her eyes, Anika said, "Well, being able to say that I'm the Altoriae's stylist would be a big boost to my future career."

"Ugh, fine!" Shari said, throwing her arms in the air. "But I get final say. And I won't wear anything I can't fight in." Turning up the path to the training ground, Shari thought she'd be able to escape the fashion-conscious girl.

"It's quite possible to fight in skirts, you know," Anika called out behind her. "I'll see you after the tests are done!" she trilled.

Groaning, Shari hung her head and slipped in through the door to meet Jon, grateful to cut off the sound of Anika's laugh.

"Are you okay?" Jon asked.

"No. I have a date with the devil later," Shari grumbled.

"Date?" Jon said, the boulders he'd been levitating pausing mid-air.

"Anika wants to be my 'stylist'. Apparently, I'm meeting her after the tests. Anyway, can we draw them out?" Shari asked hopefully.

Jon laughed. "No, Shari, we can't draw them out."

Muttering curse words, Shari got to work setting up a moat around the outer edges of the training ground. Tania was on the far side, creating seating for the viewers. Jon was placing boulders at various points that could be used for both defensive and offensive actions.

As the training ground became the testing arena that she and Jon had agreed on, she found herself planning out how and where she was going to defend. That would be her job—just defending against the others as they attempted to create a shield around her.

Not much different to every other day then.

Calem stood on the roof of his father's home. It had been years since he'd been up here alone. Even after all this time, Rakemyst still managed to take his breath away. He often found it lonely, being the only one winging through Ronah's skies, but here, flying was the way to travel.

The roof shook slightly, and he kept his eyes on the horizon. There was only one other person who'd come up here this early in the day. "How do you fare this morning, Wolf?" he asked.

"Still recovering from yesterday. Surprised to find you up here and not with the Altoriae," LoneWolf said gruffly.

"*Your niece* has never appreciated it when we hover. Jonathan keeps me up-to-date with her day, and when she needs my help. Which is less and less lately," Calem said with a wry twist to his mouth.

"Maybe you should consider staying on Rakemyst then. We need a priest. Aneon was lost to the Chirea," LoneWolf said, coming to stand beside him, his eyes on the early morning fliers.

"Shari is still too young..." Calem started.

"Just temporarily, brother. I understand that you have concerns that are more important than the people you grew up with," LoneWolf growled.

"Sometimes I swear you're more canine than avian," Calem said with a smile. "You know I never meant to–"

"Don't start," LoneWolf said, looking away from him. "Father is interviewing candidates for Aneon's role after lunch today. Just... just give it some thought, okay?"

Calem watched as his little brother stepped off the edge of the roof, falling three full body-lengths down before kicking off the side of the building and spiralling into the sky. Heart aching and weary, Calem decided that he should have a talk with Arilla to see what she thought of staying on Rakemyst for a while.

Ronah was beautiful, and a wonderful place to live, but maybe... maybe it was time for him to come home. Glancing at the very tops of the trees peeking through the clouds, he wondered if Arilla would be opposed to sharing the skies of Rakemyst with him again.

Sweat-stained and coated in dust, Shari debated shifting straight into her grandfather's kitchen for lunch. She knew her mother wouldn't care, but Anika's words about presentation mattering made her doubt what she wouldn't normally have an issue doing. Sighing, she figured she'd better go home and clean up first.

"Just got to duck home for a moment, Jon. I'll see you there?" she asked.

"Yes, yes. Don't forget that you are meant to share tonight's meal with your candidate," he said.

Shari groaned. Breaking bread with Sam was the last thing she wanted to do, but as ever, duty called. "Hey, if Yessna isn't here for Kodan, who's he meant to eat with?"

"Typically, if the sponsor isn't available, the candidate eats at the Altoriae's table," Jon said.

Gaping at him, Shari shook her head. "That would have been nice to know. How many other sponsors are going to skip out so their candidates can spend time with me?"

"They all want to be here to see their chosen one win," Jon said, "so you lucked out this time."

"Oh, how is this my life?" Shari grumbled.

"Quirk of fate, luck of the draw, or divine intervention, depending on the day." Jon laughed, twisting out of the way as she threw a pebble at him.

Poking her tongue at him, she shifted away, finding it hard to begrudge him a bit of happiness after such a stressful week. Well, year, really. Almost a decade, if you pushed it. Hearing him laugh was a good thing.

Stepping into her front door, she heard someone rustling around in the kitchen. Her bladed glove appeared unbidden on her hand. Creeping towards the noise, she peered around the corner to see Kodan unwrapping the paper from around the last savoury scone that her mother had made.

Sighing, Shari flicked her blade away. Kodan turned to her, half the scone sticking out of his mouth, broadsword at the ready.

"Really?" Shari said. "Mum's scones are good, but I don't think they're anything to kill over."

Kodan hastily chewed and swallowed. "I don't know. These are easily the best I've ever had."

Shaking her head at him, Shari snagged an apple and said, "I've got to go to lunch, but I'll see you at the tavern in town for dinner tonight?"

"A tavern. I like the sound of that," he said, nodding.

"My parents' tavern," Shari countered, and laughed silently at the look of disappointment on his face as she left the room.

A quick change of clothes later, and she shifted to SilverCloud's gardens to see Jon waiting for her at the base of the stairs.

"You changed," he said, a slight frown of confusion on his face.

"You didn't," Shari noted.

"I got the dust off." He shrugged.

"We're meant to be representing Ronah or something," Shari said at Jon's raised eyebrow.

"Do it as you, Shari. Everyone will be out to influence you. Doesn't mean that you have to do anything about it," Jon replied.

Shari nodded, conflicted. They climbed the stairs and walked through the airy halls to find her family.

They were on a terrace just off the kitchen, basking in the warm midday sun. Belfar was serving drinks, while LoneWolf was dishing out plates of food. As everyone at the table ate and laughed, Shari realised how much she'd missed her parents, even though they had only been on Rakemyst for a week.

Arilla was teasing SilverCloud and getting him to eat tiny bites of quiche, while LoneWolf looked at them out of the corner of his eye. Belfar spoke gently in his ear, causing the stoic Ilutri to practically smile. Calem was sitting next to Jon, happily chatting about what they'd planned for the candidates. Her dad was trying to keep things light-hearted, but Shari knew how concerned he was.

"So, I hear you have a new candidate?" SilverCloud asked, making Arilla look at Shari and Jon, letting the Elder scrape the rest of his food off his plate and into the maw of his pet shem'ar.

"Yes," Jon said as Arilla glanced at SilverCloud's empty plate and served him another portion. He sighed and rolled his eyes at Shari, who ducked her head and giggled. "Kodan was put forwards by the U'sala."

"An off-Realmer?" asked Belfar, spearing a roll with his fork.

"That's right," Shari said.

"Is that a first?" asked LoneWolf.

"I've been over the records, and I believe that there have been two off-Realm candidates before," Jon said.

"What do you think his chances are?" SilverCloud asked.

Shari shrugged a shoulder. "About as good as anyone else's. I've seen him in battle, and he is fast and focused, so I know he can keep his head."

"Do you think some of the candidates can't?" asked Calem, frowning.

"Actual battle is different to training exercises. It's easy to keep your head and concentrate in training, but totally different to be able to do it in battle," Shari said.

SilverCloud laughed aloud. "That's the best non-answer I've heard in a while! Enough talk of battle and candidates; it wearies my old bones." Taking a sip of his drink, he turned to Calem. "LoneWolf tells me that he asked you about staying on as our priest?"

Calem swallowed hard when Arilla snapped her head towards him, arching an eyebrow.

"He asked me this morning, but I haven't really had time to think it over yet," he said, then hastily took another bite.

"You were training to be a priest before you married Arilla, weren't you?" Belfar asked.

"Finished, actually, just before we met." Calem smiled easily at his wife. She smiled back, hesitantly.

"I didn't know you were a priest," Jonathan said.

"It's a bit hard to practise on Ronah, when the congregation and priest are one and the same," Calem replied, shrugging. "Ilutri have specific beliefs, most of which involve flying without the use of Innarn."

"That's why Dad would always fly at sunset," Shari said.

"Really?" Jon asked.

"It's to let the sun know that there will always be someone happy to see it the next day," Calem admitted, blushing slightly.

"I find other religions fascinating," Jon said.

"Really," said Shari dryly. "We never would have guessed."

Everyone at the table laughed, and talk settled onto other subjects.

Tania gasped, her eyes snapping open, the faces on the cave wall opposite her blurring as tears sprang to her eyes.

"Oh. Oh," she said. "I've got to tell..." Drawing on Ronah's energy, she shifted out of the cave and straight into the mayor's office.

"Mayor Pratt!" she called out, tears streaming down her face. "I need to talk to you."

"Tania? Are you okay?" Alan asked, rising from his desk.

"I'm better than okay!" It was like being filled with sunshine and sugar. "Ronah and Rakemyst have decided that we must join with the other Shifting Islands!" Tania brought her clasped hands up to her mouth, trying to contain her awe by breathing shakily into them.

"A convergence?" Alan asked, jolting in shock. "A full convergence of the Shifting Islands?" He sank into his seat. "We should call..." Before he finished, there was a knock at the door. The mayor waved a hand and it opened, revealing Zana and SilverCloud Dawn, who was looking rather grey.

"I believe that you wanted to see us, Tania?" Zana said, sailing into the room.

Tania envied her composure. Zana was everything she wanted to be when she was older, and her calm aura was the balm she needed to settle her jumping nerves.

After Tania explained the situation, SilverCloud asked, "Why have the Islands decided that a convergence is needed?"

'We *were not the ones to decide. Lissae was. She merely used me as her voice,'* Ronah sent to them.

"Lissae has declared this?" Zana asked. Even surprised, she merely lifted her eyebrows slightly. "Then if Lissae has said, so must it be." She closed her eyes for a minute.

"We will prepare for the convergence. It will be good for the joined to all be together again," SilverCloud said, smiling.

"You must be recalling a different convergence than the one I remember," Alan said. "The one I was at had few moments of peace."

"When all the Shifting Islands come together, it is a beautiful thing," SilverCloud said to Tania, shaking his head at Ronah's mayor. "People who grew up on the Islands generally return, and we get visitors from the mainland who want to be a part of the festivities. It is a celebration that goes on for days, and as Ronah is the middle Island, it is held right here."

"Here?" Tania squeaked, trying not to bounce in her seat.

"The Shifting Islands will be converging and quite soon. It looks like Talhan is heading to meet us even as we speak," Zana said, opening her yellow eyes wide.

"How long until he is here?" Alan asked.

"Two weeks, perhaps three at the latest. The others are not far behind," Zana replied.

"Three weeks? There's so much to do!" Tania cried.

Zana smiled at her. "We can do it together, Tania. This convergence will be remembered for generations. Now come, we have much to plan."

The two joined rose out of their seats and headed to the door, the air thick with all the ideas they were sending back and forth.

Outside the mayor's office, Zana leaped into the air, her wings pulling her higher. '*Are you coming, Ronah's Linked?*'

Tania laughed and sprang into the air, creating a gust of wind to keep herself aloft.

'*Very good,*' Zana sent, and led the way higher until they were flying over rooves and treetops.

Controlling the gust of wind she was essentially riding was easier than she thought. There was a moment after she'd crossed the bridge between the Islands when the gust almost dissipated, but she stabilised it in time.

Zana led her to the tower in the middle of Rakemyst, landing gracefully on the ground just outside. Tania touched down next to her and grinned up at the stately woman.

'*It's time we started to train together. I understand that you are still in school?*'

'Yes.' Tania tilted her head, curious.

'*And you are training with Ronah and the Altoriae as well?*'

'*Yes. Shari and I have been meeting up at least once a week, and I spend as much time as I can with Ronah in the afternoon.*'

'*Would Ronah be happy to share you? Perhaps twice a week, barring invasions and the end of the Realm, of course.*'

Tania looked at her, horrified, but caught the hint of mirth dancing in her eyes and the crinkles at the corner of her smile. 'Ronah?'

The Island sighed in her mind. *'If I must.'*

Hiding a grin at the thought that the Island sounded just like she did when she was asked to do a distasteful chore, she nodded at Zana.

'Good. There's no time like the present then. We need to test how deep your link with Ronah goes and see if we can't expand on it.'

'Alright. But will you and Rakemyst let us help you with some stronger defences? Even pacifists must hold shields occasionally.'

Looking surprised, Zana nodded slowly. *'I think I can get Rakemyst to agree to that.'*

'You like pushing me, fledgling,' Rakemyst grumbled.

The Linked shared a grin.

'First lesson: how to open the door.' Zana turned to the carved white wall of the tower and waved her hand. Tania watched in awe as a section of the wall collapsed outward, creating four wide steps that led to an arched doorway.

"Huh." Crinkling her nose, she watched as Zana reversed the process, taking care to note how she used Innarn.

Zana demonstrated opening and closing the door once more, then indicated to her. *'Your turn.'*

Tania concentrated on the wall. She thought she knew how Zana was creating the doorway—by forcing the tiny molecules of air and stone to shift and reform—but she wasn't sure. Screwing up her courage, she pictured what she wanted to happen, and waved a hand. The wall shattered outward, thousands of shards heading towards them in a deadly storm. Gasping, Tania caught them and reshaped them into stairs that were only slightly lopsided.

'Impressive for a first try. Would you like to go again?'

'Absolutely!'

First Trial – First Round

Chapter Twenty-Four

SilverCloud stepped out of Mayor Pratt's office and buried the heart that he feared was on his sleeve. Another convergence was the last thing he'd wanted to see before he left Lissae behind, and it just might happen.

A heavy hand clamped down on his shoulder, making him stagger slightly, before the hand shifted and came up to steady him by clasping his elbow.

"Elder, my apologies. You looked worried," a young man said.

"That is not so unusual these days," SilverCloud grumbled, trying to hide his shock behind a gruff voice. The slightest uptick at the corner of the young man's mouth suggested that he hadn't succeeded.

"That is something that I have noticed since I have returned," the young man said, gently guiding SilverCloud down to the street.

"Returned?" SilverCloud said. "Are you one of the..."

"Unlucky ones Anriluka decided to feast on? Yes. That would be true. I am Collis Iuvo, born on Ronah in 3715," Collis said easily, gently correcting SilverCloud when he staggered in shock.

"Ha!" the Elder laughed. "You look pretty good for three hundred and forty-four years old!"

Collis paused for a moment. "I have not thought of it that way before."

"Did you ever get to see Rakemyst before you were… detained?" SilverCloud asked.

"No, I was not so fortunate. I hear it is beautiful though," Collis said.

"You have not been to see it since the Islands joined?" the Elder asked with a frown as Collis held open a door in one hand, the other still firm on his elbow.

"It is taking a long time for me and the others to get used to the amount Ronah has changed. I do not know how I would cope with seeing another of the Shifting Islands so soon after our return," Collis admitted.

"You know, if you've never seen Rakemyst, then you won't know what has changed." There was no point in hiding the twinkle in his eye.

"Sit, please, Elder, and I will consider," Collis replied.

Taking his seat, SilverCloud realised that Collis had led him into his son's establishment. It was quiet now, with only a few other clients over the other side of the room having a silent conversation and looking deeply into each other's eyes.

For a moment, he remembered sitting like that with RainbowMist. Soon enough, he would be with her again. "You are very good at distracting an old man," SilverCloud grumbled at the Returned boy.

Collis tilted his head, a small smile twitching at his lips. "I thought we established that I was the old man?"

SilverCloud laughed a bit too hard, and started coughing. Arilla appeared at his side so quickly that he almost thought she'd shifted there.

"Here," she said, holding a pitcher of water out and pouring him a cup. "Drink this."

Taking the cup in shaking hands, SilverCloud sipped until it didn't feel like his throat had been rubbed raw. "Thank you."

"Collis, do you mind checking on the other patrons?" Arilla asked, handing him the pitcher.

"Of course, Arilla," the Returned said with a little bow. He took the pitcher and headed over to a couple to refill their drinks.

There was a moment of awkward silence between SilverCloud and his daughter-in-law, then they both spoke at the same time.

"So–"

"Won't you–"

They laughed awkwardly, and Arilla gestured for him to speak.

He smiled at her kindly. "Won't you join me?" he said.

"Thank you," she said, sliding into the seat across from him, surprisingly gracefully for a Blank. "Did you manage to slip past your bodyguards?" she asked, grinning at him.

SilverCloud groaned and shook his head. "There's only one way I'll slip past them. It makes me feel even frailer than I already am!"

Tilting her head to the side, brows drawn together, Arilla regarded him. It took him a moment to realise that she didn't know what he was speaking of.

"Don't you think it's odd that I have bodyguards when none of the other Elders do?" he asked.

"A little bit. I figured that there'd be a reason for it though," Arilla said, chewing on her lip.

"They incessantly follow me around so that when I drop dead, they can take my body to the temple and prepare it for the next life," he frowned. "Vultures, they are. Ready to pick over the flesh of an old Ilutri."

Arilla sucked in a breath, shock written on her face.

"Oh, don't act surprised." SilverCloud waved a dismissive hand. "I've been dying for over a year now. My time on Lissae is shorter than I would like. I only wish I was able to spend more time with you and Shari."

"And Calem?" she prodded.

"I know his heart like I know my own. I know he has a core of strength, and a shell of caring. I know that he still shies away from bugs, and deep water bothers him more than he will admit to, particularly considering that he lives on an island. My son may have moved away, but we have been able to send to each other to stay connected."

"You never sent to Shari?" Arilla asked.

"I learned that she was the Altoriae when the rest of Ronah did. Calem sent me the message immediately. I suspected for far longer, of course, but didn't want to put her at risk if I was right," he said, looking into the bottom of his cup as if it held the answers of the Realms.

"That must have been a hard secret to keep," she said, twisting a cleaning cloth in her hands. "It was for me."

"All the best secrets are difficult to preserve," he said with a grin, pushing his chair back to stand up. "Although I suppose that I need to be on my way to reveal the next big one."

"Next one? What secret are you hiding?" Arilla stood as well.

SilverCloud leaned in and whispered, "The Islands are converging."

Arilla sucked in a breath, excitement warring with fear.

"Relax, Arilla. If there is one thing that I've learned about Shari in the short time I've been privileged to spend with her, it is that she is the toughest, most resilient being I have ever known," SilverCloud said.

"It's true, my daughter is resilient, but that doesn't mean that she should have to continuously fight by herself to keep the Realm safe." The cleaning cloth strained in Arilla's hands for a moment as she subconsciously pulled it tight.

"Shari doesn't fight alone anymore. She has the Guardian, and his apprentice, and a whole host of others to join her guild at the end of these tests, I'll wager. Give her credit. Vebnah knows that she gets her stubbornness from my side of the family." SilverCloud clapped a hand on her shoulder as he stepped past her and through the door.

Shifting to the bridge between the Islands, he summoned an Innarnian cloud and stood atop, guiding the cloud so it was hovering directly above the bridge.

There were Elders from all over Lissae present, but he'd requested to be the one to announce the news that the Islands were finally coming together again. The other Elders had looked at him pityingly. They knew as well as he that it was likely that he'd not see all the Islands together before he entered the Spirit Realm.

Sending with the Elders had left him shaken, although he'd made sure to give no outward indication. The Island Elders understood that Shari could not possibly stop every single attack on Lissae and were doing their best to shore up their own defences, as both the Fixed and the Shifting Islands were usually the ones who came under attack first. The mainland Elders, however, were not so understanding. They were not used to being attacked and thought that Shari was failing in her duty as Altoriae. The meeting had ended when the Elders from Jinkor and Ginorti had almost come to blows over what Jinkor's Elder perceived as a failure on Shari's part to stop a major crop of toslzura beans being destroyed by an off-Realmer. Ginorti's Elder had growled that Jinkor needed to guard their provinces better, and Jinkor's Elder had leaped over the table at General Morrow.

It was not the most exciting meeting that he'd had with the other Elders, but it did come in the top ten.

Standing atop his cloud and looking at the combined populations of Ronah and Rakemyst, a sense of peace settled over his soul.

"Well met, all! I have some wonderful news to share with you," SilverCloud announced, holding his hands up. The crowd was too far away to see the slight trembling, but the Elders who flanked him stepped closer, lending him their strength the way that only Innarnians could.

"We have received the joyous news that the Shifting Islands are converging," he said, seeing no need to waffle around the truth.

Joyous noise erupted from the crowd, and SilverCloud found that he was unable to stop the smile from forming on his face. It wavered when he noticed a thread of concern twisting through the mass of people below him, but he found that he couldn't pinpoint the source with the sheer number of souls in the area.

He decided to ignore it.

When Yessna stepped through the gateway on Iabovar, the last thing she expected was an ivory arrow shot in her direction. She slid to the side and disappeared into the bush, her paw grasping the projectile sticking out of her armour near her bicep. Eyes wide, she scanned the area intently, but could not find the shooter.

Taking a risk, she glanced down at the arrow and saw that it was not, as she'd first thought, made of ivory. Instead, it was carved bone, the tip hard and sharp enough to cut through the hardest hide armour. For once, she was glad she'd given in to Jeran and worn the armour this time, as it looked like the Chirea were guarding the xarit that led to Lissae.

Yessna let out a chirruping sound, three high, two low, and kept repeating it as the rest of her team came through the gateway. They had been out scouting, but were meant to meet her at the gateway to go and watch Kodan perform in the trial for the Guardian's apprentice. She didn't think that he would particularly enjoy the experience of being a follower after he'd been the leader of a strike team for the last decade, but he'd said he wanted a chance to change the Realms for the better.

Her team made it through the portal, despite the number of arrows shot in their direction. There was a flurry of chirrups from the bushes around her, which Yessna translated. Lenyuu was down, with an arrow through his sword hand. Nerina, their medic, was treating Lenyuu, so they'd be down two members, but the rest of the team was able to fight.

Chirruping back, Yessna indicated that she wanted Kibon and Wubi to flank the Chirea, and that she would take the front with the other three. As she waited for the others to get into position, she almost believed that it was the breeze making the bushes sway, but experience told her the team was getting into the best spots to take out the beings firing on them.

The clearing around the xarit grew still. The silence deepened. It seemed that even the insects were waiting for something to happen. Then, in a flurry of movement, the U'sala team attacked.

Two of the Chirea tumbled out of the trees, downed by a throw of Wubi's spiked chain. Yessna, Felton, Zugir, and Henot burst out of the bushes and dove towards the Chirean ground troops, who showered them with arrows. They scuffled briefly, Yessna taking out one bone warrior by streaming her needle-sharp fur straight into his eyes, sending him to the ground, wailing in agony. Zugir took out the other with another spiked chain, throwing it like a lasso so it looped around the Chirea's chest, the spikes catching on the grooves of the armour and gripping as Zugir pulled the loop tighter.

Yessna held up a paw, signalling Zugir to stop.

She walked around the Chirea, fur on end, displaying her agitation. Widening her eyes, she stepped up close to the bone warrior, forcing him to look at her.

"I am the being who stands between you and crushed armour. Do you know what will happen if Zugir continues to tighten his noose?" Yessna practically purred. Scared eyes of a being too young peered out from beneath the oversized skull helmet. "No? The bones you wear on the outside will tighten around the ones under your skin, slowly splintering them until the shards start ripping apart your internal organs."

If she was right, and she usually was, the leakage streaming from the Chirea's eyes and the acidic smell coming from farther down meant that the being was sufficiently terrified.

"Now, I don't want that to happen. Do you?" Yessna waited for the being to shake its head. "I only need you to tell me why you're here, and then I can let you go."

"Those were my orders," the being whimpered. Zugir tightened the chain the tiniest bit, and the Chirea gasped. Yessna shot him a look, and Zugir smirked at her.

"Who gives you orders?" Yessna asked, stretching out a paw and tipping the Chirea's head back even beyond the point of pain. Effluvia streamed down the being's face, dripping from underneath the jawbone of the helmet.

Gasping, it said, "He does. Luttrell died, and now *he* is in charge."

"He who?" Yessna growled.

"The Light being with the purple lightning," it sobbed. "I don't know any more. We were never told his name."

"Did you ever see him?" she asked, withdrawing her paw to wipe the dripping juices from the Chirea's face onto a leaf.

"Yes, yes. Once!" It was hiccoughing now. Yessna struggled not to roll her eyes. "He's got blue skin, silver hair, and wears a purple robe."

Stepping back from the panting Chirea, Yessna growled deep in her throat. Zugir snapped the chain tight and crushed their prisoner easily.

"D'ya think that...?" Zugir asked gruffly.

"It can't be," Yessna growled, but in the back of her mind, things were starting to add up in a way that she did not like at all.

Shari tilted her head from one side to the other, stretching out her neck, as the first five candidates entered the training ground.

This should be fun.

"Well met, Altoriae, Elders, candidates, and beings of Lissae. We are here today to witness the first round of candidates," Elder Silverstone's voice filled the training ground, causing the watching crowds to edge forwards in their seats. "The first trial will comprise of four rounds, where a group of candidates must work together to attempt to overpower the Altoriae."

There was a lot of uneasy muttering from the crowd, many of whom hadn't been aware of what would be happening in the tests. Several of the Returned moved restlessly in their seats.

"The successful candidate," Elder Silverstone boomed over the crowd, "is not necessarily the one who is able to withstand the Altoriae for the longest. Instead, they will be chosen by the Altoriae and her Guardian." The Elder flourished a hand in Jon's direction. Jon nodded at the crowd, which caused a fair bit of squealing from many of Shari's classmates. She hid a smirk when she saw some of the Elders from outside of Ronah swooning.

"Now, please make welcome Talofa from Sulanta, Raven from Freeson, Dealon of the Wisara, Burke from Rohinda, and from our own humble Isle, Alistair!" Elder Silverstone called.

Some of the candidates waved uncertainly at the crowd, although Raven seemed quite at home in front of the packed stands. Talofa blended into the background, using her short stature to hide in Burke's shadow. Burke stood at the far end of the line, the farthest he could get from Raven. Alistair shifted his weight from one foot to the other, standing between Talofa and Dealon.

Shari wondered if Burke would move to the other side of the ground if he knew how powerful Alistair's fire was.

She'd find out soon enough.

"These candidates have not all worked together before, so they have gathered while we took our seats in order to create a strategy to take down our Altoriae." Elder Silverstone laughed. "I do not envy them in this trial, friends. Our little Altoriae is harder to take down than she looks."

Shari bristled. *Little.* She'd been saving his hide since her third birthday. Snorting, she flicked her hand and her war leathers appeared.

"Ah ha! It appears that the Altoriae is ready to begin. Good luck, candidates. You'll need it!" the Elder called. In the back of her mind, Shari sensed Jon raising the shield to block out the noise of the crowd, and the training ground became eerily quiet.

The candidates looked at her from the other side of the ground and she grinned at them, gave a little wave, and darted behind a nearby boulder.

Closing her eyes and taking in a deep breath, Shari centred herself. The last time she'd fought on Ronah had been to save people, and the one thing she found herself most worried about was that she would forget that this was a trial. Jon had offered to make the silencing shield opaque so that the crowd could look in, but she wouldn't be able to see them. She'd refused. Being able to see the crowd would help to remind her. Or at least she hoped so.

As she waited for the first attack, she set up a few basic traps: A tripwire between her boulder and the one on the other side of the ground that would cause a shower of plasma sparks, and a loop of vine on the ground that would draw anyone who stepped into it straight up into the tree that was only five long steps away, slamming them painfully into one of the low branches.

The ground to the left of her boulder rippled, and Shari rolled away from it without thinking. A gush of water splattered mud right where she'd been crouched a moment ago, but Shari was still pressed up tight against the boulder, and the mud only speckled the side of her foot. There was a loud thump, and she cut her breathing as Raven landed heavily on the ground directly behind her. If the boulder hadn't been there, the jet of flames the Freesonian sent out would have roasted her.

Grinning, Shari flicked her hand out, pulling the vine loop as Raven stepped forwards. The Freesonian let out a grunt as he hit the ground, hard. He should have gone whizzing feet first towards the tree, but before his feet even left the ground, Raven managed to cut the loop around his ankles. Rolling quickly to his feet, he glanced around, scowling.

Shari stifled her snigger and slid around the other side of her boulder away from the tree, only to come face-to-face with a spirit form.

"Altoriae," it said, in a voice that sounded a lot like...

An arrow hissed through the air, and Shari twisted out of the way, looking at Alistair in shock. '*When did he learn to shoot?*' she sent to Jon.

'*Concentrate!*' he admonished her.

Rolling her eyes almost cost Shari as Burke shot a volley of tiny, sharp rocks at her. Even as she raised a shield to deflect them, she grinned. Now all she needed to do was draw Dealon out and she'd know where everyone was.

Shaping a ball of plasma in her hand, she let it fly directly at Alistair as soon as he'd released his next arrow. It slammed right into his chest and sent him flying off the boulder.

'*Sorry, Jon,*' Shari sent, feeling a bit bad that Jon's candidate was the one she'd hit first.

'*Don't dismiss him yet,*' Jon sent back.

The spirit form was in front of her again. "Altoriae," it said. "Please..."

Gritting her teeth, Shari ignored it, and sprinted for the opposite side of Alistair's boulder, a hailstorm of rock shards driving into her shield as she ran, sent from Burke on the far side of the ground. Dealon added to her torment by seeping water into the ground, turning it to mud and slowing her down.

Slamming her back against the boulder, Shari saw Dealon and Raven, who both regarded her warily. If this was off-Realm, and she'd truly been fighting against them, she'd fry both with a plasma blast. A movement in the stands above the two candidates reminded her where she was.

"Come and get me!" she called out to the Freesonian and the Wisara, then slipped to the other side of the boulder before they were able to launch their attack. Raven sprinted for her, caught up in the moment, and was showered in plasma sparks from the other trap Shari had set at the start of the trial.

His panicked shouts went unchecked by Dealon, who rushed past his fellow candidate in order to reach her. Alistair, who had groggily risen to his feet at Raven's first shout, staggered to the far side of the boulder and held his hand out, drawing the plasma off the terrified Raven, while Shari took great pleasure in rounding the boulder and planting her fist into Dealon's chest.

The Wisara had been at full tilt when she'd hit him, and he crumpled into a gasping, wheezing ball, before disappearing from the ground.

Faintly through the shield, Shari heard Elder Silverstone announce, "Dealon of the Wisara has finished his part in the first trial."

Shari snorted. He'd finished his part in all the trials, as far as she was concerned. The Wisara shouldn't have left Raven to struggle with the plasma alone.

Before her again was the spirit form. "Please, Altoriae, help me," it begged.

Glaring at it, she slipped around, aiming to get to the tree she knew Talofa was perched in. Burke, still balanced on the far boulder, sent a flurry of razor-sharp leaves her way in such concentration that Shari found herself blinded for a moment. She hit the trunk of the tree hard, only to find Talofa grinning down at her from the bare branches before she was engulfed in a waterfall.

Spluttering for a moment, Shari adjusted her shield, changing it to fire so when Talofa's waterfall hit it, the water turned to steam and shot straight back up the trunk. The startled girl squeaked and scurried down the other side. Shari stepped around to grab her, but Talofa held a blade in each of her four hands and was scowling fiercely at the Altoriae.

Talofa descended on her, blades whirling. Calling forth her yellow blade, Shari managed to trap the Uleulan's lower right sword in her claws and snap the steel.

Talofa glared at her, and for the first time in this round, Shari found herself slightly worried. The Uleulan came at her again, three blades spinning in a deadly display. Shari countered each thrust as best she could, taking care not to cut the girl. Just as Shari managed to snap the upper right sword in between the tines of her claws, three simultaneous attacks hammered into the back of her shield.

Down to two blades, Talofa was open on her left side, so Shari spun, and held her yellow blade across the Uleulan's throat, the girl's slender body in between Shari and her attackers.

Breathing hard, Shari found her gaze drifting to the crowd in the stands. "Not too tight?" she murmured to Talofa.

"Isn't that rather the point?" the girl said.

"The point is to train, not to kill," Shari replied, as Alistair and Raven looked at her in horror. Burke was shaking on the top of his boulder.

"Then maybe ease off a bit," Talofa replied.

Shari eased her blade a hair away from the Uleulan's throat, and Talofa gulped in a breath. Raven and Burke attacked at the same time, and Shari shifted Talofa away before dropping to the ground and shooting plasma balls at both of her attackers. Burke shrieked and fell off his boulder. Raven drew in the plasma, but it was more than he was expecting, and he started smouldering, his eyes glowing in horror.

Rolling her eyes and sighing, Shari drew the plasma back to her and shifted Raven off the field.

Alistair shot another arrow at her, and she ducked behind the trunk of the tree.

"What have you done with them?" he yelled at her.

It took her a moment to realise what he was talking about. "They're safe, Alistair, but they're out of the trial. If you look, they'll be somewhere in the crowd," she called back.

'Burke's out,' Jon sent to her. '*He landed badly and didn't get up. Holli is tending to him now.*'

'*Does Alistair realise?*' Shari sent back.

'No,' Jon sent. She knew he was on the edge of his seat.

"I don't believe you!" Alistair screamed. Shari risked a peek and saw tears streaming down his face.

Slipping back behind the tree, an arrow passed through the air where her head had been. Despite not having fought with the other candidates in his group before, Alistair cared about them deeply. Arrow after arrow shot by her until the boy let out a frustrated cry, and Shari heard wood breaking.

Sneaking another peek, she realised that Alistair had thrown his bow to the ground, but he clearly wasn't unarmed. A tiny ball of plasma shot towards her and almost cost Shari an eyebrow.

"Bring them back!" Alistair demanded between shots and sobs. "Raven! Raven, help me!" he cried, his voice closer.

Shari sighed. She really didn't want to draw this out any longer. Closing her eyes, she breathed out and created a twister of air that spun around the tree, gathering the dry dirt from the ground and swirling it before she guided the twister to Alistair, causing him to splutter and cough as the dirt got into his lungs.

When Shari let the twister go, Alistair was tangled up in vines, and she found that she was quite proud of the fact that she hadn't caused a single fatality.

The silencing shield dropped, and Shari flinched at the cacophony that surrounded them. The crowd was cheering so loud, she imagined that the mainlanders would be able to hear them.

"Alistair Hollingsworth is the last candidate standing!" Elder Silverstone called. "Please give thanks to candidates Dealon, Talofa, Raven, and Burke for a trial round well fought!"

The crowd became even louder. Shari released Alistair from his restraints as the others stepped forwards and waved despite their grim expressions.

"Going up against our Altoriae was never going to be easy, as the candidates found out. But now, for the news we've all been waiting for. Altoriae Dawn! Tell us, who is through to the second trial?" the Elder called down to her.

Shari refrained from scowling at him. She wasn't meant to announce the candidates for the second trial until all the four rounds had been completed. The twinkle in Sampson Silverstone's eye told her that he thought he'd found a work-around for her stipulation.

Baring her teeth at him in a parody of a smile, she said, "Wouldn't you like to know?" and shifted off the field and into the safety of her parents' home.

It would be Alistair, of course. Not because he'd lasted the longest, but because of the concern he'd shown for his teammates.

Sighing, she slipped through the door of her house, glad to be away from the mental press of people analysing her every move, only to stop, head tilting to the side as she realised that someone else was in her home.

Kodan stepped into view, the hood of his purple robe pushed back, his hands raised to show the backs of them to her. She blinked. She'd thought it a Lissaen thing to not show your palms to others. Showing your palms meant it was easier to fire Innarn out of them. Maybe it was something that the U'sala did as well?

"Apologies if I startled you, Altoriae. I didn't expect the trial to be over so soon. To get into the U'sala, it is often a trial of days, not hours," he said, in a voice meant to ease wild animals and small children.

Shari laughed unconvincingly. "Just not used to having other people in the house," she said. "Mum and Dad were never much for visitors."

"I can always stay somewhere else, if you'd prefer?"

"The rooms at the castle are all taken," Shari said. "There's plenty of space here. I've just got to grab a bite to eat, and then I'm meeting with Jon."

"The Guardian?"

"That's him," she said. Shari slipped past Kodan to grab a roll out of the pantry, and some cheese from the cold box. "I'll be back later on, but please help yourself," she said, before slipping back out the door and shifting to Jon's front yard, suppressing a shiver.

There was something niggling at the back of her mind, but she couldn't quite figure it out.

First Trial – Second Round

CHAPTER TWENTY-FIVE

hari endured a restless night. Jon had insisted that she didn't patrol, and she found that her skin practically vibrated with excess energy. Wanting to be productive, she'd headed to the bookshop in the dark hours of the morning and reorganised the store, trying in vain to bring some sort of semblance of balance to her thoughts.

After shuffling the shelves for the third time, Shari decided that she needed something more strenuous to do. She started for the training ground, intent on clearing it for the morning when she and Jon would set it up for the next trial round.

Sometime in the deepest part of the night, she fell asleep under a row of seats. When the crystals of the Island chimed gently as the first rays of the sun reached them, Shari stretched as she woke.

Groaning, she stepped out of the training ground, and decided to go for a run. As the wind from the ocean blew the cobwebs from her brain, Shari began to feel more alert and ready to take on the day.

Rounding the corner, Shari sensed another fast-moving body. Before she had a chance to step out of the way, they collided.

Apologies were stuttered by both sides, and Shari found herself gazing into the startled eyes of the late candidate.

"Amara, right?" Shari said, helping the other girl up.

Blushing, the girl nodded. "You remember me?" she squeaked.

Shari smiled gently. "Yes." She didn't add that it was her job to know everyone on the Island, not to mention she'd seen first-hand Amara's fatal tripping skills.

Amara beamed at her, totally unreserved. Shari smiled back easily, a tad amused by the candidate's reaction.

Shaking her head, Amara blushed again, and tangled her words so badly that Shari didn't understand her request.

"Sorry, I get tongue-tied when I'm nervous," the Daen admitted.

"I usually end up playing with throwing knives when I'm nervous," Shari admitted.

Amara laughed. "What I was trying to say," the shorter girl said, "was do you know of any good running trails? I kinda like running where there aren't many people."

"If you don't mind a running partner, people usually leave the trails to me," Shari offered.

The Daen's jaw dropped, and she let out a high-pitched squeal that Shari swore belonged to a bat. "Really? I would... that would... yes!"

Shari grinned at Amara's unexpectedly enthusiastic response, and turned back to the trail, setting an easy pace. The candidate effortlessly kept up with her, so Shari gradually increased her speed until she'd settled into her regular stride.

When she drew to a stop at the edge of the beach, Amara ran a few paces more, and coming to a halt, gave Shari a start. She had been so lost in the beat of her feet pounding the ground she'd almost forgotten Amara was there.

Hands on knees and breathing deeply, Amara looked up at her, grinning so wide Shari thought she could see all her teeth.

"That was the best run I've had in ages!" the Daen said. Drawing one last deep breath, she straightened, and then gave a shallow bow. "Thank you, Altoriae," Amara said, and she jogged away before Shari was able to call her back.

Shari shrugged. It had been the best run she'd had in a while as well. All that excess energy that had been humming under her skin was gone. She was ready to take on the second lot of candidates.

After grabbing a bite to eat, Shari ducked back into the training ground. Jon was meeting her there to change things around for the next lot of candidates, because Shari didn't want one group to have an advantage.

She couldn't spot her Guardian. Shrugging, she figured that it wouldn't hurt to start work on the next setup.

Jon walked in about ten minutes later, munching on a pastry. "Couldn't wait to get started?" he asked sardonically.

"Sleep well?" Shari shot back with a grin, her hands twisting as she carved out a bed for the stream to run through. It was almost deep enough, but she just wanted the banks a little bit steeper. Finally, when she was satisfied, Shari concentrated hard, persuading the water running under the Island to seep up through the ground and fill the stream bed. Grinning with triumph as the ground started bubbling with water, she turned to see what Jon was doing.

He was sending a stream of olive-green energy towards the last sapling that was rapidly reaching for the sky, the trunk thickening out, so it was wider than she was able to reach around. Five massive trees inhabited the training ground now, three on the north of her stream, and two on the south. They would be transplanted to the edge of the dunes after the round was over.

Shari wouldn't admit it aloud, but she'd tried to get the trees started before Jon had arrived, and try as she might, she'd had no luck at all. Earth Innarn just didn't come easily to her.

"Ready for the testing to begin?" Jon asked her.

"I'm ready for it to be over," Shari grumbled good-naturedly. After her run with Amara, she felt different. No one would ever be the same as Mitch. He would forever be the person who taught her that it was okay to fight alongside others, and that it was okay to have friends. But maybe... maybe it would be alright if she found another sparring partner.

Jon smiled at her, as if he was reading her thoughts. She poked her tongue out at him but straightened up as the first wave of people came to take their seats.

"You know that I'll be doing the introduction after what Elder Silverstone pulled?"

"Good. How does he not understand that riling me up after a fight is a bad idea?" Shari grumbled.

Jon chuckled. The second round was about to begin.

Shifting into the stands, Jon joined the candidates who weren't in this round on the north side of the field, where he waited patiently for the crowds to take their seats. Shari watched Jon smiling with them from her spot near the middle of the field on the south side of the stream, ready to see what this lot of candidates would bring.

As the minutes passed, tension seeped into her bones. Shari shook out her hands, ready to go as Josie, Ness, Lira, Mu, and Kodan entered the training ground from the west side, directly between two big trees. She nodded to them and attempted to figure out their strategy as Jon spoke.

"Well met, all, and welcome to the second round of the first trial. Candidates Josie from Nelonia, Ness from Omina, Lira from Tevon, Mu from Nindonia, and Kodan of the U'sala are going to attempt to capture our Altoriae by putting a shield around her. If it can hold for more than a minute, the candidates will have succeeded in subduing her," Jon said, twisting his lips in a smile that was meant to reassure those who stood before Shari, but showed Shari how amused he was by the thought. "As requested by the Elders, a candidate will only be removed for essential medical aid or when the trial is over."

Privately, Shari thought that there was a good chance that Kodan might be able to take her out, but it would be interesting to see how he would go in a group he'd never seen in action.

Letting her thoughts slide over the candidates, Shari listened in. Ness and Lira had come up with the idea for the group to split up and use their strongest Innarn to try and contain her. She smirked, and a few of them exchanged nervous looks.

"No injury that results in death or permanent maiming," Jon warned them. He bowed to Shari, before saying, "Good luck, candidates." He raised the soundproof shield, and Shari lowered her head slightly, flexing her fingers, ready for the first attack.

Ness and Lira worked together to create a massive dust cloud. It covered the area between the two trees and blocked them from Shari's sight. A fire bolt shot out of the middle of the dust cloud, straight at the bushes in front of Shari. The bolt landed in the water, sizzling.

Shari blinked, then used the water in the stream to shoot in the direction of where the fire bolt had come from. From her side of the field, she heard the thud of a body hitting the stone wall of the training ground. The dust cloud settled, and Shari realised that Mu was lying slumped against the wall, clearly knocked out.

Josie and Ness were closest to her, just behind the tree in front of her, but still on the far side of the stream. Kodan and Lira were behind the middle tree on the north side.

Josie and Kodan looked at each other from behind their respective trees. Ness and Lira nodded, and the half-Ilutri and the former U'sala member shot massive blasts of air at Shari, stripping the leaves off the bushes in front of her. Kodan's blast was so strong that it sent her sprawling between the two trees on the south side of the stream. Leaves, twigs, and dust blew over her, grit filling her mouth and eyes.

Lira and Ness took advantage of Shari's prone form. Lira pulled the dust down and compressed the earth around Shari. Ness baked it to a hardened shell with a strike of plasma.

'*Altoriae!*' Ronah cried out, and the earth around Shari cracked.

'*No! Ronah, that's not fair. This has to be a fair fight,*' Tania scolded the Island.

Shari heard Ronah grumbling, but neither the Island nor her Linked did anything to tighten the previously suffocating earth around her. Shari smiled grimly as she burst out of the dirt, sending clods flying. She headed for the southmost tree, her skin feeling tender, as if she were sunburned. Grimacing at the scorch marks on her fingers, Shari slipped behind the trunk, her back to the cool bark.

Sending her Innarn around the field to see what the candidates were up to, Shari kept her eyes on the stands. *Friendly training exercise. No maiming allowed,* she reminded herself.

She felt the outer edges of a hailstorm of pebbles hit the branches of the tree she was hiding behind. *Lira,* she thought. Turning, Shari was just in time to see Kodan tripping over a branch on his way to the tree in the northeast corner.

Samuel, sitting in the stands behind the Ilutri candidate, watched the youngling out of the corner of his eye, surprised. Therdon was eyeing Kodan scathingly. The former U'sala strike leader suddenly seemed very unsure of himself.

Therdon hadn't seemed particularly good at anything so far, but a few things clicked in Sam's mind as the usually confident Sebbolen stumbled to the tree, curling up in a ball at the base and rocking. If he'd been a lesser being, Sam was of the mind that Kodan would have sobbed his eyes out.

Shari took a moment to close her eyes and recalibrate her mind.

What was the one thing that was between her and the candidates? *The stream.* Grinning, her eyes flew open. Crouching down, hands to the ground, she concentrated on sending plasma snaking through the earth. She sent it slithering just under the topsoil. Slipping into the stream, it stayed in the water. The babbling water did well to hide the occasional spark that would have given away the trap if anyone spotted it.

Ness shot a bolt of plasma at the leaves of Shari's tree, but it fell short. The leaves just the other side of the trunk Ness was hiding behind started to smoulder.

Josie turned to fan the flames that were meant to be on Shari's tree. As she pushed the air out of her palms towards the Altoriae, she set the smouldering leaves above her into a roaring furnace that made both girls' eyes go wide.

Peeking out from behind her trunk, Shari was just in time to see Josie shoot straight into the air, her wings twisting in ways that Shari hadn't thought possible, getting the half-Ilutri safely above the fire while Ness ran and dived into the stream.

For a moment, Shari felt guilty.

Ness shook as soon as her body hit the electrified water. Stunned, the Omina candidate staggered up onto the south bank, her hands and legs covered in plasma burns.

Shari pulled the branches of the closest bush snugly around Ness, taking care not to snag her burns, and sent her the thought that now would be a good time to sleep.

Drowsy, Ness seemed to fight against her drooping eyes.

Lira, still safe behind her tree, looked around to see where her fellow candidates were. Josie was hovering about the burning foliage, her feet glowing in the shimmering heat of the flames. Ness was tangled in the far bushes that ran along the south side of the bank, and Kodan was curled around himself, with his back to the northmost tree.

'*What are you doing?*' Lira sent to Kodan. '*Get up and get out there! We have an Altoriae to subdue, and we can't do it without your help!*'

Kodan started to slowly uncurl from his ball.

In the stands, Therdon leaned forwards. Sam gently kicked the seat of the candidate next to the Ilutri, who turned to glare at him, knocking against Therdon's arm and breaking his concentration. Sam sent a silent apology and turned his eyes back to the action on the training ground, trying hard not to smirk.

On the field, Kodan unwound from the tight ball he'd wrapped himself in and got to his feet. He turned to Lira and nodded once.

Darting around the other side of his tree, he headed straight for the mouth of the stream. Sliding down the bank, he slammed his hands up, the water following them to create a solid shield. It left the ground beneath his feet dry as Kodan crossed the bank. He made it to the bushes on the other side, still maintaining the shield.

'*Put out the fire,*' Kodan ordered Lira. He couldn't believe she hadn't thought of it first.

Lira turned, shotting a jet of water from her palms towards the burning tree below Josie. The jet hit the closest branch and exploded, dousing the fire in one go. Steam dispersed into the air, creating thick fog.

Ness, from her tangle of vines, saw Josie coming straight for her in a low, swooping dive. She flung her hand up, suppressing a cry of pain at the movement. The instant the two touched, the branches around Ness hardened.

Ronah sent quietly in the back of Ness's mind, '*You don't get to attack the Altoriae using my essence without some sort of punishment.*' Her words were soft and gentle—a direct contrast to the ziom-hard branches that anchored Ness to the ground.

Clearly Josie didn't get the send. She grasped Ness's burned hand and pulled, hard.

Ness screamed, agony rippling through her shoulder as it popped out of the joint. The skin on her burned hand ripped open.

Looking up at Josie's shocked face, Ness whimpered. The half-Ilutri released Ness's hand. Watching her saviour wing her way to the tree at the top of the south side of the stream, tears rolled unbidden down her face.

Behind her tree, Shari flinched at Ness's screams, and had to stop herself from sending a wave of healing to the candidate. The green of her healing Innarn shimmered around her hands, and she used it to heal her own burns and get rid of the dust that was scratching at her eyes.

Ness, Kodan, and Josie were now all on the south side of the bank. Shari would go for the strongest first. Tilting her head, she remembered the battle with the fulni and how the U'sala had paled at the sight.

She grinned, too many teeth showing. Raising her hands, she pushed forwards the illusion of six fulni bursting from the other side of her tree.

The illusion charged straight for Kodan, hiding at the bushes near the top of the stream.

In the back of her mind, Shari sensed Jon gasping for breath. The shield he'd put up to prevent outside noise flickered and fell as he succumbed to the panic. The screams of the crowd filled the field. Only the people closest to Shari—and away from the charging fulni—remained seated. Everyone else in the lower levels scampered, trying to escape the creatures that were so recently on Ronah's shore.

Kodan's eyes widened when he spotted the fulni. He dashed for the tree that Josie was hiding behind.

Josie stumbled, stepping right in the path of one of the charging beasts. Kodan slammed into the tree and reached out. Grabbing her by the top of her left wing, he heaved her backwards.

Josie screamed in agony as the radius of her wing snapped under the U'sala's hand. The pain and terror were too much to take. Josie slumped to the ground, unconscious.

The fulni charged past them.

Kodan didn't know if he should be relieved the beasts hadn't turned on them, or worried for Lira. They were heading right for her. He watched in disbelief as the fulni ran straight over the water and rounded the tree he'd been having a panic attack behind just before.

'*Lira!*' he sent frantically.

'*Working on it!*' she sent back.

Kodan watched as Lira looked around desperately. There was no way to outrun the fulni, and any movement would attract them. Her best chance of survival would be distraction.

He grinned as Lira spun circles in the air with her hands. She drew a whole swarm of insects into being between her and the fulni.

Shari, still behind her tree, saw the swarm through the eyes of the lead fulni. All the movement was enough to distract her. The fulni herd went straight through the swarm, passing through them as if the insects weren't real.

In the stands, she felt Jonathan breathe a sigh of relief. There was relief from the screams of the crowd as he raised the noise shield again.

"Isn't the Altoriae's illusion realistic?" he called. As if it were all a great joke and he didn't need to wipe the sweat off his brow at all.

Shari sent a smirk his way, before turning to see what the candidates were up to.

Lira stood frozen on the ground. Shari found herself holding her breath. Her skin turned to stone just before the tip of the lead fulni's horn cut her in half.

Eyes wide beneath the layer of rock, Lira watched in amazement as the herd continued straight on through the trunk of the tree behind her.

Shari felt Lira's thoughts. *It was an illusion.* The Tevon candidate almost sobbed with relief.

On the other side of the stream, Shari caught Kodan looking on with amazement as the fulni passed clear through Lira.

Ness whimpered in pain. In the middle of healing herself, she hadn't noticed the fulni, illusion or not, were stampeding right for her. Looking up from her tangle in the bushes, all she saw were hooves and the underneath of a large beast blocking out her light. She couldn't muster up the energy to care. She still had some serious healing to do.

Shari watched Lira make a run for the burned tree. She sensed Kodan's knives whistling through the air. The pointed projectiles rounded the corner. As they imbedded in the trunk, Shari grinned in relief that she hadn't been hit.

Peeking out, she saw Lira crossing the stream near Ness, pulling the water up to cover her torso. The instant Lira stepped into the flowing water, she was flung back by the still-active trap. Dazed, she peered blearily at Shari from the north shore.

Looking at the stunned candidate, Shari fired bolt after bolt of plasma at Lira. Lira rolled, taking cover behind the bushes on the north side. Ness, who had finally healed her burns and dislocated shoulder, weakly drew some of Shari's plasma away, but hadn't recovered enough to be successful. The bolts passed right over Ness's head, hitting the ground on the other side of her.

As her bolt missed, Shari saw Mu's eyes snap open and dart around.

Mu wasn't in luck. Shari had seen his abrupt awakening. Ducking around to the other side of her tree, she sent another powerful jet of water at the Zindarian. It blasted Mu straight in the chest and held him against the wall for a long moment. He fell in a tangle of limbs to the ground once more.

Kodan finally roused Josie. She blinked blearily at him and got to her feet. Scrubbing a hand across her eyes, she nodded.

Kodan nodded back. He ran for the tree Shari was hiding behind. He was determined to snare the Altoriae.

Ness, still trapped by the bush, must have seen Kodan's frantic dash and sent a volley of plasma bolts at Shari, laying down cover fire for him.

Lira made a bridge of earth to cross the stream and scrambled across it quickly, joining Ness by the bushes.

Back in the game, Josie used her earth Innarn to lift a stack of pebbles from the northeast corner and fling them at Shari as extra cover for Kodan.

Shields up, Shari stumbled around the south side of her tree. She made the ground beneath Josie's feet ripple like waves coming into the shore. Josie laughed at the attempt and kept her balance.

Kodan used the distractions laid down by the other candidates. He spun around the trunk of the tree, slashing Shari's bicep, splitting her armour and the skin beneath.

Shari staggered back, appearing surprised by the direct attack. She didn't get more than a pace away before her training kicked in and she slashed at him with her bladed glove.

Dodging, Kodan aimed a heavy boot at Shari's midsection.

Shari staggered back, winded and fighting for breath. She summoned the yellow short blade and slashed hard.

Her strike split Kodan from left shoulder to right hip. His blue skin bloomed with purple blood.

As Kodan staggered back from the force of Shari's blow, she knew it looked bad from Ness's distraught cry.

The blow spun Kodan around.

No fatalities. Just training, Shari reminded herself. She could feel the sweat building up a grimy layer under her armour.

Shari sensed a rush of Innarn and scooted to the side.

It hit Kodan.

The candidate for the U'sala was surrounded by a solid ball of stone.

"Adeon's flame!" Lira swore at the sight.

'Jon, monitor him,' Shari sent.

There was a mild acknowledgement in the back of her mind. *'Shall I remove him from the trial?'*

'Not unless he's in medical danger. I want to see if he can get out of it.' Shari turned back to the field.

Ness sent a stream of Innarn. Tiny spikes of rock sprouted around her ankles. Shari raised an eyebrow and looked at the candidate from Omina. Maybe she should have been generous because of Ness's wounds, but she'd expected more from her.

'*Kodan is unconscious,*' Jon sent to Shari. '*There's no air in the ball.*'

Shari half-turned back to Kodan. Josie chose that moment to stir up another dust storm. Protected by her shield, Shari watched it rage around her. The pebbles whipped through the air so fast that they managed to crack the ball holding Kodan.

'*He can breathe again,*' Jon sent to her.

Nodding, Shari turned back to the pair by the stream. Out in the open, they were currently her biggest threat. She raised the water level by drawing more water from the ocean around Ronah and adding a touch more plasma just to give it a zing.

Lira shuddered as soon as the water touched her. She fell to the ground, convulsing.

Shielding herself, Ness used the soggy ground to get out of the bush. She crawled through the mud and out of the hardened branches to stand beside the bush.

Shari gathered water from the midpoint of the stream and shot it straight at Josie. Not expecting the attack, Josie slammed against the training ground wall and collapsed. The dust swirling around Shari fell to the ground, and the field was still for a heartbeat.

By the stream, Ness sent, '*I'm not hurting the Altoriae, I swear,*' to Ronah. The Island passed the send on as Ness raised a cage of stone around Shari.

The Altoriae laughed, and the cage burst apart dramatically. Shari gathered the chunks of stone and flung them at Ness.

She dodged and fired them back at Shari.

Shari let the earth build up in front of her, forming a wall out of the stone and debris, gathering it all until the wall was as tall as her. Pushing hard, Shari sent the entire wall straight at Ness.

Eyes wide as she looked at the impossible sight, Ness didn't even attempt to raise a shield. The wall hit her straight on. The force was enough to send her flying clear over the other side of the bank, bones snapping under the force of her landing.

Panting from the effort of moving the mass of stone at such a speed, Shari dismissed the wall and looked around the training ground.

Lira lay on the bank just in front of her, the wall having just barely missed her. Ness and Mu were sprawled out on the other side of the bank, both unconscious. Slumped on the eastern wall, Josie was unconscious as well. Kodan remained trapped in the ball.

"Congratulations, candidates, on a hard-fought round! The Altoriae and I will now retire to make the difficult decision of who will go through to the next trial." Jon's voice boomed around her, loud in the sudden quiet after the battle.

Holli Doonavan was rushing onto the field, gesturing for Shari to break apart the stone ball holding the prone body of the U'sala candidate.

Shari didn't know if she should be glad that she'd beaten them all, feel guilty over their injuries, or annoyed that they'd almost gotten the best of her a few times.

The slash on her bicep stung as she flicked her hand and the stone fell away from Kodan. She was half-tempted to let it scar as a reminder to not discount what others would do when they were desperate.

'*You fought well, Shari,*' Jon sent.

'*This one was different,*' she sent back. '*Kodan got a hit in.*' Inspecting her arm, she sent a pulse of green healing at it.

'*Are you alright?*'

She could feel Jon peering at her from the stands. '*Of course. I just need to make sure it doesn't happen again.*'

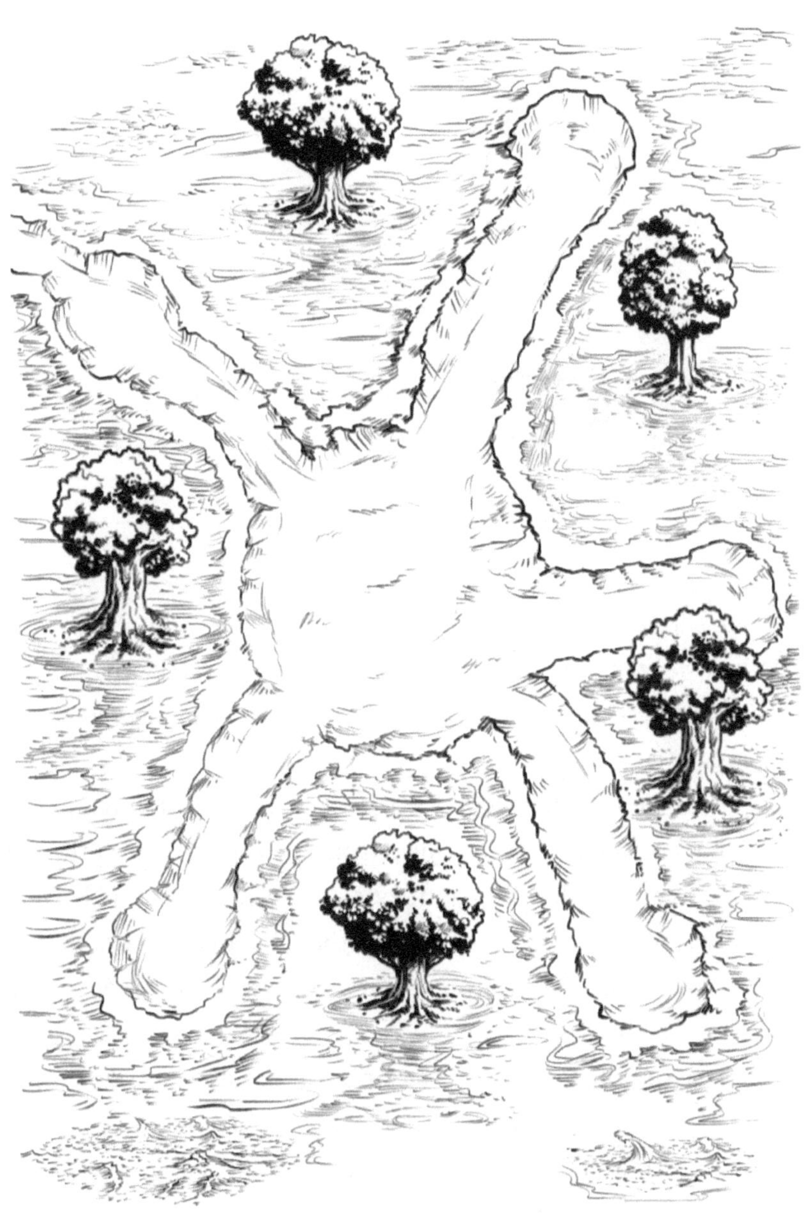

First Trial – Third Round

CHAPTER TWENTY-SIX

Sam slipped out of his seat and made it to the exit before the others had stood. He didn't know what to think. Shari had fought hard, but he knew that she was capable of more, and he didn't entirely understand it.

"You must have long legs!" a voice called from behind him.

Sam kept walking as the noise from the crowd exiting the training ground became louder. He had no idea when Kodan would be released, and he wasn't exactly eager to meet the U'sala candidate. Still, as the crowd started to swarm around him, he sent a trickle of Innarn out, searching for threats.

It was probably the only reason Lizbeth kept her hand when she placed it on his arm. "Long legs, I tell you."

Glaring down at her was pointless, but he did it anyway. She laughed at him. "Don't be like that. See me home, and I might share my rutenberry cookies with you."

Frowning, he looked at her out of the corner of his eye, trying to gauge how serious she was, and wondering exactly what a rutenberry tasted like.

Lizbeth laughed again and patted his arm. "Come now. You'll enjoy them, I wager."

Sam grumbled at her, but guided her gently to her house, letting her fill the silence with idle chatter about the beautiful day and the fine weather until they crossed her threshold and she let go of his arm, gently pushing him towards the living room.

"Sit. Make yourself comfortable, and we can eat and discuss the trials of the day," she said, walking into the kitchen, effortlessly navigating around the furniture in her way.

Settling into what was rapidly becoming *his* seat, Sam looked about the room, taking note of the ornaments displayed on a high shelf for the first time. The ledge ran all the way around the room, sitting just above the doorframe, and contained opaque containers with different Innarn swirling around inside them.

He looked from one to the other, trying to discern a pattern, and was unable to. Lizbeth entered the room, a tray full of cookies and a teapot cradled in her hands. She seemed to know where his attention was focused.

"I was wondering when you'd notice my photographs," she said, setting the tray down.

Frowning, Sam chewed over the word "photographs". He thought they were captured visual representations of moments in time, put onto paper or canvas. He hadn't realised that they were Innarn in a jar.

His host laughed softly. "Regular photographs aren't going to do me much good, are they? Here." She flicked her finger and one of the jars floated down into her hands. "Try this," she said, passing it to him.

Sam took the jar, the smooth surface cold in his hand despite the yellow and red swirling inside it. Reaching out with his Innarn, he gasped, and fumbled with the jar when he fell into a memory.

Lizbeth was younger by at least a decade, although her eyes were still clouded. She was standing in the town square, red and gold autumn leaves swirling around her. The hiss and crackle of a bonfire was in his ears, the smell of wood smoke in his nose. He felt surrounded by the thick blue coat she was wearing, and his head warm until the scarf her hair was wrapped in came loose and she laughed, turning to smile at a younger Shari, who was grinning up at her, teasingly.

Rocking back in his seat, Sam drew his Innarn away from the memory. The image of Shari so young and seemingly carefree was burned into his brain. He hadn't realised exactly how much Shari had changed; the cost of protecting Lissae rested more and more on her shoulders.

Gently, Lizbeth eased the jar out of his hands and sent it sailing back up to its spot on the shelf. "Now you see why I prefer these to bits of paper that I can't sense at all."

"So, they're memories?" Sam said, his voice hoarse as his mind struggled to grasp what he'd come across.

"Essentially, they are a copy of a memory, full of all the senses of the person who gave them to me. Shari gave me that one a few days after our autumn celebration," Lizbeth said, pouring the tea into a cup, then offering it to Sam.

Sam took it, grateful to do something with his hands again. He stared into the dark liquid for a long moment before Lizbeth gently nudged a cookie in his direction.

"Try it," she said.

"What exactly is a rutenberry?" he asked, looking at the dark spots on the cookie suspiciously.

"Delicious," she said with a laugh.

Wondering exactly how many times he would be expected to handle the tiny woman laughing at him, he took a bite. Crumbs littered his shirt, but he couldn't care less as the cookie dissolved in his mouth, sweet and rich. The dark rutenberries coated his tongue in a velvet sugary rush. He closed his eyes in bliss, concentrating on the taste. Lizbeth's laugh startled him, and Sam's eyes snapped open again.

"Eat up. If you hold them in your hand, the rutenberries will melt," she advised, reaching for another.

Sam didn't need to be told twice. His worries disappeared to the back of his mind, and he ate until his belly was full and his teeth ached from the sheer amount of sugar he'd consumed. Sitting back, he let his mind empty, content to sit in the company of someone who demanded nothing of him.

The Chirea scout watched from the vantage point in the tree across from the blind woman's house as the one calling himself Sam exited her dwelling. Sharp eyes peered from beneath the skull helmet as the being strode down the road. The scout slipped silently from his perch and crept after the dark one, determined not to lose him this time.

Jon suppressed the scowl on his face as he applied the healing gel to Shari's arm. It was not her fault that the stress of the rounds was getting to him. It was difficult to sit in the stands and watch her rather than be out there, fighting alongside his charge.

"Who do you think should go through to the next round?" he asked lightly.

Shari didn't even wince as the gel went to work, knitting her skin back together. "I thought for sure it would be Kodan, but after his performance today, I'm not convinced. He was a different fighter when I saw him with the U'sala," she admitted.

"I did expect more as well, but I think that he did better than Mu," Jon said.

"Oh, poor Mu. I really wanted him to do more! I think Josie or Lira would be a good choice," Shari said.

"Which one do you think you could work with?" Jon asked.

Shari wrinkled her nose. "I haven't really spent enough time with either of them. I keep leaning back to Kodan over the others, but I wish I could have seen how strong his plasma was."

"Then it's decided," Jon said with a shrug. He'd have to inform the U'sala. "What do you want to do for the last two rounds?"

"I was thinking a forest for round three and tiny floating islands for round four," Shari said.

Jon raised his eyebrows. "A forest for the candidates in round three would give them the advantage. Elain and Reon got top marks for earth Innarn," he said.

"What else can we do then?" Shari groaned.

"How about a whole heap of water?" Jon suggested.

"I like the way you think," Shari grinned.

The seats that surrounded the training ground were already filled to the brim with people talking in curious tones about the change of terrain— or the lack of it—when Shari stepped out and strode to the large flat disc of the middle island.

Five bridges connected tiny islands to the main one, all of them only five paces wide. Between each island was a tree on a tiny plot of land, just big enough to stand on.

Jon's booming voice filled the training ground, silencing the crowd. "Well met to all, for the third round of the first trial! Candidates Elani from Ginorti, Therdon from Rakemyst, Caeli from Akoren, and Reon from Vutana will attempt to capture our Altoriae by putting a shield around her. If it can hold for more than a minute, the candidates will have succeeded in subduing her," Jon said, winking at Shari. "Now, let's see how well our candidates can do this time!"

Jon raised his hands dramatically, the noise shield activated, and the training ground plunged into silence.

Shari shook her head at her Guardian and pushed her shields up. She waited with bated breath as the candidates crossed the bridge and stepped out onto the first tiny island, standing shoulder to shoulder.

Caeli smirked at Shari and raised one hand, sending a spray of water shooting into the air. It vaporised, leaving a thick blanket of fog between Shari and the candidates.

Behind the wall of fog, Shari felt the moment that Elani and Reon linked their minds. They were trying to raise the ground beneath the water.

Reon was struggling to hold onto Elani's mind as the ground rumbled around them. Heaving it up from depths he hadn't expected, Shari could almost feel the sweat that Reon wiped at to stop it dripping into his eyes.

Shari took to her heels. Bolting for the southwest island, she ducked down to become a smaller target.

Looking confident, Therdon raised his hands. On the newly restored land around them, a small army of perfectly duplicated candidates appeared.

The fog dissipated, and Shari pretended to be surprised at the sight of the land that wasn't there before, and the army that faced her. With a shake of her head, the duplicates became ghostlike. Spotting the real candidates easily, Shari shook her head again. She sent a small wave splashing up at their heels, causing Reon and Elani to skitter forwards.

Therdon's eyes swept the field. Shari could feel the instant he focused on her hiding place. His eyes narrowed and he yelled out, "Charge!"

Caeli and Elani took off. Reon seemed to dance nervously on his hooves for a moment before he raced after the girls. Therdon brought up the rear.

As Reon ran, he pulled the dirt behind him, using his earth Innarn to make a lumpy earthen shield to protect them all.

Shari grinned, more teeth than mirth. She slashed downwards with her hand. The land underneath the candidates slipped back below the waves.

Reon's shield didn't do anything to protect them when the ground fell away from under their feet. Spluttering and cursing, they fell back towards the water.

Elani, closest to the bridge, leaped frantically and teetered at the edge before stepping onto firm ground.

Shari wiggled her fingers in Elani's face. She felt the buzz of a send between Therdon and Elani. Unexpectedly, Elani pulled the two curving blades out from the harness on her back and charged at Shari.

Eyes wide, Shari pulled the air around herself and jumped from her little island to the tree on her right. She didn't stop. She hopped straight over to the next island, the Satyr on her heels. Giving herself an extra boost, she flew up into the next tree and teetered on the edge.

Elani drew to a halt a step before the edge of the island. Shari watched in confusion as she turned and started to make her way back to the main island.

Caeli began to whirl in the water. She used her air Innarn to create a waterspout that placed her safely on the main island, stumbling as she landed. Reon, riding a wave of water, staggered onto the main island beside her. Elani came charging up on his other side, leaving Therdon floundering in the water behind them. Shari realised that the weight of it on his wings was dragging him under.

Frantically, Therdon broadcasted, '*Help!*'

Shari watched as his teammates mechanically turned towards him. Elani stared intently at the tree closest to the floundering Ilutri. She sent a vine straight down to him, tangling it around his thrashing waist and raising him up to deposit him next to Caeli on the main island.

Shari looked at them and giggled from her perch in the tree before making the edge of the main island crumble, sending them skittering farther into the middle.

She felt another buzzing sensation of a send between Therdon and Elani.

Eyes glazed over, the Satyr turned to the Altoriae and, sword still in hand, pointed it straight at the tree. Shari could see her clenched jaw and white knuckles as the branches tangled around Shari's feet.

Earth Innarn should come easily to Elani. There was a tingling in the back of her mind warning her that something wasn't right. It would have to wait until after the trial to puzzle out.

Seeing what Elani was attempting, Reon and Caeli moved to help. Reon's eyes blazed, and the branches of the tree grew at an alarming rate, trapping Shari's legs together. Caeli pushed a gale of dust and grit into Shari's face.

Still encased in her shield, Shari wasn't bothered by the dust. She teetered in place at the top of the oversized tree before it leaned over from Caeli's gale. Almost in slow motion, the tiny island tipped, sending the tree—and Shari—crashing into the water below. Struggling briefly with the branches tangling her legs, Shari cut her way free and began swimming under the water to the far side of the field. She ducked underneath the bridges between islands to come up behind the candidates.

With a sweep of her arm, she sent them all flying to the ground, trapped against the smooth dirt by an invisible hand.

Instinctively, Reon's defensive shields kicked in and in desperation, he used an earth shield to push against the weight holding him down.

But in his panic, the dirt around them lifted and slammed down onto them, showering them with tiny, high-speed projectiles.

Another buzz of a send between Therdon and Elani, but Shari caught it this time.

'*Help Reon!*' Therdon commanded.

Elani's hands slammed down harder onto the ground beneath them and it rippled outwards before slamming up directly under Shari's feet. Shari rocked on her new plateau but remained standing.

Caeli tried to counter Shari's pressing earth attack with tears in her eyes and gasping for breath. She pushed against it so that she was able to breathe easily again.

Shari slammed her fist into the ground, shattering the earth all around them. The candidates flew back, hitting the walls of the training ground, unconscious. Shari hovered above them all in a twister of air.

'*You didn't have to do that, Shari,*' Jon grumbled at her.

'*I was going to win this round anyway.*' Shari floated, smirking slightly. The clouds above seemed to rush past at a greater speed until suddenly, cheering filled the training ground as the shield was dropped.

"The candidates have all been knocked out! Congratulations, Altoriae!"

Alistair caught up to Tania as she was walking away from the training ground, grumbling under her breath, her voice pitched too low for him to make out the words.

"So, that was quick," he said, shoulders hunched and hands shoved deep into his pockets.

Tania blinked, like she hadn't expected him to be there. "It really was. I don't know if Shari is getting into the swing of things or if the candidates in that round just weren't up to the task."

Alistair scuffed the path with his shoe. "Like me, you mean?"

Tania stopped, and the residents of Ronah poured around them, chattering about the last round, and wondering who the Altoriae would put through to the next trial. Alistair squirmed under the piercing gaze of his big sister, wishing that he'd kept his mouth shut.

"Do you know why I didn't want you to agree to be Jon's candidate?" Tania asked.

Feeling like her eyes were piercing his soul, he mutely shook his head.

"Because I've seen a teeny, tiny bit of the horrible things that Shari must do to keep the Realm safe, and I know that it affects her more than she'll ever admit. If there's anyone that I could prevent having to go through that, it'd be you. You are so..." Her hands raised as if she was trying to claw the right words from the air.

"Weak? Pathetic? Useless?" Alistair filled in.

Tania snorted. "Hardly," she said. "You are so carefree. You have a chance to have the childhood I never got in a place that is pretty much magical! I wish only good things for you, and I don't think that anyone should be turned into a child soldier, especially my brother!"

Ducking his head, Alistair took a moment to process her words, trying to figure out the best way to make her understand. "I'm not you, Tania. My life hasn't been bad. I haven't had to see the stuff that you have, and I don't have a problem using my Innarn to help protect others who don't have the option, like Mum and Dad."

Looking away from him, her arms wrapped around her middle, Alistair noticed tears in her eyes. He remembered one of the first times he'd met Tania. She'd fallen, breaking her arm badly. She hadn't cried then, even when the healers had had to wrench her arm back into place to line the bones up before they set it.

Lunging forwards, he hugged her tight, trying to convey that he was strong enough to withstand everything that being the Guardian's candidate entailed.

The candidates and their Elders were meeting up at the castle for one last dinner before the final round. Shari was late, and Samuel found himself capturing the irritated glare of several of the remaining contestants.

One of them, her red hair piled into a messy, lopsided bun on top of her head, made her way over to him, her gaze free of malice.

"Well met, fellow candidate. I'm Amara, the Daen candidate. We're in the last round together, I think?" she asked.

Samuel looked her up and down. Her fire Innarn was practically glowing around her. "Perhaps if you go and stand by the Kumaru we'd only be up against the Weaver?" he suggested.

Amara grinned at him. "I had thought about it," she admitted, "but figured it wouldn't look very good."

"Is that what you're worried about?" he drawled. There were far too many beings on this Realm who were obsessed with appearance.

"Hardly," she snorted. "More that I don't think the Altoriae would look favourably on it."

"Why do you think I suggested you do it?" he said slyly.

She blinked her big eyes at him and laughed. "Oh, I like you!" she gasped out.

Samuel raised an eyebrow just as Shari entered the room, the occupants going silent. She looked amazing in her long green dress. She gave an awkward nod at the room that had him wincing.

"She doesn't know what to do in a friendly crowd, does she?" Amara said softly, frowning in Shari's direction.

Narrowing his eyes at the diminutive girl, he nodded. It wasn't exactly a secret from the other candidates at this stage. "She really doesn't."

Amara sighed. "I wish I could..." she started to say.

"Why are you talking to him?" interrupted Therdon.

"Because..." Amara started, wrinkling her nose in confusion.

"You shouldn't," Therdon said, and grabbed at her arm.

Samuel lunged forwards and wrapped his hand around the Ilutri's wrist, squeezing. "I wouldn't," he growled, pulling his Innarn tight against his skin.

Therdon looked at him, eyes wide and chin trembling as Shari stepped up to the trio.

"Sam?" she asked, censure in her voice.

"He was going to touch Amara," Samuel growled, and the Daen shivered.

Shari's eyes flicked over the three of them, assessing the situation. "Therdon?" she asked.

"Amara and I were just going to have a chat," Therdon said.

Samuel saw the exact moment Shari sensed Therdon pressing on her mental shields.

"Really?" the Altoriae said softly.

Clearly, the others in the room remembered the last time Shari had used that tone, and they backed away. Amara looked around and, reading the room, skittered backwards too, pinwheeling her arms as she tripped over her own feet. Without looking at her, Samuel extended a tendril of Innarn and pulled her upright, allowing her to keep her remaining dignity.

"We were... we're old friends, that go way back," Therdon said, his voice low and calm, still foolishly pressing on Shari's mental shields.

Samuel dropped the cretin's hand and crossed his arms, looking forward to the punishment that Shari was going to dish out.

"Well," Shari said, her voice so soft, the Ilutri had to lean in to hear her, "I don't think she wants to talk now, but I wouldn't mind talking to you."

Therdon looked as if all his birthdays had come at once. "As you wish, Altoriae," he said, the tips of his wings scraping the floor as he bowed.

Shari walked out of the room, Therdon eagerly by her side, his chest puffed out, until he turned to see Samuel closing the doors between them and the rest of the party.

"This doesn't involve you," Therdon snarled at him.

"Actually, it does," Shari said sweetly, "because he's the one who's going to escort you off Ronah for trying to influence me." Her gaze narrowed, and she stalked towards him, the Ilutri scrambling backwards until his wings met the wall behind him. "How many others did you try to influence?"

"Kodan," Samuel said.

Reeling back as if the thought hadn't occurred to her, the shock on Shari's face was quickly replaced by rage. "Who else?" she snarled.

Samuel heard movement behind the doors and drew shadows over Shari and the quivering Ilutri. There was no wonder that he'd had it out for Samuel; not only was he the Altoriae's candidate, but there was no way Therdon's mental manipulations would work on him.

"I believe the answer to 'who else' would be me," SilverCloud said as he scanned the hall. Clearly, he'd heard Shari's question, even if he couldn't currently see where she was.

"What?" Shari said, drawing back farther.

Samuel cancelled the shadows and watched the Elder's eyes come to rest on his granddaughter.

"I told you before, Shari. I'm not sure why Therdon was chosen when there were others that are far more capable than he," SilverCloud said.

Therdon snarled at his Elder and lunged at him, but found himself looking at the pointy end of Shari's yellow blade.

"You're done here," Shari said.

Samuel was impressed that she didn't growl. Personally, he wanted to rip the limbs one at a time from the trembling idiot before him, and found that he was only stayed by the thought of Shari's censure.

Therdon opened his mouth to say something but seemed to realise that he was up against two beings who wouldn't fall for his mental Innarn tricks. Instead, he turned his gaze to SilverCloud, seemingly to plead with him.

A shiver of Innarn brushed against Sam's skin a heartbeat before the Ilutri Elder attacked.

SilverCloud smashed into him. A blast of pure Light air Innarn sent Samuel flying down the hall, limbs akimbo.

Before Samuel's head bounced off the hard stone of the castle floor, he saw Shari turning her back on Therdon to push up a shield between her and SilverCloud, who was pounding it with a fury that he wouldn't have expected from the frail Elder.

Therdon drew a dagger that flashed silver in the light.

Samuel used his Innarn to launch himself to his feet. His entire body protesting, he stepped forwards and *pushed*. A jet of pure Dark Innarn slid out of his hand, slamming into Therdon's dagger just as it pierced Shari's dress.

Therdon's gaze shot to him.

Samuel snarled, trembling from SilverCloud's Light Innarn attack and the force of keeping to his human form. A gold haze enveloped him. Roaring, he charged at Therdon.

The terrified Ilutri let out a shriek as the other candidates poured out of the room, gazes incredulous and jaws dropping as they took in the scene.

SilverCloud was still slamming an incredible amount of air Innarn against Shari's shield, intent on breaking it apart.

Samuel reached Therdon. Grabbing him by the front of his tunic, he threw the cretin against the wall next to the doors, using his Innarn to hold out the tuzar. "Let him go!" Samuel snarled when he found his voice.

"Make me," Therdon choked out. "There's a sweet sort of justice in the old fool killing his kin."

The other Elders gasped.

Shadowy wings appeared behind him as Samuel snarled again.

Amara slipped through the crowd and picked up Therdon's dagger. She glided along the wall and winked at Samuel before smacking the hilt into Therdon's temple. The Ilutri dropped like a sack of dung.

Samuel snarled at the Ilutri candidate. Gathering his shaky self-control, he nodded at her. Eyes tight, he turned to see Shari still holding back SilverCloud's attack.

"Why hasn't he stopped?" Amara asked.

Squinting, Samuel looked between the two. He saw the thread of Innarn that Linked them. The energy that he'd assumed had come from Therdon was coming from the air. "He's using air Innarn to keep his control intact."

Amara gasped, and a few of the others swore.

"May I?" said the Weaver candidate, Bren, coming to stand by them.

"All yours," Samuel snarled again, waving a hand. Really, who asked permission before entering a battle? He rethought the statement when a bony hand shot out from beneath the Weaver's robes and grabbed his arm. Samuel startled, but before he could so much as snarl, his thoughts were turned to the Ilutri Elder.

Stuck in the back of his mind, Samuel watched as Bren studied the link between Therdon and SilverCloud before it was abruptly severed.

The Elder slumped.

Only Shari's quick reflexes caught him before he hit the floor.

Now that the danger had passed, others streamed forwards, collecting the Elder and rushing him to the healers.

Exhausted and aching, Samuel leaned against the wall to catch his breath. Light Innarn was the one thing in this blasted Realm that hurt more than anything else.

Shari slid up to him. "Sam? Are you alright?"

"I could ask the same of you," he said, straightening from his slump.

"I'm fine," she brushed him off. He raised an eyebrow, and she sighed. *'Did Jon teach you the eyebrow trick?'* she snarked at him. "Shocked and scratched, but little else," she amended.

"Scratched?" he said. Remembering the dagger slicing through the back of her dress, he abruptly turned her and found the sliced material. A finger-length scratch from the tip of the dagger graced her back.

"It's nothing," she said, craning her neck to look at him over her shoulder. "I think Therdon using my grandfather to attack me is more hurtful than that."

"He is a worm and should be stepped on," Sam growled.

"Don't be silly," Shari shot back. "Worms are useful. Therdon is not."

Plans flickered to life in his mind—using the boy and discarding him. Clearly, SilverCloud was immensely powerful, but Therdon had been able to control him to fight his own family, something that mental Innarn users shouldn't be able to do. Mental Innarn was meant to encourage, beguile, and ensnare, but not outright make another being go against their beliefs. Well, not on this Realm anyway.

Sam found himself intrigued by the sharp smile Shari gave him.

"I think I'll let LoneWolf deal with him," Shari said.

Grinning back, Sam agreed that of all the Ilutri, LoneWolf would be the least forgiving of the little imbecile's actions.

First Trial – Fourth Round

CHAPTER TWENTY-SEVEN

Xanon, the new leader, looked over the Chirean army, the bloodshot eyes beneath their helmets shining as brightly as the white-knuckled grips on their bows.

Luttrell hadn't been the brightest of them, but he'd been the fiercest, and all his clan missed him.

Shocked at his defeat, they hadn't had time to mourn before they'd been whisked away by the Light Innarnian. Xannon grieved their missed chance to avenge Luttrell. He wondered if it was worth it, when every scuffle they'd had on the accursed Realm of Lissae seemed to lead to more and more Chirean deaths. He was lost in thought, wondering where his kin would be safe, when the quiet whimpers died down.

As Xannon thought of the Innarnian, he appeared, his purple robe brushing the dusty path. The male, his hood concealing his face, stepped up to Xannon, striding past the others like they weren't worthy to lick the filth from his boots.

"I take it you're the one in charge now?" the Innarnian asked, as if the death of their leader for the last twenty-three seasons didn't matter.

Xannon felt his head pounding and heard the roar of battle in his ears as he surged to his feet, charging towards the Innarnian.

"Ah, ah, ah," the Innarnian said, waving a hand as if he was going to shoo away a gnat.

Xannon froze, then slammed sideways into a kinsman, both tumbling to the ground.

The Innarnian strode forwards and peered at him from under his hood. "It seems like such a waste to have to go through all this training again. At least Luttrell was easy to manipulate. I have a feeling that you will be much harder. A shame." The Innarnian tapped a finger to his chin. "You could have been useful."

Xannon's heart raced. He tried breathing through his nose to slow it down, but it seemed to race even faster. The Innarnian was still tapping his chin, eyes locked on Xannon's as his heart beat faster still. He willed it to slow down, the way he did before a battle, but the Innarnian raised a brow, and suddenly, Xannon realised that his heart wasn't beating out of his chest from fear, but the Innarnian was making it happen.

"Stop." Xannon forced the word from his throat. "I'll do it." He wasn't exactly sure what the Innarnian wanted, but to lose two leaders in such a short time would destroy what was left of his clan.

The Innarnian leaned forwards, his nose almost touching Xannon's helmet. "Will you?" he drawled, grinning in a way that made Xannon's skin crawl under his armour.

Gulping as his galloping heart started to slow, Xannon regretted his hasty offer, but then he saw Fusstan's armour out of the corner of his eye. All that mattered was keeping his people intact enough to fight another day.

"So, here's what we're going to do," the Innarnian said, backing up and waving a hand so that Xannon and Fusstan could rise to their feet again. "You're going to send some of your friends here to keep an eye on one particular being on Lissae. He goes by the name Sam, and is close to the Altoriae, so you'll want to send someone who can blend in. This being is dangerous, and if things take a turn, he needs to be removed from the situation. Permanently. Are we clear?"

"Yes," Xannon spat out.

"Good," the Innarnian said, and disappeared with a flick of his wrist.

Xannon growled. He wouldn't put it past the Innarnian to have just turned himself invisible. "Fusstan. You're the best. Go, do what the Innarnian said," Xannon barked.

Fusstan, his childhood friend, the one who'd been there when he'd earned his first piece of armour, looked at him from beneath his blackened helmet. "As you wish." His voice sounded like rocks tumbling over each other.

"I expect you to come back and let me know when you're done," Xannon said. They both knew that the Innarnian would order this 'Sam' to die—preferably sooner than later. Fusstan quirked one corner of his mouth up and nodded before hefting his bow and heading towards the xarit.

Xannon looked after him with anguished eyes. His first command as leader was sending his friend to his death. Shaking his hands out to disguise the tremors, Xannon dearly hoped to see Fusstan again.

The crowds in the training ground were subdued as the news of Therdon's disqualification spread. People looked on, shocked and appalled. There were a few curious gazes, no doubt trying to discern Therdon's motivation by prodding at him with their Innarn.

Shari, standing in the shade of a group of trees, let it all wash over her, preparing for the final round of the first trial.

This was the round she'd been dreading. Bren and Sam were the top two scoring candidates. Although Shari had insisted on fighting them both at the same time, right now, she was wishing she hadn't. Still, unwillingly fighting others wasn't exactly unusual for her.

Jon had created a miniature forest in the training ground. The largest group of trees started in the middle of the ground and curved around to the east before coming back on itself, leaving room for three beings to pass through at the top, and a clearing for traps in the middle. There were seven other clumps of trees scattered around the outer edges, one for each of the Shifting Islands. Shari thought it was quite appropriate for the final round. Jon had even gone to the effort of including leaf litter and fallen branches, making Shari feel like she was in an old-growth forest, and not something that had sprung up last night.

The crowd rippled, heads turning towards Jon as he stood.

"Well met to all for the final round of the first trial. Candidates Haran from Dento, Amara from Cantash, Bren from Vannali, and Samuel from Ronah are the last group to attempt to shield our Altoriae for more than one minute. The remaining candidates from the previous rounds put up a valiant effort; let us see if this last lot can survive!"

There were no dramatic gestures from Jon this time, just a gentle fading of noise until Shari heard a twig snap on the other side of the small cluster of trees in front of her.

The candidates had arrived.

Shaking out her fingers and raising her shield, Shari pressed her back against a tree and waited, senses on alert, but she still blinked in surprise when a face peered at her through the trees. Haran grinned and a rough hand waved between parted branches.

"Well met, Altoriae," Haran said.

"Well met, candidate," Shari replied, then shot a blast of plasma directly at his face.

Haran frowned at her, patting at his smouldering eyebrows. "That wasn't very nice," he said mildly, and a twig snapped off to Shari's left.

Her gaze flickered for a moment, and she spotted Amara's boots, but a blast came from her right. Shari found herself caged in a spirit shield.

Eyes wide, Shari pushed air Innarn around her in a twister. She forced the shield to enlarge farther and farther until finally it collapsed.

"... only ten seconds! Congratulations, candidates, but you'll have to try harder than that!" Jon's voice boomed, before the noise from the stands was cancelled out again.

Shaken, Shari glared at where the shield had come from to see Bren, white robes removed, his inky-black skin blending in with the shadows. Bren grinned at her, white teeth flashing. He shot another stream of silvery Innarn at her, which she dodged.

Firing back a sharp blast of air to send him staggering, Shari moved into the shelter of the grove, hoping she looked appropriately scared.

The air was heavy with the sensation of the candidates' sending, and Shari hid her smile. This was what she wanted—beings who were able to work as part of a team.

In front of her, Haran stepped through the trees as if they weren't there. Bren crept closer on her right, and Amara approached from the left, but where was Sam?

She didn't have time to think about it anymore. All three candidates hit her with a multilayered shield at the same time.

As Shari pulled apart the earth, fire, and spirit shield, she started sweating beneath her leathers.

Five seconds.

Ten seconds.

Fifteen.

Finally, the earth Innarn slipped away from the shield.

Twenty seconds.

With only fire and spirit surrounding her, Shari pulled the water from the area close to her body with her left hand and used her right to make a twister of air that pushed her off the ground and through the shield.

"… twenty-five seconds, folks! Maybe these candidates will manage to trap the Altoriae after all," Jon's voice called across the ground. Shari knew it was more of a warning to her than a reminder to the crowd.

'*I'm on it, Jon,*' Shari sent him, landing in the branches of a tree on the far east of the ground. Closing her eyes, she activated the fire trap at the start of the clearing and finally laid eyes on Sam as he came around the bottom corner of the big group of trees.

Summoning the Lightest part of her Innarn, she set up a trap between the bottom east grove and one of the trees midway up the east path of the large clump. Quietly moving through the branches, she heard her fire trap to go off. A voice cried out in pain.

Wincing, Shari didn't slow down. She moved towards the top of her group of trees. A rough hand reached through the branches towards her, sliding among the bark as if it wasn't there.

Maybe I should have gone with the desert? Shari dropped to the ground. Chancing a look behind her, she saw Sam standing right at the edge of her Light Innarn trap, as if sensing it. She frowned at him. He smirked and raised his hand. A small shriek sounded from the other side of the clearing. Amara, limbs flailing, was lifted over the treetops, and placed between Sam and Shari.

She ducked as Amara shot a fireball at her. It hit the wall of the training ground and bounced off.

A startled "Oomph!" came from just around the corner. Shari turned to run in the direction of the sound, but found herself nose-to-chest against Haran. He grinned down at her and wrapped his arms around her tight.

Amara pushed a fire shield around Shari and Haran. The Kumaru looked mildly concerned. His grip didn't change.

Shari took a deep breath.

Five seconds.

Reminding herself that panicking was for later, she got to work. Pulling water from the ground, she doused Amara's shield.

Ten seconds.

Just as it flickered out, Sam twitched a finger and a Dark Innarn shield sprung into life around Haran and Shari.

Haran grunted and staggered but held tight, beads of sweat trickling down his barky face.

Fifteen seconds.

"Sorry," Shari said as she looked up at him. Closing her eyes so she wouldn't see the look of pain on Haran's face, Shari added to the Dark Innarn shield. Haran's grip went slack.

Thirty seconds.

Shari pushed a bit more. Haran groaned and toppled over. His eyes rolled backwards, his bark-like skin was blistered and peeling.

Forty seconds.

She pulled the Dark Innarn into her in a move that few others on Lissae could do.

The shield faltered and fell. Shari twisted, blasting Amara with Dark Innarn.

The young Daen dropped.

Sam, still standing on the other side of her Light Innarn trap, raised a brow. "Impressive," he murmured, "but can you contain this?"

That was all the warning Shari got.

Sam slammed her with jet after jet of pure Innarn, elbows bent and resting near his hips. If it wasn't for the black streaming from his fingertips, he'd look like he was casually standing around in a forest.

Dancing backwards, Shari moved out of Sam's line of sight. He just strolled into the shade of the south eastern clump of trees, continuing to fire Dark Innarn at her.

Summoning her yellow blade, Shari used it to reflect the streams back at him. She slipped around the corner when she paused in surprise.

Bren was waiting for her.

The Weaver looked at her with narrowed eyes. "You are too used to being the strongest in a battle. You must use everything at your disposal," he said to her.

Raising her eyebrows, Shari said, "Everything?" and used a flick of air Innarn to smack a rather solid tree branch into the back of Bren's skull.

Bren slammed forwards. A second low branch caught him across the stomach and rotated him, so he landed face up. Creeping closer, Shari coaxed reluctant tree roots up to entangle the unconscious Weaver. She created a trap designed to catch any unfortunate being in a bubble of water around him.

Hearing heavy boots behind her, Shari sprinted towards the middle of the ground. She came to a stop right near where she had started the round.

Jon's voice boomed over the ground. "Candidate Haran has been removed from this round for medical reasons. Good luck to the remaining candidates."

Shari's face fell. She reminded herself that Holli and her crew of healers were on standby. If Haran was out, and Bren was trapped, then she had only Amara and Sam to contend with.

There was a shriek and the wet plop of her water bubble trap being activated. Now she just had to contend with Sam.

Speak of the candidate. He was running at her, his face twisted in a furious scowl.

Before Shari had a chance to counter, his fist swung and landed a solid blow to her belly. She gasped and landed flat on her back. She looked up at Sam as he stood over her. He had one leg either side of her prone form, fists cocked and ready to go.

"That was my team," Sam snarled at her. He waved a hand through the air and a thick spirit shield cut them off from the outside world.

'*Shari?*' Jon sent.

'*I'm fine,*' she sent back.

On the inner walls of the shield, silvery outlines of Bren, Haran, and Amara appeared next to Sam.

Five seconds.

Shari got to see them conversing and coming up with a plan, which Shari had inadvertently foiled. Sam's guilt at letting the Dark Innarn shield build to the extent that it had, his surprise when Shari had added to it and used the power against his own teammates. His fury when Amara had let him know that Haran was unresponsive and severely burned from the Dark Innarn were all played out for her.

Shari looked up at him, still gasping for breath.

'*Twenty-three seconds, Shari,*' Jon prodded.

'*I spoke to Bren,*' Shari sent to Sam as she continued to struggle for breath. He'd put every bit of momentum into that punch.

"And what did the Weaver say?" Sam snarled at her.

Thirty-five seconds.

'*That I should use everything at my disposal,*' she said. She punched up at his unprotected groin, using the air inside the shield to push her, adding even more power behind the strike.

The effect was instantaneous.

Sam's eyes went wide. Something golden and feral shined behind his carefully crafted façade. His hands snapped down to cup his groin even as he went flying up and off her.

Forty seconds.

The spirit shield fell apart as his concentration was shattered.

Shari fell back to the ground, straining for breath again. She'd called on every skerrick of air from inside the shield—that had included what was in her lungs.

'*Shari!*' Jon shouted in her mind.

'*I'm fine, Jon,*' she sent back even as she struggled to draw air into her lungs. She could feel the tendons in her neck standing out in stark relief as she drew in breath after much needed breath, the odd look in Sam's eyes forgotten for the moment.

'*Anything broken?*' Jon asked calmly. Shari could still sense the concern and anger buried underneath the placid question.

'*All in one piece,*' she added, trying to ease her Guardian's worry. Figuring she should see if that was accurate, she mentally checked that all her bones were indeed in the right spots.

'*So, should I announce the next trial then?*' Jon sent back, only half teasing.

Sam moaned on the ground. Shari pushed herself to her feet and staggered over to him, resting the tip of her blade against the hollow of his throat.

Shari groaned. '*I think we both know who the winner is, Jon.*'

Left unsaid and unsent was that Shari didn't think she could withstand another pounding like the one Sam had just given her.

In the far recesses of her mind was the niggling thought that it hadn't seemed like he was trying too hard at all—at least not until the end. She really didn't want to find out what it was like to be beaten by Sam when he was trying.

'*Maybe one of the others will surprise you?*' Jon offered feebly.

Reviewing the other successful candidates, Shari found herself shaking her head. Alistair had been good but had won his round because of the care he'd shown for his teammates. Kodan had worked hard in round two. Therdon had won round three because of his leadership, but there was no way that she wanted to work with him. Kodan was the closest to Sam as far as technique and power went, but there was something that Shari found disconcerting about the former U'sala member.

Sam, however, had worked with his team effortlessly, supporting them in a way that no one else had. Even as they'd fallen to her, he'd done his best to ensure they were somewhere safe to recover. None of the others had done anything like it in the rounds before. Sam, newcomer though he might be, was the clear winner in every capacity.

'Really, Jon? That's your argument?' Shari said, pulling in an easier breath. Jon fell silent, brooding in the back of her mind. She snorted. *'Tradition would be the next argument, right?'*

"Congratulations, Altoriae! The round is complete!" Jon announced, and the sound shield dropped. Shari cancelled the water trap around Bren and Amara, sparing a flicker of Innarn to make sure that they were okay.

The roar of the crowd was deafening, almost dampening the relief coming off Jon. Breathing heavily, Sam heaved himself to his feet, ignoring Shari's outstretched hand.

'Fine. You may as well announce the next trial now,' Shari grumbled at him. She sensed Jon's apology but brushed it off along with the dust that was coating her clothing. "Sorry for the low blow, Sam," Shari said softly.

"It was nothing. I was merely... unprepared. How are you faring?" Sam asked her, his voice low and concerned.

Looking up at him, she saw there was a strain in his eyes that she hadn't been aware of before. "I'm fine, candidate."

Shutters fell, and Shari found that she almost regretted her formality.

Shari sighed. "Sam..." she started to say, but the rest of it was lost as Jon's voice boomed out over the training ground.

"On behalf of the Altoriae, I would like to thank all of the candidates who have taken part in the first trial. It is no easy feat to go up against the Altoriae, but you all took to your task bravely. The second trial will start momentarily and consist of..." Jon broke off.

For a long moment, Shari thought that the dramatic pause was going on for too long.

The *twang* of a bowstring being released reached her ears, and she shoved Sam to the ground, leaning over the top of him to get a look at the shooter.

"Are you trying to throw me off my game?" Sam quirked the corner of his mouth up, back to being his usual annoying self.

Scowling at him, Shari hissed, "Hush. We're completely exposed out here."

"I think, Altoriae, you have to worry more about what I'm going to do than any of the others." Sam laughed.

"Egotistical, much?" Shari snarked, looking down at him.

Sam effortlessly flipped them so she was stuck underneath him. Immediately, she jabbed her fist into his side, so if she called her glove in, he'd be breathing through a few new holes. He raised an eyebrow. "What do I have to do to win?" he said.

"Take out the bad guys and make sure no Lissaens get killed in the process. Same as always." Shari frowned at him.

Frowning back at her, he ducked lower as an arrow whistled overhead. "No Lissaens? What about me?" Face-to-face, he stared down at Shari for a long moment before he abruptly shifted away.

'*You're of Lissae now, Sam!*' she sent. As much as Shari wanted to lie there and figure out what that was all about, she knew she had to move. Sam's form shimmered before her and he disappeared.

'*Shari! The Chirea!*' Jon sent out, his thoughts heavy with where to aim his crossbow next.

"Again?" she muttered aloud, shifting to relative safety behind one of the big trees Jon had grown in the training ground. '*They sure are persistent!*' Shari groused to Jon.

Peering out from behind her tree, she noted the absolute panic in the stands as the residents of Ronah and Rakemyst rushed to escape their attackers. Shari squinted, trying to see what was blocking their exit, and a huge purple dome grew from the ground up above the training ground, trapping everyone inside.

As a few Ilutri fled through the top of the dome before it closed, Shari realised that everyone included her parents—her family.

Shari was exhausted; there was no doubt about it. She'd just gone through four straight days of fighting so intense that she had seriously considered taking Jon up on his offer of not patrolling tonight, but now, she was needed again.

With a tired flick of her hands, Shari's weapons appeared. The familiar heft of the yellow blade was comforting. Before she stepped out from behind her tree, Tania shifted to her side.

"Hi, guild buddy," Ronah's Linked greeted her. "You're looking tired. Here." Tania blasted her with a massive jolt of healing energy that sent Shari staggering backwards.

"Sorry." Tania winced, shifting her weight restlessly. "Think I had too many of Mum's cakes."

Just like that, Shari was alone again.

Blinking, she rolled her shoulders, the excess energy running down her spine. Now, she was ready to tackle anything.

Chapter Twenty-Eight

Sam moved through the trees of the training ground, wincing with each step. He was glad that he'd had the presence of mind to shield himself from sight, as he was sure the other candidates would be laughing at him. Who designed human bodies to have such an accessible weakness? Although he was glad Shari was willing to use everything she had to win, he found himself currently unable to appreciate her tenacity.

Slipping sideways through two tree trunks, he mentally grumbled. When he'd first laid eyes on the modified training ground, he'd had to suppress a shudder. The close quarters of the forest were no good for flying, and more than once he'd gotten his wings tangled or torn fighting in woods like this. He'd had to sternly remind himself that he didn't have wings to tangle him now, and that *no*, he couldn't burn the trees to the ground, however much he'd wanted to.

Now, he was finding himself grateful for the cover they provided. Pausing just behind the last tree before the exit, Sam gathered himself, shaking off the lingering pain of Shari's punch. Ready to fight, he stepped out and found himself on the pointy end of a Chirean arrow.

"Careful, beast," the Chirea rumbled, its voice like a landslide. "This arrow's marked for you."

Sam cocked a brow and held his hands out at his side, palms up, trying to show that he was harmless. "I was just leaving."

"You'll be leaving the living if you so much as twitch," the Chirea rumbled.

Sooner or later, the Chirea would falter, but could he afford to wait him out that long? Sam blinked. It seemed that they were at a stalemate for the moment.

'*How do they keep getting onto Lissae?*' Shari grumbled.

'*It's a portal. I'll see if I can close it,*' Tania replied, her Innarn fairly buzzing through their mental link.

Shari shook her head and concentrated on centring herself. More from instinct than awareness, her blade came up and deflected an arrow, the shooter hidden somewhere in the treetops.

'*Ronah, can you get the non-combatants out of here and remove the trees?*' Shari sent.

'*Maybe? The trees, yes. But I'm not sure about the people. The plasma shield... it's so Light, it burns,*' Ronah whimpered down their connection.

Breathing deeply and swatting another arrow out of the air, Shari swore.

'*What about pointing out where the Chirea are?*' Jon suggested. Shari could almost hear the Island frowning.

'*They must be shielded. I can't see any Chirea at all!*'

'*I've got one over here shooting at me,*' Shari said, sending the visual to Ronah.

Looking through the spectrum of Innarn, Shari saw that the Chirean archer was shielded, likely by the same Innarnian that had covered the training ground with the plasma shield. The signature seemed familiar, like she'd come across it before, but she couldn't figure out where.

Putting it out of her mind, she flicked another arrow away. Surely the archer had to run out at some stage?

He did. There was a thump and rattle as the archer jumped down from the trees. Shari tipped her chin, ready to take the Chirea on. He stepped out of the shadows, a bone broadsword hefted in one hand, a bow in another. The strap of his quiver slung across his chest, dark against his ribbed armour. Almost too late, Shari realised that he held daggers in his other hands, which were rapidly spinning her way.

Shari moved to counter. Bren stepped up to her left side, a staff as dark as his skin lashing out and connecting with a dagger a foot before it would have hit her. Amara was on her other side and merely blasted the dagger out of the air with a fireball. She rapidly shot a storm of fireballs, the tiny missiles slamming into the Chirea with surprising force.

Bren peered around Shari and looked at Amara for a long moment. Nodding, he turned back to the Chirea and joined in, his added attack forcing the Chirea back. Shari grinned and added her own volley of fireballs. The Chirea dropped his bow as he involuntarily stepped out of the way, lest he be flattened by the onslaught of tiny, fierce fireballs.

The trio didn't pause until they had the Chirea up against the wall of the training ground. Shari *pulled* on the rock the wall was made of, capturing the Chirea so he couldn't move. Bren looked hard at the Chirea for a few counts. Their attacker slumped, going still in his bonds.

Someone made a choked noise. The three turned with varying incredulous expressions to see another Chirea who was holding Sam at arrow point. Sam shrugged a shoulder, but then blasted his captor with a burst of air so ferocious that it tore the front of the Chirea's armour apart.

"Took you long enough," Sam grumbled, plucking the arrow from the ground, and stabbing it viciously into the Chirea's belly.

As his captor gurgled through his last breaths, Amara crossed the short space between them and shoved Sam. "You didn't have to do that!" she cried.

Sam looked at her, unmoved by her shove or her cries. "Am I meant to let him live when he'd kill us all if he got the choice?"

"Death isn't the only answer!" Amara cried, turning to the Chirea who was scrabbling for a dagger despite the blood spurting out of his mouth. He raised his hand and sliced at Sam, but his eyes rolled back, and his arm thudded limply to the ground before he made contact.

"Fusstan!" cried the Chirea trapped in the wall. He snarled and seemed to grow before their eyes, bursting free of his restraints and barrelling straight for Sam.

Bren swung his staff out and caught the Chirea around the ankles, toppling him. The Chirea merely tucked his limbs in and rolled, jumping up directly in front of Sam, who'd retrieved the dagger and was waiting.

Coldly, he thrust forwards in a sharp, swift jab, leaving the Chirea to drop writhing to the ground.

"I thought it must be poisoned," Sam noted idly as the Chirea at his feet spat green foam from his mouth. He scrabbled at the dagger. Sam kicked the hilt of the weapon, driving it in deeper.

Shari stared at the scene, not sure what to make of it. Cries from the stands caught her attention. She'd have time to mull things over later.

"Split up. We need to cover as much ground as possible. Keep the residents safe. If you see any other candidates, get them to help. One shields, one attacks. Go!" Shari commanded, and used a twister of air to raise herself into the stands, landing lightly on her feet.

The others scattered. Shari turned to see one of the withdrawn candidates, Esme, drawing an arrow from her quiver and shooting it into the trees. The crystals on the fletching sparkled in the light. The arrow curved, but Shari couldn't sense any Innarn guiding it. It curved again.

Shari moved in time to see a Chirea fall to the ground, arrow protruding from the eye socket of his skull helmet.

Blue leathers blending in with the sky above her, Esme grinned down at Shari. She drew another arrow and took aim again.

'*Keep it up*,' Shari sent, grinning back. Narrowing her eyes, she built a shield around Esme, making sure that any return arrows would glance harmlessly off her. Behind the withdrawn candidate, a family crouched, and Shari was delighted to see they were crafting arrows for Esme, refilling her quiver before it got too low.

Leaving them to it, Shari moved higher in the stands, trying to see where she was most needed. Dealon was in the first row of seats and had created whips from water Innarn which he was using to flush out the hiding Chirea. The whips would pass painlessly over anyone from Lissae, but Shari watched as a Chirea got caught in one.

Dealon raised the whip high and slammed it down into the side of the training ground wall so hard it shook the armour from the being. Another slam and the Chirea was dead, lying discarded at the bottom of the wall in a steadily growing pile.

Moving upwards, Shari spotted Alistair at the top of the stands, pushing pure Innarn at the plasma shield, trying to break through using sheer brute force. Haran's face appeared on the other side of the shield, looking rather healthy, even with the purple glow from the plasma. He nodded to Alistair and held up a hand, fingers coming down slowly. Alistair nodded, and when Haran formed a fist, the two blasted the shield from both sides together. They managed to create a hole big enough for a single being to squeeze through. Alistair let out a whoop of triumph, and one of the people closest to him cheered as well, before they started ushering others towards the hole.

'*Esme, can you cover them?*' Shari sent.

The archer below nodded, using air Innarn to push up through the stands, moving so her back was against Alistair's. Dealon saw what was going on, and he disappeared for a moment, reappearing below Esme, out of her range of fire but in the perfect position to stop any ground troops from getting to the newly created exit.

Shari nodded at them and moved along, spreading the word of the exit as she took out the Chirea in her path. At the southwest point, she came across Burke and Talofa fighting back to back. Shudders wracked Burke's frame, and tiny Talofa murmured words of comfort even as she stripped the leaves off the closest trees and sharpened them with earth Innarn. She used them to slice through the Chirea's armour as an eight-being-deep phalanx converged on the pair.

Leaping over two rows of seats, Shari came to their aid just as Mu joined them from the other side. The trio of candidates seemed determined to show Shari just what they were capable of.

Talofa's leaves continued to slice effortlessly through the Chirean ranks. Burke's sword flashed out, lopping fingers and limbs off indiscriminately whenever one of the Chirea got too close.

Streamers of plasma shot out of Mu's hands, past Burke's shoulder, taking down five of the Chirea in one hit. It startled Burke so badly that he turned, edge of his sword out, and slashed Mu's torso.

Horrified, Burke pulled his weapon back, a fountain of blood spraying him. Mu looked at him, purple eyes wide as he dropped to his knees and Shari rolled her eyes at the pair.

Pushing her way between them, Shari ran her hands over Mu's wound, stitching organs and skin back together, cleaning and pulling the blood back into the Zindarian's body.

The remainder of the Chirean phalanx crested the wall and descended on the four of them.

Swiftly, Shari finished healing Mu.

Talofa yelped and ducked under a seat, disappearing. Burke's sword was smacked out of his hand, clattering uselessly to the ground.

Rolling her eyes again, Shari did something she hadn't done since she was a child. Screaming, she used every tremor in the air to magnify the wall of fire she built between the candidates and the Chirea. Her scream echoed across the training ground. With each echo, another blast of fire Innarn slammed against the Chirea until the phalanx was a melted, unrecognisable mess.

Idly, Shari wondered what Amara would think of what she'd done. Talofa crawled out from the seats in the row above her, and Mu stood on shaky legs. Burke hurried to help her, shaking, apologies pouring from his mouth.

"There's an exit." Shari pointed. "Spread the word and get as many as you can out." She wished that she could just do a mass send but she didn't want to alert the Innarnian who'd let the Chirea onto Ronah know.

The candidates nodded at her, and Shari moved on, leaping into battle with Bren, who was at the southernmost tip of the training ground.

After they'd dispatched a few of the more stubborn Chirea Shari had come across, she told him of the exit. Bren nodded, smiling widely as he waded into the crowd of Lissaens, touching each one lightly on the shoulder to send the news to them.

Shaking her head, Shari couldn't help but grin along with the Weaver who seemed to be thoroughly enjoying the chance to shape and flex his Innarn in an actual fight. Leaving Bren, she started to make her way up the other side of the stands.

Sulak was fighting alongside Josie and Caeli. All three were doing an admirable job of holding the Chirea off from a large group of unarmed Ilutri, until they saw Shari. Sulak continued to throw and recall his daggers with scary precision. Josie, however, faltered, the silver hoops on her jacket flashing in the light, her volley of sharpened rocks clattering down on the heads of the Ilutri, causing several to cry out.

'*What is it about me that turns the candidates into fumbling fools?*' Shari sent to Jon.

'*Well, to be fair, you turn a lot of the Chirea into fools as well,*' Jon sent back.

Huffing out a breath, Shari gathered Josie's projectiles and lifted them off the startled Ilutri. She sent the message of the exit to them. Flinging the sharpened rocks at the oncoming Chirea, Shari wondered when the horde would end.

As soon Tania had healed Shari, Ronah grabbed Tania and sucked her straight into the ground, along with Zana. The Island had spat them out in what she'd come to think of as *her* training caves.

"Ronah, no! I've got to get back!"

'*You must stay safe.*'

"What about my family? My friends?" Tania pleaded.

"Hush, child. We must wait out the fight here."

Swinging around, Tania stared at Zana in shock. "How can you say that? We've got to do something! Those are our people dying in there!"

"Our people are fighters. It is our job to keep the peace between them and their home."

"No! No, it is our job to keep them *safe*! I can't stand by and watch as people are murdered!"

"What do you propose we do?"

"Fight!" Tania threw up her hands. She barely believed they were having this conversation.

"Rakemyst does not fight." Zana's wings rustled.

"Rakemyst doesn't *have* to fight. But he can aid those who do," she pleaded.

Zana wrinkled her nose. "How can we support our warriors?"

'*Alistair has opened a hole in the wards,*' Ronah supplied helpfully.

"I see it! There! If we push hard enough, we'll be able to widen the hole and more people can get out!"

"Very well," Zana sniffed. Conjuring up a stool, she settled down. Tania sensed the moment she connected with Rakemyst. Hastily, she tapped into Ronah. Together, the two Linked pushed the power of their Islands into expanding the hole in the wards.

As her Innarn pulsed into the wards, Tania found a purple glow niggling at the edge of her concentration. Turning her head did little to move her astral form, but when she did, she gasped.

'*I found it!*' she sent to Shari.

'*I found it!*' Tania sent, thoughts tumbling over each other so that the rest of her send didn't make sense.

'*Slow down,*' Shari coaxed, blade flashing as she cut down a Chirea aiming for Caeli's back.

'*One of the candidates let the Chirea in. I found one of the Ducibus... he... she... ze. Ze said that the 'purple one' forced them to open the doorway,*' Tania sent.

'*Purple one?*' Shari asked. Purple skin, purple eyes, purple what?

'*I get the impression that ze was talking about a super high-level plasma user,*' Tania sent.

Shari's eyebrows rose. '*Like the one who made the shield around the training ground?*'

'*Yeah! Oh. That kinda doesn't help. But Ronah helped me to put a trap around the portal they've been using, so no more can get in, and anyone who tries to leave will arrive at your side,*' Tania replied.

Shari nodded. '*Thanks for the heads-up. I need you to stay there and guard that portal. Is there anyone else with you?*'

'*No. I think it's best to keep it that way,*' Tania said.

'*Okay, but you or Ronah need to contact me or Jon the instant you need help,*' Shari ordered.

'*Will do, Altoriae!*' Tania sent, with an image of her saluting.

Shaking her head, Shari turned back to the fight.

Josie seemed to have gathered herself and was back to using earth and air Innarn to fling tiny shards of rocks in a storm of pain towards the Chirea.

Sulak's blades were dancing, slipping between ribbed armour to deal as much damage as possible.

Caeli was twisting her hands in the air. It took Shari a moment to realise that she was freezing the water inside the Chirea's bodies. The only sign of her work was a stiffening of their limbs, and frost covering any exposed skin before they dropped to the floor, hearts unable to keep beating.

Nodding to them, Shari moved on, determined to work her way towards Jon. She snuck up on a Chirean archer who had bunkered down in the seats, and dispatched him.

"Shari!"

Head snapping up, Shari saw her parents at the very top of the stand, sixteen rows above her.

Arilla was wielding a length of metal. Calem was dealing devastating blows with fireballs that expanded every time they encountered the bone armour of the Chirea. LoneWolf was crouched down, shielding a protesting SilverCloud, firing off volley after volley of air and fire Innarn, felling any Chirea who dared to glance in their direction. Belfar was crouched, his back to LoneWolf, a flurry of exploding arrows leaving his bow with each *twang* of the string.

Shari vaulted the first row of seats, using the backs of the rest as steps as she fairly flew up to them.

"You sure you don't have wings?" Belfar grinned at her. He let loose another flurry of arrows that took out the Chirea who'd tried to follow Shari up the stands.

"I am *not* too old for this!" SilverCloud was grumbling from underneath the press of bodies around him. He broke free of their circle and jumped into the air, wings spread, firing a volley at the Chirea.

LoneWolf pulled him back down by the ankle with a sigh.

Containing her grin, Shari sent her dad and LoneWolf the directions to the exit. She went to move on, but froze at Arilla's voice.

"Shari!" Arilla cried. "I saw one of the candidates go down over there." She pointed towards what was now a gap in the training ground wall.

Nodding sharply, Shari set off, her feet skimming over the rows of seats. Pushing gusts of wind at the Chirean soldiers in her way, she blew them off their feet and out of her path. Dropping over the wall, she landed silently in the makeshift forest.

Arrows thudded at the earth along her path. One came so close, it bounced off her boot. Scowling in the direction of the stands, Shari strengthened her shield. She took off deeper into the forest, looking for the remaining candidates among the thickening vegetation.

Muffled sobbing came from up ahead. Shari carefully peered through the leaves to see Lira wrapping Raven's upper arm in a makeshift bandage.

"Will you be quiet?" Lira was hissing, "You'll bring down the Chirea on us if you can't shut your mouth!"

Sending her Innarn around the tiny clearing, Shari sensed that Lira was right. There were three Chirean soldiers closing in on them. Four more approached from the middle of the training ground. As Raven whimpered again, Shari focused on trapping the Chireans. She used roots and branches to bind the bone warriors and move their weapons away from their reach.

It was almost too easy, Shari thought, until she turned around, and came nose to arrow.

"Oh, by Zoemer's Rocks!" Reon swore, lowering his bow but leaving his arrow ready, his gaze sweeping the trees around them.

"You could say that," Shari muttered. "Do you know about the exit?"

Reon raised an eyebrow, but still didn't look at Shari directly. "Yes. I'm here to help you."

"I'm pretty self-sufficient," Shari remarked.

Glancing at the Altoriae from the corner of his eye, he said, "Of course you are, but two bodies can clear more than one."

Shari opened her mouth to protest, but found herself nodding. Later, she would justify it because the corner of Reon's mouth twitched up, reminding her of the way Mitch would try and get her to smile. Ruthlessly suppressing the memories she'd been fighting so hard to ignore, she sent the location of the exit to Lira and a wave of healing to Raven.

Turning to Reon, they kept going. In the next clearing, Ness was slamming flaming plasma boulders at a score of Chirea who were trying to surround her.

Tossing her hair out of her eyes, Ness stomped her foot down. Another boulder spat out of the ground and spun in the air before her. The heels of her palms together, she shot a bolt of plasma out, setting the boulder on fire. Spreading her fingers wide, she abruptly pulled her hands apart. The boulder split into fragments.

The Chirea stopped in their tracks.

Tossing her hair again, Ness flicked her fingers. The burning rocks pelted the Chirea, going right through their armour as if it weren't there.

Ness smirked at the fallen soldiers and strode forwards, completely ignoring her back. Shari raised her eyebrows at Reon, who rolled his eyes. Grinning, Shari scooped up a pebble and sent it straight into the small of Ness's back. Ness flicked up a rock and sent it spiralling at Shari before she even turned around.

"Impressive," Shari said, looking at the rock that was hovering in front of her nose, stopped by her shield.

"Altoriae! I apologise, I didn't realise…"

"Don't ever apologise for defending yourself. Do you know where the exit is?" Shari cut her off.

"Yes, but Elder Zetta may need help. I must get to her," Ness said.

Shari searched out the Elder from Omina. *There*, helping to guard the exit. "Hold on," Shari said, and shifted Ness to her Elder's side.

Reon blinked at the abrupt dismissal of the other candidate. Ducking his head, he moved on.

They were almost three quarters of the way around the ground when thudding and grunting came to Shari's attention. She traded looks with Reon, and the pair split apart, making for the sounds.

Peering through the trees, Shari saw Kodan leaning over Therdon, punching the Ilutri viciously. With a sickening crack, Shari knew the U'sala had broken Therdon's nose. As his fist rose again, Shari stepped forwards, shielding Reon as he raised his bow, arrow notched and ready to fire.

"What are you doing?" Shari asked, blade at the ready.

Kodan had drips of sweat running down his flushed face, the veins in his neck and arms standing out in stark relief. "He snuck up on me," Kodan gasped. His purple robe was stained with sweat. Drops of Therdon's blood had splattered the front, and mud clung to the hem.

Below him, Therdon gurgled something. The vicious grip Kodan had on the neck of his tunic, and the blood that was no doubt trickling down his throat, was making him unintelligible.

"Let him go, Kodan. Therdon isn't the enemy," Shari said, trying to reason with the U'sala.

Looking at her for a long moment, Kodan finally growled and shoved Therdon away from him as he stood. "You can't trust him," Kodan bit out, almost growling.

Shari raised her eyebrows, and Kodan looked away. She sent a wave of healing at Therdon, who whimpered and passed out. *'Can you take him to the exit please?'* she sent to Reon.

Reon sent back his wary agreement, but then added, *'Look at his feet.'*

Frowning, Shari lifted Therdon up in preparation to shift him out and looked at Kodan's feet. Etched into the ground were glowing purple symbols she'd never seen before. Blinking as if to clear her eyes, she committed the symbols to her memory. Surely if she sketched them out, Jon would be able to tell her what they were.

Opening her mouth to tell Kodan about the exit, Shari was distracted by a high-pitched scream. She took off running. Crashing through the bushes with a lack of finesse left her scratched and sore. She kept going, until she saw Elani pulling a dripping green blade from her shoulder.

Despite her left arm hanging limply at her side, the Satyr wasn't about to let the Chirea get the upper hand again. Her sword flashed out, sparking against the Chirea's chest armour.

Shari twitched her nose. The ground beneath the Chirea's feet became sticky, making it hard for him to move. Elani took the advantage. She slammed the tip of her sword into the neck joint of her opponent's armour and levered it up. The skull helmet popped off. Green eyes, the same colour as the poison dripping from Elani's wound, widened even as the Satyr slashed again. The Chirea's head rolled off his shoulders.

Slumping to the ground and dropping her sword, Elani gasped in pain. One hand came up to hold her injured shoulder. Shari rushed to her side and pushed her healing into the wound. It frothed and bubbled as the poison rushed to the surface. Elani swayed on her knees, her face going white as her mouth opened in a silent scream. Carefully wiping away the last of the poison, Shari started to knit Elani's muscles and skin back together.

Shakily, Elani rose and bowed to her. "Thank you, Altoriae."

Looking at the Satyr critically, Shari nodded. "You're pretty amazing to keep fighting after being stabbed with a poisoned dagger."

"Just keep that in mind when you're choosing the next apprentice," Elani said with a smirk.

Shari grinned at her, but sobered quickly. "Can you head back the way I came and make sure that everyone gets to the exit?"

"There's an exit?"

Nodding, Shari pointed out where it was, and showed Elani the way she'd come. "I missed part of the wall. Make sure everyone gets out."

"Except the Chirea."

"Except them," Shari agreed.

Picking up her sword, Elani nodded and jogged off. Shari admired her tenacity for a moment, before Tania's voice filled her head.

'Incoming!'

Surrounded by Chirea in less than a heartbeat, Shari breathed in and got to work. There was no way that the bone warriors were going to win today. Not even with a plasma Innarnian on their side.

Jeran led the U'sala through the portal and into the halls of Lissae. The Ducibus scattered out of their way, suspicious gazes far from what he was used to from the guardians of the gateways.

'What has happened here?' Yessna asked.

'The Chirea led by your Light Innarn has stormed our halls. We were able to keep losses to a minimum, but they have no regard for us.'

'My Light Innarn?' Yessna looked at Jeran, fur standing on end.

'*They are attacking Ronah right now. Your Light Innarn leads them into battle, unwillingly.*' The Ducibus pulled the hood on zir robes forwards. '*You must fix what your Light Innarn has broken, or the U'sala shall not walk these halls again.*'

Jeran felt pale under the furious scowl he was sporting.

"U'sala, with me." He gave the signal.

Grimly, Yessna nodded. Shifting the group out, she deposited them in the middle of chaos.

Jeran hefted his sword, ready to wade into the fray.

Shari pulled her blade from the belly of the latest Chirea to fall to her sword and was scanning the area to discern the flow of the fight when she heard it.

A whimper.

Head snapping in the direction of the sound, Shari caught a flicker of movement and charged. Leaping over a bone heap and skirting a boulder from the trial, the tip of her blade came unerringly to rest against the hollow of a lone Chirea's throat.

"N... n... no," he gasped out, hazel eyes large under his skull helmet, the colour reminding her so much of Mitch's eyes that she paused.

"Give me a reason not to," she snarled, trying to hide the quiver in her voice.

Hazel eyes blinked, and he gasped out, "I know how to stop the Chirean army."

Shari froze, her blade steady against his throat. All sound of the battle seemed to rush away before returning twofold. "And why would you do that?"

"Because we need to stop. We've been fighting for eons and have yet to find a place to call our own. I... I don't want to fight anymore," he admitted.

Shari's mouth twitched to the side, eyes narrowed as she properly took in the young Chirea before her. He was shivering, making the bones of his armour clank ever so slightly, the oversized skull on his head missing the jawbone. His bottom two arms were crossed protectively across his belly, pressed so tightly that Shari saw there was no armour protecting his stomach at all.

With a sharp move, Shari pulled her sword back, making him flinch. "I don't really want to fight either," she admitted. "Tell me how to stop them."

CHAPTER TWENTY-NINE

here's a man, one with purple flames. He approached my father when he was leader of the Chirea. Told him that there was a place we could call home. Somewhere we'd be safe and free, and we'd only have to share with a few others," the Chirean youth said.

"You're the son of the leader?" Shari asked. The youth's armour hardly told the story of a great warrior.

"I was his second son. But the name Kanntal now means less than dirt," he said, his head bowed. "The new leader stripped me of my armour because I failed to stop my father's death."

Shari chose not to comment on the number of bones the youth had collected since then and focused on the immediate problem. "So how can I stop your kin?"

"It's not them you need to stop; it's the one with the flames." Kanntal shivered.

Shari found that she almost felt sorry for him. "Why him?" she asked instead.

"He's the one who's determined to take over your Realm," the youth spat. "He's the one keeping our troops going and pulling more in when we don't want to fight anymore, or when we die. If he's gone, we'll stop," Kanntal said, his voice pleading.

"How am I meant to stop a plasma Innarnian when I've no idea who they are? Do you know how many there are just on this island?" Shari said, running a hand through her hair, her fingers getting snagged on a tangle.

"I know his name." He nodded his head, his too-big helmet bobbing crookedly.

Shari froze, and looked at the youth. "What is it?"

When Kodan's name spilled from the Chirea's lips, Shari saw the purple marking around the U'sala's feet in her mind's eye, and it suddenly made sense. Furious, Shari practically screamed in Yessna's mind, '*How could you!*'

The second in charge of the U'sala sent, '*How could I what?*'

Yessna felt close, and Shari whirled, finding Yessna and a large group of the U'sala behind her, weapons pointed at the Chirean youth.

Ignoring the weapons, Shari strode up to Yessna, forcing the information from the Chirean youth into the Ferah's thoughts.

"No," Yessna said, shaking her head. "No. Kodan would never do that!"

Jeran stomped up next to her. "Do wha'?"

"Why don't we find him and ask?" Shari growled. "I'll bet you a new blade that he's still in the middle of the training ground."

"You're on, healer," Yessna growled back. Together, they strode off.

"You lot figure out who's guarding tha'." Jeran spat in the youths direction as he stomped off.

There was a brief scuffle among the U'sala over who would guard the prisoner. Two, bearing blooming bruises, stayed. Pointing the tips of their weapons at the prone form of the young Chirea trembling on the ground, they watched the others trail behind Yessna and the Altoriae.

When they were in sight of the clearing in the middle of the training ground, Kanntal's words seemed to be true.

Kodan was standing in the direct centre, the purple symbols glowing in a ring around his feet. Streams of plasma shot from his hands as he sought to repair the holes in the shield keeping them captive.

Yessna gasped.

The soft sound alerted Kodan, who whirled to face them. Smirking, he turned to see the clearing surrounded by his former comrades, weapons all pointed in his direction.

This close to him, with plasma literally streaming from his body, Shari finally identified the familiar Innarn signature.

Despite the tears prickling at her eyes, Shari snarled, "Take the shield down."

"What? Like this?" Kodan asked, false pleasantry thick on his tongue as he shot out another thick stream of plasma.

Instantly, the air directly behind the other side of the clearing shimmered, and Shari saw that just beyond the U'sala were row after row of the Chirea. Their eyes burned uncomfortably into her back. Rolling her shoulders, and trying to ignore the heat from their gazes, Shari sent to Yessna, '*Take them out. Leave Kodan to me.*'

The second in command growled at her, but turned and slashed down hard, stopping an arrow from hitting Shari's back.

As the sounds of battle took over, Shari stalked towards Kodan. "So, Therdon didn't attack you then?" she said, trying not to snarl at him.

"As if he could. That weakling tried to influence me again. He wanted to stop me and be the hero. You saw how that worked out." Kodan laughed.

"You think I've got the same chance as Therdon?" Shari asked.

"I think you've got less, Altoriae." He grinned at her, far too many teeth on display. "I've been in your house, remember? I know exactly where to hurt you the most."

Another thick stream of plasma shot out of Kodan's hand, connecting to someone. As the plasma stream recoiled, dropping a figure with trembling limbs and shaking wings at Kodan's feet, the tip of Shari's blade came up.

"I wouldn't," Kodan said, foot lashing out as his own blade came to rest against the wing-joint of her grandfather's sprawled form.

Shari's eye twitched.

Kodan's smug face overtook her vision as she debated her options. She didn't so much as flinch when SilverCloud cried out weakly.

A flicker of uncertainty crossed Kodan's face.

Shari struck.

Pulling on the ground beneath the traitor, she made it jump beneath his feet.

SilverCloud attempted to scramble away but couldn't get past the circle of symbols on the dirt.

Kodan laughed, and aimed a bolt of plasma at Shari.

She ducked and skewed his shot, so it took out half a dozen Chirea behind her. The smile dropped from his face and became a snarl.

"You think you're so good," Kodan growled at her. "But I've seen you, Altoriae. When it comes to those you care about, you're sloppy." Bolt after bolt shot towards Shari.

"Don't be ridiculous," Shari panted as the next bolt hit her, the energy making the fine hairs on her body stand on end. She only needed a few more, and she'd be able to pour it into the symbols and break them. "I'm far from sloppy when it comes to the ones I care about."

For a moment, Kodan paused. He noted her staggering form, the smouldering holes in her armour from his plasma bolts showing the skin beneath.

Shari took in a ragged breath, wishing he'd hurry up, because his Innarn was burning at her insides.

He started laughing, and rapidly fired off the last three shots she needed.

Staggering forwards, Shari shoved her fingertips into the soil right at the edge of his symbols and poured his own power into them, breaking the elegant lines apart with careless, jagged rips.

"Think you're so good," she panted, parroting his earlier words. Unsteadily, she rose to her feet, holding out a hand for her grandfather to take.

As their hands met, Kodan cried out. Shari whirled SilverCloud away and slammed the hilt of her sword into Kodan's temple with the same move, dropping him to the ground.

Shari abruptly shifted Kanntal into the middle of the fray. He cowered at her feet until she hauled him up.

"Tell them to stop while you still have some kin left," she growled at him.

"They won't listen to me," he protested.

"Try," she snarled, shaking him by her grip on his upper arm.

Kanntal whistled, long and high. The Chirea stopped fighting.

A few of the U'sala attempted to take advantage of their opponents' sudden lack of fight, surging forwards for the kill. Shari pushed up a shield between them, isolating the Chirea on the training ground.

"It is time for us to look for our home elsewhere!" Kanntal announced, shaking off Shari's arm to stand tall despite his lack of armour. "This is a fight that was never ours, but his," he spat on Kodan's sprawled form.

Shari found that she couldn't summon the indignation she probably should be feeling at seeing Kodan disgraced in such a way. After the trust that he'd broken, she felt a bit like spitting on him too.

The Chirea seemed to chitter at each other for a moment. Miraculously, one by one, they sheathed their bows and swords.

"Let us take our dead and wounded, and we won't return," Kanntal said, turning back to Shari.

Shari eyed the young Chirea, her knuckles white around the hilt of her sword. "Where will you go?"

"Altoriae, no," Yessna protested. "The Chirea are..."

"Wounded and desperate. Dying out. Going to find something other than the bones of their victims to use for armour," Shari's voice was hard.

Kanntal lowered his head but nodded slowly. "Our traditions are old, but I think it's time they were updated," the youth said slowly.

"That's a really good idea," Shari said, her eyes held a hint of warning.

He gulped. "We will go where we were before your scout found us. The Realm appears deserted, and we had intended to set up our new home there," Kanntal said.

"There are others on Gerhar," Shari frowned.

"Not Gerhar, Altoriae. Zokleran."

Shari raised her eyebrows, but slowly nodded. "As you wish." *'Tania, Ronah, a hand, if you could?'* she sent out.

'What are we doing?'

'Sending the Chirea back to Zokleran,' Shari sent back.

'All of them?' Tania asked.

'Every last one,' Shari replied, her features hardening for a moment, before smoothing out.

"Ready?" she asked Kanntal.

The Chirea nodded, and Shari took a deep breath in. As she breathed out, she found every last bone-covered warrior on Ronah and Rakemyst.

Breathing in again, she sought out the Link between Ronah and Tania, and joining with them, the trio shifted the Chirea to the Realm of Zokleran.

'*Lock down the portal and ensure that there are guards at the gateway. A guard needs to go with any and every Ducibus that needs to enter Zokleran,*' Shari sent to Ronah and Tania.

'*Will do,*' Tania sent faintly. There was a general murmur of agreement from Ronah before Shari turned her gaze back to the sprawled form of Kodan.

By the time the traitorous U'sala had come to, the last of the Chirea had gone, and his plasma shield was only a memory.

Standing over Kodan with a blade against the hollow of his neck, Shari blinked when Sam smirked at her.

'*You look rather like an avenging warrior angel, especially with one of the Ilutri behind you,*' Sam sent.

Flicking her gaze into Jon's eyes, she caught sight of Belfar behind her, his wings spread out as if to shield her from the view of curious onlookers.

"Why?" Shari growled at Kodan. The tip of her blade at his neck drew a bead of blood that slowly dripped down, staining his tunic.

Kodan surged to his feet and laughed at her.

Yessna lunged forwards and backhanded him hard across his face, her tail fluffed out in fury. "You are–"

"Why?" Shari's blade was steady against the base of his neck, despite her obvious exhaustion.

"Because the U'sala need a permanent place to rest!" Kodan growled back at her, pushing forwards slightly so the drip became a small stream. Shari glared at him and he laughed. "The Chirea came to me when I was patrolling. They wanted help to right a wrong, and when I heard what was happening, how could I not assist? A son killed? A father in need of a home for his people? That's what the U'sala are all about," Kodan said, smirking at her, his teeth stained by the blood from Yessna's backhand.

"The U'sala are not about displacing people who are already on the land," Yessna growled at him.

"Oh, you'd like to think so, wouldn't you?" He spat at his former team leader, his face contorted in a fierce scowl. "Jeran's pet would never dare be given the task of 'displacing' people. That fell to *me*."

Yessna stumbled back from him, aghast.

"Don't pretend you didn't know," Kodan scoffed. "How do you think Jeran kept us in coin?"

Eyes wide, Yessna turned to Jeran, who stared in horror at Kodan.

"The U'sala and the Chirea both needed a place to call home. Where better than the Mother Realm?" Kodan continued.

"Yer off ya rocker, Kodan," Jeran said gruffly. "Tha Mother Realm ain't nuthin but a bedtime tale."

Kodan laughed and pressed harder onto the tip of Shari's weapon.

She shifted back slightly, not letting him cut any deeper. "Mother Realm?" she asked, her eyes flicking between the bickering U'sala.

There was a moment of silence, and Kodan laughed again. "Are you telling me that the Altoriae doesn't know what she's fighting for?" He grinned. Shari scowled at him but didn't answer. "Oh, that's just too sweet. The Mother Realm—*your* Realm—is the birthplace of—"

He never finished.

A hard shove of air Innarn came from out of nowhere.

Kodan's next words were lost in a gurgle of blood as he fell onto her sword. His eyes went wide as blood bubbled up and out of his mouth before he slumped. Shari felt his soul slip away.

She wanted to scream in frustration but settled for thrusting her blade roughly back into the scabbard. The U'sala around her flinched.

"What did he mean?" Shari ground out.

Yessna was pale, large eyes flickering all over the place, clearly scanning for threats.

Jeran gulped back tears and shook his head. "I donna think he was in his right mind," the leader of the U'sala said softly, attempting to lay a hand on Shari's shoulder.

Twisting away from him, she scowled. "So, what he said about displacing people was a lie?"

"Tha's sumthin' I ne'er asked him tae do. Tae move 'em so they'd be with their own kind, aye, but naught tae displace any o' 'em," Jeran said. "There were a few groups tha dinnae wan' ter go, but Kodan was always good at persuading 'em."

Shari harrumphed at him and turned her gaze on Yessna. "Why did he die?" she asked the Ferah, who was squatting next to Kodan's body.

"I think he was allergic to your blade," Yessna said, her voice trembling.

Dipping into her thoughts, Shari realised that Yessna was devastated by Kodan's betrayal. Slowly, she backed out of the Ferah's mind, leaving her to grieve her fallen comrade.

"Shari!" Jon called from the edge of the clearing.

"I've got to–"

"Go," Yessna said, her voice thick with unshed tears. "We will gather our fallen and leave."

Heart aching, Shari was torn.

"We will meet as allies again, no doubt, little healer." Yessna looked up at her and dredged a weak smile.

Shari offered a nod and shifted out to Jon's side, leaving the U'sala alone with the body of the traitor.

Does she truly not know? Jeran signed to Yessna.

'*If she doesn't, someone is making sure she fails to learn it,*' Yessna signed back.

Samuel sauntered by, smirking at them.

Jeran's eyes followed the Dark being. '*I wonder who?*' he signed, and then began the heart-wrenching job of gathering his fallen.

Yessna found her eyes glued to Samuel's back as he moved to join the Altoriae and the Guardian. Just what was he playing at? Even as she helped Jeran gather their fallen, her mind was busy trying to figure out who was free to keep an eye on the dangerous being without being found out.

Neither the U'sala nor Shari saw the green eyes peering down from a tree at the edge of the clearing. Nor did they see the way the eyes tracked Samuel's movements, narrowing as the Golden One threw back his head and laughed.

With her digits clasped firmly around the blade that had killed Fusstan, Pallen narrowed her eyes further. No one killed her life-mate and got away with it.

CHAPTER THIRTY

"Shari?" a voice said softly by her side.

"Hmm?" Caught up in the sight of the decimated training ground, Shari barely acknowledged the speaker.

Trees had been toppled, and the air reeked of blood, sweat, and Innarn. Or maybe that was just her.

When Anriluka had attacked on Lissae, Shari had felt like she was failing, but this was even worse. She'd let the attacker in, welcomed him into her home, and smiled about it. For her troubles, he'd betrayed her and killed dozens of the people she'd sworn to protect.

Anriluka's attack had been predestined, but this was personal, and Shari couldn't help but feel that she'd been responsible for everything.

A hand lightly touched her elbow, and Shari knew it was Jon. It was the dark presence hovering behind him that brought her back to the present. Her eyes snapped over Jon's shoulder, Innarn at the ready for another attack, only to relax when she met Sam's gaze.

She felt Jon's Innarn brushing out against hers. Frowning at the amount of wild Innarn he sensed buzzing beneath her skin, Jon guided her over to an exit. "Let's get you home," he said, gently pushing her out of the training ground and away from the stench of the battle.

"Why did I trust him?" Shari wondered, unable to keep the thought bottled up.

"Because he knew just how to play a hatchling like you," Sam rumbled.

Shari dipped her head down, wishing away the tears that threatened to spill. She felt the silent, fierce conversation that Jon and Sam were having over her head.

"I won't let that happen again," Jon said vehemently.

"Neither will I," Sam said, and when Shari looked up, she caught the flash of shock on his face, like he'd spoken without thinking.

She may have been exhausted, but she didn't miss the sceptical look Jon gave the man he called an 'acquaintance' but treated as a friend. "I am quite capable of ensuring it doesn't happen again myself, you know." Shari slid out from between the two men, heading for a hot shower and her bed.

"Shari! Wait!" someone called, and Shari, recognising the voice of her tormentor, groaned.

The last person Shari had ever expected to see on the battlefield caught up with them, teetering on one high heel. Her other foot was bare, the missing heel in her hand, dripping with blood.

"Anika?" Shari asked, taking in her splattered appearance and the gore entangled in her usually pristine hair.

"You'll be announcing the new apprentice soon, won't you?" Anika asked, picking out a chunk of... something from her hair and flicking it to the side.

"Um... yes?" Shari said, blinking as she failed to process the sight before her. "Are you alright?"

Anika looked up from grabbing another handful of whatever it was and paused, then looked down at it again. "Having my skin stripped from my flesh over and over has given me a surprisingly strong stomach," she said, quirking her brow and pursing her lips. "About most things that is. If you show up to announce the new apprentice looking like you usually do, I'll probably lose my lunch."

Shari rolled her eyes. There was the Anika she knew. "I do have a few things to do that are more important than looking good," Shari said, but there was no heat in her comment, and Anika knew it.

"Impressions are important. I would say first impressions, but we're way beyond that now." Anika shooed away the past with an elegant wave of her hand.

"Alright, what do you want me to do about it?" Shari asked with a shake of her head.

"Meet me before the announcement, and I'll make sure that you don't totally disgrace Ronah," Anika said, flicking a chunk away into the bushes, before waggling her fingers at Sam and sending a sultry smile at Jon. "So, two hours... well, maybe three hours before, okay?" Anika limped away before Shari found the energy to come up with a convincing argument.

"What just happened?" Shari whimpered.

Sam smirked at her. "You were walked all over by a girl who fought off the Chirea with a shoe."

He was laughing at her; she just knew it.

"Let's just get home," Shari grumbled. Sam's eyes seemed to flicker golden for a moment, but Shari passed it off as a trick of the light when LoneWolf landed behind her.

"Shari," he said, and something in her insides froze over at his tone.

"Who?" she asked.

"What?" LoneWolf's head jerked back, wings rustling as he adjusted his balance.

"Who was killed?" Shari asked, trying to brace herself, but knowing it would be useless at the same time.

"No one, I just... Your father sent me to make sure that you got home safely," LoneWolf admitted.

'But...' Shari prompted.

'*I am worried about SilverCloud. The battle has weakened him, and Therdon's betrayal has sapped his strength even further,*' LoneWolf sent.

'*Where is he now?*'

'*Resting, at your parents' house,*' LoneWolf sent, and with a powerful downward push of his wings, he was airborne again. '*I will race you there.*'

Shari reached out and grabbed onto Sam and Jon, shifting them in a heartbeat. '*I win,*' she sent to LoneWolf.

His good-natured grumbling down the link made her smile again, even as her legs felt like jelly and the gurgling of her insides were a reminder that she either needed to eat or throw up.

"Come inside for something to eat?" she implored Jon and Sam. Sam's eyes flicked to the door and back to her, clearly torn. By what, she didn't know.

"I think you need to be with your family right now, Shari. We'll leave you to it, and I'll see you in the morning for a report." Jon's eyes dashed over her face as if he wanted to catalogue every wound before he left for the night.

Stifling a sudden yawn, Shari nodded. "See you in the morning then," she said, and slipped inside.

Outside, Jon and Sam stared at each other for a moment.

"You're planning on making sure that no one will play Shari again?" Jon raised an eyebrow.

Sam took a deep breath, his nostrils flaring. "That's what I said."

Jon tilted his head, and Samuel felt it like a slap to the face. In this form, his face was not strong enough to handle the blow.

Shadows grew and stirred behind his back and he stalked forwards. A small part of his mind was impressed that the Guardian refused to back down. "How many times have I saved your ungrateful hide? How many times have I paved the way for you to make a clean escape from my kin? How many times more will I have to prevent your untimely demise before you trust me to have your back?" Sam growled, his eyes flashing gold.

"Oh, I trust you to have my back. I won't pretend to understand the fascination that you have with me, but Shari is different. She is my sole reason for being. My duty and my life are hers to command, and you... I wish you would tell me what you want with her."

Sam tipped his chin up, his scowl hiding the hurt. "You don't understand? Then let me help you." Leaning close, Sam whispered a word into Jonathan's ear and watched the man go pale.

Another unspoken conversation later, and they both shifted away. They needed to rest and prepare for the day ahead of them.

Neither of them was likely to get much sleep.

Shari made her way into the kitchen, smiling as she heard voices. Reaching for the door handle, she heard the sudden scraping of a chair being pushed back and a pounding of feet. The door burst open and her mum tumbled out, followed closely by her dad.

"Hi," she said.

"Shari," Arilla breathed, and she found herself wrapped in her mum's arms. Shari's dad grinned at her even as he drew them into his embrace.

"Glad you're in one piece, Shari," he said softly.

Shari was swept away at the concern and trust underlining his words, and just grinned, reaching out to wrap an arm around him as well. Calem flinched, and Shari, without thinking, sent gentle waves of healing at him.

Belfar, leaning in the kitchen doorway, grinned at them, feathers rustling as a door opened behind him.

Shari sensed LoneWolf enter the kitchen and smiled, closing her eyes. SilverCloud's heartbeat from downstairs sounded loudly as she pushed her Innarn out, trying to place where everyone was. Her family was all in one place, and mostly uninjured. Opening her eyes, she saw Belfar and LoneWolf draw apart, the stunned look on LoneWolf's face a direct contrast to the smug smile Belfar wore.

Leaving her uncle as he wrapped his brain around Belfar's kiss, Shari slipped away from her parents' arms. She spied SilverCloud leaning over the handrail guarding the passage upstairs, a soft smile on his face as he took in Belfar and LoneWolf.

"Took you long enough, Wolf," SilverCloud goaded his son.

LoneWolf raised an eyebrow at his father before grabbing Belfar and dragging him into the kitchen, the door closing firmly behind them.

Shari laughed as she stumbled up the stairs.

"How are you going, little Altoriae?" SilverCloud asked her, his eyes dark with concern.

"Tired," Shari admitted. "I think my pride and ego copped the worst of it." She shook her head. "I trusted him. I let him in and..."

"Not everyone is good, Shari, even when we want them to be," Calem said as he came up the stairs, Arilla on his heels.

Shaking her head again, Shari couldn't prevent the yawn that cracked her jaw. "I think that..."

"Thinking can wait until the morning. A bite to eat and then bed for you, young lady," Arilla said sternly, even as she wrung her hands.

"I'm okay, Mum," Shari whispered as she gave Arilla another hug.

"I know, Shari," Arilla said. "Now go rest. Actual, proper rest, not fighting in your dreams. There's a tray for you in your room. Make sure you eat something first."

"Muuuummmm," Shari groaned.

Arilla raised an eyebrow and pointed at Shari's door. Reluctantly, Shari shuffled her way off to her room, her feet dragging. She couldn't remember the last time she'd been this tired.

Mechanically, she lifted the tray of food. Some far off part of her brain told her it smelled delicious. She managed to eat a few mouthfuls of vallan pie, but the tray started to slide off her lap, and she was too tired to catch it.

Her dad appeared as if summoned, and rescued the tray before it hit the floor, expertly saving the food.

"Sleep," her dad said, and it was the last thing Shari knew.

Morning rolled around before Shari was ready for it. She rose, feeling as though her mind had rested even though her body was still sore.

After working quickly through her morning routine, Shari headed downstairs to the smell of breakfast cooking. Calem, Arilla, SilverCloud, Belfar, and Jon sat around an enlarged table as LoneWolf manned the cookers, grilled tomatoes and poached eggs on the go, fresh bread ready and warm on the bench. Shari snapped up a slice as LoneWolf playfully swiped at her with a spatula.

"No fighting in the kitchen," Arilla said. It was a phrase that Shari and her father had heard often.

Shari looked at her dad and grinned. "But Mum!" they chorused, LoneWolf and Belfar joining in.

Arilla opened her mouth to tell them off, and just groaned. "I'm outnumbered," she said, hiding her head in her crossed arms.

"You've always been outnumbered." Calem grinned, kissing the top of her head.

LoneWolf was a surprisingly good cook, and they passed the meal pleasantly, laughing and talking. It was a slice of bliss that Shari hadn't known she'd needed.

"Thank you for breakfast; it was delicious. I'm afraid I have to steal Shari away for a bit now," said Jon as he rose from the table.

Just like that, Shari's bubble burst. Despite wanting to grumble and curse, Shari managed to rise from the table and thank her uncle, tucking the memory of the perfect morning away as she gave everyone at the table a quick hug, even Belfar, before she joined Jon at the door.

"Lead the way, Guardian," she said with a flourish of her hand.

"Would you like to do the honours?" Jon asked.

For an instant, Shari was reminded of a time when she was about twelve. Jon had tried to shift her somewhere without her being ready, and she'd almost split Ronah in two. Ever since, Jon let her shift them wherever they needed to go. Shari hadn't thought about it in a long time. She hesitated, debating if she should let Jon shift them to the bookstore. A flash of Kodan's smiling face in her mind's eye hardened her gaze and she shifted them to the back of the bookstore in the next instant.

The abuse of her trust was still too fresh for her to think about letting another take control.

Shari immediately slumped into 'her' chair, drawing her legs up and resting her head on bent knees.

"I'm sorry," Jon said softly. "I know that this is the last thing you want to do today, but..."

"It's something that needs to be done, isn't it?" Shari asked. She blinked at the heavy, bitter tone that came out of her mouth. "Sorry," she said softly.

Jon lowered his eyes, waiting for her.

Shari's thoughts rolled around in her head as she figured out what their best course of action would be. The training ground would need to be cleaned and cleansed. She had to check on the Returned, and maybe check in with the U'sala and the Ilutri. Where was Tania? How was her link with Ronah? Maybe she could...

"Shari," Jon said. Blinking, Shari looked up into her Guardian's eyes. "What's on your mind?"

Slumping, Shari realised that she still needed to go through the second trial. "Jon, I don't think that I can do it."

"Why not?" he asked gently.

"What he did... Kodan... I vouched for him. I trusted him. I fed him. He stayed at my house! I'm worried," Shari admitted, "that if I have to fight the other candidates, I won't hold back."

"They are not him," Jon said.

"I know that. But what if one of them was working with him?" Shari asked, leaping to her feet. She started pacing.

"They are not him. We can't judge others by what he's done," Jon said calmly.

"Then what should we do?" Shari pleaded.

Jon was silent for long enough that Shari had paced the length of the room and back a dozen times before he answered. "We can cancel the second trial on the ground that they were tested during the battle against Kodan. We could claim that he was brought in to test them," Jon said slowly.

"So, the all-knowing reputation of the Altoriae and her Guardian isn't questioned?" Shari laughed humourlessly.

"Something like that," Jon admitted. "It also means that you wouldn't have to see how your resolve holds up in another fight against the remaining candidates."

Frowning, Shari slumped back into her chair. As much as she disliked the thought of lying about why Kodan had been there, not having to fight the other candidates would be a relief. The stress of battle was one thing, but the additional strain of having to pull her blows to make sure that she didn't permanently injure or kill one of the candidates weighed heavily on her.

"If we cancel the second trial, how are we going to figure out who the next apprentice will be?" Shari asked.

"I'm sure that you have someone in mind," Jon said. "I have a few likely candidates myself."

"I'll tell you mine if you tell me yours." Shari grinned.

Jon crossed to his desk, rummaging through the papers. Leafing through a thick stack, he muttered, "Let's see. Wesin, Esme, and Sulak never competed, so they're out of the running. I think it's safe to say that Therdon is out as well?" Jon asked, glancing up.

"So is Kodan," Shari growled.

Jon nodded and crossed another name off the list. "I get the impression that Reon doesn't really want to be here."

"Me too. I'll not team up with someone who doesn't want to work with me. It could cost their life," Shari said flatly.

"Well, that's six down. Who would you say is in your top three?" Jon asked, looking up from his papers.

Idly, Shari picked at the seam of the chair as she went through the first trial in her head. "Dealon's out. He should have helped Raven."

Another name crossed off the list.

"Talofa was impressive. She'll be hard to defeat one day," Shari said as she stared into the dust motes floating around the back room. "Alistair has heart, but he lacks the fortitude for battle. I think he would collapse if someone died in front of him."

"He did well when the Chirea attacked," Jon reminded her.

"True. He has a massive amount of raw Innarn but needs a lot more training before he'd be ready for the role of your apprentice."

Jon's pen scratched across the paper. "Did you find anyone else worthy from the first round?"

If it had been anyone else, Shari would have thought he was being sarcastic, but it was Jon. "Nope. I wasn't particularly impressed with the lot in the second round either." Shari was scowling darkly, thinking that this time yesterday, Kodan's name would have been on her lips.

The pen scratched again; four more names gone.

"Take off Elani and Caeli too. If they can be held in such total control by Therdon, there's a chance that they'll need time to heal before they're ready for off-Realm battle," Shari said.

Two more names gone.

"What about the last lot of candidates?" Jon asked.

"Take off Bren and Haran as well," Shari said, thinking back to the last round. Bren worked admirably during the Chirea attack, but Shari wasn't sure that he was ready to go off-Realm either.

"That only leaves us with three names," Jonathan said. "Did you want to remove anyone else?" he prompted.

"Who do we have left?"

Jonathan glanced down at the parchment. "Talofa, Amara, and Samuel. I would agree with the first two, and would replace Samuel with Alistair."

Shari wrinkled her nose. "Why? Sam showed significant care with his teammates and did well against the Chirea. He's also shown restraint off the field against Therdon, and he healed me when the soul-sucker arrow hit me," Shari said.

"He's..." The reason Samuel Caragnton couldn't be *his* apprentice was on the tip of Jonathan's tongue. Here was his chance to tell Shari exactly who Samuel was, but telling her now, so soon after Kodan's betrayal, might just break her. Shari would find what Samuel had done was far worse than Kodan's actions, and rightly so, with the monster living in their midst. The only way to save her was to dissuade her from picking Sam as her preferred candidate. "He's stubborn. He'll not work with me without a fight, and my energy could be better spent."

Looking at him with narrow eyes for long enough that sweat started to form under his collar, Shari finally shook her head and laughed. "That'd probably be good for you, Jon," she said. "Sam might just shake you out of your comfort zone."

"I'm quite comfortable in my zone, thank you," he said with a sniff.

"That's why it's a 'comfort zone'." Shari laughed. "Amara is brilliant, but I think training with her would be dangerous. That girl tripped over air and killed someone. Talofa is amazing. She has some serious skills, but I worry about how young she is," she admitted. Jon raised an eyebrow at her, and Shari laughed. "Stop it! I mean it. I know what it's like to have to protect your Realm instead of having a childhood, and I don't wish that on anyone."

"So that leaves Samuel or Alistair," Jon said.

Why was Jonathan being so stubborn about this? "Not Alistair." Shari shook her head. "Just Sam." She conjured a ball of light and tossed it in the air as if the matter was decided. She'd seen how ruthless he was in a fight and hoped that he could temper his reactions somewhat.

Jon opened his mouth but seemed to think better of what he was going to say. He paused for a moment and tried again. "I don't feel comfortable working with him."

"It's because he's Dark, isn't it?" Shari asked, her eyes following the path of the ball as it rose into the air, and almost missed Jon's shocked look. "It's not like he's the darkest being out there, Jon. I know it's disconcerting to work with someone who's Darker than you, but you work okay with me."

"Shari..."

"He's my final choice, Jon," Shari said. "I want someone who can fight in a team, someone who can lead when one of us can't, someone who can work seamlessly with others, and someone who cares about the rest of their team making it home. And that's what Sam has shown every step of the way."

"I still don't think–"

"Jonathan."

Well, this was it. Jonathan knew for sure that he was going to be the first Guardian killed by his Altoriae, and history would paint her as being right. He would say that she was right too, if she'd let him leave his spirit behind.

"There's still a chance he'll refuse," Jonathan said, hoping Samuel would, but doubting it at the same time.

"Amara would be my next choice. I'd like to ask her to stay on Ronah anyway. Add her to my 'guild'," Shari said with a quirk of her lips.

"What about the other candidates?"

"I'll see if they want to join as well."

"Even Therdon?"

Shari glared at him. "I never want to see him again."

"You know he'll be at the ceremony, don't you?"

"No, he won't. I don't want him there."

"Shari," Jonathan ran a hand over his face. "I don't want him there any more than you do, but it's tradition."

"Tradition?" she looked at him incredulously. "Really?"

"Yes. All of the surviving candidates will be there."

"Far be it for me to break with *tradition*," she huffed. "I need to get going. I'm reserving the right to kick Therdon out if he tries anything."

"Very well. I shall release you into Anika's clutches. I'll see you at the town square this afternoon?"

Shari groaned. "Ugh. I'd forgotten about that. Fine. I'll see you at two. If I survive."

Jonathan's smile was strained as Shari shifted away, but she didn't notice. After she shifted out, he crossed to the Handbook and opened it to the Guardian's section. He ran his hand down the list of Guardians who had come before him. He wondered if any of them had ever created such a blunder that made them suspect the very Realm was going to implode.

Sighing, he poised his pen over the book, ready to add Sam's name to the list of Guardians' apprentices, but found that he just couldn't do it. Maybe he'd add it after the announcement. Or maybe it'd be a good idea to get Shari to update the book, and he wouldn't have to run his eyes over the names of all of those he'd failed.

"Well met!" Anika trilled at Shari, who was still poised with her hand raised to knock on the door. "What are you doing? We have sooo much to do," Anika said, grabbing Shari's wrist and pulling her inside.

Anika tugged her through the Thornes' house and up the stairs to her room. "Okay, sit there. I have a whole range of outfits for you to try on. Now, what style calls to you?" Anika asked, tapping a long nail against her lips.

Shari blinked. "Um... my leathers?" She cringed as it came out as a question.

Anika's chin dipped and she peered at Shari in horror. "Your... leathers? No. No, absolutely not! You're making an exciting announcement, not fighting! Here." Anika scooped up a hanger and thrust it in Shari's direction. "What about this?"

Eyeing the form-fitting dress, Shari shook her head. "I won't be able to move in that," she protested.

"Who do you think you're going to be fighting? The Chirea are all gone, and so are the U'sala and the traitor. You're safe," Anika said earnestly.

"I need something that I can move in," Shari said instead of answering Anika's question.

"Is that why you never wear skirts?" Anika asked.

Shari blinked, not used to the idea of someone scrutinising her wardrobe so closely. "Yeah, pretty much."

"Hmmm. That makes sense, I suppose. Let me see what else I've got," Anika said, flicking through her wardrobe. "Oh, how about this?" She flung a hanger with an orange floral thing onto the bed. "Or this, or this, or this?"

More hangers joined the first, and Shari stared with growing alarm at the pile on the bed.

'*Help*,' she thought. In the back of her mind, Jon gently laughed.

"Aha!" Anika emerged from the depths of her wardrobe with yet another hanger. "This is *so* you!"

With quite a bit of trepidation, Shari looked at the outfit that Anika had pulled out. Black slacks and a flowing emerald-green blouse. "That's... not too bad, actually."

"Get these on while I put the rest away," Anika said, passing the clothes over to Shari.

Shari slipped behind a screen and pulled the outfit on before marvelling at the range of movement she had in it. The shoulders didn't pull when she stretched her arms up. She was even able to slip a dagger into the sleeve without it showing. There was the hint of a scar at her collarbone. Her fingers trailed over it for a moment, a smile shining in her eyes.

"Okay, ready?" Anika asked. "That was the first colour I saw after you brought me back to Ronah, you know." Anika's eyes were on the top.

"I didn't," Shari said softly.

"Oh, don't baby me," Anika snapped. "Everyone is too scared to talk to me about what happened. Anriluka was *my* fault, and I can't say a word about it to anyone!"

"What do you mean 'your fault'?" Shari asked.

"She... I..." Anika slumped down, her face pale and her chin quivering. Shari hovered awkwardly, unsure of what she was meant to be doing.

"I've known since I first started school that I was a Blank. Do you remember the testing on the first day? I came up with nothing. When I told my parents, they were devastated. They sent me to my room, and I heard them arguing for hours. I cried myself to sleep that night, and when I dreamed, a voice told me that it would be my power. It would show up for tests and lend me Innarn and my parents would never cry about their pathetic little Blank ever again." Anika swiped at the tears welling and fanned her face.

"She tricked me. Anriluka. It was years before I put the voice together with the name, and then it was too late. I needed her. I didn't know how to tell anyone, and I figured that the Altoriae wasn't going to be around for years more. And then, I was getting ready to come and tell you about it all and... and she grabbed me." Tears were coursing down Anika's face now, and Shari hugged herself. She knew Anika wouldn't welcome another's touch right now.

"I've never... there was so much pain..." Anika sounded broken, but sniffed and straightened up. "No one is ever going to feel like that again. I'm going to use how I felt and turn it around. No Blank is ever going to feel so unwanted that they reach out to a monster like Anriluka."

"You know what?" Shari asked.

"What?" Anika turned to her, her eyes blazing with determination, her jaw set.

"When everyone thought that I was a Blank, people would cross the street to get away from me, and they'd flinch if they accidentally touched me. I get why you'd reach out, and I think that if anyone has the determination to change the way that people think about Blanks, it'd be you," Shari said softly.

"And I'll look damn good doing it. Now, we need to get you ready," Anika said, sniffing as she rose and crossed to her dresser. Picking up a brush, she turned back to Shari and grinned. "Hold still," she warned.

Shari wondered if she had a chance to escape before Anika descended on her.

Jonathan stood at the double doors of the room the candidates were in. Resting his hand on the wooden panels, he sighed.

Last time he'd had to announce his apprentice, the Elders of Ronah had thrown a massive feast, and he'd been almost giddy with the thought that he'd be able to share his burden with someone else. The ceremony they'd held when Mitchel's name was announced as apprentice had been a grand affair, and the Island had celebrated for days.

Shari had hidden herself away from the others, claiming to be sick. She'd patrolled instead, her escape from all the pomp and circumstance.

Mitchel, though? He had worn a grin for weeks. His parents had been so proud of him, and his siblings had teased him even as they fairly radiated with delight that he'd been chosen. His apprentice had always worn a smile, even when Jonathan had put him through the most gruelling training sessions he'd been able to devise.

Now...

Jonathan wondered what sort of mistake he was making. Maybe he should have more faith in Shari? Surely, she wouldn't have picked Samuel without good reason?

Opening the doors, he stepped inside, the cheers of the candidates ringing in his ears.

Tugging at the neckline of her blouse, Shari stood behind the podium in the town square.

"Do *not* ruin all of my hard work." Anika slapped her hand away.

"I'll try not to." Shari rolled her eyes. The clatter of shoes sounded around the corner.

"Good. I'll see you after," Anika said, and slipped away just as the first of the candidates rounded the back of the podium, led by Jon.

Jon, who'd been forewarned of Shari's transformation, gave her a quick smile. '*It's not as bad as you were saying,*' he sent.

'*I look like a painted clown.*' Shari scowled at him.

Behind Jon, Burke whistled when he caught sight of Shari. Someone nudged him, hard, and he cut off.

"Candidates," Jon said. "Please excuse the Altoriae and I. When I summon you, please come forwards onto the stage."

There was a general murmur of acceptance and Jon grasped Shari's elbow, leading her up the stairs.

'*Out of the frying pan and into the fire,*' she sent to Jon. He masterfully ignored her.

"Well met, all. Today, we shall be announcing the next Guardian's apprentice. Many thanks to the Altoriae for her tireless efforts in testing the candidates put forwards," Jon said to the assembled crowd.

There were noises of surprise as they realised that this wasn't the announcement of the next trial, as well as a few exclamations over Shari's appearance, mostly from classmates who were used to seeing her in far more casual clothing.

"As a result of the unexpected attack by the Chirea, the Altoriae was able to see how all the candidates performed in a real combat situation. As such it has been decided to forego the last of the trials, and announce the new apprentice today." Jon let the applause go on for a long moment, before holding a hand up to quieten the crowd. "Let us welcome the candidates to the stage!"

Raucous cheering erupted again, and Shari fought against flinching from the sound as the candidates made their way up the podium stairs.

The Elders of the candidates shifted to the stage as well, each standing behind their candidates. Sam moved to stand behind Shari, and Alistair moved to stand behind Jon. Shari turned slightly to look at the candidates and caught SilverCloud's gaze. He smiled at her, his eyes misting over.

Shari lowered her gaze and turned back to Jon. Sam stepped slightly closer, and she sensed his heat against her back.

'*Therdon is planning something,*' Sam sent to her.

Dipping her head slightly to acknowledge Sam's words, she sent her Innarn out, and was able to taste the tension around Therdon. It was different to the anticipation of the other candidates. There was a thread of desperation that made him dangerous.

Jon droned on, mentioning accolades for each of the candidates, and they each stepped forwards, beaming, until Jon got to Therdon.

"The Ilutri candidate, Therdon of Rakemyst, has been disqualified due to unscrupulous use of his Innarn on the other candidates," Jon said.

If Sam hadn't have warned her, Shari would never have been able to shift SilverCloud out of the way of the dagger Therdon turned to stab into his heart. As it was, the shift was inelegant, and SilverCloud was only moved to the front of the crowd.

"You!" Therdon was almost inarticulate with rage. He turned on Shari, eyes blazing, but her shields were already raised. "You're in danger!" Therdon screamed at her, spittle flying out of his mouth. "Can't you see?" He gestured wildly, almost slashing the Wisara Elder in his rage, his blade bouncing off the shield Sam hastily created.

"He'll be the death of you! I tried to stop SilverCloud when the Chirea first attacked. The Ilutri need a stronger leader, not an ailing fool! I made him and the other Elders pick me as a candidate, even though they wanted Belfar instead of me! Then, I stopped Kodan long enough for you to finish him off, and it's only right that I do the same for him!

Samuel Caragnton is a danger to everyone on Lissae!" Therdon screamed.

Shaking her head, Shari tried being diplomatic. "We've gone over this, Therdon. Sam is—"

"He'll kill you!" Therdon screamed again. "He has to be stopped! I must protect you!"

It seemed to happen in slow motion. Therdon lunged forwards, the tip of his dagger cutting through the cloth of Sam's shirt.

"I don't think so," Shari growled, raising a hand, releasing a jet of flames so strong that the beings closest to Therdon screamed in terror, beating at the stray embers that drifted from his smouldering body.

Sam looked at her in shock.

There was a long moment of silence when Therdon's skin could clearly be heard crackling from the intense heat. Shari hadn't even given him a chance to cry out; she'd cooked him where he'd stood.

LoneWolf, Belfar, and her parents lunged forwards out of their first-row seats. Belfar and Calem gathered Therdon's ashes as they fell. LoneWolf shot into the air, landing beside SilverCloud with his bow in hand.

Grimly, Shari smiled at Sam, who looked at the crumbling form of the Ilutri candidate.

"Remind me not to stab anyone when you're around." Sam smirked at her.

"Well, you'll have plenty of chances to remind me, won't you?" Shari asked smartly.

"Things are never boring around here, are they?" Jon said brightly to the crowd, as if a body hadn't just burned to ash before everyone. *'They didn't see it happen. As soon as you shifted SilverCloud, I created a shield and played back some of the footage the Silverstones took of the first trial.'*

Shari gave a choked laugh.

"Now, I suppose we'd best get down to the lucky one who will be working alongside the Altoriae and training under yours truly. This being showed tenacity, cunning, and a skill that overshadowed the others. May I present to you, the next Guardian's apprentice..." Jon paused, and Shari wanted to kick him. The noise of the crowd fell away. Into the quiet, Jon announced, "Samuel Caragnton!"

The crowd exploded and Shari couldn't hide her flinch this time as the sound overwhelmed her. Sam caught her gaze and raised his eyebrows. She smiled at him and nodded, and he allowed himself to be drawn forwards to shake hands with Jon.

"I suppose this means you want to see the back of me?" Amara teased her good-naturedly.

"Of course not," Shari replied. "Who else is going to run into me?"

Amara laughed, grinning up at Elder Billi.

Shari shot her a smile but found her gaze straying to Sam as he soaked up the accolades of the other disappointed candidates.

She'd made the right choice. Hadn't she?

Chapter Thirty-One

Tania sat in a tree on the highest point of Ronah, near where the bridge to Rakemyst was connected, looking out at the waves breaking as the Islands soared through the ocean. Without thinking, she knew how fast they were moving.

Sighing, she guided the puff of air from her lungs, adding it to the wards Ronah used to prevent the strong breeze that would have blown her from her perch. Pulling her knees up, she wriggled back until the hard, smooth trunk of the tree cradled her, and stared out sightlessly, trying to come to some sort of peace with the battle against Kodan and the Chirea.

Even when she'd been held captive by Besfu and Opar, Tania didn't think she'd ever felt so helpless as when her family were stuck inside Kodan's wards and she had been on the outside. Her family, her friends, her people all trapped, and she didn't know enough to get them out without help, and without some of them dying.

Wiping uselessly at the tears streaming down her face, Tania remembered Zana's words after the battle was done.

'*You have the soul of a warrior.*'

The way she'd said it, it wasn't meant as a compliment.

Mournfully, Tania looked out over the ocean, trying to still the tumultuous thoughts rattling around in her head.

Rustling sounded in the leaves below, and Tania peered down, seeing her brother's copper head as he climbed higher to reach her. She said nothing as he heaved himself up onto the branch next to her, struggling to catch his breath.

They sat, shoulder to shoulder for the longest time, neither speaking until the sun started to dip below the horizon.

"I'm glad Shari didn't choose me," Alistair said at last.

"Me too," Tania said, and slung an arm around his shoulders. They watched the sky turn darker, pinks and purples overtaking blues to form a spectacular sunset.

"Time to head home, hey?" she asked. Alistair nodded and turned to slide off the branch. Tania gave him a cheeky grin and stood, balancing carefully.

"What're you doing?" he asked. Winking at him, Tania threw her arms out, and jumped. "No!" Alistair screamed, his free hand reaching frantically for her as she slipped past.

Laughing, Tania pulled the air around her, making a dense cushion of it at the bottom of the tree. She bounced off easily and landed on her feet with a smile.

"Jump, Al!" she called.

Worried face peering at her from between the leaves, Alistair shook his head. "You're mad!" he yelled down at her.

"Jump!"

With a shriek, he let go, and landed safely on her cushion of air. Together, brother and sister turned and headed for home, neither of them spotting the hulking shadow that watched over them.

Shari sat in the cushy chair, looking around the back room of the bookstore. So much of her training had happened here, but there were times when she missed her sanctuary, her little pocket Realm where she could practise as much as she wanted without the constraints of other people, or having to fulfil some of her traditional duties.

The Altoriae's Handbook was open on her lap to the Guardian's page where she had to enter Sam's name under Mitch's.

One hand held the ridiculous quill that Jon wanted her to use, while her other hand almost subconsciously smoothed over the pages of the book, her fingertips trailing over Jon's name. She wondered what thoughts had gone through Joshua's mind as he'd entered the name of the then seven-year-old boy who would grow to be one of the most influential and respected people on all Lissae.

Had he had an inkling of what Jon would grow into? Or had it been just another duty that he completed without thought? She'd spoken to his spirit a few times before she'd first revealed herself to Jon, but found him overly stuffy and difficult to take seriously when he'd glide right through her.

What had gone through Jon's mind when he'd entered Mitch's name? Had he been relieved that the testing was over, or worried about what the future would hold?

Shari had to admit that she didn't know how to feel. Sighing, and acknowledging that she'd put off an easy task for long enough, she dipped the quill into the inkpot on the side table and swiftly wrote Sam's name. As soon as she lifted the quill from the page, the ink glowed with the same golden light that she thought she saw in Sam's eyes sometimes.

Glad to mark one more thing off her list, Shari closed the book and put it on its hidden shelf, her hands trailing reverently over the cover.

Time to go and face the latest apprentice to the Guardian.

"So, it's official then," Shari said as she came out of the back room, stuffing her hands into the pockets of her pants.

"Official?" Samuel pushed off from the counter to stand in front of the one he'd just sworn to guide and protect.

The thought of annoying Jon was the main reason that he'd agreed to become Shari's candidate, but Samuel was quickly discovering that there was more to it. His desire for a purpose to remain on Lissae and to get closer to the Altoriae was a large part, to be sure, but he was finding that the more he was around Shari, the more he wanted to help her, to keep her safe. Idly, he wondered if she emitted some sort of passive Innarn that he hadn't thought to check for that would make him act like that.

Shaking his head to dismiss the thought, he turned his attention back to the general who now commanded him.

What could he say? His training was hard to break, and even though Samuel had thought himself long removed from his early years, apparently some of the teachings of his Elders had pierced even his thick hide.

"You're in the book, so it's all official. I'll leave you and Jon to set up a training schedule, and I think that you're more than competent to go out on patrol, which will help take some of the strain off Jon. He's working too much," Shari said, frowning at Jonathan who was studiously ignoring them in favour of going over one of his lists.

"I'll sort out the schedule, Shari, but I'm not sure about patrolling yet," Jon said, acting as if he hadn't heard her last remark.

"Jon," Shari started, but the Guardian looked up with a glance that made her stop.

Samuel found himself watching the interaction between them avidly. He didn't think they'd ever been quite this unguarded around him before.

"Fine," Shari said shortly. "I need to go do a few things, but I'll swing past later and drop off some of Mum's soup."

"Thanks, Shari," Jonathan said, and his tone indicated that it was not the last time the issue would arise.

Nodding his thanks, Samuel watched as Shari slipped out the front door before turning to his new teacher.

"So, when do we get started?" Samuel smirked at him.

Dropping the pretence of concentrating on the list, Jonathan looked at him fully for the first time since he had made the announcement in the town square.

"What are you playing at?" the Guardian asked.

For a moment, Samuel thought about feigning innocence, but of all the people on Ronah, Jonathan Buan was the last one his act would work on. "I find that I want to get closer to the Altoriae and to help her protect Lissae," Samuel chose his words carefully.

"You can't be serious," Jonathan said, making an inelegant sound that did not suit him at all.

"I am," Samuel said, raising his chin, and peering down at Jon.

Jonathan studied him for a moment. "Why?"

"I... I do not know," Samuel admitted.

"Are you going to kill her?" Jonathan asked harshly, his breath coming in agitated pants.

"No... no. I don't think so," Samuel said slowly.

"You don't think so." Jonathan turned away from him, scrubbing his hand over his face. "I caught you once, Sam, and if you hurt Shari, I'll do more than just cage you next time."

He fought the instinctive words that threatened to bubble up out of his throat—that Jonathan had been lucky, that he'd be the one doing the catching next time, that he had no intention of hurting Shari, that couldn't Jonathan just *trust* him? He knew, better than most, that actions indicated more than words.

"Time will show you that I mean what I say," Samuel settled on instead, and slipped out of the store.

CHAPTER THIRTY-TWO

A few weeks ago, before everything had happened with the Chirea, Fiona had mentioned a Light Realm that was amassing an army, and he'd been putting off patrolling there, but tonight was the perfect excuse. He'd caught scouts from the Realm of Atlantis torturing the Ducibus at Lissae's doorway, and there was no way that he was going to stand for that.

Jonathan didn't think he'd ever been so glad that he was the one on patrol. A tiny part of him had been hoping that Shari wasn't entirely serious about choosing Samuel as his apprentice, but he'd sensed it in his bones when she'd entered Samuel's name into the Handbook.

He had a small group with him tonight: Elder Thorne, Uista Zeypher, Ashlen Shansky, and Katie Doonavan. As he led them into the fight with a scouting group, he couldn't help but thinking how well they worked together as a team.

The rest of his patrol group were fighting one-on-one with the Atlantians, leaving the others to Jonathan. The scouting group was not large, only about twenty human men. They were no match for his crossbow, nor the heavy blows of Innarn he was sending their way. There was no compassion in him tonight.

The Atlantians fought well, their grasp of tech Innarn far outstripping his own. As they threatened the others in his patrol group, neither they nor their machines were able to match him in raw power. Jonathan blasted one after the other out of the sky.

Shooting off one last devastating blast of fire Innarn, Jonathan realised that the battlefield was quiet except for the panting of the patrol group as they recovered from their fight.

Jonathan found that the fight had only taken the edge off his frustrations, but that edge was enough. He would learn to work with his new apprentice, and Samuel would learn to work with him. He was not above using Samuel's fondness for Shari to keep him in line.

"Guardian?" Elder Thorne was saying, bringing Jonathan back to his current battlefield and out of the metaphorical one in his mind.

"My apologies, Elder. We need to remove the bodies and take one of the machines back to Lissae to study," Jonathan said.

The Elder nodded, and Jonathan moved to prod at one of the machines with his boot. It sparked and hissed at him, and he swiftly shielded the device, making his way back to the doorway to Lissae as the others carefully laid out the Atlantians' bodies, gathering up other parts of the machines as they went and destroying them. The back of Uista's coat was gently smouldering, but Katie put it out by giving her a hearty thump.

Watching the interaction between the rest of his patrol group made him grimace. If he ever let Samuel off Ronah to be a part of the patrol, Jonathan knew he'd spend the whole time wondering when Sam would turn on him, or turn on Shari. He couldn't let that happen.

As his patrol joined him at the doorway, Jonathan guided them all through, motioning to Ashlen and Katie to gather up the Ducibus and take him back for healing. Throwing one last look around Atlantis,

Jonathan wondered if the idyllic vista held someone who wanted to kill him.

Snorting at his self-absorption, Jonathan shook off his sensation of gloom and stepped through the doorway.

Shari watched as her Guardian closed the doorway to Lissae behind him, the stunning view now seamless once more. She'd been curious as to why Jon had wanted to come to the Light Realm, but it appeared he'd wanted to blow off some steam from the way he'd been fighting.

There were not too many foes Shari had faced who were as accomplished at tech Innarn as the Atlantians were. The machines that they'd sent to guard their doorway ensured that they were well protected with a minimal loss of life. She'd dipped into the Ducibus' memories and seen what they'd done to ze, and was horrified. With the Ducibus phasing in and out due to the pain ze'd endured, Shari had only caught some of the questions, but there was a definite interest in Lissae and her protections.

She needed to get back to see what Jon had learned, and to figure out how to stop the Realm of Atlantis from attacking her home.

Slipping soundlessly from behind her tree, Shari made her way slowly towards the doorway, keeping an eye out for more of the machines. Reaching the doorway without being stopped, Shari swiftly opened it and stepped through to Lissae, sealing it firmly behind her to make sure that nothing could get through. The last thing she wanted was another situation like they'd had with the Chirea.

Stalking through the corridors, she realised that she was going to be late if she didn't hurry, and she shifted out.

Jonathan, who was showing the next patrol group, sensed Shari's distinctive Innarn signature as he strode back down the corridor to the doorway to Atlantis. Frowning, he wondered how long she'd been there before smoothing his features and showing the group which doorway they were to protect.

Nodding in satisfaction, he slipped away to attend the funeral of the Ilutri candidate.

Shari felt like a fraud. Tugging on her formal tunic, she looked around at the bowed heads of the Ilutri. The upright collar stood too close to her throat, and the embroidered Innarn symbols emblazoned in a circle on her chest were itchy despite the layer between her skin and the tunic. The laces on the sides were pulled too tight, making it hard to breathe. Jon stood on her right, with her mum on her left, gently tugging Shari's hand down.

Calem raised what was left of Therdon into the air. "We are borne from the air, we live our lives in the air, and with a final breath, we give you back to the air from whence you came!" Calem said. The entire flock of Ilutri breathed out, swirling Therdon's ashes as they rose higher and higher into the sky.

A low crooning noise came from her father's throat, and slowly, others joined in. Shari watched in awe. With every voice that joined in, her father's hand sparked with a touch of the Innarn they were lending him, until the clearing rang with the sound of the crooning and Calem thrust his hands upwards, igniting the ashes in a spectacular showcase of colour.

Shari had never seen her father in his role as Ilutri Priest, and she understood, perhaps a little bit, why LoneWolf was so upset that he had left everything behind when he moved to Ronah. Her father held the Innarn of others like it was as easy as breathing. Shari knew from experience that it was an almost impossible task to do, let alone to complete it without breaking into a sweat.

It still didn't help her feelings of unease. SilverCloud had specifically asked for her to be here, but she'd rather be anywhere else. There were not many beings who would invite the deceased's killer to their funeral.

She stood still as her father turned his gaze onto her.

"Therdon of the Ilutri tried to die with honour, but failed to ensure his duties were upheld. We all swear to protect the Altoriae. Therdon's actions did not match the duty he swore to, forcing the Altoriae to kill him in self-defence."

All eyes turned to Shari, and she felt the weight of them judging her.

"The Altoriae acted within the terms of her duties, and Therdon acted outside the terms of his. The Altoriae is not held responsible for her reaction to Therdon's actions," her father intoned. A peculiar relief filled her. She'd never totally accept that what happened to Therdon was the only option she had, but she did feel slightly better knowing that the rest of the Ilutri would not hold her responsible.

The rest of the ceremony passed in a blur of colour and motion, and Shari found herself joining in the celebration for the joy Therdon had found in life rather than mourning the last thing she'd known him for.

She shared a smile with Jon, who seemed far more at ease than he'd been when she'd seen him on patrol, and forced herself to concentrate on the good things.

After the ceremony was over, Shari slipped away to leave some of her mother's soup for Jon and Sam. Although Arilla might have been a Blank, she cooked with so much love that Shari would swear up and down that her food was pure magic.

She and Jon had gone through so much lately, and Shari knew Jon would forget to eat, pushing thoughts of self-care out of his mind until he was satisfied that an attack like the Chirea couldn't happen again. She knew, because she was the same.

Slipping inside Jon's house, she set down the first bowl of soup, putting a heating ward around it so it would remain fresh, hot, and ready, tempting Jon with the smell as soon as he came through the door.

'*Jon! I need to talk to you!*' Shari sent.

'*Where are you?*' Jon sent back. Even his thoughts sounded weary.

'*At your house,*' Shari said. Swiftly, she set up her note: *Eat, we'll talk in the morning.*

Giggling, she slid silently out the back door as Jon came through the front. Shari shifted to Sam's new house, following the same procedure before slipping away to have dinner with her parents.

Pallen snuck out of the copse of trees, moving low and letting the dappled light warm her hide. She'd stripped her armour off after Fusstan fell. If she couldn't save her mate, then she wasn't worthy of it. She'd waited and waited for the Golden One to be alone, and now she finally had her chance to earn her armour back.

While Fusstan may have preferred the blade and bow, Pallen far preferred her potions and poisons, and she knew just the thing to add to the Golden One's dinner. Slipping in through the side door of his abode, Pallen scurried through the rooms until she found where his meal waited.

With a care that belied her need to be quick, she added three drops of a luminous yellow gel from a blue bottle to his soup and stirred it quickly. There was the slam of the front door and Pallen dropped to the ground, scurrying under the table, and bracing herself.

The thud of his boots became louder as the Golden One entered the room. The scrape of the chair made her teeth ache in her skull. All was quiet for a moment before the thump of his body hitting the floor made her smile in triumph.

Until she looked down and saw him smirking up at her.

His mouth moved, but Pallen didn't hear the sounds he made. She scrambled to her feet. Throwing the table off her back, she smashed the blue bottle at his feet.

The Golden One raised an unimpressed eyebrow.

Pallen shrieked and rushed at him. He stepped out of the way, and she slammed into the cupboard behind him. Before she rushed at him again, she felt something piercing her hide, and a burning, sticky liquid dripped down her torso. Looking at the floor, she groaned, and her eyes rolled back into her head.

The last thing she ever saw was the Golden One smirking at her as he licked his fingers clean of her blood.

Sam thought about ignoring Shari's summons, but she was his commanding officer now, and no one disobeyed a command from the general and lived to tell the tale. At least, not where he came from.

He strode quickly through the town and into his house, expecting to find Shari, but only smelling something enticing in the kitchen.

He breathed in deeply. The aroma of the soup was tantalising, but there was an underlying smell of burned leather and seared bone that made him frown. Looking at the pile of discarded clothes that lay in a heap in the corner, where he'd shed them after the battle with the Chirea, he shrugged and sat down.

The first spoonful of soup was so good, it almost disguised the taste of the poison. Throat closing over, he dropped to the floor with a thud. His fingers scrabbled at his neck before he engaged his brain and morphed just his throat into his natural form and back again. As he regained his higher function, he looked up, and saw an armour-less Chirea smiling down at him.

"You've got to be kidding me," Sam growled, "I thought we got rid of you lot." The Chirea threw a blue bottle at his feet. The fumes made his eyes water and his throat threatened to close over again, but Gods be damned if he was going to show it.

Predictably, the Chirea rushed him. Sam stepped to the side, watching impassively as she crashed into his cupboards. Deciding he'd had enough, he changed his hands and throat to his natural form. Grabbing her torso with his claws, he breathed hard on the wounds.

Pulling his talons free as she slumped down, he licked his fingers clean. As the room began to spin, he hoped the incompetent poisoner had enough antidote to whatever was in the smashed bottle left in her bloodstream to affect him.

As he landed heavily on his knees, he figured that she didn't.

Just before his world became dark, he sent out a weak call, 'Shari...'

Chapter Thirty-Three

Shari poured all of her healing into Sam as she shifted them both into the Healers' Centre.

"Don't think you can get out of the job this easily," Shari said, trying to hide the quiver in her voice.

Sam's listless form didn't reply.

"Stand clear!" a healer said. Shari stood back and watched as the healer slammed Sam's chest with a bolt of pure Innarn that set Sam coughing and made a vibrant yellow liquid spray across the room.

"Is that...?" another healer asked.

"Hydrusfel," the first healer replied. "You're lucky you found him when you did."

Poison. Shari stood with her arms wrapped around her stomach and her head bowed low. Sam hadn't even lasted a day as the Guardian's apprentice without being attacked.

Just what had she gotten him into?

Shari slept standing against the wall beside Sam's bed, only startling awake when Jon waved a cup of azehal under her nose, the tantalising aroma bringing her out of her stupor.

"Huh? Oh, thanks, Jon," Shari said, rubbing at her tired eyes with one hand and taking the proffered cup with the other.

"I got the townsfolk to search every bit of Ronah and Rakemyst last night. There are no other Chirea left," Jon said, taking a sip of his own drink.

Gaze dark, Shari nodded before taking a long drink and closing her eyes in bliss. When she opened them, she automatically sought out Sam's sleeping form.

"Why don't you go get some rest?" Jon offered. "I'll watch over Sam."

For a moment, Shari thought about protesting, but she was still feeling drained after the battle and the week-long fighting beforehand.

"Alright, but if you need me, I'm only a send away," Shari said, and slipped out of the room before Jon changed his mind.

As soon as she was clear of the healers, she shifted home, eager to spend as much time with her family as she could.

Before she reached the door, SilverCloud burst through it and wrapped his arms around her, crying, "Shari!"

Shari stood awkwardly in her backyard, arms pinned to her side, SilverCloud squeezing her so hard she thought a rib might have cracked.

"I told them no, but they're not listening." He let her go gently.

"Not listening to what?" Shari asked.

"They want to move to Rakemyst to help Wolf keep an eye on me. Bah! They need to keep an eye on you!"

"What're you talking about?" Shari asked, confused.

"They think I'm too old," he grumbled, and started tugging her into the house.

"I'm lost," Shari admitted.

Her parents were seated at the kitchen table. LoneWolf was clanging pots and pans in the sink in a way that made Shari think he was trying to reshape them rather than clean them, and Belfar was watching them all with a concerned look.

"What's going on?" Shari asked.

"Tell them you still need them," SilverCloud demanded.

"Of course I still need them. They're my parents," Shari said. She was sure there was a huge part of the story she was missing, and that impression was only confirmed when LoneWolf banged a pot so hard against the side of the sink that the sink cracked and began to leak. Shari fixed it with a flick of her hand.

"Your parents have offered to move into the Dawn residence on Rakemyst," Belfar said. "SilverCloud needs more help now, and they know you are only ever a shift or a send away."

Shari felt a bit like she was Astral travelling and was half a step out of sync with her physical body. "Oh. Well, if you need to…"

"Oh, Shari," her mother cried.

'SilverCloud is dying, Shari. And he's as stubborn as you are. I want to spend the last few months that he has left with him, but not if it means leaving you behind,' Calem sent to her.

Searching her father's stricken face, Shari was torn. She knew SilverCloud's life force was ebbing, and the stresses since Ronah and Rakemyst had joined were only exacerbating his condition, if you could call 'old age' a condition.

There was only one thing for it. "Oh, I don't mind. Now it's all official and everything, I'm meant to move into the castle anyway. So you're free to make sure that LoneWolf doesn't smother SilverCloud too much," Shari said easily.

It was probably the hardest statement she'd ever had to make.

"Oh, Shari," her mum said again, this time granting her a watery smile between the tears.

"Not you too," SilverCloud grumbled, sinking into a seat at the table. "I'll be surrounded by babysitters!"

"Hardly." Shari snorted. "I bet you know all the secret passageways in and out."

Even as SilverCloud's eyes lit up, LoneWolf and Belfar groaned in unison. Shari grinned wickedly. If she was going to be living by herself in that big old castle, then at least her grandfather would be able to sneak away from his carers and visit her on occasion.

Chapter Thirty-Four

Jonathan looked at the still form in the bed beside him.

He'd never known how much a poison like hydrusfel would affect a Q'Aralide, but clearly the Chirea who'd chosen it did.

Before he had the chance to contemplate his new apprentice for much longer, Samuel startled awake and blasted a fireball at the curtains surrounding his bed. The explosion was absorbed by Shari's shield, which seemed to make Samuel more inclined to violence.

He struck out three times in rapid succession, attacking the top of the shield and trying to get through that way, hoping to create holes big enough for his wings, Jonathan noted. Shari was nothing if not thorough in her shielding, and the blasts merely glowed against the ward for a moment before being added to it, making it stronger and more immune to Samuel's Innarn.

Finally, Samuel seemed to realise that he wasn't going to make any headway on the shields and looked around his bed frantically before his gaze came to rest on Jonathan.

With a burst of speed that said nothing of his attack and subsequent recovery, Samuel was up and on his feet, fists clenched in Jonathan's sweater as he lifted him off his toes and pushed him against the wall.

"Where is she?" Samuel snarled, his eyes as black as the Darkest Realms.

"Shari is safe, and the Chirea who attacked you is dead," Jonathan said calmly. Samuel's eyes searched his face for a long moment before he abruptly released Jonathan and slumped onto the bed.

"How did we miss her?" Samuel asked, his voice hoarse from the swelling the poison had caused.

"She'd removed her armour. Best we can figure is that we swept for Chirea with bones on the outside and missed her because of that. I've had the rest of the Islands searched, and there are no more left."

"Lucky me." Samuel snorted, and moved to put his boots on.

"No way. Healers' orders. You are to stay in bed until deemed fit," Jonathan said, trying to keep the satisfaction out of his voice.

From the dark look that Samuel gave him, he hadn't quite succeeded, but Samuel did subside, and lay back in the bed, one hand behind his head. "Tell me what I've missed," he demanded.

Jonathan looked at him askance but answered anyway. "Atlantian troops attacked and tortured a Ducibus, trying to gain information on how to enter Lissae."

"Atlantians?" Samuel frowned. "They can't be allowed on Lissae. Not even one of them, and absolutely not one bit of their machinery should come through the doorways."

"Why not?" Jonathan asked. "How are we meant to understand how to fight them if we don't figure out how they can connect with their machines?"

"Because the machines are evil. They'll wipe out everything and everyone on Lissae, and there'll be no one left to stop the Atlantians taking over," Sam warned.

"Don't be dramatic," Jonathan snapped. "The machines need tech Innarn to power them, and even Shari couldn't power one from a Realm as far away as Atlantis."

Samuel shook his head. "Don't come crying to me when Ronah is overwhelmed by the machines then," he said, and closed his eyes.

Jonathan stared at the man before him and sighed incredulously. *What a ridiculous thought.*

Shari shifted straight into the back room of Books 'n' More. Jonathan sat at his old, dented creamy-coloured desk. Shari sat down cross-legged in *her* armchair.

The bookcases that lined every wall of the room were in a shocking state of disarray. Books had been piled haphazardly on the floor; apparently, the man before her had searched frantically for something. Even the hidden bookcase door to the back room had carelessly been left open.

"What's going on? I thought you wanted me to make a good impression today?" Shari asked. Rising, she went to peer over Jon's shoulder. It took only a few more turned pages for Shari to realise what she was looking at.

"The *Hekkor Mafae*," she breathed, meeting Jon's eyes. The Dark Innarn pouring out of the pages was almost visible from where she sat. Each time he turned a page, Jon would flinch. If he were exposed to Dark Innarn for too long, it would take him days to recover from. Essentially a Light Innarnian, the Dark could taint and change him in unexpected ways. Shari was a Grey Innarnian, and as such, the Dark Innarn would take much longer to affect her.

"The one and only," Jonathan replied, his voice tight with control. Shari gently nudged him out of the way, turning the pages of the book for him when he tapped her shoulder. As he skimmed the text, Shari couldn't contain herself any longer.

"Jon, I know this is important, but I still think it's more important to find out what crossed over. That happened *before* Anriluka. You can't tell me you've found nothing on it."

"Him," Jonathan said absently as she flicked through the book, rapidly skimming the text, trying to find the exact location where the conclave would be held.

"Him? So, you have found something! Just when were you planning on telling me?" Shari griped, fingers subconsciously tightening on the pages.

Although his body froze, Jonathan's mind went into overdrive. What in Na'reh's name was he going to tell Shari now? He couldn't very well admit what race the creature was, and it was imperative that Shari was not concentrating on anything else while at the conclave. So, he did the very thing he swore he would never do.

Lie.

"It was—he was a shape-shifter. He changed himself into something ferocious to scare us. I'm days away from removing him from Lissae. By the time you're at the conclave, he'll be gone." Deep, deep down, in the recesses of his mind, he added, *and when you come back, so will he.* "Now that we've covered that, can we get back to the matter at hand?"

If there was a hint of anything other than impatience in his voice, Shari did not catch it.

"Wait, conclave? What conclave?" Shari asked.

"The Dark Conclave," Jonathan said. "Every few eons, the leaders of the Dark Realms meet and decide upon alliances and strategic plans. Due to the number of attacks we've had from the Dark Realms, I think it's a good idea if one of us is present, and disguised, at the conclave. And we both know it can't be me."

"What about Sam?"

"He still needs training." Jonathan's gaze darted back to the book.

"So, I get to go alone into a place where a fair few of these beings won't hesitate to kill me?"

"Don't be ridiculous. You'll have backup," Jonathan scolded, tapping her on the shoulder to turn the next page. "It won't be that dangerous, unless it's–"

"Unless it's what?" Shari asked when Jonathan broke off.

He gulped. "Unless it's on Altum," Jonathan said hoarsely. His breath seemed to be caught in his lungs, unable to escape.

"Altum? But isn't that the home Realm of…"

"The Q'Aralide," Jonathan said.

Shari pushed back from the book abruptly. "I need to go outside and think."

"Shari, wait!" Jonathan called and rushed after her.

In the sudden quiet of the back room, there was no one to hear the series of beeps from the pile of metal lumped on the desk. No one saw the single red light flick on, or the spindly arms start to pull the body of the machine back together.

GLOSSARY

Adeon – The God of the Element Fire and husband of Ke'ra.

Akoren – One of the sentient Shifting Islands on Lissae. Originally home to Lissae's Deities, now it is inhabited by a few, select representatives of the races that came from the other Shifting Islands.

Altoriae – Protector of the Realm of Lissae. Traditionally a female role, although there has been one male Altoriae. Previous Altoriaes have included Kay'imi, Muran Curtis, Jali Thorne, and Fiona MacAde. Forces of nature cannot kill her. They must swear to uphold the seven duties of the Altoriae. They are: 1. Protecting the Realm; 2. Protecting Ronah and its residents; 3. Calling Ronah's residents to arms in times of need; 4. Teaching Ronah's residents; 5. Maintaining peace on Ronah; 6. Ensuring that Ronah's young remember their Elders' pledges to the Altoriae; 7. Maintaining the Altoriae's Handbook for the use of future Altoriaes.

Altum – The home Realm of the Q'Aralide.

Anriluka – A U'tan from Rataeo who is older than Lissae's calendar and the being Shari had to stop to prove she was the Altoriae. Anriluka almost devoured Ronah's entire population before Muran Curtis' Guardian banished her back to her home Realm.

Apprentice – The Guardian's apprentice traditionally undergoes testing in order to be chosen. Testing for the Guardian's apprentice is made up of three trials that have four rounds each. The apprentice must undertake intensive training in order to ensure the safety of the Altoriae. Once a Guardian falls in battle or dies of old age, it is up to the Apprentice to take on all of their roles and responsibilities.

Atlantis – A Grey Realm with a predominantly human population, Atlantis is famous for its tech Innarn and wide variety of Innarn-powered machines.

Baenge – A Dark Realm with a giant shell for a door.

Bereni trees – Trees that are grown to be used as buildings. The size and design of the tree can be controlled by an Innarnian or by one of the sentient Islands.

Blank – A person who can't use Innarn.

Bone warriors – see *Chirea*.

Books 'n' More – A store on Ronah that the Guardian runs when he's not saving the Realm of Lissae.

Boon – Something that is granted for a completed task or heroic deed.

Cantash – One of the sentient Shifting Islands on Lissae. He is home to the Daens.

Castle Bachelor – The centre point of Ronah and the traditional home of the Altoriae, the Guardian and their respective families. The base of it was made up by a huge volcanic crater, one that had ceased its activity on Kay'imi's command. This left incredible natural catacombs beneath the castle that were mostly used for storage or the occasional prison cell. Merged with the top of the crater was a wall of plasma, with a doorknocker that boomed every time it was used. Windows of clear air dot the structure, and those inside can choose to darken or lighten them at will. A bereni tree grows at the heart of the castle, making not only a secure place for the Altoriae to train, but a solid structure should the outer walls fail. The branches and leaves of the tree made up the majority of the rest of the castle, except for the top, which sprouted turrets of flame, and the floor of the second floor, which was made of blue-green water.

Chirea – A race of warriors who use the bones of their fallen enemies to make their armour, weapons, and other items. The Chirea show status and power through the amount of bone armour they have collected. They use golden arrows soaked in a special mixture created by the Q'Aralide to steal Innarn. They are also known for poisons and soaking their weapons in potions that make healing by Innarn impossible. The Chirea made their base camp at Iabovar, near the Niverwell Ranges.

Clans – Family lines.

Crihimos – A Light Realm.

Crystals – Hold energy which is turned into electricity. Often installed in clusters to gain more power and last longer. Different coloured Crystals do different things. White Crystals are used for communication. Black Crystals gather power and Orange Crystals connect currents to create fences. Crystal necklaces are given to young children and Blanks for them to manipulate the Crystals.

Crystal See and Speak Communications – Or CS&SC, also called Crystal Send. Similar to Earth's video telephones.

Crystal Video Screen – Or CSV, is similar to Earth's televisions.

Curses – Several curses are common on Lissae, including: Adeon's fire; By the Life of Lissae; Ke'ra's Flash; Zoemer's Rocks; Rasshnae's Floods; Vebnah's Breath; Na'reh's Ghosts. Other curses from the Realms include: ketarr; dathae; tuzar's arse; tongue of a Ne'fora; whales' arse; basalt-chewing hemmit-loving buzzard; cestoray; slime vattar; hanotqe; slime filled cedore; feseor; gozochas; thrice-damned.

Daen – A short, fierce, and loyal race with amazing control over the Fire Element.

Dakleozen – A Dark Realm.

Da'mar – A humanoid race with lizard-like features who reside in the caves under Lissae. They live by a warrior code that is difficult for other races to understand.

Deities – Lissae has six Deities who are said to have lived on Akoren. See: Adeon, Ke'ra, Na'reh, Rasshnae, Vebnah and Zoemer for more details.

Dento – A fixed Island on Lissae. Home of the Kumaru.

Ducibus – The Ducibus guard the gateways between the Realms. No one really knows what they look like, as they all wear dark cloaks. There is a theory that they come from different Realms and are made up of all sorts of races. They ensure the safe travel between Realms and that those who aren't meant to get through, don't.

Duties – Ronah's residents must swear to uphold five duties. They are: 1. Protect the Altoriae at all costs; 2. Assist the Altoriae in any way she asks; 3. Answer an Altoriae's call without hesitation; 4. Ensure a safe place for the Altoriae to train; 5. Help to maintain peace among Ronah's residents to the best of your abilities.

Eazithan – A Dark Realm with a bristle hide-covered door with a bronze handle and hinges.

Elders – Those who have, through age and experience, managed to survive the Realms long enough to guide their people. They also act as advisors to the Mayor.

Elements – Lissae has seven main elements that Innarnians can manipulate: Earth, Air, Fire, Water, Plasma, Spirit and Technology.

Femto-crystals – The latest in healing technology for Talhan. They can help a patient recover from any damage they've sustained, and decrease recuperation time.

Ferah – Humanoid beings with cat-like features, including fur, tail, whiskers, and claws.

Feseor – Often used as a curse word, and refers to ravenous creatures that live in scum-filled ponds.

Fizzpot – An insult used by the older generations.

Freeson – A fixed Island on Lissae.

Frito – Small, bird-like animal with wings similar to a dragonfly. They live their lives in the air, only returning to the ground to lay their eggs or die.

Fulni – An animal similar to Earth's buffalo, but carnivorous and with two heads. The last fulni herd went extinct over two hundred years ago. Their tails are attached to a major artery, and if the tail is removed, they will bleed out in seven seconds.

Gerhar – A grey Realm near Lissae.

Gihalan – A Dark Realm.

Ginorti – One of the sentient Shifting Islands on Lissae. He is home to the Satyrs.

Gondnotia– A continent on Lissae.

Guardian – The rank for the person who oversees training and caring for the Altoriae, and for Lissae. In cases of emergency, the Mayor and Elders defer to the Guardian.

Harvvens – A race inhabiting the Niverwell Ranges, on the Realm of Iabovar.

Healers – Similar to Earth's doctors, they heal patients who are sick or injured, usually using Innarn, although they also use the old methods.

Healers' Centre – Also called the Hospital. A place to go when sick or injured.

Hekkor Mafae – A book about Dark Ones that Jonathan is very uncomfortable about having on Lissae.

Hinioxar – A Dark Realm.

Hospital – Also called Healers' Centre. A place to go when sick or injured.

Hulios – A fixed Island on Lissae.

I bid thee well – A traditional phrase when two or more people part ways.

Iabovar – A Grey Realm, home to the stunning Niverwell Ranges. The Realm where the Chirea made their base camp.

Ilutri – Winged humanoids from Lissae. They are usually found on Rakemyst and are high-level Innarnians. They include some of the finest archers on the Realm.

Innarn – (said Inn-*ar*-n) Predominately Elemental magic which is present in all Realms to varying strengths. Innarn is split into three main groups: Dark, Grey, and Light. Each variant of Innarn has its own specialties. See Elements for more information. There are also other disciplines of Innarn, including Animal, Crystal, Mental, Realm, and Time.

Innarnian – (said Inn-*ar*-ni-an) A person who can use Innarn.

Iomnuroz – A creature with razor-sharp claws.

Jali Thorne – The tenth Altoriae. She held the title for three years, before being trampled by a herd of ullfin.

Jinkor – A fixed Island on Lissae.

Kay'imi – The first Altoriae. She lived until she was 1217 years old when she was killed by a lone Ahana archer.

Kenorvia – A continent on Lissae.

Ke'ra – God of the Element Plasma and husband of Adeon.

Kumaru – Tree-like humanoids from Lissae. They are usually found on Dento and are high-level earth Innarnians. They pride themselves on their connection with earth and spirit Innarn. A long-lived race, the Kumaru rarely step off-Realm.

Kunun soup – Thick orange soup served with plates of crisped bread.

Lawrgaea– A continent on Lissae.

Lefo – A Realm that is said to hold the *Hekkor Mafae*.

Linked – A soul joined with that of one of Lissae's Shifting Islands. As the Shifting Islands are sentient, it was decided long ago that they should link with a being on their Island to ensure that they remain in touch with the current needs of their population, and not remove themselves from the trials and tribulations of everyday beings.

Lissae – A Grey, sentient Realm who is defended by the Altoriae. Comprised of six continents, seven sentient Shifting Islands and multiple fixed islands, she is home to ten races. She is said to be a Mother Realm. There are two moons in her orbit.

Lissaen – A person who lives on Lissae.

Luerix – A Grey Realm.

Muhara– A fixed Island on Lissae.

Na'reh – Goddess of the Element Spirit and wife of Vebnah.

Neharn – A desert Grey Realm with two suns.

Nelonia– A continent on Lissae.

Nindonia – A fixed Island on Lissae. Home of the Zindara.

Nine Hells – The name given to a particularly nasty set of nine Realms.

Niverwell Ranges – A stunning mountain range on the Realm of Iabovar. The range has a myriad of tiny, naturally created holes going from one side of the range to the other. It allows for the static build-up of two Elements, creating a whistling noise. Local legends claim the noise is caused by the souls of the departed.

Obirium – A Dark Realm with a door of deep black wood that seems to glow.

Omina – A fixed Island on Lissae.

Opestila – A fixed Island on Lissae.

Osin berries – Small, sweet yellow berries.

Palon – Native to Lissae, the palon is a small, six-legged creature descended from wolves. They have soft fur and long tongues, with a preferred diet of insects.

Panagar – A Dark Realm with a metal door.

Patrol – Any Innarnian resident over fifteen is required to help the Guardian and the Altoriae patrol the Realms to watch for any possible threats.

Pedutia – A large green leafy plant that freezes well.

Piggyback – Mentally piggybacking is something that telepathic Innarnians can do. It is a way of gathering information and listening to conversations. It can be stopped by strong mental shields.

Pocket Realm – A small Realm that is attached to a larger one.

Q'Aralide – A vicious Dark race who wielded spirit, earth, plasma, and air Innarn. Approximately thirty feet tall, their social status depends more on their colour and abilities than anything else. Quite apart from their Innarn, their breath is something to watch out for, as it can strip the flesh and the life from someone in just one exhalation.

Quass juice – a sweet bubbly orange drink, served cold.

Rakemyst – One of the sentient Shifting Islands on Lissae. She is home to the Ilutri.

Rasshnae – Goddess of the Element Water and wife of Zoemer.

Raval – A Realm reduced to cinders at the hands of the largest Dark Army ever seen.

Realms – Planets which inhabit various parts of the multiverse on three main levels, Dark, Grey, and Light. Although there can be many sub-levels and a mix of Dark and Grey, or Grey and Light within the same level. Dark Realms are places with little to no natural sunlight. Most lights in these Realms are made by Innarn. Grey Realms are places with a similar amount of light to Lissae and Earth's equator. Light Realms are places where there is an abundance of natural light.

Returned – The name given to those from Ronah who survived being eaten by Anriluka.

Rezem – A building built out of a mound of earth. The size and design of the mound can be controlled by an Innarnian or by one of the sentient Islands.

Ridden Hall – The school on Ronah.

Rohinda – A continent on Lissae.

Ronah – One of the sentient Shifting Islands on Lissae. She is home to a variety of races and the traditional home of the Altoriae. Traditionally, Ronah selects a being to be her spokesperson. Ronah is one of the six gateways to the Realms. Ronah also has duties to the Altoriae, which are: 1. Ensuring a safe place for the Altoriae to live; 2. Ensuring a safe place for the Altoriae to train; 3. Maintaining peace among the residents to the best of her abilities; 4. Training the Altoriae if asked; 5. Guiding and guarding the Altoriae when no Guardian is available.

Rutenberry – The frosted dark-purple skin of the rutenberry hides the chocolate-like fruit inside. It can be eaten raw, although the skin can be bitter. Skinned, mashed, and cooked, it can be added into cakes, biscuits, and other sweets, including drinks.

Ruzayra – Native to the Realm of Iabovar, the ruzayra is a large, flightless bird with cloven feet. Able to walk great distances over mountainous terrain, the ruzayra are highly prized for their meat and feathers.

Satyrs – A humanoid race from Lissae with legs and tail similar to a horse. They are usually found on Ginorti. They include some of the finest crack troops on the Realm.

Sebbolen – A race of blue-skinned beings with pointed ears.

Sedolic – Green, scaly dog-like animals with two large pincers at its front that are a favoured food of the U'tan.

Send/Sent – The word used for telepathic communication.

Sephina silk – Collected from silk worms that feast on the Darfionious Oak tree, which is only found in the Sephina Ranges. It is the warmest, softest, strongest fabric on Lissae, and there's just something about it that makes it immune to Fire and Water Innarn.

Shem'ar – Shem'ar are small dragon-like creatures, no bigger than a large dog and about as intelligent as canines as well. Kept most often as familiars, guard creatures, messengers, and family pets. They have soft, furry hides that come in almost any colour. Although incapable of Innarn or talking, owners of the shem'ar can communicate telepathically with the creatures, some of whom understand more than others.

Shifting – The Innarn art of mental teleportation from one space to another.

Shifting Islands – The name for the group of Islands that travel around Lissae's seas, seemingly on a whim. They are sentient beings who care for the residents who make them their home. See Akoren, Cantash, Ginorti, Vannali, Rakemyst, Ronah, and Talhan.

Sinfrons – Creatures who can use Fire Innarn.

Soul-seeker arrow – Once upon a time, there was a Dark Priest who created the perfect weapon to destroy Innarn on the bequest of his Elder. He created a mixture that when an arrow of iron was doused with it, it would turn golden, and be able to transfer the Innarn from one to another. The Elder insisted that the soul-seeker arrow be tested, and used it to steal the Innarn from the Dark Priest's mate, attempting to take it for himself. The Innarn of another turned the Elder mad, and the Dark Priest fled before the Elder could take his Innarn as well.

Spirit Realm – A Realm that is found alongside Lissae, where the spirit or souls of the deceased go when their physical bodies are no longer needed.

Sulanta – A fixed Island on Lissae.

Talhan – One of the sentient Shifting Islands on Lissae, and the only one to start with an all-human population. He now accepts immigrants from all races on Lissae.

Tevon– A fixed Island on Lissae.

Tiaclorune – A Dark Realm.

Toslzura beans – A major crop on Lissae's Jinkor.

U'sala – A group of beings from all over the Realms who have banded together to protect the Realms from creatures who wished to change them for their own benefit. Currently led by Jeran Metasta Voutar, and his second in command is Yessna. The numbers of the U'sala vary because of the high turnover rate.

U'tan – A race of extraordinarily powerful strategists who reside on Rataeo.

Uleulan – A race of four-armed humanoids from Lissae. Usually found on Sulanta, they have distinct features: a single, large eye and translucent skin. They contain some of the Realm's high-level water and spirit Innarnians.

Ullfin – Herd creatures. Jali Thorne, the tenth Altoriae, was killed by a trampling herd of the creatures when trying to save her family.

Vallan – A creature bred for its hide and meat. Vallan flesh is particularly delicious roasted.

Vannali – One of the sentient Shifting Islands on Lissae. She is home to the Weavers.

Vastilda – A Dark Realm with an ice door. Its inhospitable cold weather made it the perfect place to hide the *Hekkor Mafae*. Home to the four-armed Vastildian cyclops.

Vebnah – Goddess of the Element Air and wife of Na'reh.

Vendalbara – A continent on Lissae.

Veti Cant – Or Cant, is a sign language that uses hands and facial expressions to communicate. It is often helpful when overcoming language barriers. There are variations for beings with more limbs, but the essentials of the Cant remain the same.

Vutana – A fixed Island on Lissae.

Wards – Innarn shields designed to protect specific areas.

Wastigg – A large beast with a body and head like a bull, and a scorpion's tail and claws. They stood ten feet high at the wither.

Weavers – A strong Innarnian race from Lissae. They reside on Vannali and usually keep to themselves. They are regarded as one of the oldest races and are often considered mythical beings as they rarely leave Vannali or allow visitors.

Wikkur – A race of tripedal Dark beings, both cunning and savage.

Wisara – Wisara are primarily ocean-dwelling beings whose bodies–although humanoid–look like the tangled roots of lotus flowers. Their 'hair' is the leaves of the lotus, and the flowers act as adornments. Wisara can change form to a more traditional humanoid shape and inhabit land areas in either form. They move around as gypsies and trade between the continents and Islands of Lissae by walking the ocean beds. They are the perfect oversea (or in this case, undersea) merchants, as storms have little to no effect on them. Custom dictates that the Wisara are offered fish and bread and other items to restock their larder by the towns they visit. As payment, the Wisara would tell the Tales of Lore. Only the Eldest of the Wisara is given the title of 'Lore Keeper', although anyone could tell one of the tales.

Xarit – A special portal which enables travel to and from neighbouring Realms. There are only a handful of Realms that have xarits leading to them. Only one side of the xarit is a Realm where Innarn is possible, the other side is completely neutral.

Yaston – A fixed Island on Lissae.

Yuham cheese – Cheese created from the milk of the Yuham.

Ze/Zir – A gender-neutral pronoun.

Zindara – A race of humanoids from Lissae. They are usually found on Nindonia and are high-level plasma and fire Innarnians.

Ziom – The hardest metal in the Realms, found on Lissae. Used for the creation of housing frames, precious jewellery, and weapons.

Zoemer – God of the Element Earth and husband of Rasshnae.

Zokleran – The Grey Realm the Chirea were banished to.

LIST OF CANDIDATES

Alistair from Ronah

Amara from Cantash

Bren from Vannali

Burke from Rohinda

Caeli from Akoren

Dealon of the Wisara

Elani from Ginorti

Haran from Dento

Josie from Nelonia

Kodan from the U'sala

Lira from Tevon

Mu from Nindonia

Ness from Omina

Raven from Freeson

Reon from Vutana

Samuel from Ronah

Talofa from Sulanta

Therdon from Rakemyst

FIRST TRIAL ROUNDS

First round:

> Talofa from Sulanta
> Alistair from Ronah
> Raven from Freeson
> Dealon of the Wisara
> Burke from Rohinda

Second round:

> Josie from Nelonia
> Ness from Omina
> Kodan from the U'sala
> Lira from Tevon
> Mu from Nindonia

Third round:

> Elani from Ginorti
> Reon from Vutana
> Caeli from Akoren
> Therdon from Rakemyst

Fourth round:

> Amara from Cantash
> Bren from Vannali
> Haran from Dento
> Samuel from Ronah

MAP OF RONAH

N
BEACH STREET
BEACH STREET
SUMMER CLOSE
RIDDEN ROAD
TEONAE DRIVE
BARKLEY STREET
CALLOWAY STREET
DEW DRIVE
BARKLEY STREET
SHORT STREET
ARBOR STREET
SWAN STREET
RIDDEN ROAD
WINIAR TIOTH ROAD
Castle Bachelor
Tania's house
SPRING STREET
Jonathan's house
Shari's house
WEAVER DRIVE
WEAVER DRIVE
WEAVER DRIVE
RIDDEN ROAD
AUTUMN DRIVE
FERN ROAD
ASTRAL ROAD
BARKLEY STREET
BEACH STREET
RIDDEN ROAD
Ridden Hall
METTA STREET
ASTRAL ROAD
RIDDEN ROAD
IRONY WAY
BEACH STREET
RONAH

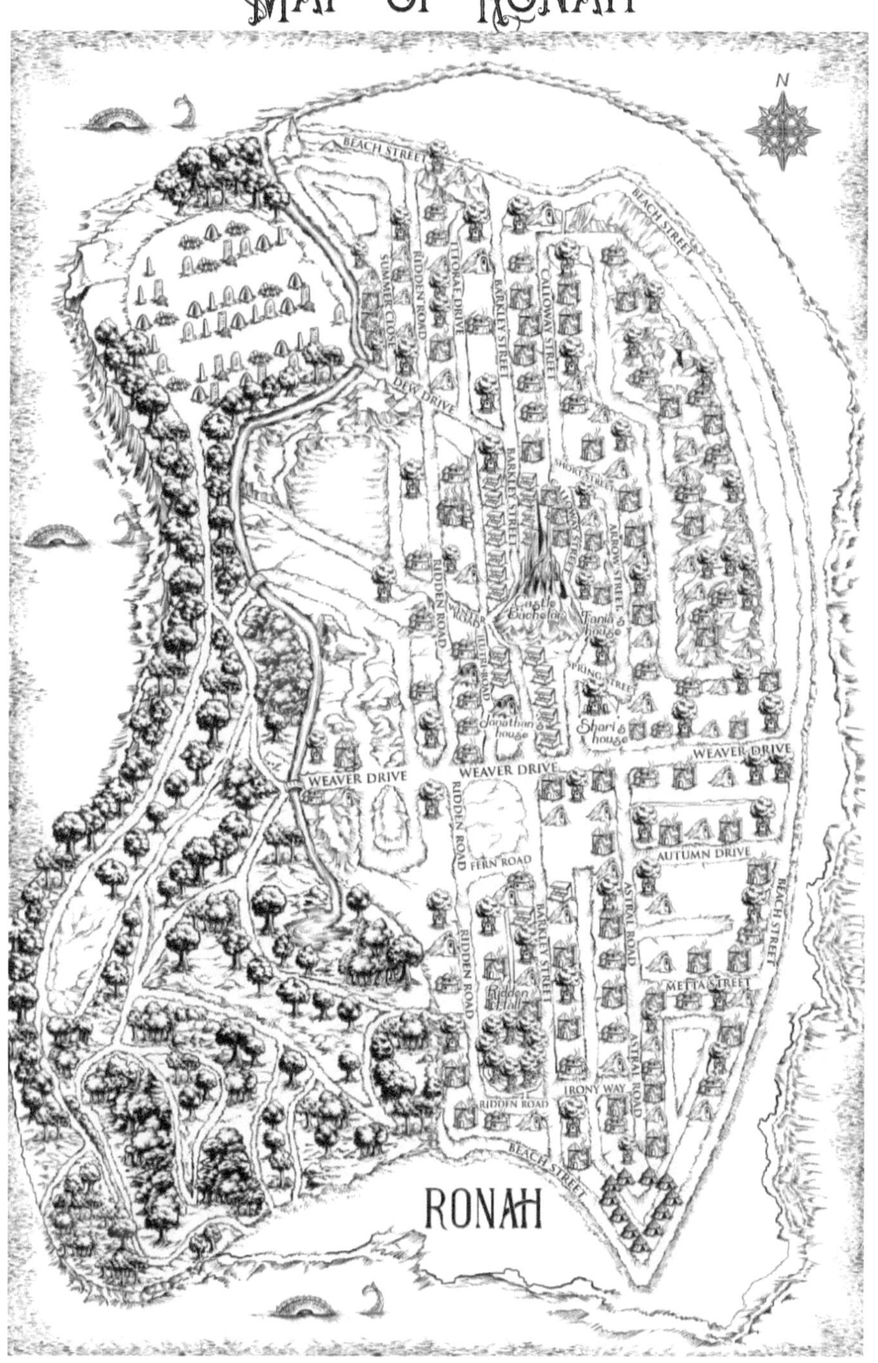

N
RAKEMYST

MAP OF FIRST TRIAL ROUNDS

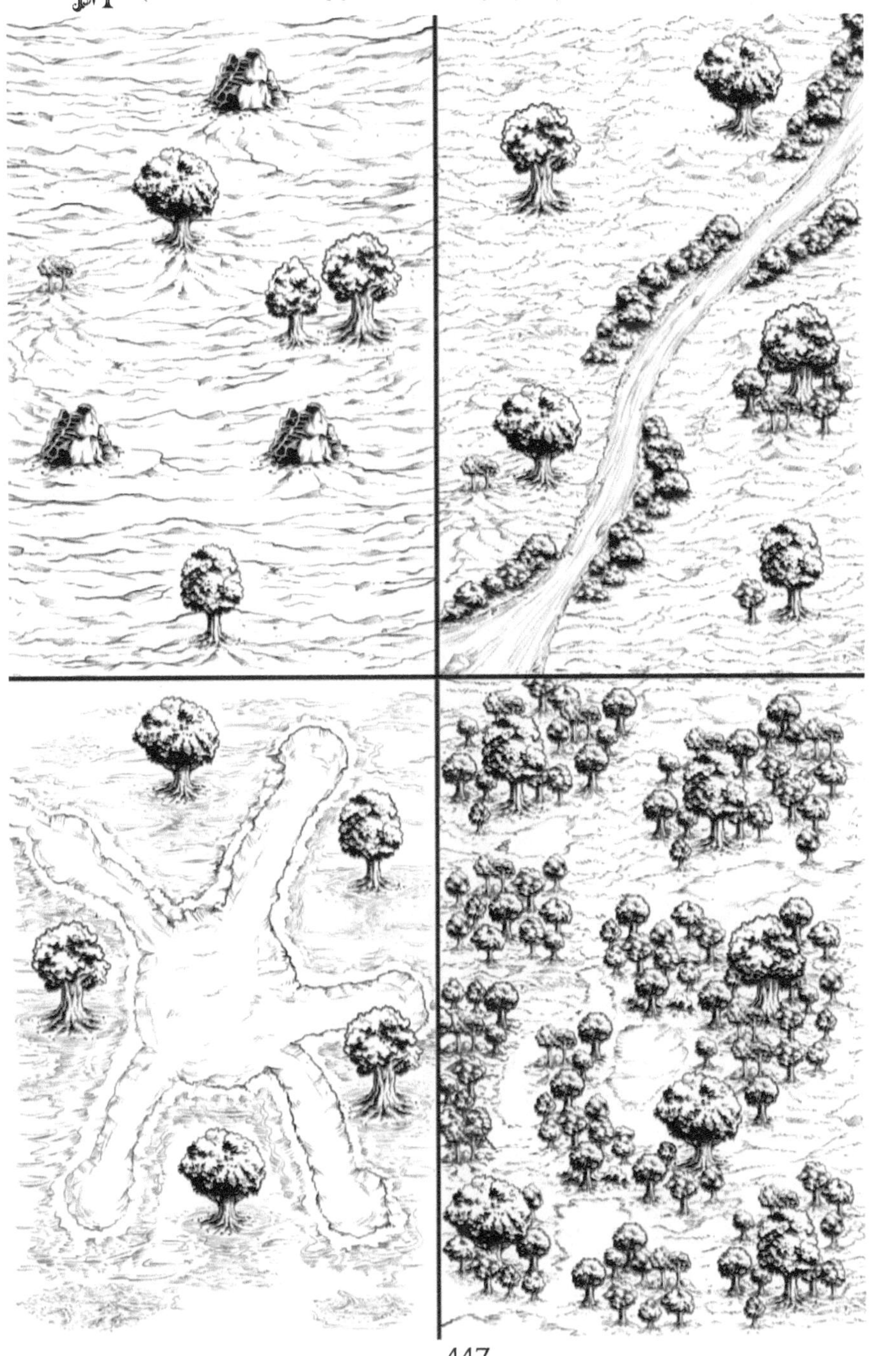

ACKNOWLEDGEMENTS

Writing a book is never a solo effort. There are a whole host of behind-the-page helpers to whom I owe my eternal gratitude.

Thanks must go to Corin, for the concept of the bone warriors. You continue to enrich my world just by being you. Never stop.

Cyrus, Lisa, Kathy, Jodie, Ruth – thank you! Your nit-picking and pulling things apart has made Rakemyst a better book.

My beautiful editing team – thank you Anna from Creating Ink for fine-tuning the manuscript, Lauren for putting up with endless questions and Desanka for proof-reading and offering wise words.

I can't thank Vanesa enough for the stunning cover – and adding the gold feather. And Ricky Gunawan for the amazing maps! Lissae wouldn't look the same without both of you.

Of course, thanks go to my family and friends – for the endless support, probing questions, and giving me the time to write.

Savannah, your eternal enthusiasm keeps me going. Watching you devour the books means the worlds.

Danielle and Ashlee – your comments, questions and expertise has helped to shape the worlds both in the book and the ones without.

And, I cannot forget you, the reader! Thank you for exploring the worlds within these pages.

About the Author

R. Lennard is the Australian author of the young adult fantasy series *Lissae*. She is an avid fantasy and sci-fi reader, and in her spare time, she works as a librarian. She enjoys learning about ancient civilisations, cosplaying and drinking endless cups of tea.

Residing on the beautiful Sunshine Coast in Queensland, Australia, Rebecca enjoys the natural beauty of both the beach and the bush, finding hidden writing spots as a makeshift office. She lives with her family and is ruled over by her cat.

Rebecca is a fan many things, including Doctor Who. She loves each Doctor just as much as the last, and cosplays as the Tenth Doctor on numerous occasions.

After more to read?

The Eni Inside is a short story prelude to the *Lissae* series included in the 3rd Australian Pen anthology, *The Evil Inside Us*.

The Headmaster of Ridden Hall, Lawrence Anderson, went out on patrol, but never returned. Instead, a being bent on taking over Lissae came back in his place.

Full of stories about dark secrets, you'll want to join the masses and buy your copy of *The Evil Inside Us* now!

Available at: lissae.com/short-stories

When evil walks, there must be a Guardian to save them all...

After his father was killed protecting the Realm, Jon Buan became just another street rat. Now, Jon must face the same menacing darkness as his father. Following the guidance of his strict mentor, Jon discovers his magic is stronger than he ever thought, but will he be strong enough to protect the whole Realm?

Will Jonathan survive the deadly Realms, or will he be forever changed?

If you like fierce heroes, pulse-pounding action and unique magical worlds, then you'll love R. Lennard's page-turning introduction to the Lissae series.

Buy *Guardian* to bend the elements to your will today!

Available at: www.lissae.com/short-stories

A looming evil. A hidden saviour. A young protector will rise...

Shari Dawn is no ordinary seventeen-year-old. In a world desperate for a defender, she could be the answer. But revealing her innate powers to the non-believers of her hometown could spell death for everyone she loves...

Battling against the guidance of her by-the-book mentor, Shari unveils her magic—and unleashes a curse designed to push her to breaking point. And now she must hone her strengths if she has any hope of defending her Realm from a bloodthirsty entity bent on destruction and revenge.

Will Shari defeat the primeval menace, or has she doomed her world to eternal darkness?

Buy *Ronah* to bend the elements to your will today!

Order now at: lissae.com/ronah

Keep up-to-date with the Lissae series, and receive exclusive extras
by signing up to the newsletter at:
lissae.com/welcome

www.ingramcontent.com/pod-product-compliance
Lightning Source LLC
Chambersburg PA
CBHW020539120726
47903CB00001B/40